I0535044

The Forbidden Courtship

Castle Road Series

Phylis Caskey

Petite P Imprint

This is a work of fiction. All characters and events portrayed in this novel are either products of the author's imagination or are used fictitiously.

Petite P Imprint

Website: phyliscaskey.com

Cover Art by

Kim Killeen Graphics

No part of this publication may be reproduced, stored in a retrieval system, or transmitted in any form or by any means electronic, mechanical, photocopying, recording, or otherwise without the prior permission of the copyright owner.

The Forbidden Courtship

Copyright pending

By Phylis Caskey

All rights reserved.

This book wouldn't be a reality but for the endearing support of four spectacular women.
Amy Liz Talley and Jennifer Moorhead plot with me, encourage me, and unapologetically push me beyond my self-imposed limits.
Sam (Sandra) Haynie and Scotty Comegys read my chapters when the paper is so thin with erasures, they see the sky and still discern promise.
We dream together, we sigh together, we succeed together.

Contents

Introduction

Pitre, France–1175

Chapter One

Orange light threaded its way through a narrow arrow split and illuminated Catherine de Gray when she stepped from her sleeping chamber into the upstairs common area. Dressed in a tight-waisted bliaut, she crept down the main staircase to the shadowy Main Hall on the bottom floor.

Mordieu! The great room smelled of farting men and soured ale. Dried rushes crackled with each step, and Catherine strained her eyes looking through the darkness for any movements other than her own. She had chosen this midsummer morning to venture out with good reason. Fête de la Saint-Jean had ended the previous night and nothing short of an earthquake could wake her father.

She maneuvered past one sleeping man whose pug-like snout hung open; a lazy snore droned over his thick lips and covered her escape. Relieved, she let out a sigh. A quick turn, and her hunting bow clacked against a trestle table. Frozen in midstride, she kept her wits, fighting to stay calm while her inner voice urged her to bolt. A cough rang through the room. She remained perfectly still like a hart caught in the line of an archer's aim.

Only last week, her father's thunderous voice had confined her to her room for sneaking out at dawn. Yet here she was again. This time she had no choice. She'd promised to meet Perrine and Rayne on this auspicious day. If her father caught her, she would have to kneel, or lie prostrate at prayers for days on end. Checking the room one last time, she spied a honey-colored man with a triangular beard slumped over a bench, his blue eyes rolled in her direction. Her stomach clamped down, releasing an untimely growl. She grabbed her middle. The man swiped his nose, appearing not to see or hear her. Coals hissed in a man-sized fireplace at the end of the room, but no one else stirred. With one cautious step, she wished for invisibility.

Last night, Catherine had wanted to join in the frivolity instead of being stuck on the second floor with the women sucking on chicken bones. But, as much as she desired the freedom to drink and spit like the men, there was justification for not mixing with them— she knew what darkness lay in their hearts. She had seen knights, belonging to her father, boot lame peasants to clear a path, shoving the most vulnerable into muddy puddles or steaming piles of horse manure. As if that weren't bad enough, as a child, she had peered between her fingers when beefy men hacked off the hand of a hungry child for stealing food. Only days ago, during the midsummer festival, she hid behind the castle wall while men dressed in armor forced a scrawny old man to strip naked and lay beneath hot coals for practicing sorcery. His screams filled her nightmares despite the convivial spirit usually associated with the celebration.

"These men will protect you until their dying breath. They may be ruthless, but they are pledged to me and that includes my family." Her father's words heated her ears. Brutality and justice went hand in hand. She did not want to think about their protection right now.

Beyond the kitchen, away from the slumbering, swollen men, she crept from one shadow to the next in the Outer Bailey. The gatehouse appeared just ahead. Once past the gatekeeper, she could finally relax, but first she needed to draw him away. She fished a rock from her pocket and hurled it into a feathery gaggle of geese, plumped up just outside the gatehouse door. The indignant birds squawked loud and long while flapping their wings like so many sheets on a line. A grin stretched across her face.

"Noisy Birds! Shoo! Shoo!" An ale-bellied man trundled out of the narrow building, waving his hands above his head. A startled goose turned and blasted him with a cautionary honk.

With the gatekeeper's back to her, Catherine slipped under the portcullis. She patted a pouch draped across her body. Two white paws appeared over the embroidered lip and a furry black head, about the size of a rabbit, rose until it nudged the knob of her chin. Her dog, Bijou, went everywhere with her. With her skirts lifted, she tapped the drawbridge with the toe of her thin leather day slipper. The boards could be slippery. Once before, she had fallen painfully on her bottom, her pride hurt more than the actual injury.

Straight ahead in the lower fields, smoke curled over a dying, blistered bonfire. Castle Road wended between two sparsely wooded hillocks. Catherine hastily tramped over ripe barley toward Bracken Woods. Matin bells would soon ring, and the road and fields would fill with thirsty, hungry bodies. Pinks and yellows peeked through the tree line and promised a peaceful day. Catherine felt her soul open, and her breath quickened.

If only she lived nearer Gabriel's Stream with its vibrating air and fat-bottomed trees. The castle was so confining, so hectic. The Outer Bailey bustled with noise. She easily envisioned bakers hoisting breadbaskets on their thick stomachs at the same time ale brewers groaned against creaking grain-heavy carts. Clanging hammers from the blacksmith's forge would pound out a hot rhythm while grooms swept stables and brushed spirited horses.

Catherine had a spring to her step now that she was beyond the castle. Always in a hurry, she would need to double her efforts. The salt caves lay exactly halfway between Rayne's family and the de Gray's castle. Hidden deep in the woods, the caves proved to be the perfect meeting spot. Still, Catherine had to hurry if she wanted to arrive before midmorning. She lifted her small dog from the pouch and stared into adoring black eyes surrounded by a fringe of dark fur.

A moist, pink tongue darted over her cheek, and Catherine smiled down at the one creature she loved above all others.

Ferns and wild mint muffled each rushed footfall. Sunlight filtered through fiery red leaves like heavy smoke. Soon Catherine crossed into an ash and willow copse.

"Stop!" a woman shouted.

Catherine ducked and pressed Bijou farther down into the bag. In one smooth motion, she rotated her bow into a ready position. With another furtive movement, she nocked an arrow into place. She moved with innate stealth and transferred her weight to the balls of her feet. Unlike the castle, the woods brought out her natural instincts. Her body became liquid motion moving from tree to tree.

Listening for another provocation, she emerged past crusty-tipped reeds. Beyond the reeds was a small rippling pool connected to a branch of Gabriel's Stream. Catherine's eyes narrowed when a woman came into view. With a shake of her head, Catherine clicked her tongue against the roof of her mouth, dropping her bow to her side and rolling her eyes.

"Hail Perrine! A welcome sight. For a moment I thought you were the one-eyed witch who wanders the woods stealing children."

A young woman, dressed in a nubby brown robe, scattered dried seeds over the moist ground. Her hair resembled dandelion thistles fluttering in the wind, her round irises a translucent pink. She laughed then said, "I have two eyes as you can see. They may be an odd color, but they suit me well." Watching a disheveled black and gray swan in dismay, she continued to speak. "This crazed swan eats half the seeds before they meet the ground. You had no difficulty leaving?"

"It was perfect. Just as we'd planned." Catherine pushed back a curtain of starred jasmine and stepped into darkness. The swan followed her inside, wiggling its tail. The bird plopped into a grass nest and made a noise like a yapping puppy. Catherine was never sure if it was a welcome or a warning.

She drew in the air around her. She loved the cave's interior. It smelled salty like the inside of the seashell her father once gave her–a precious gift he found as a young man on the Second Crusade. She suspected the light scent had to do with the cave's brackish stream that dove and dipped throughout the chamber. The cave itself was a treasure, and if anyone besides she, Perrin, or Rayne ever discovered it, God's wonders would be destroyed. As girls, they dreamed up ceremonial vows, then performed finger pricks, leaving bloody prints along the pale rock walls. The cave became their secret, their refuge––a magical place.

"Shhhh." Perrine pulled her hands from her sleeves; her pink eyes deepened to the color of fresh raspberries in the dim light. She cleared her throat and closed her eyes. After a brief pause, she rose on tiptoes and snapped her fingers near the torch. "Lumiere!"

The torch sputtered to life with a blue flame gliding up the pitch until it became a pulsing violet light.

Catherine ducked. "Light! Magic?"

Perrine ignored her, stepped to another torch, closed her eyes, and ruffled her hands inside her sleeves. Catherine feared interrupting, but her curiosity was piqued. Perrine again rose on her toes and touched the torch. A blue flame shot from her fingertips. Light swirled around the torch, curling into a deep indigo flame. Catherine inched closer to Perrine, scrutinizing the smaller woman's every move. A spray of moisture dotted Perrine's upper lip. She repeated the gesture exactly as before–snap. Nothing. No spark, no flame.

Perrine's face registered disappointment but she nonchalantly shrugged. "Best be content. Wondrous results for a first try."

"If I had not seen it, I would not have believed it possible." Catherine bit down on her lower lip with worry. "I know it is a small thing, but magic...."

"Simple observation. I found a special rock in the cave after the last rain. It sparked when struck with other rocks. I wondered if I ground it into powder, would it create fire? Alone it did nothing, but by accident I spilt another element into it and... Voila! A spark. Is only torch lighting, there is not enough flame to even start a piece of wood."

"I will tell no one." Catherine was serious, too. She would never tell anyone. Though a small thing, Perrine could be accused of sorcery. The idea of her friend stripped, tied to thorny branches, her skin melting under pressed coals... no she wouldn't consider it.

And yet, the flaming torches were a wonder and brought the cave to life. Part of Catherine couldn't help but marvel at Perrine's ingenuity. Violet light fluttered over walls shot from ceiling to floor with glittering, crystalline veins. When she and her friends first came upon the cave, the space measured barely enough room for the three girls to sit and share a cold meal. However, with each rain the cave walls melted and reformed, joining with adjacent hollows and bays until a huge cavern existed with salted pools and secret nooks.

Red clay pots ringed with Roman markings claimed a half-moon recess. Catherine's father allowed her to study with the priests. Their stories rang in her head, and she suspected ancient Cilician or Roman pirates' booty filled the containers. Most likely, her imagination crowded out reality. They were too far inland for a true treasure.

But then again, the cave was magic.

Above them clumps of dried herbs and flowers hung between braided strands of hemp. A rock shelf tipped forward, a home for sparkling glass ampules filled with herbal potions, effervescent concoctions, and flowery perfumes. Perrine used the cave to store her potions and elixirs for healing. Ampules crowded together, organized by brilliant blues and greens to soft canary yellows and dark ancient blacks. She ran her index finger over several glass vials, counting them, taking inventory.

A highly polished copper mirror captured in a metal frame leaned against the south wall of the cavern. Catherine valued it more than colored rocks, crystals, vials, or ampules. The panel measured larger than the doors on her father's castle and reflected the entire cave. She often wondered how the mirror, impossible to move, came to exist in that spot and was absolute proof that parts of the ever-changing caves had once been occupied. Catherine gently placed her pouch on the hard floor. Bijou rolled out and pranced over to Perrine. Catherine chuckled–her dog knew who had food.

Resting her bow and arrows against the mirror's rim, Catherine stared at her image. She flipped her braid. Her hair seemed more like yellow silk thread than Perrine's wispy white thistle. Running her hand past her waist, she hit a soft curve, new evidence of her maturing body. She sighed and pressed her head to the mirror. The cold burned against her forehead as she studied two green-gray eyes. She stuck out her tongue. Her stepmother, Sabina, warned her about vanity. According to Sabina, the church should have included vanity in the seven deadly sins. The looking glass belonged to the cave; she hadn't placed it there. True vanity lived in one's heart, and she only wanted to see how she looked.

A movement in the mirror caught her eye. A shadow crept over the cavern floor. Catherine spun around. Rayne! Without a trace of self-consciousness, she grabbed her friend, hugging her hard. Rayne usually returned the embrace, but not today.

"I left before the first cock crowed. Would not be possible to slip away later. My mother placed a guard at my door, but he is a sleepy fellow. I had to pay the stable boy to secretly meet me with a horse beyond the gates." Rayne held up her hands showing a slight tremor. "I have known my entire life this time would come. Nothing can stop my wedding, and I am resigned to my duty. If I could but eat without my throat closing or speak to my mother without crying, I am sure my Lord and father would be happier."

Catherine turned Rayne by the shoulders toward the mirror. Catherine's empathetic face hovered next to Rayne whose morose visage stared back. Catherine spoke over her friend's shoulder, "Frère Cyril teaches that Saints and Angels created duty. It's what separates us from the beasts, an honor to be cherished."

Rayne glared deep into the polished surface. A wrinkle split her dark brows. "I've heard the same said, but Saints withstand torment beyond mere mortals, and priests are men who care little for women.

Within a week, I will be wrapped in silk and married to a man I only know by reputation, then carted away to live with him in Normandy. Escape is impossible. Duty has wrapped me in dread."

Rayne hung her head. Catherine feared she might cry. She could not take it. Mayhap she could distract Rayne long enough for her to forget her troubles. For years she had made her friends laugh with her antics. An idea came to her–just this one last time. She untied the cincture at her waist, dropping it to her feet, kicking off her shoes before her soft linen bliaut hit the floor. The air felt cool against her exposed skin, and she hurled herself into a dark pit, hugging her knees to her chest at the last second.

Perrine yelled, "Stop!"

Catherine heard the exclamation before she hit the water. Warmth surrounded her, encasing her like a mother's womb. All worries dissipated, and she floated in nothingness. The water tasted faintly of salt. She surfaced and spewed water in an arc. Some of it hit Perrine, who sputtered, water dripping from her chin. She glared at Catherine, running her hand beneath her jaw and slinging droplets from her fingertips. Rayne laughed until she doubled over.

Perrine's eyes narrowed. "You are a devil!"

"Anger does not suit you. She did it to make me laugh." Rayne loosened her cincture and then pulled her wool and silk bliaut over her head.

"At my expense," Perrine huffed. With a jerk, she drew her hand over her open mouth.

Rayne looked down and thrust her hands over her sex. Catherine swam to the rock ledge unable to see. "What? What are you hiding?"

Rayne spun around, her hands still in place, and slowly removed them. Her tuft of dark hair had vanished, a fleshy split in its place. Catherine gasped. She could not take her eyes off Rayne.

"It will be easier for my new husband to inspect me. At least that is what my mother says," said Rayne.

Catherine couldn't speak if she had wanted to. Duty, like justice, could be cruel. It meant subjugation to the will of others: scheming parents, a dominating church, an omnipotent God. It meant Rayne would leave, and Catherine might never see her again.

The idea strangled her. They were near the same age, at least five summers past their first blood. Sometime this coming year, Catherine would also be prodded and poked, but until today, she had never guessed she would be shaved. Of course, she had heard of it. How else could her new husband inspect her like a freshly sheared ewe? If he thought she was not pure, he could throw her away, fresh offal tossed on the road. She'd always accepted her duty as a noblewoman. But now with Rayne exposed... Catherine wondered if Perrine, not promised to anyone, were not the lucky one. At this moment, the idea seemed a good one.

A thud jolted Catherine from her thoughts. Perrine had collapsed to the floor, clutching her head. Her eyes rolled back in her head, the whites wild and exposed. Her arms flopped at her sides.

Catherine scrambled out of the pool on Rayne's heels. She had seen her friend do this before. Abruptly, Perrine stopped jerking.

"It's always this way before a premonition." Catherine felt for her skirt and balled it up, placing it under Perrine's head, then knelt beside her while taking her hand.

Perrine opened her eyes. They were hugely dilated. She clutched Catherine's arm, until her fingernails blanched white.

"A monstrous boar chases someone through a fallow field. I can smell its angry rage. It will not be satisfied until it has tasted blood. I pray no one has been killed... but... I fear the worst."

Catherine and Rayne gaped at each other and joined hands. Perrine's premonitions were never wrong.

Chapter Two

Sir Gregoire Le Sage's chain mail dipped at his waist when he bent over the lifeless body of a young man who looked deceivingly healthy until rolled over. He must have died in agony; his mouth frozen in a terrified grimace. His eyes had been open for so long, midges had planted eggs among the lashes after buzzards had pecked away his eyes. A jagged gash ran the full length of his body where his guts spilled out in a glistening and gaseous heap. Gregoire jumped back just in time to prevent the putrid mess from splashing onto his pointed leather boots.

It wasn't as if violence were new to him, the only surviving son of William the Wise, he was famous for his courage and agility on the jousting circuit. People admired his angular jaw, his full lips, his wavey hair and boldly called him handsome when he traveled to fairs and festivals. For all his confidence, his shyness was more oft than not mistaken for conceit, a presumed trait he used to his advantage.

"We cannot leave him to be torn apart by buzzards." Dru Devreux pulled on his horse's reins. It was to his father's castle they traveled. He had not bothered to dismount. An early ray of sun bounced off his shoulder armor, highlighting a dark curl resting against his muscular neck. He frowned at the dead body. "Behold his tunic. He is no peasant."

"A boar did this. A horrible death." Gregoire shook his head in bewilderment while his squire stuffed the man's insides back into the gash the best he could. Arduous to move, the man wore a tunic in the style mi parti, the front and back sections cut from two different colors, usually worn by the seneschal's staff in a household. A light-weight woolen cloak twisted around his neck. Gregoire was troubled over the man's death even though unfamiliar with this section of Aquitaine. "Do you recognize him?"

"I have not been in Pître for years. Perchance he came from Castle de Gray, but he wears not their colors. Mordiable! The stench." Dru covered his nose with a gloved hand. "We should take the body to Lord de Gray since the death occurred on his land before continuing to Devreux Castle."

Gregoire nodded. He ripped the soiled cloak off the body and examined it. Dyed a vibrant orange the cloth did not suggest nobility. Nonetheless, Gregoire checked the man's tunic and discovered a hidden pouch. He pulled out two flat lumps of sliver.

"What was he doing on the road alone?" He tossed the silver to Sir Dru.

"Who says he traveled alone?" Dru tucked the silver in the leather pocket of his chainmail. "Friends are the first to leave when trouble arrives."

The statement seemed odd, coming from Dru. Gregoire passed it off and mounted his horse while his squire, along with a few lesser knights, wrapped the man in his mantle then boosted the unwieldy body onto a packhorse.

Once again on the move, Gregoire drifted into his own thoughts. They had been crossing Pître, the land belonging to Lord Robert de Gray, for the past two days. He had never been this close to the Loire River. Wheat fields alternated with plain oats, tangling green at the borders. He marveled at the drooping brown lentils and bulging pea pods planted earlier and ready for harvest. Sheep dotted fallow fields, their droppings to be turned into the soil. He noticed an interesting new concept: onions and edible greens lining the roads for anyone to easily pick when passing. New agricultural postulates were being tested, and he assumed under Lord de Gray's authority. The sense of community impressed him. The entourage had passed through two villages belonging to the lord along with several small rustic hamlets. Hearty men worked alongside women lugging baskets and harvesting fresh crops.

Dru had all the luck. He was betrothed to Catherine de Gray. Even though Gregoire had never met her, the stories about her were close to fantastical. She was not the typical nobleman's daughter. Her mother had died when she was but a girl, and no one had tried to restrain her. According to some, she ran wild and lacked courtly manners, while others claimed her a prodigy capable of learning a new language by hearing it only once. He heard she hunted with a bow and could hit a target better than most men. There were stories about her disappearing into the forest faster than a fairy. Lord de Gray supposedly sent out search parties daily, only to later find her in the castle shadows innocently reading. One description stayed with him, that of a young woman, her blonde hair fluttering behind her like wings, bolting through fields on a copper-red horse, carrying a vicious black dog on her shoulders. Which parts of the legend were true, and which were false? He wanted to see her with his own eyes—one of the reasons he agreed to attend the wedding of Dru's sister Rayne.

"Did you hear me?" Dru's saddle creaked when he leaned in.

Gregoire jerked his horse to a stop, embarrassed he'd been caught musing. "Pardon. I thought—"

A flash of color caught his eye at the edge of Bracken Woods.

"We've reached Castle Road. To the left is Castle de Gray. To the right are the Devreux lands." Dru clicked his tongue, veering his horse left.

"Did you see something?" Gregoire flicked his chin toward the woods. The image drew closer. A young girl emerged from the forest. She raced toward them, frantically waving her arms.

Dru pulled up. "Christ's Blood. What is she doing here?"

The girl sped up, her legs pulling against her skirt's fabric. The closer she approached, the clearer it became she was no girl, but a petite woman. Her brows knitted together. Lifting her hand, she shielded her face from the sun, then stepped onto the road. With her free hand, she shook out her dress before straightening her shoulders, daring the men to reprimand her. Dru made no sound, just watched along with the others, his horse sidestepping and prancing.

"Time changes all things, but nothing changes you, Catherine de Gray."

Gregoire watched Dru closely. His greeting showed no sign of affection or devotion. Neither seemed particularly thrilled to see the other.

After all the stories Gregoire had heard about Catherine, he had to admit, seeing her in person was a disappointment. She did not appear mythical in any sense, more waif-like than wondrous. The stories featuring her hunting prowess were exaggerated. Her hands were too small to hold a sizable bow, and her arms too thin to power an arrow. He suppressed a laugh when he beheld the fabled dog that supposedly sat on her shoulders. The tiny animal resembled a hairy rat, its nose sticking out of a padded pouch.

Catherine tilted her head, her gaze traveling past Dru. A slight buzzing told Gregoire flies had discovered the body, and he could tell by Catherine's face that she had, too.

"John! Oh Mon Dieu. John!" She ran to the horse, stroking the man's body with one hand and slapping at the noxious flies with the other. A whimper escaped from her when she pressed her face against the ghostly cheek of the dead man. Her shoulders shuddered, and she hid her face, but she could not block out the sound. Her sobbing was so raw it was hard to watch.

Dru threw his leg over the wooden pommel and slid to the

ground, placing his hand on Catherine's shoulder. "We found him a league down the road. Appears a boar killed him."

With her palms, she ground the tears into her cheeks.

"Do you know why he traveled on Bracken Road? If he journeyed alone or with others?" asked Dru.

Catherine sniffed but rested the weight of her body against the palfrey.

"No? I have no idea?" Her answer was a question not a statement. As if Dru knew more than he said.

Gregoire expected Dru to act as was his habit and comfort her because, as every servant in Lord Henry's court knew, he had comforted any woman who held his favor: short, tall, plump, thin, clever, silly—it made no difference. Instead, Dru removed his hand and tucked it behind his short sword, seemingly uncertain of what to do next.

Hooves pounded on Castle Road, and Gregoire looked from the couple to the road. Approximately ten men on coursers rode toward them, led by a silver-haired man tipped so far forward in his saddle he intended to either charge them or fall off his horse. He rushed them, circling them twice before he reined in.

Gregoire ran his hand over his horse, Fiérsabo's mane, and then casually fingered the hilt of his sword so he conveyed no overt threat. The animal's muscles tensed, preparing for a fight. A sense of pride filled him; not only was his horse dependable, but he also sprinted faster than most coursers.

A well-trained horse meant the difference between life and death on the battlefield according to his father. Gregoire could not take the chance on an animal that lost its head during a jousting match either. He took his father's words to heart and trained Fiérsabo from a foal. He taught the animal to ignore clanging swords, piercing screams, and the scent of blood. He put the horse through every imaginable scenario short of his own death. Fiérsabo had never failed him.

The silver-haired man threw back a shock of hair escaping from a leather thong tied at the nape of his neck. At first, he appeared angry, but as he circled Gregoire and the other men, his expression changed to bewilderment. He dismounted off a black and white roan stallion. Most men appear commanding seated on a horse, but when this man vaulted to the ground, he was still intimidating. Towering over the animal, he gave the impression the horse had shrunk. Gregoire slid from his mount, unnoticed. His hand went to his waist and rested on his dagger.

Catherine turned from the packhorse, exposing the dead body. Dru bowed. "A surprise to see you, Lord de Gray. We were on our way to Castle Road when we found this unfortunate man. By all manner of means, seems a boar killed him."

Catherine bolted to her father and clutched him around the waist. Her upturned face shone with tears. Gregoire stood close enough to see that freckles dusted her nose, and her eyes were tinted blue like a field of lavender on a stormy day.

"Oh, Papa. It's John. Faith's John."

"A loyal man. A terrible loss." Lord de Gray made the sign of the cross and unlinked Catherine's arms from around his waist. "The second such killing along this road. Time to send out a warning."

Lord de Gray grumbled then slipped past Catherine to examine the body. When he finished, he clapped Dru on the shoulder. "These boars have become treacherous along these roads of late. This boy was my seneschal's son—an educated, responsible young man. I will take him to his father. I do not relish it. He was his only son."

"More's the pity." Dru gave the standard response.

"A knight returning home deserves a better welcome. Would you do us the pleasure of staying the night with us before continuing?"

Dru glanced at Gregoire, then returned his attention to Lord de Gray. "Thank you. We did not expect to come this far but felt we must once we found the body. I have already sent a messenger ahead. My father will expect us by day's end."

"Yes. Of course." Lord de Gray motioned for two of his men to transfer the body to the back of a horse. "How did you come upon my daughter?"

Gregoire watched the shift in Catherine's demeanor. Her back stiffened. "I was returning home from Gabriel's Stream when I spied them on the road."

De Gray's gaze never left Dru. "Did you hear something? A mouse perhaps?"

Dru grinned for the first time. "Yes, Your Grace. A very small mouse."

Gregoire wondered if it was a good idea to taunt Catherine. She showed no fear of her father, yet she did not defy him by stomping her foot or puffing out her chest. In fact, her face remained impassive. A horse, more copper-colored than red, nuzzled her shoulder, and she reached up to soothe it. Gregoire noticed the horse when Lord de Gray pulled up, mainly because it lacked a rider and bucked against de Gray's man.

Catherine scrutinized Gregoire with hard eyes and seemed to notice him for the first time. Yet, her face remained passive. Not the response he was accustomed to. Most women fluttered their eyelids or fiddled with their hair, others turned crimson, while some pulled at their neckline, allowing him a peek at their breasts. He'd even had two women faint when they laid eyes on him. It struck him Catherine excelled at hiding her emotions. Either that or he hadn't impressed her by looks alone.

Dru cleared his throat. "Allow me to introduce a fellow knight from the court of Henry le Liberal de Champagne. Sir Gregoire Le Sage, son of William Le Sage de Champagne—or as some call him, William the Wise."

Gregoire bowed. "Lord de Gray."

When he lifted his head, he considered not the man, but his daughter and nodded. She dipped her chin, again, her expression unreadable. Something in him shifted. Maybe the sunlight hit her just right, he was unsure, but she seemed prettier than she did a moment ago. And her eyes went from a watery, steel color to intense blue. He almost shook his head to clear it.

"After the wedding, we have planned a hunt to celebrate your return." Lord de Gray spoke mostly to Dru and then regarded Gregoire with a smile. "Perchance you will stay. William the Wise's son is always welcome at Castle de Gray."

"Would be my pleasure."

Lord de Gray helped his daughter onto her saddle, and then threw himself atop his roan, bringing the animals side by side. As he leaned toward his daughter, he said in a low voice, "The entire castle has been searching for you this morning. You know the dangers that lie beyond the castle walls and have just witnessed my worst fears. We will speak of this later."

Gregoire realized Dru had mounted his horse. He bowed once more and immediately followed suit.

Lord de Gray tapped his chest with the flat of his hand. "Until we meet again."

His entire entourage galloped away with the dead body. The horses kicked up so much dust they disappeared before the first rise.

"We need to make up the distance if we are to arrive by night-fall." Dru turned his horse and bolted in the opposite direction. Gregoire spurred Fiérsabo, allowing him to stretch, and in a flash, they caught up with Dru like mist on water. The two knights slowed to a trot, laughing until the others reached them. After a while, they reined in on a wooden bridge over a bubbling stream, the cool spray refreshing them. Red clover stretched across the landscape and flanked the stream. Sheep moved across the landscape like woolly clouds.

"Hawk's Bridge. Take a breath. Smell that. Fresh clover. Feels good to be free of that stinking body. When King Louis VII redistributed lands after the Second Crusade, he awarded Lord de Gray all the land we crossed before reaching Hawk's Bridge. Upon his father's death, he became the largest landowner in Pître. My father owns all past this bridge. Gabriel's Stream is the border between the two lands. The castles are but a full day's ride apart, and water is plenty near the stream. Too close for comfort if truth be told." Dru stretched in his saddle. "What did you think of Catherine de Gray?"

Good question. What did he think of Catherine de Gray? He had to remember this was the man betrothed to her, not merely his jousting partner. "A small woman, smaller than I expected."

Dru roared with laughter. "Who cares how little she is, as long as she can shift her hips below me and give me sons. My father worked long and hard to talk Lord de Gray into a wedding alliance. Her father has been in the favor of both kings, first Louis VII and now Henry II. Although our castles aren't far apart, it took us three days to cross his land and reach Hawk's Bridge. He may seem hardy, but he has yet to produce a male. Catherine is heir to all her father owns. Not long from now, all you see around you will belong to me."

Gregoire's gaze swept over the countryside. The land was lush, and the water below them churned silver. Gregoire joined in the laughter. Dru was a braggart of the worst kind. He boasted more than any other man Gregoire knew, but he found him amusing and mostly harmless. There had never been a reason to doubt his sincerity. However, Dru was susceptible to planetary movements, especially Mars, and when chance played with his moods—anger followed close behind.

Chapter Three

She smelled Death's rotting breath all over John, yet the sun continued to shine when the world should have wrapped itself in grief and shut out all light. She had felt the same when her mother died, when her baby brother died, and when Nana died two springs ago.

Regardless, Castle de Gray stood steady. Her father sent a messenger ahead. Chapel bells pealed, announcing the passing of a soul. Villagers and servants lined the road leading to the castle, their heads bowed; their hands signed the cross as they passed. Her father rode ahead; John's body rode behind. She dreaded seeing Faith, John's father, more than anything. Her stomach started to cramp. She felt sick.

Four fat towers rose in the air like thick fists warning enemies away. But they did not scare away the boar that killed John. He had been her childhood playmate. Ever since his father became seneschal, the priests educated John alongside Catherine. He showed her how to hunt, and shoot his bow, an unwieldy man-sized thing, then surprised her with a recurve bow made especially for her smaller hands. But after her first blood, things changed. She was no longer allowed to be with him alone. He stopped meeting her on the castle parapet to study the stars and never hunted or rode horses with her again. Once he became apprentice, he claimed his father kept him busy, but she knew the real reason—she was Catherine de Gray, promised to Dru Devreux. She missed John's friendship more than she ever admitted to anyone.

An oily moat coiled around the castle; its foul odor caught in her throat. In the Outer Bailey bells clanged so loudly the sound vibrated in her chest, competing with her heart. She caught sight of Faith, supporting his wife with one arm and himself with his cane. His face was a mix of anxiety and desperation. When he saw Catherine, his face crumbled. It seemed as if all the bones in his body melted. He folded over, nearly falling to the ground. Catherine averted her eyes.

Faith was kinder than most men. He loved his wife and tended to her when lesser men would have put her out. She raved some nights like a rabid dog. Sabina said an accident occurred when the sickly woman gave birth to John under a full moon. His poor mother was cursed, never able to have another child and compelled to howl from vesper bells at dusk until Matin bells at dawn. What would happen to her now?

Once the death knell ceased, the castle grounds were briefly silent. Lord de Gray's knights lifted John and gently placed him on the ground. Faith's wife fell on top of him, hysterically pawing at her son. With enormous effort, Faith held his dignity and dropped into a kneeling position beside her, leaning hard on his staff. Frère Cyril silently stood behind the couple and clutched a silver cross to his chest. Catherine leapt from her horse, heading straight for Faith, but her father grabbed her by the arm.

"Let them be. You will have plenty of time to comfort them later." Lord de Gray touched Catherine's hair. "That could just as easily have been you. Boars roam and establish new territory in summer, and this year has been worse than most. I have warned you before. Do not leave the castle alone."

"I am always careful, Papa. I have the luck. You have said so yourself." Catherine felt the strain in the back of her neck from staring up at her father.

"Do not tempt fate or God, my child." Lord de Gray put a hand in the center of Catherine's back, guiding her to the Inner Bailey. "I am not asking you. I am telling you. Boars care not whom they kill. All they need is your scent. But you are my heir, and there is greater danger beyond these walls. Should you stumble into a nest of thieves, you can bring a large ransom. My dear, there are more unpleasant ways to die than being killed by a boar.

"Sabina will be waiting for you. I know it is hard, but if you would only allow her to guide you. Your stepmother is a woman well worth imitating. And think about what I said to you." Her father patted her shoulder before turning on his heel to rejoin his men.

Catherine's throat ached, and she wanted more than anything to go to her bedchamber and cry. John's death was fresh and needled her heart. But his death was not the only rock in her shoe. The expression on Rayne's face when they were in the cave talking about duty had stayed with her as well. Encountering Dru and his knights brought up more questions than answers. What kind of man had he become, this man who would one day be her husband? Perchance, had his life of privilege left him judicious or foolhardy, compassionate or heartless? What would her life be like after the nuptials? Her aching brain felt as if it had been stitched to her skull.

The moment Catherine entered the Inner Bailey, Sabina stopped pacing on the raised platform attached to the Keep. She pressed the folds of her saffron tinted bliaut then smoothed the matching silk veil covering most of her hair. Her gaze followed Catherine as she came up the winding steps.

Dread pulsed through her, and Catherine resisted rolling her eyes to the heavens, already resenting her stepmother's anticipated reproach. Lord de Gray had said his piece, but Sabina let matters fester until they reached Biblical proportions. She was an ardent follower of Frère Cyril and never, ever broke fast before her morning prayers in the chapel.

The best thing about Sabina was her daughter, Catherine's half-sister, Isabelle. At least, her stepmother expected perfection from both and for that, she remained thankful. Her stepmother was too self-possessed to ever raise her voice, but her severe words cut to the bone. No matter how hard Catherine tried, she would never be able to please the woman. Catherine's mother had died delivering a still-born son. Her father waited a respectable two seasons before marrying Sabina. Her stepmother slipped into her new role without hesitation, but Catherine was the wasp under her wimple.

"Christ sees all and is merciful. We will visit the chapel later today and pray for John's soul. He has been such a comfort to your father of late." Sabina hid her hands inside the lining of her angel sleeves, but her eyes softened. Her stepmother rationed out kindness with practiced humility, considering it her Christian duty. Her compassion caught Catherine off guard.

"Your father never admits his failings, but he has difficulty seeing the written word, especially near the fire at night. John had been reading and interpreting documents for your father of late. He was the most trustworthy of men." Sabina reached down and helped Catherine up the last step. "To encounter Sir Dru must have been a shock as well. You have not seen him in more than a good five summers."

Catherine kept her mouth closed, too tired and too desolate to answer. She tried to pull together some energy, but it was no use. Her shoulders drooped, and death's weight settled there.

"We were worried. Did Papa tell you his men killed a boar near the castle this morning? No. I can tell by your expression he forgot to do so. Come, the dressmaker is waiting. We leave in a few days for the Devreux wedding." Sabina held out her arm to hasten Catherine.

Best to keep her thoughts to herself. No need to explain it was the very reason she left the castle—her last chance to be alone with

Rayne before all the festivities. To add to her uncertain feelings, her happiness had been obliterated by John's death.

Sabina called it the Devreux wedding, not Rayne's wedding. But that is what it truly meant: the joining of two families. No matter how much the troubadours sang about love and longing, duty trumped everything, even affection and admiration.

But Catherine knew love existed; every young girl knew about it. She had witnessed it between her parents before her mother died, in the way her father touched her mother's hair, the quickening of her mother's steps when her father entered the castle, the way they held each other and laughed before the fire. Perchance their relationship was more confusing than comforting. Her mother fell ill long before her last pregnancy. Confined to bed during her final months, she embraced Catherine, holding her close as she told stories of mythical dragons that melted forests with a single fiery breath, but she also showed Catherine how to weave a basket just like the one used to float the baby Moses down the river. She could still hear her mother's voice, and it brought her great comfort on the worst days.

She followed her stepmother into the Main Hall. The servants had been busy. All the filthy men and sleeping hounds were gone. The scented dried rushes Sabina had insisted on scattering over the floor before de Gray's men took over had been swept away and replaced. Trestles and benches were pushed neatly against the plastered walls.

Chubby-cheeked Dagena thumped out of the kitchen holding an empty tray on her ample stomach. "Ah, Catherine. You returned and not a moment too soon. What did you have for breakfast, porridge or cold beef?"

Catherine smiled. Dagena made oats early in the morning for the servants but served bread and leftover meat to the de Grays and their guests. Her comment revealed a little secret. She knew Catherine had escaped early that morning.

"I had neither."

"Missed the noon meal, too. Hips are not made of stones and

grass. If you come by the kitchen later, I will find a morsel or two." Dagena winked at Catherine as she thumped the tray on the trestle table. Her daughter, Alice, had grown up with Catherine, hiding and playing in the kitchen and gardens. She left the castle and married the village miller. Everyone said he was quite the catch, but Catherine was never sure. He seemed pragmatic about the marriage, more interested in whether Alice could lift ground wheat or not. But she seemed content with a new baby in her arms and a smile on her face.

"Are you coming?" Sabina stood with her hands tucked into her sleeves at the top of the stairs. Her voice carried from the second floor. Reaching the top step, Catherine noticed nothing changed from the morning. No one stayed on the second floor but the family and their private guests.

Sabina reached out and stroked her arm. "I know John's death is a great shock. But you are Lord de Gray's daughter, and you must conduct yourself in a manner befitting a lady. You have not been a child for a long while and can no longer run off to the woods. I am sure your Lord and father warned you of the danger, but have you thought about the impression it gives, the gossip that follows... you have a younger sister, your actions affect her, too."

Catherine's mouth went dry. Sabina hit her in her most vulnerable spot, her half-sister, Isabelle. Sabina knew Catherine would never do anything to hurt her sister, not knowingly anyway.

Her stepmother epitomized perfection. She made beautiful tapestries embroidered with tiny stitches so perfect the fronts and backs were identical, but she could be colder than a steel blade in winter. Isabelle never mussed her mother's lap, to read, cuddle, or play. But Catherine made time for her innocent prattle and always held her affectionately close. She was clever for a child, watchful and, something no one ever claimed of Catherine—sensible.

"I'll try my best." Her voice sounded flat, drained. She always promised to do better, and she truly meant it, but somehow, it never worked out that way. She opened the door to her bedchamber.

Two women, dressmakers, stood in Catherine's room and before she knew it, she stood on a small stool, mindlessly turning while they snipped and stitched and pinned. The only window in her room, an arrow slit, let in a narrow shaft of sunlight.

She forced herself to reflect on something other than John's death. Thinking about Dru only made her anxious, but she needed to understand more about him. After all, he was the man she would marry within the next year. She had to get past her insecurity and accept her duty, become the lady that Sabina and her father expected. But at the same time, she wanted Dru to mean more to her than an alliance between families.

Since the last crusade, love and chivalry were infused in every conversation. Eleanor of Aquitaine and the Courts of Love had started it. But Dru never showed the least bit of concern for her. Yet to be fair, he had been away at Henry de Champagne's court. He more than likely had known other women, whereas she had known no other men. Mayhap they needed to spend more time together. She would find an opportunity at Rayne's wedding.

Dru was handsome by most standards. His jaw defined his face more than any other feature, powerful and angular. On Castle Road, she noticed his height when he stood alongside her father. His dark hair and violet eyes were stunning like Rayne's. But no matter how hard she tried, she felt uncomfortable in his presence.

Another face crowded her mind, that of Gregoire Le Sage. She noted her father's reaction when Dru introduced him. Everyone had heard of William the Wise. He was a fair, intelligent man. Kings and nobles alike often sent for him as a sage adviser. Apparently intrigued with French politics, he had penned a book entitled: *Chronique de Res Publica.*

She had heard of Gregoire, too. He and Dru traveled the jousting circuit. Last year they survived a tournament mêlée that killed over twenty knights. She caught the quirk in his stance when he was introduced. He expected her to be impressed; apparently many women were. Luckily, she was betrothed. He was nice to look at though. His green eyes shone like watery moss-covered stones. Obviously, he trained regularly. He leapt on his horse without effort, his leg muscles straining against his tan gambeson trousers. She noticed something else, too. He had deep scars around his wrists. Not surface scratches made by a rope, but thick fibrous slashes. A painful story lingered underneath those scars, and she wondered if she would ever hear it.

Chapter Four

The next day, mid-morning sun lit the Devreux Castle Keep. Gregoire sauntered down the spiral stairs, checking the castle grounds from each keyhole window. Tents of all sizes covered more than half the Outer Bailey and stretched past the Outer Wall for leagues down Castle Road. Striped green and white standards, bearing a yellow Devreux Griffin, flapped above each tent, resembling squat ladies waving in the wind. He almost choked. He was certain this was not the impression Dru's father was trying to achieve.

A drop of water landed on his shoulders, and he stepped back from the narrow window. He shook his head, and water dripped down the front of his shirt. He had taken a tepid bath from a basin and changed into a deep green tunic given to him by a certain lady from de Champagne's Court. She swore it matched his eyes. He smiled; he liked the attention, but the lady was clingy and made him cringe. With all the road grime scrubbed off, he felt a stone lighter. As was his habit, he rubbed the scars crisscrossing his wrists. Today, his scars were numb, but some days they itched so badly, he scratched them until they bled.

Unexpectedly, hounds clamored past him nearly knocking him over. A beleaguered servant followed with a leather leash failing to catch them. The heavy wooden door hung wide open. Gregoire exited the Keep and spotted Dru just beyond. Servants carried towering poles painted in rainbow colors. Copper bells dangled from spiral ribbons and jingled with each step.

Lord Devreux stood on one side of the courtyard and snapped orders to his seneschal. Dru swung his wooden crop in the air, completely uninterested. Devreux raised his hands in the direction of the castle. He spotted Gregoire.

"Dru? Is this the vagabond you brought in with you last night?" Lord Devreux swaggered over to Gregoire, leaving his seneschal to convey his orders. "Welcome. I apologize for not greeting you earlier. You arrived so late; we had gone to bed. Tell me, have you ever seen such a sight?"

"I once attended a celebration for King Louis in Paris. It was a grand affair with jugglers and performers. But it could never compare to this."

Gregoire prepared himself for a sturdy hug. Strangely, Lord Devreux held his arms absurdly wide, then he stopped short as if reconsidering the gesture. Clearly uncomfortable, he grabbed Gregoire's shoulder and shook it. "A hearty welcome."

Then he cleared his throat and addressed his son. "You asked about the hunting earlier. Never better but be wary near Bracken Woods. Lately, the boars have been active and attack without provocation. Gossip has it they are the size of bears."

"Lord de Gray's servant was a wicked sight. He looked worse than someone trampled to death in a mêlée." Dru picked up a loose flower from the ground and sliced it in half with his crop. "I know we discussed this when we arrived, but it is unusual you didn't know de Gray's man."

Dru's father ran his finger over the bridge of his nose. "You say you found him on the old Bracken Road, not Castle Road. He was more likely heading to one of Lord de Gray's villages. Odd though, he had no one with him. And no one found his mount? Extremely unusual."

Gregoire opened his mouth to agree because he also thought it strange not only was the man alone, but curiously dressed. However, before he could comment, Lord Devreux glowered at a disruption over Gregoire's shoulder. Servants made loud clucking noises joined by Dru who slapped his crop against his thigh, flapping his arms like a duck until he noticed a side-eye from his father.

"Rayne." Lord Devreux muttered under his breath, then he glared at Dru. "Stop that noise, you lout. She needs no added attention. My own daughter gathering flowers beyond the castle grounds unescorted. Rayne is beginning to act like Catherine de Gray, but an oiled leather strap will correct that."

Gregoire eased to Dru's side. The young woman skipped into the courtyard, hugging a clutch of fresh flowers. Her smile stretched across her face in a good-natured greeting. Her hair fluttered, unbraided, behind her. She was a refreshing sight after all the perfumed false women around court. Lord Devreux spoke about Catherine with such disapproval; it not only surprised Gregoire but alerted him to possible discord between families.

"Catherine is young and can be subdued. But a leather strap leaves marks. There are other ways." Dru's voice was low so that only Lord Devreux and Gregoire heard. "Darkness, cold, and hunger are powerful deterrents."

"Catherine is strong-willed, not easily broken. A woman never respects a man who lets her run wild. But never forget. She is key to everything de Gray owns which should have been mine from the beginning. Luck was with him the day he defended the king. Many men returned home for the crusades rewarded with new land." Dru's father gave a rumbled whisper. "Not much can be done with her until she takes the name Devreux."

Uneasy with this openly hostile admission, Gregoire massaged the back of his neck. Rayne abruptly stopped before her brother, then slowly extended her hand. Dru ignored it. At first Gregoire thought him rude, then he noticed Dru's chin twitched as if holding back a smile. With an exaggerated frown, she stomped her foot, then her lips tipped up at the corners. After a slight pause, she bowed, deeply. "Welcome home, saintly brother."

Dru guffawed, pulled his sister to him, and twirled her around. He set her down and flipped the cuff of her trumpet-shaped sleeve, exposing her wrist. Servants murmured when she reached on tiptoes and fluffed Dru's hair.

"You give the magpies too much food to gossip with, my dear," Lord Devreux groused. "The castle is full of wagging tongues. Your new husband might not like what he hears."

"My Lord." His seneschal reappeared, harried, unrolling a scroll of vellum, and pointing to a particular line.

"Mon Dieu. I must do everything. Rayne, come with me." He spun on his heel, bustling the man away. Rayne raised a brow, giving her a determined look, then she tucked her hands into her sleeves, following her father.

Lord Devreux freely insulted Catherine de Gray, openly expressing his contempt. Dru had never insinuated that there was anything problematic about the girl. Yet, if word of their disdain ever reached Catherine's father it would cause a considerable rift. Not that Gregoire had plans on telling Lord de Gray, but she belonged to a nobleman and deserved the respect given to any woman. Devreux appeared not to care whether he might be too outspoken. In fact, his eyes held a gleam, suggesting he would enjoy the challenge.

All the years Gregoire had spent with Dru had left him unprepared for the strained relationship between father and son. Perchance he did not know Dru as well as he imagined. He would have to watch both men to determine the reason.

Dru stalked toward the stable. "The Master of the Hunt is waiting for us near Gabriel's Stream. My horse is chomping for a run. If we hurry, we can get in a hunt this afternoon."

Gregoire never turned down a hunt. Truth be told, he loved Fiérsabo's quick response to blaring horns, yapping dogs, and bolting horses, but Dru's young horse was skittish, and unpredictable. This would be interesting.

* * *

The hunting park ran parallel to Gabriel's Stream. The meadow so thick with red clover, Gregoire felt as if he walked on a living carpet. In the middle of the meadow, a flat-topped boulder clearly served as the meeting point. A shaggy-haired huntsman rested against it gripping the leash of two anxious hounds, waiting for news from forward scouts.

Once dismounted, Dru immediately traced a map along the boulder surface. Gregoire watched as he outlined the hunting park. Hills and the nearby stream made natural borders.

The Master of the Hunt, dressed in drab green from head to toe, approached leading a massive dark brindled Lymer. Gregoire eyed the dog, admiring the animal's slick, black nose, especially bred for tracking deer and other large game. The dog whimpered, pulling toward an evergreen grove near the stream. It strained so hard against its leash, the Master of the Hunt had no choice but to let the dog lead.

Dru pointed to a line of swaying trees. "Anything on this side of Gabriel's Stream is ours. The other side belongs to Lord de Gray." He continued with a wide sweep of his arm, pointed to a knoll left of the woods. "The largest Stag I have ever seen was right there. A most splendid beast. His antlers measured more than seven hand-lengths We tracked him a full day and night. He led us well into the hills, but we never caught him."

"He must be huge for his neck to hold up a rack that size. And you say no one has ever killed him?" Gregoire had to shout above the yelping hounds.

"Despite many sightings, no one has ever drawn blood. According to Devreux someone spotted him in this very meadow less than five days ago. He had wide scars across his flanks. Appears he fought a bear." Dru mimicked a great claw raking the air.

31

Gregoire whistled. They mounted their horses, waiting for a signal from the Master of the Hunt. Dru brought out a bladder of watered wine and tipped it back before offering it to Gregoire. The wine was warm and mellow. Suddenly, a huntsman dressed in dirty brown, ran out of the wood, straight to Dru. Gregoire wound the wine bladder to his saddle.

"The Stag!" The man panted, puffing out a word between breaths. "The Lymer has its scent."

Gregoire glanced at the woods and identified the Master of the Hunt. He could barely contain the Lymer. Its pointed teeth ground between his massive jaws, its muscles shivering with anticipation. The huntsman, standing in the center of the field, made a circular motion above his head and several men rushed the forest, dividing the remaining hounds into relay teams, two dogs to each man.

Dru's horse pawed the ground, clearly ready, biting at the bit. Fiérsabo never moved, his eyes never blinked, he focused on the Master the Hunt. Gregoire petted his neck, leaning close and whispering, "Not long now, fellow."

A huntsman blew a long blast from a tinny horn. The Lymer, once released, shot through the woods. A high-pitched whistle sounded, and the first wave of barking dogs trailed the powerful Lymer. Dru's horse darted into the woods with Fiérsabo on its heels.

The last shrill notes of the whistle rang in Gregoire's ears as they bounded deeper into the woods. Then, he saw him. Just ahead. The Stag. The most magnificent creature he had ever seen. A thrill ran through him, and his breath caught. The Stag stood perfectly still; sunlight glinted off his numerous branching antlers. With the twitch of an ear, it bolted. Crashing through the forest, the Stag showered the ground with bark and leaves, yet he never slowed.

Gregoire flattened his body against Fiérsabo, dodging low-hanging branches as they picked up speed. Dogs bayed and dove ahead.

Dru raced ahead, whipping his horse with the stiff crop, prodding the animal to keep up with the hounds. The Stag sprang over tree trunk after tree trunk, causing the dogs to stumble and dart between horses. Gregoire gained on Dru. The Stag bounded for freedom across Gabriel's Stream.

Gregoire knew the Master of the Hunt had stationed his men at the water's edge. They would trap the Stag before it crossed. Hounds howled at a fever pitch, hooves pounded faster, and trees sped by in a blur. Anticipation filled the air like sparks shooting from a fire.

Hounds escaped from the handlers, frenzied, ready for the kill. The Stag bolted ahead in full view of the stream. A distressed note from the huntsman's whistle split the forest, and the dogs bit at the Stag's hooves. They churned around him. He bucked at them, caught a few, flinging blood. Yet, he appeared unstoppable, rushing toward the gurgling water.

Gregoire dug his heels into Fiérsabo. Once the Stag bounded over the stream into de Gray territory, the understory would swallow the animal whole. It zigzagged down the line of huntsmen who stretched out nets meant to force him back toward Dru and Gregoire.

The noose tightened. The Stag lifted his head in a regal nod, then vaulted over the men, sailing past hounds, landing on the opposite side of the stream. Gregoire had never seen anything like it, and he thought for a moment his eyes deceived him. The deer leapt an unnatural height, as if it sprouted wings and flew. It immediately disappeared into Bracken Woods.

Horns bleated. Dogs skidded into each other. Hounds thrashed in the deepest part of the stream, rolling under the water caught in the very nets meant for the Stag. Huntsmen fell into the tangled dogs, hauling them reluctantly to the muddy banks. Dru flew off his horse in a rage.

"Who was in charge of the hounds by the stream?" He whipped his crop against his leg.

No one answered. Hounds continued to yelp, men refused to meet Dru's eye, instead offering dogs pieces of meat to calm them. Dru's horse whinnied and pranced, unable to calm down. His crop beat against his leg faster and faster. Suddenly it stopped.

"That Stag should have been mine!" Dru shouted.

Gregoire had seen Dru angry many times before. He liked to have his way no matter what it took. It's what made him the foremost partner when jousting.

Dru Devreux desired only the best, and he'd stop at nothing to get it. It is how he won his young horse. A passion for dice was how it started. Dru was losing, and his opponent pressed him for silver. As a last resort, Dru bet his jousting horse. His luck turned and by the end of the night, his opponent, now losing, bet his young mount. When the dice rolled, Dru stood the winner. The defeated man raged and accused Dru of cheating. Jumping the drunken man and easily pummeling him to the ground, Dru walked away with the young stallion.

This outburst was different. Gregoire studied his friend His eyes were black with anger, and his neck bulged against his collar. He jerked up the nearest man, a boy really, and struck him with the crop. The child's tunic split, exposing a jagged red slice down the middle of his smooth back. His cries cut through the forest. Gregoire shifted uneasily in his saddle, hugging his heels into Fiérsabo. He knew better than to interfere though. He was a guest, and Dru was Lord Devreux's son.

Dru went wild, hacking and battering the boy with his bloodied crop. The huntsmen wound their dogs and leashes tighter. Two or three of the men stared at the ground. Others watched Dru, frightened expressions spreading across their faces, a few regarded Gregoire, their eyes large and questioning. The boy struggled until his legs went limp, and he dangled in Dru's grip.

Gregoire had enough. He leapt off his horse and planted himself between the boy and Dru. He lifted the crop in a high arch, defying Gregoire, glaring at him eye to eye. But Gregoire never moved. He never touched Dru, just stared him down. Dru threw the crop wide, dropping the boy to the ground. His jaw tight with rage, he flung himself on his horse and charged away.

Gregoire gently touched the boy's shoulder yet made no move to lift him. As the other huntsmen moved closer, he removed a blanket from beneath his saddle and covered the child, talking to him in hushed tones. No one said a word. Gregoire swaddled the boy's body, carefully tucking the ends. He gently lifted the child and handed him to the Master of the Hunt.

"Boil wool, then dip it in wine. Clean his wounds and take him to the healer. He will live. It looks worse than it is." It was all Gregoire could do without appearing to oppose Dru's actions. Regardless of his feelings, Dru was a fellow knight. His father was Lord—therefore the law of the land.

"Thank you, sir. It was his first time out." The Master of the Hunt took the boy and held him to his chest. "The Stag is devious. No one has come close to trapping him, much less killing him. Some say he is a wizard."

"May be some truth to it. I've not witnessed anything leap that high in the air before."

Gregoire climbed in his saddle and backtracked to the meadow. He wanted to give Dru time to cool down. As boys, Gregoire and Dru had arrived at the same time in Champagne. They trained together from their early teens. Normally, Gregoire could read Dru's moods but since they had arrived in Pître, he had become unpredictable. Dru tensed at the sound of his father's voice, as if he were afraid of the man, but that was ludicrous. His father sent him lavish gifts and visited him more than any other noble. Gregoire had never seen them at odds, never.

One thing was certain. Gregoire had not ever known Dru to administer such uncontrolled violence. Yes, he had put his fist through stable walls, and flung weapons across the room. But underneath, he was always in control, at no time going too far. Gregoire needed to find out what was bothering him before they jousted or fought together again. He had to know he could depend on Dru. It was never a good idea to go into a mêlée with an erratic partner. Instability affected perception and timing. A sword delayed by a slow flick of the wrist meant death.

Gregoire emerged from the woods and squinted at the sudden bright light. He found Dru perched on the flat-topped boulder in the middle of the meadow, hurling rocks into the clover. Gregoire approached him.

"If I had killed that boy, Devreux would be furious. I swear he cares more about those servants than he does his own offspring." Dru tossed a rock in the air still not making eye contact with Gregoire. "Sometimes my temper conquers even me."

"I hope to never be on the other end of your fury. Would be the end of me, I fear." Gregoire eased up in his stirrups and scanned the woods. "The hunting party is coming back. I checked the boy. The Master of the Hunt will care for him."

Dru threw another rock, clipping several heads of clover from their stems. Then he fixed Gregoire with a scowl, suddenly brightened, and gave Gregoire a contrite smile.

"Race you to Hawk's Bridge." He jumped off the boulder, landing neatly on his horse, and prodded it with his heels.

"Fiérsabo can beat your bristly bone of a nag any day!" Gregoire shouted.

He leaned forward until his chest touched his horse. Brushing the reins on the back of the animal's neck, they took off instantly. Before long, the horse's gait fell into a familiar rocking motion. They could have been flying.

Dru galloped ahead, but not for long. Wind ruffled Gregoire's hair as Fiérsabo picked up speed. Dru's horse flicked onto Castle Road. In their wake Gregoire smelled sweat coming off the animal and knew he was a hand's breadth away from overtaking Dru.

Level with Dru, Gregoire called out, "Last one to Hawk's Bridge has to kiss his horse's ass!"

He grinned as Fiérsabo blew past the younger horse.

"That will be you!" shouted Dru.

Fiérsabo snorted and his stride lengthened, pulling ahead. As they rounded the final curve to Hawk's Bridge, something white, ghost-like darted off the road. A woman screamed.

Fiérsabo skidded. Gregoire grabbed the reins and held tight. Despite his impeccable training, Fiérsabo bucked and stuttered in the middle of the road. Gregoire was certain he had heard a scream. He searched the road but saw nothing. An empty ditch ran beside the road eventually joining Gabriel's Stream.

Dru pulled up at the bridge.

"A woman screamed. Didn't you hear it?" Gregoire smoothed Fiérsabo's mane while the animal pranced in a circle. "There. There. See?"

"That was no woman. Your lame horse stopped for a cat." He slapped his saddle, roaring with laughter.

Something moaned in the ditch. Gregoire leaped off his horse and ran to the side of the road. In the ditch, a young woman lay face down, her arms stretched out like a cross. She still held a small basket filled with flowers.

"Corbleu! A woman." Gregoire quickly reached down and grabbed her hand, pulling her up to the road. Dru trotted back.

As soon as he touched her, he was struck silent by her appearance. Her hair was completely white, whiter than an old woman's hair. She was overly fragile, too. The tiny birdlike bones in her hands felt like cool glass. She spit dirt.

"Do you always command the road, forcing harmless villagers off the road?" Despite the edge to her voice, she sounded amused.

She tugged at a hooded woolen robe with yellow flowers embroidered around the neck and sleeves. She didn't wear the trumpet sleeves of a noblewoman. Her skin was so pale Gregoire could count every vein in her hand. He studied her eyes. They were the color of seashells, pink pearl. What kind of creature was this? She gave him the shivers.

Dru pulled up. "Perrine the Fair."

He eased off his horse to stand beside Gregoire. "You scared his horse. Did you end up in the ditch? Are you injured?"

"Only my pride." She dipped. "'It's good to see you home, Sir

Devreux. Hope your travels were safe. My parents and I are counting the days until the wedding festival. How is Rayne?"

Her eyes sparkled when she mentioned Rayne. Gregoire stroked his chin. There was tension between them. What exactly did she mean to Dru?

"You should know. Somehow you always do." Dru's forehead wrinkled. "Boars are active. Do you need an escort home?"

Perrine laughed. She sounded like a flute playing a musical scale, then she turned serious. "Have I ever needed an escort? I have been collecting herbs, and I can surely follow the stream alone."

She dipped to them, then walked toward the bridge, wiping her palms on her dress.

When she was out of earshot, Dru grabbed the reins of his horse and muttered.

"Trouble on two feet. Not only her appearance. Strange things happen wherever she is. Her parents had no children for years and years despite being healers. When her mother finally conceived, the babe came early. A pale and sickly creature. Her mother nursed her, using every elixir and concoction she had at her disposal, even hired a young wet nurse, and gave her special food and brews for extra milk. Her parents had a living child, but one without color, and they invented the name Perrine the Fair for her. She has no fear because no one dares go near her. Magic. She controls magic."

Gregoire rubbed his fingers. It did seem as if they still tingled where he touched her. "Do you think she cursed me?"

"More like she would curse me. She is friendly with Catherine de Gray and my sister, but not many more. They have some secret pact. Once when I returned to Devreux Castle, I overheard my sister say she was meeting Perrine the Fair. I followed her to Bracken Woods, but she walked behind a tree and disappeared into thin air. My sister has no magic, but I swear, that woman does."

Chapter Five

Catherine shivered as Frotlina, her nurse, scrubbed her back. Frotlina hummed a nonsensical tune. Probably to draw attention away from the freezing water.

"Hurry. My back has become a turtle shell it's so cold." Catherine spoke through clenched teeth. "Ice crystals are forming. Hurry."

"How can your back be cold? The water is warm." Frotlina blew out an irritated breath through the gap in her two front teeth. "You should set an example for your sister instead of complaining."

Catherine glanced over at her sister, caught her eye and grinned.

Isabelle clutched a doll made from faded silk scraps to her chest. Her cheeks were fever bright, a sure sign she had been running. She swiped her auburn hair with her hand. "Ty-Ty, you are too slow. You promised to dance with me before we leave."

Frotlina plopped a rough cloth in the copper tub. Then hastily draped Catherine with a wool blanket. "Dry off, before you catch your death."

Catherine hugged the blanket to her, plucking a rose petal stuck to her thigh, then tossed it into the water. Tucking the wool around her, she watched Isabelle dance in a circle with her doll. There were few people in the world Catherine trusted. Isabelle, though only five, was one of them. She had the innocence of a child loved by everyone. She eagerly folded into to Catherine at night in their bed. No one else seemed to care about the stories handed down by Catherine's mother, but Isabelle begged for them. Catherine wondered if she could love anyone more.

She had a tender place in her heart for Frotlina as well, but she could never trust her. When her mother died, Frotlina was heartbroken. She cared for Catherine and indulged her by letting her have more freedom than anyone else, but once Sabina inhabited the castle Frotlina changed. For one thing, she insisted Catherine wear silk bliauts instead of her wool tunics. She found it impossible to keep the hem clean, much less account for the countless rips and tears. Isabelle was clearly Frotlina's favorite. She often brought her treats from the kitchen. Her allegiance had changed from Catherine's mother to Lady Sabina. Frotlina had done the smart thing, but it still hurt.

Isabelle climbed on the bed near Catherine and started jumping on the goose down mattress. "Catch me."

Isabelle sailed into her arms. Catherine held her high in the air, then swooped her over the bed like a bird. Isabelle grabbed Catherine around the neck and gave her a crushing hug. She looked down and fingered the tiny silver deG on Catherine's right shoulder.

"Why are we the only ones with a mark?" Isabelle asked.

"Why do you always ask, ma petite minou?"

"Because I like the story."

"Time for you minou." Frotlina took Isabelle from Catherine and pulled her chemise over her head before the girl's feet hit the floor.

"When I was a little girl, smaller than you, just a baby, robbers stole children from their homes and kept them. They were returned only if a ransom was paid. And before you ask, a ransom is gold or silver traded to release for someone held hostage." Catherine tugged a white chemise over her head, smoothed it in place, then pulled on a brown linen bliaut for travel. The sleeves were lined with soft linen and had a bell shape instead of the usual full-length angel sleeves to prevent them from dragging on the ground.

Isabelle shivered in the water. Frotlina whispered between her teeth. "One baby boy was taken in the night, right out from under Lord Forest's nose. No one knows how the scum broke in. No one in the castle heard a thing. But it snowed and giant footprints led up to the parapet and disappeared. Evil magic."

Catherine rolled her eyes. "Years later. A man entered the castle and told the Lord he had found his son. The Lord asked to see the boy. It had been eight long years, and he had no way of knowing if the boy really belonged to him or not. He asked for proof, but the man had none. No marks on the child, nothing. So, the boy left the castle with the man. It was so sad. No one will ever know if the child belonged to Lord Forest or not."

"When your sister, Catherine, was born, your papa insisted on a mark, a mark no one could deny." Frotlina lifted Isabelle from the water and wrapped her in a soft cloth and gently placed her on the bed. "I was there the day they branded both of you. Proud I was. Lusty cries you had."

Catherine rubbed Isabelle with the cloth, touched the tiny deG, on her sister's right shoulder, in the exact spot as her own. "No one can ever take us away from Papa. He made sure of it. He said it is the mark of nobility. Therefore, we never have to worry."

"I never worry." Isabelle grabbed her doll.

"Not yet," Catherine said under her breath.

The door flew open, and Sabina swept into the room. She was dressed to travel with her hair hidden beneath a covering so heavy she could have passed for a nun if not for her close-fitting tunic. She glided over to Catherine. "You may wear your hair in a braid, but one of the servants will dress it with a bit of gold thread once we prepare for entry into Devreux Castle. Your dresses are packed and on their way. The tent will be ready before we arrive. Your papa has seen to everything."

Sabina set a locked box on the bed. She removed a key from one of the folds in her dress and unlocked the box. Isabelle and Catherine peeked inside. Several strands of gold thread wound into skeins were in one corner. Small black jewel pouches arranged in two distinct lines ran down the middle. Sabina locked the box and went to the door, allowing a young woman with a slight limp into the room.

"Turn around." Catherine felt her stepmother's fingers in her hair, probably measuring the amount of gold thread she would need. She felt her hair go slack, then smaller hands picked up her hair and began braiding it, finally tying it at the base.

"We will stay the night in the Manor House near Hawk's Bridge. Tomorrow we will continue to Devreux Castle. The horses and cart are waiting in the courtyard. Your papa is ready to leave."

Devreux Castle was a full day's ride from de Gray's Castle. If pressed, they could arrive just after dark. However, a late arrival robbed her father of a grand entrance. Therefore, their entourage would start from Hawk's Bridge first thing tomorrow morning.

Sabina locked the box, then slipping it under her arm, she left the room. Catherine felt light-headed. This was it. The last time she would see Rayne. Isabelle patted her on the back.

"You're beautiful, Ty-Ty."

Catherine glanced down at her sister. Tears formed near the corner of her eyes. She sniffed and took her sister's delicate hand. The wedding would be spectacular, lasting for three full days. But she dreaded seeing Dru. If she only knew what he thought of her it would be so much easier. She would know how to talk to him and how to respond. No matter, she was betrothed to him, signed, sealed, and one day soon, to be delivered.

* * *

The next day, Catherine wound her fingers through the red ribbons braided in her horse's mane. She rode behind Sabina whose horse was draped in blue and red check—bold colors clearly designed to proclaim the de Gray's nobility. Two knights, with matching banners, led the entourage down Castle Road. They would arrive at Devreux Castle before noon.

Catherine turned in her saddle and winked at Isabelle who rode beside Frotlina in a rumbling cart that seemed to seek out every stone along the road. Before leaving, Isabelle had begged to keep Bijou with her, and Catherine had consented, but only if Isabelle held the tiny dog in her lap. Catherine had given Isabelle the pouch containing the dog with some apprehension. The tiny pet, a puppy once, now silver-bearded, was the last gift from her mother.

An indigo finch landed on the top of a banner. Sabina cleared her throat and pointed. "Girls, we have a sign. We will have good luck."

Catherine stared ahead as the horses trotted onto Castle Road. The finch remained on the banner, which was odd, but Catherine looked past the bird to the banners near the front of the line. Her father's lean, dark stag rippled across the two front banners, signifying strength in battle. She shifted in her saddle and sat a little taller.

Anticipation made Catherine want to spur her horse and dash down the dusty road, but the morning passed quickly. A few leagues down the road, Devreux banners, sporting yellow griffins against green and white striped backgrounds, guided unfamiliar travelers to an open meadow. Tent cities had sprung up over the last few days, neat blocks of red, blue, yellow, and green with small alleys in-between.

Devreux Castle dominated the rise. Beyond a massive stone wall, a single turret overlooked the rectangular wooden structure. A steady drainage channel ringed the hill's base. Alongside the water ditch, a spiked-wood fence undulated up to the stone wall. Iron gates yawned wide. Guests dressed in festive colors bustled between the main entrances. Inside the spiked-fence a tent, half-red, half-blue, dominated the grounds. Stags dotted the flags along the seams, making it appear that they leapt from one side of the tent to the other. No question about it, the de Gray emblem stood out from the others. Their entourage moved closer.

While the de Grays advanced to the castle, fast paced tunes

played on flutes and drums floated in the wind. The music thrilled Catherine. She wanted to dance, whirl, touch hands. Her eyes could not take it all in. Her head buzzed with all the distractions. Troubadours wandered through crowds, shouted out love poems, pulled doves from under their robes, produced flowers from seemingly nowhere, and swallowed flaming sticks. A man on stilt-legs towered above everyone and threw flower petals like raindrops.

Lord de Gray trotted ahead to the iron gates, and Sabina dropped back to ride through the entrance with Catherine.

"I have never seen so many people. Are they all here for the wedding?" Catherine asked her stepmother.

"Some are here for the wedding. But most of the knights are here for the tournaments. I heard they came from as far south as the Kingdom of Sicily and as far north as Denmark." Sabina adjusted her sheer wimple made from silk so light it gave the impression a spider had spun a web over her dark auburn hair. A far cry from the traveling cover she wore the day before.

"Do you think Dru will be in the tournaments?"

Sabina dropped her chin so that her eyes stared straight into Catherine. "If you spent more time sewing than in the woods you might know more about your betrothed. He is famous for jousting. Some say he is the best in France. Just remember your duty is what you make it. You have the opportunity to talk with him during the wedding festivities. Make him want to be your betrothed."

"What does that mean?"

"A man is like a fish. You must catch him, but he must think you were the one who fell in the net, not him." Sabina raised a brow. "These are the things women talk about while sewing tapestry and planning meals. We are not just silly cows."

Catherine viewed Sabina in a new light. Was this true? Had her stepmother caught her father in her net? This sounded ridiculous, but Sabina seemed to be giving her genuine advice. The biggest problem: What to do if she caught Dru. She had never practiced being coy. For that matter, the idea of being insincere bothered her. Why would a woman want someone to think she was someone else, some silly brainless goose?

She had consciously paid little attention to interactions between men and women. It seemed not to matter much with her betrothed gone, but with her marriage so close and the prospect of being a wife right before her nose, she realized how totally inept she was. This was hopeless. Surely there would be other women her age at all the festivities, and she would see how they fished for men. She stifled a giggle.

Sabina snapped into position, her back straight and shoulders stiff. "Here comes your Lord and father. Prepare to enter the castle grounds."

Catherine checked her gown, making sure it draped over the back of her horse and her demeanor changed. She followed Sabina's lead, stiffening her shoulders, and noticed her horse sidestepping, a sure sign of nervousness. She brushed the animal's mane. "Hush. We will go to the stables straightaway, and you will have a bucketful of oats. Show the Devreux who you are. Calm and easy."

Her horse seemed to respond and stopped prancing. She had just enough time to turn and nod at Isabelle who rose in the cart, pointing at something on the parapet.

Catherine's gaze drifted above the gatehouse. Gregoire stood solemn and still, only his hair ruffled in the breeze. His stance was wide with his hands behind his back. He wore a tunic of deep indigo reminding her of the sky at sunset. Unable to pull her gaze away from him, her eyes stung. She should have averted her eyes, practiced being coy, but she was no good at pretense. Only when the stones from the castle arch blocked her vision did she stop staring.

Strange, she felt disoriented. Heat flooded her face, and she felt light-headed. She dropped the reins to feel the warmth in her cheeks. No sooner had she done so, than quick, precise drumbeats echoed off the entry walls. The rhythm sped up and circled her. Catherine clapped her hands over her ears. The noise muffled, but the beat rumbled all the way through her chest to her backbone.

She felt some relief, but just as she exited the arch, a tremendous roar ripped across the courtyard. Smoke shot past. Her horse bucked and hit the horse pulling the cart behind them. Isabelle screamed. Before Catherine could grab the reins, the animal reared. She clutched the material draping its mane and held on, while her heels dug into the animal's sides. Her saddle slipped. She knew if she fell, the horse would trample her. The horse bucked again, hitting the castle wall. Isabelle screamed, again, and Frotlina joined her. Pandemonium followed.

Catherine crept up the horse's neck and attempted to cover the its eyes. Someone tossed a blanket over her mount's head, holding it still. Catherine swallowed hard and eased back in her saddle. The din around her quieted, the smoke dissipated, and she exhaled. She tried to hide her nervousness, but her hands shook when she grasped the reins, giving her away. Another breath, and she looked for the person holding her mount. At her knee, Dru glowered at a contraption made of painted pottery. It resembled a fire-breathing dragon. Smoke continued to seep from its gaping mouth and settled along the uneven stones in the courtyard.

"I told Devreux not to bring that Erupter into the courtyard, dreadful beast. I tried to tell him it would be dangerous." Dru gripped the cloth covering her horse's head. He groused something, but Catherine barely heard.

"I think she's calm now." He removed the binding just as de Gray reached them.

"Ma petite puce. Are you safe?"

"Thanks... to Dru." Catherine spoke haltingly, unsure of how to act. Her horse's behavior troubled her, but not as much as the crowd. The narrow entrance was packed with frolicking people. They seemed not to notice the danger her horse presented. Her palms started to sweat.

"You should have ridden another horse. This one is not much more than a filly." Lord de Gray shook his head moving past Catherine to the cart.

A tearful Isabelle cried out. "Papa!"

"Minou, nothing to fear. Just a belching false dragon." He sounded agitated.

Catherine's arms and legs tingled. The trapped, closed-in feeling she experienced in a confined space was not far behind. If she stayed in the archway, it would appear to narrow, a false notion, yet her apprehension grew. Must be a curse or a spell. What else could make her react so? Dru clasped her hand and helped her off her horse. The movement broke her fixation, and the warmth from his hand brought her back to the festival.

"Even if her horse was a full-grown mare, it would have bucked at the sound of the Erupter." Dru released Catherine and scanned the courtyard. "There is never a squire around when you need one. I will take your horse to the stable."

Dru seemed preoccupied, never fully focusing on her face. Should she have fainted and put on the act her stepmother told her about? Maybe she should have grasped his hand; he would have noticed that surely.

"May I go with you?"

Dru gave a perfunctory half-smile. "Of course, stay close."

Catherine heard a scuffling sound from behind, then felt a light hand squeeze her shoulder.

"I was standing near the Keep and heard the commotion." Perrine was at Catherine's side. "The smoke was too thick to see, but I heard someone call your name."

Catherine immediately relaxed where Perrine's fingers touched; a friend's reassurance was worth more than gold. Perrine wore a thick linen wimple, usually reserved for married women or nuns. Catherine knew Perrine wore it to hide her hair. Over the years, she had discovered the less attention, the better.

They left the arch and walked inside the Upper Bailey. Fresh flowers were strung above them in giant diamond patterns over the entire courtyard. Perrine pointed at two performers surrounded by fascinated men and women along with a few small children. A thick-chested man rammed swords down a scrawny man's throat. A lump slid down the inside of the thin man's neck. With each thrust the lump grew and the mesmerized circle of people let out a unified AH....

Up ahead was a woman seated in a conical striped tent that reminded Catherine of a billowing scarf. A line snaked along the castle wall, and those waiting chewed their nails or stared blankly, waiting to hear what the seer had in store for them. A few people pointed at Perrine and scuttled away.

When Dru, Catherine, and Perrine were even with the tent, the seer paused and stared at Perrine. But not for long. She jumped up and folded her small table, shooing away potential customers. The woman gaped and thumbed a bubble shaped amulet hanging around her neck. With a frightened grimace, she collected a mouthful of phlegm and spat it at the ground.

"What did you do to her?" Dru asked Perrine.

"It happens all the time. Once they notice the color of my eyes, they think I will give them the evil eye or curse them."

Dru gave a nod before leading the horse into the stable. Perrine and Catherine stood at the entrance. Catherine placed her hand on her friend's waist, pulling her close.

Catherine noticed Dru watching them. "If they only knew what a great healer you are. Maybe they would stop some of their silly superstitions."

"They will never stop." Perrine sighed, then stepped back. "It smells strongly of horse dung inside. Too many animals are crowded into this stable. Are you sure you want to leave your filly?"

"Where else would I put her?" Catherine watched Dru take the horse to a clean stall near the middle of the stable. "Look. He found a place for her. She will be fine."

When he came from around the gate he yelled to Catherine. "Your mount seems calm now. I will find my squire to brush her down and feed her. Will take only a moment."

"Thank you." Catherine let go of Perrine and slipped past the stable entrance. "You worry needlessly. She will be well taken care of. I'll check her."

"What are you doing?" asked Perrine. "You should wait. Let the stable boy or one of your father's squires do it." Perrine paused. "You will soil your dress. Be careful. Remember you have Rayne's wedding."

Catherine waved her off, reaching the gate to the stall, upsetting a small empty bucket on the ground. The horse's coppery head and smooth velvety muzzle came over the gate. She spoke to it. "No need to be afraid. They will care for you here."

She pressed her cheek into the warm smooth spot above the horse's nostrils. She heard a clatter and glanced up. Gregoire sauntered over as if he owned the stable and everything in it. He carried a length of leather connected by metal rings. He was bold enough to walk right up to her. His confidence made her squirm.

"Beautiful horse," he said, tossing the bridle over his shoulder.

Catherine didn't want to seem intimidated and looked straight into his eyes. She wanted him to know he meant nothing to her. Maybe other women led him to believe he was the stuff of dreams or tossed out their net as her stepmother would say, but she was at least savvy enough to know he was trouble. "She is unaccustomed to crowds."

She decided to say as few words as possible. He might go away. Instead, he stepped up to the stable and scratched her mount behind the ears. "What is her name?"

Catherine tucked her lips between her teeth as a preventive measure. She knew he was making polite conversation, but she was unsure of his motives. Best to answer him with as little information as possible. Besides, she had told no one the horse's name. So why start with him? She wished he would move back. He was too close, and she could see the golden stubble on his cheeks. It made her uncomfortable, especially the slight sheen on his lips where he had just licked them. Unexpected desire startled her, and she wanted to reach out and touch his lower lip, wanted to feel the warm moistness clinging to it. What was happening to her? She kept her eyes on him, afraid if she looked away, she would give herself away. Her stomach flipped on itself, and the area between her legs flooded with sensation. She had stopped breathing.

His gaze traveled over her body. Her face caught fire. She scanned the stable, searching for something to distract her. The wooden bucket she spied earlier was just at her feet. Catherine went for the rope handle, as did Gregoire. He was faster, and her hand collided with his. Before she had time to think, she jerked her hand up to her chest. But not fast enough, his touch reminded her of lightning and shot up her arm.

"Sorry. Did not intend to startle you," he said, his smile turning him into the little boy who kicked ant beds for sport.

She tried to answer; her tongue stuck to the roof of her mouth as if fastened. All she could do was shake her head. She needed to fan the heat from her face, cool her cheeks, but then he would know for certain his effect on her. The ridiculousness of the situation made her want to cross her arms and stomp away, anything to give her time to gather her wits. Instead, she glanced down at the bucket. He still gripped the handle; his wrists were clearly exposed. She grimaced at the scars. Up close they were even more hideous than when she first saw them.

Catherine shot him a look. He was watching her, but his smile had vanished.

"I hear bells." Her mouth finally worked, but what came out was idiotic. She wished she were anywhere but here.

Gregoire's mouth lifted into an amused smile. "That would be the chapel bells."

An odd feeling of accomplishment flashed through her. He liked her, yet she had not started out wanting this outcome. The heat in her face vanished, replaced with a glorious feeling of satisfaction, and she liked it.

Perrine called into the stable. "A call to the chapel. The wedding is beginning. We must hurry."

Catherine wanted to wink, tease a bit, but she practiced restraint, and started for the stable door. She called over her shoulder. "Her name is Moncadeau."

"Who?" He gave a light chuckle.

"My horse. You asked her name." A smile rose inside her, and she felt as if she were at the edge of cliff about to fly. She had never felt so alive.

"Watch out!" Perrine shouted.

Too late. Catherine slipped on a reeking clump of horse manure and flung out her arms to steady her balance. How could she have been so stupid? She should have been paying attention instead of... making sheep's eyes. She had never been so muddle brained in her life. She scrunched her toes to avoid the ends of her shoes, which were already soggy. She glanced down. Her new slippers, the blue embroidered ones were ruined.

"What are you going to do now?" Perrine hopped from one foot to another, obviously not about to enter the stable. "If you embarrass Lady Sabina, she will preach to you and pour wax in your ears to seal it."

"What can I do?" Gregoire was at her shoulder.

"I have clean shoes in a sack tied to the saddle." It was a huge effort to sound calm with his gaze on her. With a hard blink, she cleared her head.

She picked up her bliaut, holding it above her ankles, fearing the border or her sleeves might touch the ground. She nearly sighed with relief. At least her dress was spared. The stench assaulted her nostrils. Odd, she had not noticed it before. She had smelled the inside of stables all her life. But today, every scent smelled stronger, every touch felt more alive, each word held a hidden meaning. It reminded her of reading a new passage and discovering a new concept that changed how she viewed the world.

The next thing she knew, she was in the air. She could have sworn she had fallen from a cliff. Dru had scooped her up and cradled her much like a babe. One of her shoes fell to the ground, and the air licked the souls of her foot. Instead of embarrassment, laughter bubbled inside.

"Leave you for a breath, and you somehow find trouble." Dru teased her.

Catherine fastened her attention on Dru, afraid to look at Gregoire. Her feelings bewildered her. One minute she was euphoric, the next giddy, and now distressed; it was like riding the tail of a fox, whipping over hedges and under bushes.

Dru lifted one hand in the air, holding Catherine with the other. His upper body was solid, and she felt his steely muscles beneath her grasp. Gregoire tossed him the bag, then left the stables and stood in the outer courtyard. Activity beyond had ceased and those not invited into the chapel milled around the open doors.

Dru eased Catherine to the ground, knelt, and slipped off her shoe. Grasping her ankle, he replaced her silk slipper. His fingers could have wrapped around her ankle twice they were so long. His touch though warm, did nothing to her, at least nothing like she experienced with Gregoire. He replaced her other shoe, and she was again in his debt.

Before she expressed her gratitude, Perrine grabbed her by the hand and yanked her into a run. "Wake up! You act as if you are in a trance. We must hurry. The bells have stopped, the wedding has begun."

Catherine glanced back. Dru and Gregoire sauntered to the chapel, each with a different expression. Dru seemed amused, but Gregoire ran a hand through his hair as if perplexed. "Should we not wait for them? They were so kind." Her voice sounded hardly above a whisper.

"Catherine, you need your wits about you. I had a bad feeling earlier." Perrine's fingernails dug into Catherine's palm. "Listen to me. I have never been fond of Dru, but he is your betrothed. I saw the way you looked at Gregoire, and the way he looked at you. He is an experienced knight. Do not think you can play games with him and get away with it. He will be the death of you."

Chapter Six

The sun hid behind a chorus of rain-fed clouds when Gregoire traipsed behind Dru into the chapel. He could not explain his reluctance at entering. Once inside the dark room, his eyes adjusted to the low glowing candles. Ahead, Catherine and Perrine genuflected, tracing a cross on their chests. Gregoire took in the simplicity of the chapel, yet his mind remained distracted. When he had touched Catherine de Gray, he sensed a change in her. Her reaction to him was so swift, it startled her. Afterwards, she tried to hide it. Inexperience only added to her attraction.

Unaware of her beauty, she had tilted her head when befuddled, just like the first time he had seen her. The way her blue eyes caught the light completely undid him. Still, he had to remind himself she was unavailable, betrothed to a fellow knight. The vows he had recited with Dru kneeling beside him bound him as surely as a brother. He would do best to remember his oath, the same taken by Charlemagne: to honor his fellow knight and respect the honor of women. The ritual meant nothing if he were to act on the feelings he had for Catherine.

His musings were interrupted by a row of young women who

stood in the middle of the hall, all dressed in colors meant to dazzle. Catherine stood out among them, mostly due to her small stature, which seemed in direct contrast to her disposition, or at least what he had seen of it.

Perrine sidled quietly over to Catherine, and he noted how the other women immediately took a step away from her. The healer, unlike the other women, hid her hair completely beneath a wimple. Her plain dress hung from her shoulders instead of defining her waist. If her aim was to be invisible, she had failed.

The ceremony proceeded with a prayer. Gregoire inched next to Dru on the front row just behind the bride and groom, leaving a visual path between him and Catherine. Dru's mother, Lady Amée, clasped her hands at chest level, yet nothing about her looked saintly. She appeared pinched and in pain. Taller than her husband, she wore a halo-shaped headdress, her hair pulled back until her wrinkles extended under the coiled fabric. She glared at Gregoire and Dru, her hard dark eyes admonishing them for being late.

When the priest instructed everyone to kneel, Gregoire wondered if Rayne's rib-hugging bliaut would accommodate the movement or if she would faint. He had seen it happen before. Women went without food for days to ensure a narrow waist. Lord Devreux had spared no expense when it a came to his daughter's attire. She had been stitched into exquisite red silk; gold thread looped across her floor-length angel sleeves. The cincture at her waist was gold, too. She reached up and adjusted the simple gold ringlet resting above her brow, tucking a diaphanous red veil behind her ear. Clearing her throat, she repeated her vows.

Gregoire had met the groom before during a tournament. Edwin was the son of a Normand Lord, Edmond Fécamp. His coastal land was rich with fishing and trade. Recently, he had doubled his holdings when he absorbed a lower Count's land. Lord Devreux had chosen wisely. With his daughter married to a Normand, he would be privy to any changes occurring along the coast while expanding his own land through his son's marriage to

Catherine. Well done. Gregoire felt as if he should applaud the old man and his ambition.

He slipped away from the family and stood against the wall behind other noblemen so he could study the other attendees. Gregoire was good at reading people. He had an honest face and people often opened themselves to him. It made him easy to trust and a favorite at court. For this reason alone, his attention to Catherine was troubling.

His eyes swept the room, and he again found her. She stood next to a dark-haired beauty, her green eyes widening when Catherine whispered in her ear. Reflexively, she giggled, and a large dimple appeared on her right cheek. She had to be Cristobel. Dru had spoken of her, and from what he relayed, she was promised to no one. According to him, her father still weighed his options. He had a small feudal estate and hoped her beauty would attract a wealthy landowner with a dowery large enough to protect her even in widowhood. Gregoire nodded watching her. Cristobel's gaze roved about the room when she spoke to Catherine. Her eyes stopped on Gregoire, and she gave a shy smile before bowing her head. He could not be certain, but she seemed neither innocent nor shy.

The ceremony was nearly over. The groom slipped a gold ring on the middle finger of Rayne's right hand. The priest instructed them on the kiss of peace, the final symbol of unity between the families. Edwin's family stood on the opposite side of the chapel, their backs to Gregoire so he could not determine their reactions. He was curious what advantage the Fécamp gained from this marriage. Perhaps Lord Devreux provided the funds for Fécamp's newest land acquisition.

Catherine brought her hand up, a sudden motion, and Gregoire's attention flew back to her. She ran two fingers swiftly along the edge of her bottom lip as if deeply in thought. When Rayne leaned in to kiss Edwin, Catherine leaned in too, but a frown deeply creased her face. Her fingers pinched the center of her lip until she flinched. This was one of the strangest responses to a kiss he had ever seen. Dru claimed his sister and Catherine were friends. She should be happy;

Rayne had made a good match to a prosperous man. At least, this was the thinking. But times were changing.

As a child Gregoire's ideas connected to marriage were directly bound to duty. However, his father William the Wise had invited Andreas Capellanus to live with them and share his philosophies long before he wrote his famous *Treatise on Love*. Though William still adhered to the concepts of duty to one's family, he was also a convert of Capellanus. For this reason, he had never betrothed Gregoire to anyone. A filial son, Gregoire wanted to bring someone into the family who shared their values, someone who would bring honor to them. There were women at court who would have broken their engagements, they told him so. But he never seemed to get past the initial attraction. Often, he wondered if he should have his father choose a bride for him and be done with it.

The ceremony ended, and guests flooded the forecourt. Catherine gathered with her family, hugging a young child, apparently her sister before heading to the hall for the feast. Someone bumped him from behind. Gregoire spun around, ready to take on Dru.

"Excuse me," Cristobel smiled, coiling a black curl around her finger. "A rush to the feast, I fear. Would you mind?" She held out her hand, clearly wanting him to accompany her.

"Of course." He tucked her hand into the crook of his arm. Reluctantly, he found himself searching for Catherine through the crowd. Cristobel fanned her face, and Gregoire caught the scent of something exotic and expensive. Since the first crusade, new trade routes proliferated from Antioch, and oils perfumed with spices had become commonplace.

Near the chapel, an old man with a knobbed staff walked up to Perrine. His long beard swung past his waist and was tied at the bottom with a red piece of string. A woman joined them, her hair hidden beneath a beige linen wimple that trailed past her shoulders, an old style worn by pious women. The couple dressed in course-spun woolen robes. Dried herbs and flowers dangled from their packs, easily identifying them as healers. After the tender greeting, Perrine, along with the couple, left the forecourt through a small, recessed door.

"The healers must be old enough to have known Jesus, and they dress like it, too. You would think they would dress differently today. It's a joyous occasion." Cristobel sniffed. "I heard you and Dru are competing in the mêlée tomorrow. Lord Devreux has planned it for months. My father said it will be the largest tournament ever seen in this region."

"Danish knights arrived in the tent city just last night." He drew in a deeper breath. Her perfume swirled around him, and he felt his blood heat. He studied the sky looking for a diversion. "No clouds. Should be a fine day for a tournament. And if what you say is true, which I believe it's so, Lord Devreux will not be disappointed."

"Word has it, you and Dru are the favorites." She dipped her head against his shoulder. "I understand you are an unbeatable team in the mêlées. Is it true?"

Gregoire covered her hand with his. A smile spread across his face. He had reason to be proud. They had trained hard, many times sleeping only a couple of hours. "We are a good team if we avoid injury. The Danish knights have a reputation for bravery and ruthlessness. They train to the death. We shall see who fares better."

"The seer made a prediction earlier today. She gave odds in your favor. Would you argue with a seer?"

Gregoire laughed. "No. I guess not."

As they approached the castle's entry, Cristobel swirled her fingernail against his palm, a subtle, but suggestive move. She spoke as if bored. "Maybe we should stay out and watch the stars appear. It is so noisy in Main Hall."

Gregoire regarded Cristobel with interest, but her eyes were not searching the heavens, they were pinned on him. She slid her hand up his arm and fingered the lacing at his shoulder. He touched the tip of her chin.

Catherine burst through the door, nearly knocking them over.

"Excuse me. Have you seen Perrine?" Her words tumbled out, and she lifted up on her toes.

"Yes. She left with an older couple dressed like they were on their way to Bethlehem." Gregoire gestured toward the small door in the castle wall. Cristobel tugged his arm; with her other hand she smothered a giggle.

Catherine gave Gregoire a scowl that would have killed a lesser man, then ducked back through the massive iron doors. Cristobel rolled her eyes.

"They have some mysterious connection. Best to stay away from them," she said.

* * *

Catherine awoke to bells clanging, flutes trilling, and drums beating a lively rhythm. She bounded from her sleeping mat and tore open the drapes to her tent. Soon, Sabina stood to her side, craning to see the spectacle appearing on the lane between camps. Two women stuffed into yellow gowns waved a bloodstained sheet and danced to the musicians' merry tune.

"Rayne's marriage is complete." Sabina drew a green robe embroidered with fall leaves over her shoulders. Isabelle slipped between her mother and Catherine. A small gasp left her lips.

"Yes." Catherine kept her voice low. Rayne's blood. She cringed, thinking what Rayne's night was like. Old women repeated tales about men with staves longer than swords.

If it was only life and duty, where did love fit? Was devotion limited to God?

"No doubts about her purity. Her mother will be pleased when the sheet is presented to her later this morning. With any luck she will have many sons." Sabina cupped her hand under Catherine's chin and gave a gentle smile. "It isn't all bad. Is ordained by God and a woman's joy to present her husband with children."

For some reason, the idea rankled Catherine. A marriage had to be more than children; she was worth more than that. Surely, Sabina thought differently despite what she just said. Unable to conceive more than once, Perrine's mother had visited their home many times, leaving packets of herbs and special instructions for Sabina, but nothing had helped. Still, Sabina slept with Lord de Gray, and Catherine often heard them groaning through the wall that separated their bedchambers.

Sabina closed the flap and beckoned the girls inside. Frotlina entered a while later, carrying a rectangular tray with steaming slices of beef and a dark bread loaf along with a small basket of fresh berries. "From the cooks in the castle. No dried meat for the de Grays today."

Sabina waved her over to a small collapsible wooden table between two sleeping mats made of linen pieces stuffed with hay. Linen sheets lay crumpled across the mats, trailing onto packed earth, strewn with fresh reeds. Frotlina smiled once she set the tray down, then plopped onto the sleeping mat she shared with Isabelle. She reached into a fold in her skirt, extracting a piece of stringy meat and pulled it through her teeth.

"Isabelle, you will stay with Frotlina today in the tent city. Tournaments are not for children. It can be dangerous." Sabina popped a berry into her mouth and puckered her lips. "Tart! Too tart for me."

Catherine's eyes lit up. "More for me."

Sabina picked at the grain topping the bread, gazing unenthusiastically through the slit in the tent. Light peeked along the tent seams. Isabelle flopped beside Frotlina with a fistful of bread. They whispered to each other, obviously making plans for the day.

Sitting cross-legged on her hay, Catherine munched on the tart berries while her mind wandered. She had attended only a few small tournaments where the winner walked away with a few pieces of silver. Rumors suggested the prizes for this tournament would surpass anything ever given in a single tournament. The festive atmosphere was contagious. She became anxious to start the day. She stood and gingerly stepped around her temporary bed, looking for her clothing.

Sometimes mêlées lasted until sunset. She had heard the ground sometimes became so thick with blood, the horses slid, crushing a knight's legs beneath them. Despite knowing Dru was one of the best tournament knights, she worried. It was a strange feeling, worrying about him. Perhaps her concern was the beginning of a deeper feeling. Whatever happened, she had a suspicion she would never forget today.

Catherine sat among the young women, waiting for the tournament to begin. Thanks to Sabina, she wore a periwinkle silk dress. Her fingers played with the delicate white flowers stitched at the neck and along the waist. She and Sabina had never been close, but maybe that was as much Catherine's fault as her stepmother's. When her father brought Sabina home, he introduced her as Catherine's new mother, and she had felt betrayed. There was never any doubt he would remarry. Sabina was better than most he could have chosen. The true problem was this: he may have needed a new wife, but Catherine neither wanted nor needed a new mother. Frotlina fed her and Dagena cared for her at the castle, met her daily needs. As for confidantes, she had Perrine and Rayne.

As children, the girls developed a system of communication using dried flowers. They gave blossoms particular meanings then sent them to each other through servants. Later they used messenger doves. Catherine eagerly anticipated those days of sneaking away to meet in the salt cave. Over time, the girls developed a bond and were closer than most sisters; it was all the love Catherine needed. But overnight, everything had changed. Rayne was leaving the very next day to live in Normandy with Edwin. Catherine might never see her again. She weighed the information, heavy in her heart.

Catherine mused about the wedding feast the night before.

Perrine had disappeared at the beginning of the feast. Sabina had played the lady, and Catherine felt more alone than ever. Dru had tousled the hair on a young servant carrying a tray crowded with full goblets, then snatched up a fresh goblet and stopped at the table where Catherine was seated next to her father. "Lord de Gray, I understand you have planned a hunting party after the wedding festivities. It will be a great pleasure."

His eyes slid toward Catherine with the last statement.

Her father answered, "We were blessed with a mild winter and game is plenty. Lady Sabina has been after me to organize a hunt since the season's change. While home, you have use of the hunting park whenever you like."

Dru nodded and plopped down next to Catherine, his body swaying uncertainly on the bench. His breath reeked of wine and onions. The combination surely could not sit well in his stomach.

Drawing attention to herself, Sabina tapped the table with a horn-handled knife. "Seems Cristobel went with Gregoire to the courtyard to view the stars. Her mother overheard them talking and is worried; her daughter has not eaten all day, but who could turn down a view of the heavens."

Catherine's back stiffened. Was Sabina suggesting that Dru escort her out to view the stars? She faced him, and he gave her a self-satisfied smile. She wondered how many women had experienced his attention and given in to his charms. He was handsome, and his shiny black hair curled around his forehead, the ends wet with sweat. For the first time, she realized how hot the Main Hall had become; a single drop of sweat trickled down her backbone, adding to her discomfort.

"Good luck to her. No woman holds his attention for long." Dru slapped his leg and guffawed, holding his sides. "Cristobel thinks she's about to be queen bee, using all her honeyed words and practiced wiles. Gregoire leaves behind a trail of broken hearts. Good luck to her."

Sabina sipped her wine, watching Dru over the rim of her cup.

61

She studied him planning her next move. Catherine had no doubt her stepmother enjoyed the gossip about Cristobel. Perhaps she was intrigued by this new information about Gregoire.

Catherine glanced back at Dru, her future husband, sitting to her right. Did he think about her very much or just take it for granted one day she would be his? He gave her no inkling of how he felt. For such a long time he spoke to her only if she were with Rayne. She had observed that at times he seemed endearing, captivating everyone around him, while at other times he seemed angry, his words quick and fiery. He kept her off guard, unsure what to expect of life with him.

To add to her confusion, during the wedding, she had glanced up twice, and both times, Gregoire had been staring at her. She had felt flattered, never once attempting to attract his attention like so many of the other women. If Dru had looked at her the same way, she would not be having these thoughts.

So... Gregoire left behind a castle full of broken hearts. Cristobel needed to watch her step. Mayhap, she should warn her. Then again, perhaps she should not be thinking of Gregoire at all. Certainly, he was a rogue and led women astray. Good thing she was promised to Dru; Gregoire would never have the chance to break her heart.

A tournament horse neighed, the sound bringing her back to the present. She self-consciously cleared her throat and scanned the grounds. The railing in front of her had been draped with a fluttering periwinkle cloth to match her dress. Uncertain how long she had been daydreaming, she bent over the railing to see if any knights had entered the field.

"Catherine must know." Cristobel covered her mouth when she yawned. "Excuse me. A late night."

Caught in between sentences, Catherine had no idea where the conversation lay. On the other side of Catherine sat Emma, one of Cristobel's close friends. She giggled and nudged Catherine. "Tell us. Surely you spoke to Rayne this morning. She has the radiance of a new bride, the blush of a first jostle."

Catherine blinked and turned her head toward the stands. On the high middle platform, Rayne and Edwin sat among their families and several neighboring nobles, including the de Grays and Cristobel's parents. Rayne kept her eyes on the field, her face was unreadable, but her skin did flush pink.

"I have always thought she was beautiful." Catherine's voice was soft. Rayne sat quietly, her hands resting against a vivid emerald dress. She wore a matching wimple edged with chartreuse piping, her head covering the sign of a married lady.

A white linen canopy fluttered above Catherine's head. The Devreux had seen to every detail, draping fabric overhead to prevent the women from freckling. Pages ran among the guests pouring cups of sweet wine and handing out palm-sized honeyed pastries.

"I was so excited about this tournament, I hardly slept." Emma laced her fingers together like a little girl. Deep hollows ran below her cheekbones, and her rabbit teeth protruded over her lower lip. She was older than Catherine, well into her childbearing years. Three years ago, her father had made a match between her and a wealthy Parisian. She expected a splendid life at King Louis's court. However, upon meeting his new bride and her family, the groom begged weariness and retired to his sleeping chamber. The next morning, a grand wedding feast lay before hundreds of guests, but the groom had disappeared. Emma waited in her bedchamber while her father seethed over the insult with friends and neighbors in the courtyard below. He vowed he would get satisfaction, both sides threatening violence. Eventually, the matter was settled, but in the interim no other nobleman had stepped forward to ask for Emma's hand.

"I hope this day doesn't end with ten men lying lifeless on the grounds like the last tournament." Cristobel dabbed her face with a scarf as if she had just witnessed the spectacle.

"You act as if you were there. Who told you?" Emma tipped her head to the side, a clear indication she didn't believe Cristobel.

"Gregoire. Last night, he showed me the stars. The sky reminded him of the tournament field, and he described the contest in detail. A frightful experience." Cristobel brought her hand to her throat in exaggerated shock. "Huge war horses were killed, too. So much blood, everywhere... the moat turned red."

Emma leaned in to hear more and Catherine pursed her lips together while Cristobel continued, "It was the longest mêlée he had ever been in, lasted three full days. These tournaments are not for the faint of heart."

Normally, Rayne would have pinched Catherine over that statement. Cristobel would find a way to faint before day's end. It always brought her attention. Catherine wondered how Emma stood her. She decided to ignore Cristobel.

"Most tournaments last two days. Why three days?" asked Emma, her eyes bright with interest.

"Gregoire said Henry de Champagne offered a large purse for a jousting tournament before the mêlée." Cristobel yawned when she answered. Her words were laced with false boredom. She was dying to share every drop of conversation she had with Gregoire from the previous evening. "So many knights arrived, they had to be divided into six teams. There were so many people they ran out of food and had to slaughter new animals to feed everyone."

Emma held her hands to her chest. "And to think, those same knights are here in Pître."

Catherine's interest piqued. A young woman behind them edged so close trying to capture a bit of gossip, she fell off her bench. Cristobel's grin grew so large her back teeth showed. "Gregoire let me in on a secret."

"What pray tell?" Emma's mouth formed a perfect circle.

Cristobel stretched, coyly shaking her head. She loved the attention. Emma shifted away from her tiring of the game.

"Dru must tell you secrets, too. Do share." Emma squeezed Catherine's shoulder.

Catherine shrugged out of Emma's reach. Dru rarely spoke to her, much less discussed anything of importance like his training or their betrothal. However, last night, she discovered he had a wicked wit that came at the expense of others. Something like that wasn't developed without practice She wondered how many women at court had felt the sting of his humor. Emma would need to stay out of Dru's path, or she would be an easy target.

Swallowing hard, Catherine turned to a noise on the field. Squires dressed in similar jewel-tones lined up along the wooden platforms. Some of them not much more than boys, helped older teens spread out special mêlée equipment. Tournament lances stabbed the ground alongside shields. Blunt metal swords replaced sharpened weapons to prevent bloodshed in an already dangerous sport. Catherine thought about the times Dru must have been responsible for the weapons as a boy in training. Knighthood brought honor to his family, and yet, she'd never heard him speak about it.

Horns blared, the tinny sound jarring her back into the moment. Knights sauntered onto the field leading everything from creamy broad-backed war horses to fast, inky-furred coursers. Catherine spotted Dru's young charger and Gregoire's stunning Fiérsabo at the front of the parade. The crowd cheered. Without realizing it, she jumped to her feet, stood tall and joined in the uproar. Cristobel bent toward her and yelled over the din to be heard.

"Did you bring a ribbon? Surely, Dru will ask for your favor?"

Catherine touched the narrow strip at her waist. She had almost forgotten. Sabina had wound it around her twice, once tightly then loosely with a complicated knot so as not to fall to the ground over her hips. She placed her hand at the knot and untied it. The ribbon fluttered in her hand, and a thrill raced through her.

Tournaments made men into legends–their names uttered around soldiers' campfires, their feats sung among women stitching tapestries, and their triumphs heralded by troubadours. Here she stood waiting to watch her betrothed spar with men she'd heard of all her life. She'd never imagined this much anticipation. Across the field, she spotted Perrine, dressed the same as yesterday and planted calmly beside a tent with her parents. Injury and death were part of the draw. Excitement flew, multiplying with each foot tap and shout.

Spirited horses tramped and snorted when mounted. Squires clung to bridles as armor clinked against saddles. More horns mixed with the bum-de-bum of drums, and what should have sounded musical became a cacophony of instruments. The noise plucked at her nerves. No one else seemed bothered.

"Did you bring a ribbon? As soon as Gregoire asks for your favor, every woman in Pître will want to be you," Emma shouted to Cristobel.

Her eyes glittered beneath her lashes as she slinked her body around the ribbon like a kitten with a string. "Only the stars know for sure."

Emma giggled, then lowered her voice, but Catherine still heard. "Gregoire confides in you. Did you see the scars on his wrists? Did he tell you what made them?"

Catherine's ears tingled. This was something she had wondered herself. She noticed he rubbed his wrists while walking to the ceremony yesterday.

"He did. But he said it was for my ears only" Cristobel pivoted away from Emma and waved her arms in Gregoire's direction, arching her back when she dipped her ribbon over the wooden railing. Catherine strained to hear but shouting from the stands drowned out Cristobel's voice–a single finch chirping in a tree of crows. And Catherine wished the crows would peck her friend into silence.

Chapter Seven

G regoire searched the crowd for familiar faces, his heart pounding over the roar of the crowd. It was always like this before a tournament. Energy coursed through his muscles so hard he could barely sit in the saddle. He lived for these events. They put everything he ever learned to the test and prepared him for battle better than any practice session ever could. The men he was pitted against endeavored to win, especially with the rumored golden suit of armor as a prize. He would have to cut down challengers before they had a chance to strike. Of course, no one had ever seen a golden suit of armor, but that never seemed to matter.

Lord Devreux waved a silver goblet, sloshing wine on his wife. Lady Amée clapped her hands but kept her lips pressed so tightly together she looked like she might break her jaw. Rayne rested her hand on her husband's arm and nodded to Gregoire and her brother, hesitating the proper amount of time between each nod almost as if she had practiced sitting in her chair, presiding over the games her entire life. Her husband Edwin gave an enthusiastic toast, letting it be known he expected his knights to win.

Gregoire took the toast to heart; he never underestimated a challenger, foolish to do so. The opening ceremony continued, and he scanned the remaining faces until his gaze fell on the last section of spectators and a sea of ribbons fluttering in the air. He ran his hand, encased in a thick glove, over his tunic, admiring the two colors: crimson and gold, Le Sage colors. He searched the crowd for Cristobel. Her waist-length hair drifted on the wind like a dark ocean wave. Catherine stood next to her with a peculiar expression on her face, not a scowl, but something close. His gaze left her, brushing over the other women on the platform. Her peculiar expression pulled him back. He wondered if she were concerned about Dru, but he'd not seen them interact but once since he arrived. Her face had turned from him, and his attention returned to his taut muscles, stiff and ready for action.

Directing his horse closer to Dru, he mused about teasing him and asking for Catherine's favor. It wouldn't be out of character. They often teased one another over a woman's favor, but then he thought better of it–Dru had been acting strangely since the day of the hunt. When Lord Devreux spoke to his son, especially if they were out of Gregoire's hearing, Dru reacted by flicking his crop rapidly against his leg, a sure sign his father aggravated him. He twisted his mouth in a familiar grimace that Gregoire had seen at court from time to time when someone disgusted Dru.

The relationship between Dru and his father affected everything it seemed. An unusual strain had developed between them. The camaraderie they shared on and off the field had disappeared. Gregoire prayed it did not affect their performance today.

The horns stopped and a solitary drum beat out a tempo until two lines formed facing the crowd. Gregoire and Dru led the first row. When the drum roll stopped, all the men from the first row trotted to the stands. The crowd shouted out their favorites' names. Shrill whistles shot through the air. Several women ran to the railing with ribbons, tossing them so high it appeared the heavens rained colored streamers.

Stopping directly in front of Catherine, Dru tipped his lance. She tied a blue ribbon to the end of his weapon. He popped the green lance to his shoulder, met her gaze for a moment, and bowed. Her eyes sparkled, then darted to the ground when she stepped back. She seemed a little unsure, a little bewildered. Gregoire wondered why. After all, she had just affirmed Dru was her favorite by giving him her good luck ribbon.

Once Dru returned to the line, Gregoire goaded Fiérsabo. He stopped in front of Cristobel and lowered his lance to her. He thought it best since he had kissed her last night under the guise of stargazing. She had not only let him kiss her, but she also guided his hand beneath her chemise. He tapped Fiérsabo, and the horse lowered his head, tucking his front leg into a deep bow. The crowd clapped, while clacking heels and stomping on the boards to sound like thunder. He grinned. His horse was a bigger crowd pleaser than he was.

Cristobel sprang forward and returned an outrageous bow with her hands held straight back. She shook her hair and rolled her shoulders emphasizing her swollen breasts. Her actions were excessive; the crowd tittered. From the expression on her face, she realized her mistake. She was competing with a horse, not another woman. She lowered her lashes, slowly peeling the ribbon from her sleeve, then tying it to the lance.

Fiérsabo rose when Gregoire tugged at the reins. Raising his lance, he nodded at Cristobel with respect. He didn't care to make her a spectacle for others to chatter about in the future. He returned to the line of knights and waited until the last man had received his favor. There were plenty of knights to receive ribbons or scarves, no need for anyone to be left out.

One knight, a solid-suited man with a shabby horse, waited for a young woman to give her colors to him, but she turned her head and refused to look at him. He went to another young woman and received the same response. Finally, he stopped before Emma, and the relief on her face was followed by a huge grin. She tied a violet ribbon to his lance and clapped as he backed his horse away. Gregoire could almost feel the knight exhale. If she had held onto her ribbon like the two maids before her, he would have been disgraced. Without a ribbon he would have no luck.

Gregoire's legs cramped from sitting in his saddle for so long. He hadn't realized the number of men competing in the mêlée. It seemed to take forever for the second row of knights to receive their favors and line up across the field. Finally, the last man returned to the opposite line of waiting men. The drums stopped and another, faster beat began. Gregoire shifted in his saddle. Over his left shoulder he observed the crowd return to their benches. Pages and servants bustled between them, offering fresh wine and savory treats. The squires scurried on the sidelines, readying extra weapons—lances for some, swords for others. Ready for the signal to charge, the knights on the other side of the field stilled.

Rayne rose, clutching a lemon-colored scarf. Horses quivered, threatening to bolt; in response cheering increased. Knights sat ready and high in their saddles. They focused on the yellow scarf flicking beneath Rayne's raised hand as if it were a snake ready to strike. Gregoire licked his lips, tasting the tension in the air.

"A good match for all today." Rayne lifted her chin and wiggled the scarf for good measure. "May the best man win!"

She released the bright scarf. Energy surged through Gregoire; he dug his heels into his horse, charging across the field, his lance pointed dead ahead. Dru crowded close. Fiérsabo pounded over the ground, his ears perked and alert, but Gregoire knew better than to let the initial commotion and agitation distract him. He crossed the field within two full breaths.

The opposing knights coming toward him picked up speed, and he braced his lance against his body, guiding Fiérsabo with his knees. He angled his body slightly into his lance, reducing his core as a target. He chose the man he would bring down and went straight for him. Knights crashed ahead of him. Metal clanged, echoing against the stands. God, he loved that sound. Blood poured into his muscles; power surged through him.

The knight he'd targeted came into range. Gregoire rammed his lance into the man's shoulder with such force he knocked him cleanly from his horse. He had enough time to whip around and strike another opponent. The man registered disbelief and fell to the ground; he never had time to prepare.

A horn blasted one sustained note. The first round was over. Gregoire reigned in and returned to the starting position. He took his time trotting past the crowd, absorbing the energy they threw his way. Dru galloped ahead and played to the crowd, holding up a single finger, then pointing to his chest. Gregoire chuckled at Dru who normally admonished him for such behavior.

Once they were back at the starting point, Gregoire faced the field and assessed the damage. Four knights trotted over to their squires, replacing broken or shattered lances. At least thirty men had been knocked from their horses. One knight staggered in the center of the field, obviously stunned. After much pulling and pushing, his squire led him away. Several horses trotted aimlessly about the field. It would be a while before the next charge.

"Well done!" Gregoire yelled to Dru.

"Who is that giant knight in the black and white check? He went after you straightaway. Would have knocked you from your horse, too, had not one of his own men crossed between." Dru removed his helmet and swiped his hair. "Have we come across him before?"

"Humph. He was at the last tournament, but seems he made an early exit and was none too happy. Brute, I think he was called." Gregoire pushed his helmet back, letting the breeze cool his face.

"What do you think? Should we do away with him right away or make it more exciting and leave him for last?"

"Best not get too bold. I know you want to show how heroic we are, but he is the size of a bull. It might take more than a couple of tries to bring him down," Gregoire said. He counted the number of men from their team still mounted and compared them to the numbers on the other side of the field. "This is going to take all day.

They have just as many men left as we do, plus the brute. This may be a tournament worth watching."

Dru huffed. "The Master of the Tournament knew what he was doing. He put you and me on the same team, though. There is no doubt which team will ultimately win, but what if the last two men standing are on the same team?"

Gregoire dodged the question. He would never lose for Dru's sake. There were limits to any friendship. He glanced over at the young women. Cristobel caught his eye. "I may need to lose something other than this tournament soon, or I might be trapped into a marriage."

"She thinks she has you already. Her mother boasted about you taking her to see the moon or some such. She has probably visited the healers and has something special to put in your drink tonight. The women at court scheme, and women from the country may seem innocent, but be warned, they are clever. Careful what you drink, or you may not wake up in your own bed."

A horn trilled, and Gregoire tugged on his helmet. Through the narrow opening vent in his helmet, he studied the other team. Pushing any distracting chatter to the back of his brain, he closed his eyes, then slowly reopened them. He was ready.

Edwin held up his arm for what seemed forever, finally dropping it to signal the next engagement. Fiérsabo was so fast Gregoire reached his mark before anyone else and flipped his first opponent just steps beyond his own starting line. When he spun around, he collided with the rear of another horse, bolting away. He charged the fleeing knight, his lance held securely out front.

Without warning, a blow knocked his helmet askew; the narrow vent rotated over his cheek, resting above his left ear. Without the slit stationed above his nose, not only was his vision completely blocked, he also couldn't breathe. The jolt knocked him awry with one leg wrapped across his saddle's ridge. His other foot dangled in the air, frantically searching for a stirrup. He clung to the saddle horn, struggling to remain on Fiérsabo.

Wind whistled past his helmet. Fiérsabo took off at a full gallop. He clutched his lance and hung on, wishing he could see anything but darkness. The whoosh inside his helmet grew. He held on for his life, praying Fiérsabo would lead them to safety.

The horse stopped, and Gregoire nearly fell off. He was so disoriented for a moment he thought the vent above his ear was still whistling until he realized Fiérsabo heaved rapid breaths right next to his head. He tried to make sense of it and heard distant yelling. Fiérsabo remained steady. Gregoire gripped the saddle horn and swung into his seat. He heard urgent screams, his name called, a horse pounding toward him.

There was no time to adjust his helmet. He flipped it off, dashing it to the ground. His head was completely exposed; a lance strike would certainly kill him. Fiérsabo had taken him away from the mêlée, near his starting position. He saw the knight in the black and white check bearing down on him. With his lance cradled against his side, Gregoire dug his heels into Fiérsabo. They galloped toward the charging knight. He had the distinct advantage, but Gregoire had no choice. He goaded his horse. They had to pick up speed. The brute came at him so fast it appeared as if his horse's hooves never touched the ground.

Just as they were about to collide, Gregoire tapped Fiérsabo with his heel. They darted right. The brute's lance whizzed a finger's width from his face. He smelled the fresh paint on the wood. He never looked back, kept heading toward the mêlée, listening for the brute behind him. Just as he reentered the fray, he heard the horn signaling the end of the second round. His shoulders dropped in relief.

He passed the brute on his way back to his starting position. The man's eyes narrowed through the slits of his helmet, and he said, "You are a dead man."

"Surprised a talking ass can sit on a horse." Gregoire laughed, saluting the other man, then trotted away.

Gregoire's conceit nearly killed him. He felt his shoulders slightly sag. He pulled them back. He couldn't afford to give away a mental advantage. The moment he pulled up next to Dru, they clinked lances. Wearing his helmet, Dru made some muttering, but Gregoire could not make it out.

"Are you injured?" Dru lifted the lower visor, but his voice still sounded like he was underwater.

"Could have been worse." Gregoire's squire appeared and handed him his dented helmet along with a dipper of water. He poured it on his head, the bracing chill bringing back his senses. He was handed a second dipper, and he gulped sweet water, then swished it in his mouth before swallowing. "I would have hit the ground if not for Fiérsabo."

"No doubt, they are after you. When you crossed the midline at least three men charged you. But two backed off and let the brute take you. I saw him hit you from the corner of my eye. He wants you down."

"Seems so." Gregoire bristled. Partly his fault, the brute had met him with terrific force, but he should have been prepared. Later when they crossed paths, the brute sounded committed to wounding Gregoire. Malice poured off the man like steam from boiling water.

Rubbing the edge of his helmet with his finger, he needed a distraction and considered the crowd. Catherine was staring at him, her hands on either side of her head. The anguish on her face was so plain, it sent a jolt through him. He looked away, and a movement caught his eye. The healers were hurrying to the center of the field, followed by two men carrying a litter. A wounded knight lay still, deadly still. His thighbone was splintered in half, the larger portion pointing straight up. Blood spurted with each heartbeat, staining the ground beneath him.

The other women stayed in the platforms, but Catherine left the stands and approached Perrine. They shook their heads as the men carried the wounded knight off the field. Nothing could be done for him, and the spectators had gone silent. Catherine turned her head, averted her eyes as the man passed. Gregoire swallowed hard. It could have been him. He pushed the thought back hard. He couldn't let it affect him. He vowed not to look Catherine's way again.

The mêlées continued with a slight break around noon. By the end of the day, just as the sun was sliding into evening, several wounded men were being helped from the field. Three men remained. Dru and Gregoire faced the brute.

"We know he will go for you." Dru clicked his tongue at his horse, moving closer to Gregoire. "You go first. He will think he has you. But slow down just before you reach him. Hopefully, his focus will stay on you. I will flank him from the left easily and knock him off his horse before he knows it."

Gregoire agreed with a bob of his head. His shoulders were screaming as much as his butt. Wooden saddles, no matter how much padding, hurt at the end of the day.

Rayne lifted a red scarf, signaling the last round, and let it flutter to the ground. Gregoire charged forward with Dru on his heels. Just as they expected, the other knight went directly for Gregoire. He leaned forward on Fiérsabo, so his eyes met evenly with the slits in his helmet. He continued to goad Fiérsabo forward, but Dru's horse should have been near him by now. The brute was closing in. Where was Dru? Gregoire slowed, and the brute charged him, barely missing. Instead of the brute flipping back to take down Gregoire, he continued past and went for Dru.

Gregoire had not expected it and whipped around. Not two horse-lengths behind the brute, Gregoire pushed his horse to capture him before he reached Dru. As Gregoire moved into position, the brute hammered into Dru knocking him full in the chest and flipping him off his horse.

Gregoire roared and plowed into the brute with all the power and speed he could muster. Hs lance slammed into the brute; the blow rang through the stands. A gratifying sound. The brute, knocked askew, dropped his lance He clung sideways to his saddle, but it was useless. Gregoire rammed him a second time. The brute crashed to the ground with such force the earth beneath him burst open, showering him with dirt. He attempted to rise, but his legs gave out and he rolled over like a bug flipped on its back.

Gregoire yelled and pumped his fist in the air. He goaded Fiérsabo, and they galloped a full circle around the field. The spectators jumped in the air, some stamping feet like marching soldiers; others clapped and chanted his name. The cheering suddenly stopped.

Someone screamed above the rest of the crowd. "He killed his squire. Mordieu! He has gone mad!"

Gregoire spotted the brute near the stands, a bloody lance in one hand and a sword in the other. With hardly a thought, Gregoire vaulted off Fiérsabo, grabbed his sword from its scabbard, and landed lightly on the balls of his feet.

The brute closed in fast, swinging his sword over his head. Gregoire was faster. He thrust his sword into the ready position. Sacrebleu, what was wrong with this man? He had been in enough tournaments to see some men go crazy after fighting all day, but this man had lost all his senses and was more unpredictable than a trained man in battle. Badly wounded, the brute's squire was on the ground, clutching his shoulder and screaming in pain.

"I want what is mine." Blood ran down the brute's face, the front of his checked tunic smeared with filth, grass, and blood. He swayed, yet still managed to point his sword at Gregoire. "The reward belongs to me."

"You hit the ground first." Gregoire kept his sword angled at the brute. "The fight is over. Think of your honor."

"Honor." The brute's words slurred together. "A cheat has no honor."

Gregoire stepped back. The man's injury had obviously affected his movement and speed. But what stopped him was the hatred kindled in the brute's eyes. It would bring back speed and agility in a snap. The brute wiped his face with a shaky shrug, then swung his sword in an arch, cutting the air ahead of him. He followed with a full body thrust. Gregoire was ready, but this knight was nearly twice his size. He would have to be fast. He jumped to the side, but not far enough; the brute nicked his shoulder. Gregoire lost his balance and fell to the ground.

Blood rolled over his tongue. He clasped the hilt of his sword with both hands and leaped to his knees. The brute had stiffened his back with his sword held high, giving Gregoire a clean target. He aimed his sword and prepared to run the brute through.

"Hold!" Lord Devreux stood on the field with a small army of knights.

They surrounded the brute before he had a chance to react, seizing his sword and pinning his arms behind him. Loathing sizzled in his eyes, but he made no attempt to escape. Gregoire rose, spitting blood.

Lord Devreux pulled on the end of his beard, watching the healers lead the injured squire from the field. His eyes slid back to the brute. "We do not hold for such dishonor. You forfeit any prize you may have had. My men will escort you until you are out of Pitre. I order you never to return."

The brute narrowed his eyes. He opened his mouth to protest, but Lord Devreux stopped him, putting up two fingers. "I said go. There are men here who would just as soon see you strung up. But it is my daughter's wedding, and you will not disgrace it. I am giving you leniency. Now leave, before I change my mind."

Gregoire watched as Lord Devreux's knights took the brute away. He could have handled the man, but they would surely have killed him, too. And this was a celebration. Any men who entered the field and died did so with honor. Lord Devreux grabbed Gregoire's hand first, then Dru's hoisting them high in the air.

"The winners of the Devreux Tournament!" Lord Devreux motioned to the crowd.

Their horses were led to them and once mounted, they circled the field with the spectators going wild. This had been the closest to losing Gregoire had ever been. Despite the win, he felt disheartened. He hid it well and pumped the air with his fist.

After a full loop of the field, he galloped over to Cristobel to collect his favor. She stood on tiptoes to plant a kiss on his cheek. And for a second his eyes slid to Catherine at the side of the field. She scowled at him with her arms crossed over her chest. His heart jumped into his throat. If he had not known better, he would say she was jealous. And for all the world, he wished she were.

Chapter Eight

After the mêlée, Catherine went back to the tent city with mixed feelings and dressed for the evening festivities. She had gone to tournaments for the last few years, but this one affected her more than usual. Before, it all seemed like a grand adventure. This time, the men were more than names, they were men she had known or heard of for years. The danger struck her with real fear, and she thought she might be sick. While inside the tent, she rested for a few minutes before Frotlina thrust her bliaut over her head.

As prearranged, she met Perrine at the Main Hall. Flutes and harps played soft tunes under a white flowered swag. Greenery twisted from the rafters and smelled powerfully sweet. A griffin made from late-blooming sunflowers dominated the wall behind the wedding table. Huge metal sconces cast a golden glow across the room.

Despite the grandeur, Catherine's mind returned to the tournament. She couldn't let go of the anxiety and wished she had never gone. But something else niggled at her when Gregoire claimed his winner's kiss from Cristobel. His arrogance astonished her. Was he simply collecting more than hearts on a string? She remembered the warmth she felt when he touched her earlier. When she watched Cristobel reach up to give Gregoire the kiss, something like anger bubbled up in her heart, and she wished she were giving the kiss. Emotionally inexperienced, she didn't understand her feelings. Catherine touched her forehead. Surely, she must have a fever. Perrine shook her arm, bringing her back to the festivities.

"I need to return and assist my mother with the injured. It is selfish to want to see Rayne once more when so many men fill the tent with wounds." Perrine's hand disappeared into the sleeves of her robe.

"Can you not stay until she and Edwin are presented?" Catherine watched all the people coming through the great door, dipping their heads under the ribboned grapevines and ivy. In truth, though, she was searching for Gregoire and Dru. She spotted her family's table at the front where Isabelle sat alone. "I must see to Isabelle. She is so excited to come to her first feast."

"Before you leave, I want to ask you something." Perrine's gaze wandered the room before settling back on Catherine. "Do you have true feelings for Dru? For Gregoire? You must know it shows. If I notice, others notice. You must be mindful of your actions."

Catherine shifted closer to Perrine. Her emotions seemed in continuous flux. Did Perrine sense her confusion? She had not known it was obvious. Yet, Perrine analyzed every move she made and would recognize the slightest difference. "You should worry less about me and more about Cristobel. Dru told me Gregoire had broken many a heart at court. Is as much his reputation as a winning knight in the mêlées. He is toying with her. He could hurt her."

"I care not a fig about Cristobel." Perrine inflated her chest while her hands snaked around under her sleeves. "It's for you I worry. Your mood changes when you are around him. He has a strange effect on you."

"I..." Catherine pinched herself. "I must admit, I do feel odd when he is around. It is as if he cast a spell. Do you think it possible? He has cast a spell over not only Cristobel, but me as well."

"Sometimes you are a goose. Do you think you are the only woman to have these feelings? I have seen my mother give women potions to help them cease caring for a forbidden man." Perrine took Catherine by the hand. "You have to protect yourself."

"But, how?"

"You must never find yourself alone with him. Never let him touch you." Perrine slipped a little vial of liquid to Catherine. "Slip this into his drink tonight. I promise, he will not bother you again."

"What is this?" Catherine asked. But inside, she questioned whether she wanted him to leave her alone. No other man had ever made her question her motives, her future.

"Nothing to hurt him, only herbs." Perrine thrust her hands back inside her sleeves.

Catherine wondered what Perrine kept inside those sleeves; they must weigh at least a stone. She was always pulling out things like tokens, a packet of compounds, or needles for rupturing boils. If Perrine was so worried about her, why not give Dru an elixir for falling in love? That would seem the logical choice. Truly, she wished someone understood her dilemma–life was naught for love, but duty.

Rayne and her new husband entered the Main Hall. The music stopped and Lord Devreux took over a raised dais. The giant griffin's talons appeared to be moving. Catherine wondered if anyone else saw it.

"This is the last night we celebrate the union of two families, the Devreux of Pître and the Fécamp of Normandy." He raised an ornate copper goblet, regarding Rayne and Edwin with a wide grin. "May your days together be prosperous, your nights amiable, and your years together peaceful."

He drained his cup before gesturing to the couple; they drank from silver goblets engraved with a griffin entwined with a dragon. Catherine and Perrine had sidled closer to the door and now they stood directly across the hall from the young couple.

Rayne glanced over the rim of her goblet. She smiled and raised her thumb, nudging it toward the left side of the room. Catherine laughed. The gesture was their secret code. When they were children, they used the signal to meet under the stairs or in the gardens. Rayne would meet them in the left corner by the stairs as soon as she could get away.

"Now that I have seen her for the last time, I must leave. If I stay any longer, Lady Amée will notice me and have me removed." Perrine pushed a wafer into Catherine's palm. "This is for Rayne. Tell her I soaked the wafer in a concoction made from the roots of scopolia. When her time comes to give birth, she must put this under her tongue. It will cut her pains."

"She will want this from you, not from me. Stay." Catherine grasped the edge of Perrine's robe, unintentionally drawing her hood back. People near the door gasped and stepped away.

With great forbearance, Perrine bowed her head and pulled the hood around her face. She gave Catherine a look of resignation. "Meet me at the cave two days after you return home."

Perrine left before Catherine blinked. She examined the wafer and the vial of clear liquid in her palm. The priest taught that forgiveness is a virtue. Perrine would forgive her, but she should have been more mindful. Perrine had enough difficulty moving about unnoticed without Catherine's carelessness. She felt pressure on her shoulder and snapped her hand shut.

"Lord Devreux will be giving out prizes for the tournament. Would you like to sit with me?" Cristobel cocked her head to one side and twirled a curl near her collarbone.

Catherine wanted to sit as far away from Cristobel as possible. After all, Gregoire would be with her, and Catherine was avoiding him for certain. She slipped the wafer and vial into a secret pocket sewn to the inside of her sleeve. "This is Isabelle's first feast beyond our castle. I promised her I would sit with the family."

She had promised no such thing, but she had to get away from Cristobel and fast because the knights were filing in. She made a step toward the de Gray table, and Cristobel squeezed her shoulder, again.

"Emma is coming this way. We shall sit with you. The festivities will be more fun with each other." Cristobel smiled a little too sweetly.

Catherine felt sure Cristobel was sitting with her for another reason, perhaps to flaunt Gregoire. After all, he buzzed about the silly girl like a newly blossomed flower.

Perrine was right. Catherine was no good at hiding how she felt. And tonight was shaping up to be an evening she would be tested. Luckily, Perrine had given her the elixir. She might have to use it.

Catherine sat down next to Sabina. Her stepmother swayed and blinked. She smelled more of alcohol than the rose-scented perfume she put on earlier in the day. Cristobel sat on the other side of Sabina. Unexpectedly, a narrow space between Catherine and Isabelle appealed to Emma. She relaxed enough to whisper something in Isabelle's ear. Her sister suppressed a laugh, and Catherine loved that Emma made Isabelle feel a part of them.

Cristobel gave some lofty compliment to Sabina, and they began to talk over Catherine. She had no reason to listen. Neither woman meant a word they were saying. Rayne caught Catherine's eye and nodded. Catherine lifted the folds of her bliaut, carefully making sure her sleeves were high enough not to drag the ground, a tricky business.

"Excuse me."

"You will miss the reward presentation. You want to see Dru receive his prize, do you not?" Cristobel had poured each woman a goblet of wine and placed Catherine's in front of her.

"I will be back in time." Her hair swung freely behind her. She ran her fingers through a strand at the base of her neck. An odd sensation as she was so used to her heavy braid. "I would not miss it for the world."

She quickly wended her way through the tables to meet Rayne. Mon Dieu, she was going to miss her once she left for the Normand coast. As she approached the wall near the stairs, she was struck by Rayne's beauty. Her hair was held up in sheer netting crisscrossed with gold thread, and her dress was the color of mulled wine, the sleeves lined with creamy silk. Her cheeks were the same color as her dress.

"Oh my, this has been a whirlwind." Rayne reached for Catherine pulling her into a soft embrace.

Catherine took a step back. "How are you? Truly well?"

Rayne laughed and held onto Catherine's hands. "It's not what you think. All the old wives' tales are so frightening, but Edwin is gentle and somewhat shy. Take another step back and let me see you."

A little self-consciously, Catherine took another step back. Rayne continued to hold her hand and gestured for her to turn around.

"But what about duty?" Catherine asked.

"I now know why they say duty first, love later. We said only two words to each other before the ceremony. We will grow to love each other. But you have always had the luck. You have known Dru since childhood. You will grow to love him before you marry."

Catherine felt her face heat up. She wanted to discuss love and duty, but not with Rayne. Dru was her brother, after all, and Catherine hadn't grown up with him. He had been at court most years and she barely knew him, felt little for him. How could she tell Rayne she would rather be with another?

The thought frightened her. She hated to admit it, but Perrine had brought it to the surface. Mordiable! How did she do that? Catherine had fought the idea, but the thought kept returning, especially if she tried to replace it with thoughts about the wedding, the crowds, even the tournament. This was a dilemma she needed to solve before she made a fool of herself. She just needed to remind herself Dru was her future. Her father had chosen well for her, and she had pushed those ridiculous feelings for Gregoire way down. Besides, she knew he collected women like girls collect dolls and thought no more or less about her than any other woman. The notion should have made her mad, but it only made her sad.

"Where is Perrine?"

"She had to leave. Her mother needed her help with the injured."

Catherine thought it best not to remind Rayne that Lady Amée would have removed Perrine from the Hall.

Rayne hugged her again. "I will miss her, but you and I... we will be sisters soon. I will be here for your wedding next year. We will be together again."

"Not if you are with child." Catherine lifted the wafer from her sleeve. "Perrine forever foreshadowing our lives gave me this. She did not say if she had a premonition or not, but she concocted this wafer from the roots of scopolia and said to put this under your tongue to cut the birthing pains. That must mean something."

Rayne raised her brows and took the wafer, slipped it under a thick gold bracelet. "Time will tell. If she is right, then we may not see each other for a while."

"My friends..." Lord Devreux boomed across the vast space. He spread his arms wide in welcome.

Catherine grabbed Rayne, and they hugged so hard she felt her friend's ribs against her own. She hated to let her go, but if she stayed any longer, she might want to hide in one of Rayne's trunks on its way to Normandy. Without another word, they made their way back to their tables. When Catherine sat down, Cristobel perched on the edge of the bench. She had several goblets in front of her. Catherine sipped from her own goblet, letting the honeyed wine roll over her tongue.

"Greetings noble lords and ladies. This is a momentous day. By the grace of God and the King of France, two noble families have been joined. It is with great affection and appreciation we celebrate this union." The roof to the Main Hall seemed to rise with all the noise; deep male voices shouted strong words and goblets pounded the tables. Pages and squires darted between tables pouring wine, clinking metal to metal. Isabelle covered her ears with her hands.

"The tournament today was the largest and boldest Pître has ever seen." Again, the shouting and pounding started. Lord Devreux put his hand up. "Awards are not given for winning alone. Knights must set standards for other men. They must be honorable and deserving men. They are living example for others to live by, not always an easy task. However, it is by winning we determine who are the best men."

It struck Catherine that the tenor of Lord Devreux's voice was slightly off. He spoke flowery phrases, yet they came off as insincere. But this would not be the first time she had heard a man speak of bravery and then cower at a hunt. Drink brought out false bravado in many.

Four beefy men entered the Main Hall carrying a wooden chest decorated with yellow griffins. Lord Devreux popped open the lid and held up a shiny cup. "To each man on the winning team, a silver cup."

The men fighting with Dru and Gregoire surged to the front. The seneschal threw a cup to Dru who caught it midair; he held it overhead for everyone to see. Gregoire caught the next cup. He lobbed it high, nearly touching the ceiling. As it descended, he spun completely around, catching it just before it hit the floor. Clapping and thumping started again.

The room seemed smaller with all the people packed into it. A tingle crept up Catherine's neck. A trapped sensation crowded her. She wiped her sweaty hand along the side of her skirt and searched for a distraction. She spotted Dru juggling three cups in the air. A young woman, not much more than a child, dressed in thin wool—probably a servant's daughter, swept past him. He clasped his hand to her shoulder causing her to stop. He took something shiny from his pocket and dropped it into the cup. With a grand sweeping gesture, he gave her the cup. The young woman giggled behind her hand, dipped to him, and left. Catherine was unsure what to make of the scene. A silver cup would feed a servant's family for many years. That along with a silver coin would buy clothing for the entire family. His generosity surprised her. She had never seen this side of him.

Gathering her skirts in her hands, she wondered if there was more to Dru than met the eye, more for her to learn. He strolled with Gregoire over to the table, then positioned himself behind her and placed the two remaining cups next to her goblet. Gregoire did the same to Cristobel. She tilted her head back toward Gregoire, and he cupped her chin.

Catherine pinched her wrist. The room seemed to close in around her. Dru leaned over her to pour wine and the air felt heavy. Then the strangest thing happened. The air floated past her, smelling of Dru–a manly musk of leather and sweat. He gave her a heavy-lidded look, then he turned toward Gregoire and clapped him on the arm.

He lifted his cup. "To us."

Cristobel handed Gregoire a goblet. Near the base, Catherine noticed white powder. Cristobel's gaze was pinned on Gregoire, her posture and face gave nothing away. He had barely taken a sip when his eyes returned to the dais. Lord Devreux held up his hand. The room grew quiet, again.

"Not everyone can be the last man standing. Many men showed great worth today, but only one man can be the best man, the next to the last one standing. The best man must also show true regard for his fellow knights during the competition. To this end, I present the prize for the best man from today's tournament..." Lord Devreux motioned to the back of the room. "To Dru Devreux! The best man! A silver handled sword and matching silver gauntlets!"

The crowd erupted into wild shouts and congratulations. The seneschal brought in a magnificent sword on a red silk cloth, followed by a boy with a matching red pillow. Silver gauntlets rested in the center.

Dru bounded to the dais, lifted the sword from the pillow, and brandished it over his head. Then he clanged the gauntlets together. His father laughed heartily, standing to the side.

Gregoire nipped Cristobel's neck, and she kissed him at the base of his ear. Catherine's eyes were drawn to them when she turned from the dais. Cristobel knew better. Catherine scanned the room to see if anyone else noticed. Sabina certainly had, but she had drunk so much all she could do was form her mouth into a tiny "O". She had seen Gregoire the knight, now it seemed, she was getting an eyeful of Gregoire the lover.

Catherine had to clear him from her mind. She shifted her eyes back to the front of the room. Dru lifted the sword over his head, and his father grinned from ear to ear. The crowd applauded when he pretended to run his father through. Lord Devreux gave a false grumble and raised his fist in pretend anger.

Dru returned to Catherine with his gifts in hand. Several fellows clapped his back on his way to the table.

"Well done." Gregoire said studying the sword. He handed it back to Dru.

"Behold the handle engraving; it's a hunt scene." Dru held it at Catherine's eye level.

She ran her hand over the cool metal, tracing the dogs and deer in the hunt. "It's beautiful. Can you use it?"

"Is it functional?" Dru smirked. He hit Gregoire's backside with the flat of the sword. Gregoire laughed so hard he fell in between Cristobel and Catherine.

He brushed against Catherine, and she felt pressure from his body. His closeness made her uncomfortable, and his scent overwhelmed her, something like sweat, but spicy. It made her dizzy. She felt as if the area between her legs would explode with warmth. She wanted him badly. Perrine was right. She had to get away from him. Before she turned away, he leaned into Cristobel and kissed her. Catherine's heart cracked. She rummaged into her sleeve and wrapped her fingers around the tiny vial. Her heart thudded, and she wondered if she should pour the vial into her wine. Was not she the one who longed to be free of him?

Dru placed a hand at her waist, drawing her away from Gregoire and Cristobel. She lifted her chin to him, but he was focused on the front of the room. A gong sounded, and its vibration rippled about the room. Lord Devreux had left and returned. Clomping onto the dais, his hands cradled a striped fish with a flat blue-black hat on its slimy head.

"Just as a gale surpasses a breeze, one knight eclipses all others. Therefore, the last prize of the day goes to the last standing knight." Lord Devreux faced Gregoire. "Gregoire Le Sage!"

Devreux held the fish over his head. The room went silent. Then a chant began: "Gregoire... Gregoire... Gregoire!" A few women grabbed candles and hoisted them high, tapping in time with the chant. Men thumped their goblets on the table.

Catherine watched him with interest as he strode up to the dais. Now was her chance to use the liquid Perrine gave her. Gregoire's silver cup, now empty, sat next to her goblet. All she had to do was pour wine into the cup and empty the vial into it when she lifted hers. She could do it. But she had seen powder on the base already. If Cristobel gave him a love potion, would this just cancel out her potion or would it work as Perrine described? She tapped the vial's stopper while watching the front of the hall.

When Gregoire jumped onto the dais he had a quizzical expression on his face, especially after Lord Devreux shoved the fish in his arms. "Thank you, Lord Devreux. A unique prize, but it's too much."

He held the fish like a baby, removed the cap, and kissed it. The room shook with laughter.

"The fish has something to say." Lord Devreux gave an exaggerated wink.

While all eyes were on Gregoire, Catherine reached for the wine. Her hand collided with Cristobel's, who held a thimble filled with white powder. Cristobel put her finger to her lips while shaking the thimble over Gregoire's goblet.

"We all need a little help from time to time." She gave Catherine a conspiratorial smile and poured wine into the cup, stirring it with her index finger. Then she whispered to Catherine. "Would you like to test it on Dru? You really should taste the grape before making wine."

Catherine had her answer as to why Gregoire was so amorous. She shook her head, and Cristobel giggled. Had Perrine given Cristobel the powder thinking Catherine would not use the potion?

Perhaps Cristobel was so desperate she used a love potion to snag Gregoire, and Perrine knew nothing of it. Catherine slipped the unopened vial back into her sleeve.

The room hushed. She glanced back at the dais. Gregoire was talking to the fish. She thought she heard him ask it to open its mouth. She watched as he slipped two fingers down the fish's throat.

Then his face lit up. "Ah. He does have quite a lot to say."

He pulled his hand out. He clutched a black money pouch. People in the back were swaying on benches to see. He loosened the strings and poured five of the blackest sapphires Catherine had ever seen into his palm. He pressed his fist containing the gems to his lips.

"Lord Devreux. This is too much!"

Devreux glowed and pounded Gregoire on the back. Everyone clapped, yelling congratulations. Cristobel hugged Catherine, pushing her against Dru. He steadied her with his hand around her waist.

"Cristobel is in for a shock," he said to Catherine, watching Cristobel make her way to the dais. "Too many women before her have wished for a proposal from Gregoire, but it will never happen."

"I thought he was bound to no one." Catherine stepped in closer so she could hear Dru clearly. Seemed as if everyone pushed to the front.

"True. But his brother died of dropsy last year leaving a young widow. His father wants him to marry his sister-in-law."

"Ah. So, he is promised?"

"Not like a betrothal, but he will do what he has to do." Dru removed his hand from her waist. "We all do what we have to do."

His tone struck her as complacent. He bowed to her and made his way through the cheering crowd. All this talk of love, proposal, betrothals, and marriage—her brain was muddled. Dru had never encouraged her, and she wondered why. Other than a steady hand at her back or a kind word he never attempted to woo her. Love might never enter their relationship. His father and mother never touched. They rarely smiled or gave a kind word to each other. Was this her fate? That Dru and she would represent nothing more than the melding of two families. He was polite, but his heart might never be hers.

Catherine wanted more. The full weight of her future was too much to bear. Her knees almost collapsed under her, and again, the room grew overly warm. She bent over the table. There was no escape, even for someone like Gregoire with the freedom to choose. Isabelle had moved to her side of the bench and stroked Catherine's hair. She reached for her sister and pressed her tiny hand to her cheek, wishing they could leave.

Lord de Gray accompanied Gregoire and Dru as they ambled back to the table. Cristobel held up Gregoire's cup, panting with excitement, her eyelids fluttering. She gave Catherine pause with her obvious desire to be with him. Sabina insisted men wanted a woman who was chaste and demure, yet Gregoire seemed totally enthralled by Cristobel.

Lord de Gray made a circle in the air with his finger. "The finest hunting park in all Pître. Would be my pleasure if you wanted to come stay with us a few days. Invite all Pître." He rocked back on his feet like he always did when he had too much wine. Any other time Catherine would have thought the idea of guests and a hunt were exciting, but not today. She cringed at the idea of Gregoire being at the castle for days. How would she endure it?

Dru spoke first. "A kind invitation. What do you say Le Sage?"

"How can I leave with all the amusements Pître has to offer?" Gregoire tapped his silver cup while smiling at Lord de Gray.

Music started for an Estampie. Catherine rose, lifting Isabelle with her. The pages, squires, and other servants pushed several tables against the walls and voila, a dance floor appeared in the middle of the Main Hall. Isabelle stamped on Catherine's toes.

"Why did you do that?"

"I was trying to get your attention. Hear the music. Your favorite dance started."

Catherine tried to act excited, but what she really wanted was air. Taught to read at an early age and listening to the traveling troubadours, she had come up with her own concepts of love. She had assumed attraction and seduction a straightforward affair, but tonight she had learned it was anything but. With all the bodies dancing and swishing about, heat ballooned, the room shrank, and air evaporated.

"Come little one. I promised you the first dance." Lord de Gray clasped Isabelle's swaying hands and gave Catherine a teasing grin. If he only knew the turmoil swirling in Catherine's head, he would not be so jolly.

Couples were lining up to dance. She was smothering in this grand Main Hall. She pushed through the crowd, her chest burning with need each time she pulled in a breath. She pinched her wrist, knowing full well she was making a bruise, but she could have cared less. She vaulted for the door and the cool air outside.

Catherine felt like a simpleton. She had convinced herself all the tales recited by the troubadours were true. She sucked in a lungful air, shuddering as her body rejuvenated. She truly believed the story her mother recounted about meeting her father, how they never wanted to be separated from the first moment. But love was nothing more than sex sheathed in silk. What a fool she'd been.

She peeked into the hall at all the partners lined up to dance. Gregoire stood to one side. He stared at her and started toward the door, but he made it no farther than a couple of steps before Cristobel clipped his arm and ushered him into the dance. The doors to the Main Hall closed, and Catherine felt more alone than when she first arrived.

Chapter Nine

"Please, come with me." Catherine sat by the cave's warm pool. She made a trough with her hands, dipping them into the water. Bijou lapped up every drop, tickling Catherine's palm with her slippery tongue.

Perrine ground a bright green herb into paste with a mortar and pestle. "Why do you want me there? You know how people view me."

"No one will think anything unusual. You know well that injuries occur at a hunt. Papa will be glad you came. You can stay in my sleeping chamber. No one will suspect it is for any other reason. Sabina says I must go to the hunt, and you warned me to stay away from Gregoire. You control magic, but so far, I have yet to see you occupy two places at once."

She had to persuade Perrine to come with her. It was one thing to be dubious about Gregoire, but nightmares involving him woke her up at every turn. Images so real, she feared falling asleep. The resulting fatigue made her jittery. She was the one who needed a healer.

"There is more to this than you're admitting. You do realize you bring up Gregoire's name more often than anyone else." Perrine placed the mortar down on a rock ledge. A slight mist hung above it like a small cloud. "I gave you the elixir. You decided not to use it."

"You gave Cristobel something, too. He followed her around like a buck during rut." Catherine tucked her feet under her and shivered, then picked up Bijou and nuzzled her ears. "Do you want him with her so much?"

Perrine sighed, coiling her white hair into a bun at the base of her neck. She wore a beige linen bliaut fitted at the waist with a braided tie made of dried flowers. "I never gave Cristobel any powder, but I wish she would run off with him. She is a silly woman, who only worries about whether she will be loved. Such a strange concept. Like all the women this side of France, she listens to the troubadours and believes their every word. You discussed the very topic with Rayne until I was sick of hearing it. Do you ever think about people who worry where their next meal comes from, or if there will be enough food to last through the winter?"

"I think about those things. And I leave alms and food for the pilgrims passing this way. But this is the only place where I can truly say what is on my mind. With Papa and Sabina—and sometimes, even Rayne it's only about duty." Hot tears gathered at the corner of her eyes. She was so tired, the moisture felt good under her scratchy, parched eyelids. It hurt her that Perrine viewed her so shallow. She would have to tell her the truth. Rubbing her arms, and trying to calm herself, she finally spoke. "I can't sleep. My dreams scare me. They are so real that I wake up in pain and sometimes, I smell dead rotting animals. Something else. My dreams linger with me well into the day. Perchance they are a forewarning?"

Perrine's eyes flashed the color of frost-covered roses in the cave's low light. She clasped Catherine's hand and isolated one finger, then placed it against her own fingertip. "Can you reveal your dreams to me?"

Energy flowed from Perrine to Catherine like the thrum of a lyre. She shifted closer to Perrine and lowered her voice as if the spirits might hear. "In one dream, I am falling fast. Which is common enough, and I think it will be all right. Normally, I fall until I hit something soft, jarring me awake. But not in this dream... instead, I land in a bone-filled pit. When I struggle to gain purchase, jagged pieces cut my arms and legs. No matter where I turn, there is nothing to grasp, nothing to hold, and I slide deeper into the heap. I panic and no matter how hard I fight it, I fall deeper. Then everything goes black. The cave or room, wherever I am closes in on me, and I jerk awake."

Perrine pulled away from Catherine. She studied her fingertip. "Your dream came to me without hesitation. I could see the hole, the bones, the light shifting to darkness. It's simple. You remember the sensation you had at Rayne's wedding when you were surrounded by people and fought to breathe."

Catherine nodded, wrapping her arms around herself, and hugging tightly. How could she forget that sensation of being smothered?

"This has to do with the hunt. You dread it. All the guests your Papa has invited to the castle make you uneasy. The bones represent people, the more of them, the larger the burden. As the hunt gets closer, the dream becomes more real, thus the pit, a place you cannot escape."

"Are you sure this is what the dream means?" Catherine couldn't shake the feeling that something was wrong.

"Nothing is ever certain, but it is the closest I can come to an answer right now. Just remember, in a dream your pain is not real. It's but a false shadow. Be mindful of your breathing. Bring yourself into the present. Remind yourself you are not in a pit but in your bed. Touch your face, your coverings, then open your eyes and search for light. Then the dream, along with your disquiet, will slip away."

Perrine slid something into Catherine's hand when she helped her up. "A small token... will keep you safe. Let me gather a few things, and I will go with you to the castle."

Catherine examined the piece of green marble Perrine had given her—a sleek bird suspended from a black silk ribbon. Relief rushed through her when she turned the token over in her palm. She made so much of the dream. Strange how the mind works, she thought, replacing one fear for another. Despite Perrine's explanations, her disquiet persisted.

Perrine transferred the green paste into a sealed clay pot and placed it on the crowded stone shelf, then she picked up her satchel, mumbling to herself, "Something for pain and something for a blistering wound." She dropped hemp seeds into the bag, before tying a strand of chrysanthemum buttons to the outside.

Catherine hugged Bijou, while Perrine pulled on her robe, tucking her hair deep into the hood. Now that Perrine decided to come with her to the hunt, she felt relieved. The little dog scrabbled at her pocket and dove inside, mewing more like a cat than a dog. For the first time in several days, Catherine felt like she might finally sleep.

Gregoire led Fiérsabo out of de Gray's stable. He had brushed and groomed him without the help of his squire. Sometimes he liked to ruffle the courser's coat with his fingers, massaging the hard muscles below. He walked around to its muzzle and blew into dilated nostrils. The horse snorted its approval.

The old seneschal came around the corner. Because of a crippled foot, he walked with a limp, using a wooden cane carved with a wolf's head. Though his son had been killed without escort on a road posted with boar warning flags, Gregoire had been around enough castles to know things were not always as they appeared. Gregoire was wary of the old man. Had he sent his son out on some clandestine errand? Or was his son beyond the castle gates without his father's knowledge?

"Sir, let me find a groom to help you." Faith leaned on his cane, crooking his frail body to one side. His voice was unexpectedly strong. "You should be eating breakfast with the rest of the guests."

"Plenty of grooms and squires were ready and willing to help, but

I like to feed and brush my horse before a hunt. Makes for a closer bond between man and beast." Gregoire stepped closer to Faith and noticed a medallion on his chest. The metal was covered with superb engravings. "Your medallion is well-crafted. I have never seen anything like it."

Faith winced and covered the medallion with his hand. "It belonged to my son, but I wear it now. The cool metal against my chest reminds me of what was. I have never been able to thank you for finding him and returning his body to us."

Gregoire envisioned the young man lying gutted in the road. The poor fellow experienced a horrible death. "My condolences. It must have been a shock. He appeared healthy otherwise."

"Young men die as easily as old in this world." Faith gestured to the castle entrance. "There is still time if you want to meet the others for breakfast. I can have your squire ready the horse."

"Seems crowded in the castle. But thank you." Gregoire went back to brushing Fiérsabo, a mindless activity.

He had avoided breakfast, even though the scent of roasted lamb filled the entire bottom floor. Tables overflowed with small Brie tarts, bowls of eggs in green sauce, and platters layered with jellied fish. Leaving through the kitchen, he caught the eye of a woman with a chesty laugh; she gave him roasted chicken stuffed with leeks. He had not seen Cristobel since his arrival at the de Grays, but he had no doubt she put something in his drink after the Devreux tournament. He had never wanted a woman so badly in his life. His blood was so randy he could have taken her right there in the Main Hall. Luckily her father had approached him about marriage, and it sobered him up faster than a mouse in a cat's paws.

High-pitched voices rang out into the courtyard. At first, Gregoire thought the servants were quarrelling. Two women crossed over to the sitting gardens. One patted the other in a consoling manner, while the other shooed her away. As she backed away, her hood slipped, and white hair shone in the morning light. He recognized Perrine at once. The other girl turned. Catherine glared at him and flipped her braid over her shoulder before she straightened to her full height.

He tried not to stare and quickly pulled his gaze in another direction, but not before he saw Catherine narrow her eyes, They shifted from blue to black. The effect startled him. Instead of distancing himself, he felt drawn to her. His senses came rushing back to him. This was Dru's future wife, and he had no business considering her thoughts or actions. They had nothing to do with him.

Before Rayne's wedding, he had envisioned Catherine as some mythical person, but she was real. She was not what he expected, but something about her, maybe her feisty nature or her independence, made for a curious young woman. He felt as if he could love her if given the chance. The thought jarred him. Again, he reminded himself she was betrothed to his best friend. If he wanted to keep the peace, he needed to let those thoughts go.

Just then, Dru stepped into the castle forecourt with several other men, laughing and clapping each other on the back. They spilled farther into the courtyard, and squires started delivering horses. Dru made his way over to Gregoire.

"The rumors are flying about you and Cristobel." Dru stroked his chin like a fox that just raided a rabbit hutch. "Soon your bride to be. Her father is convinced of the same."

Gregoire ground his teeth. "I said nothing to make him think I would marry his daughter. Where are they? I need to make this right."

This had gone too far. All he did was ask for her favor, and yes, he had gone out to watch the stars with her, but she was eager to do so, too. In fact, she had offered him more than a kiss and a hasty feel, but he knew better than to fall into that trap.

"Lord de Gray invited the entirety of Pître at the wedding, but in reality, he only included the families neighboring him. Cristobel's father was not one of them. Much the pity." Dru snickered as he mounted his horse and glanced down at Gregoire. "If you could see your face. After all the women who desire to be Lady Le Sage, to think she might have outmaneuvered your sister-in-law into becoming your bride."

"Cristobel may make a fine lady one day, but Lady Le Sage she will never be." Gregoire swung up into his saddle and rode to the front of the Inner Bailey beside Dru. Odd how much his friend loved reminding him about his sister-in-law. It was as if Dru enjoyed the fact that Gregoire had no feelings for the young woman one way or another. He had never promised his brother to protect his sister-in-law should anything happen to him. Regardless of his father's wishes, he still hadn't gotten past what his brother's death meant to him. Maybe he had delved into it too much and chewed it tasteless. His sister-in-law, a virtuous woman, would no doubt make a fine wife and would bear him several sons, but he had never been able to strike up a conversation with her about anything beyond the weather. His father liked the girl and her family, so it would make an easy match. He needed to let his father know his decision in the weeks to come.

Across the courtyard, Catherine and Perrine had mounted and moved to the front gate. Musicians congregated near the arch ready to parade all the guests to the hunting park. The resulting music sounded neither melodic nor regal.

Lord de Gray burst through the castle doors, talking with Lord Devreux, gesturing at a new stone wall reaching around the Outer Bailey. When Sabina entered the forecourt with the ladies, she skirted around a small flower garden and picked a fresh rose, placing it under the piping of her wimple. Gregoire found the courtyard brimming with something close to happiness, and the idea surprised him. The concept wasn't one encouraged over loyalty and duty which was all he heard about at Henry de Champagne's court.

The courtyard quickly became overcrowded and noisy once the castle emptied. Gregoire guided his horse, taking it all in. Dru was just ahead. He sat tall in his saddle. Once they were even with Catherine and Perrine, drummers rattled out a rhythm. Without any warning, Catherine spurred her horse.

Dodging musicians, she headed straight through the gate,

galloping through the Outer Bailey. Audible gasps rushed through the crowd. Two lines of people had already formed near the portcullis, and she bolted between them. In no time, Perrine goaded her scruffy palfrey. Sabina covered her mouth, her face set in disbelief. Gasps of disapproval hung in the air. Gregoire was slightly amused to see Dru's mother Lady Amée, pressing her bottom lip with her finger, a noncommittal look pasted on her face. Despite all the commotion, Lord de Gray shook his head with a grin as if he expected nothing else. The man gained Gregoire's respect by the day.

Dru huffed. "Vin Dieu! Is she deranged? Ho!"

He spurred his horse and chased after her, but instead of avoiding the musicians he ran right through them. Instruments clanged to the ground as men dove out of the way. Gregoire pressed his lips between his teeth to keep from laughing. Now, this was the best start to a hunt he had ever seen.

Catherine dashed beyond the Outer Bailey, and Perrine fell farther behind. Castle Road stretched before them like a brown ribbon. Dru shouted over his shoulder at Gregoire. "She needs to see what a real horse can do."

Dru pushed his courser into a gallop. Gregoire let Fiérsabo have his way and for a while they were all racing down the road like dry leaves in the wind. Once even with Perrine, he reined in his horse. Showing up Dru in front of friends and family was not what Gregoire was about.

Fiérsabo cantered, and Gregoire leaned in Perrine's direction. "Is this the usual way to start a hunt in Pître?"

"Nay." Perrine kept her eyes on the road.

"Appears Dru has turned this into a race. Do you think he has a chance?"

"What do you think?" Her answer mocked him, but there was no twinkle to her eye, no amusement.

He would try to bring her around. "I understand you are an exceptional healer. Some say wise beyond your years."

Perrine did not respond. She kept her visage noncommittal.

Gregoire made another try. "Catherine has a good head start, but Dru is fiercely competitive. She does know that?"

"Have you never seen her ride before? It's like she is part of the horse. Not to worry." Perrine finally looked his way, shielding her pale, pink eyes with her hand. "Why did you really stay in Pître?"

"Lord de Gray invited me to hunt."

"I think there is something else, some other reason." She kept her spooky eyes trained on him. Then she raised her hand, forking her first two fingers and pointing them toward Gregoire. "Catherine must be left alone."

Was she giving him a command or a hex? He swallowed. She gave her horse a kick and galloped ahead of him. If she cast a spell, he felt no changes. Perchance he misread Perrine. No, he hadn't. She showed contempt, not fear. He was perplexed. As far as he knew, he had said or done nothing to offend the odd healer. Tu Dieu! He had only been around her once or twice. How could she make such judgments about him? Cristobel, as much as he hated to admit it, was right. Perrine was strange, much stranger than just her white hair and pink eyes.

He trotted ahead. Dru's horse strained to catch up with Catherine. Just as he neared her, Catherine veered off the road and clipped across a meadow toward three blue tents set up in a clearing. Dru struck his horse with a crop and charged into the meadow closing in on Catherine. Even from behind, Dru's stiff posture betrayed his anger. Gregoire's heart pounded in his chest, and he urged Fiérsabo into a gallop, whizzing past Perrine. No sooner had he entered the meadow than Dru charged at Catherine as if she were a tournament challenger. She slowed her mount. He reached out and grabbed Catherine's reins, guiding her to a halt. Once stopped, he slapped her reins against his thigh.

"Such reckless behavior. I thought it was an accident during the wedding, but I see now you have no control of your horse. Someone needs to tame you before you hurt someone." Dru's voice carried over the meadow as he faced her. "This behavior will not hold once we are married."

Gregoire had seen Dru angry so many times since they had arrived in Pître; he had almost begun to expect it. At first, Catherine seemed astonished at his outburst. But then she tensed her shoulders, stiffened her back, and glared down her nose at Dru. Clearly, she had no intention of allowing him to intimidate her. Instead of thinking her disrespectful, Gregoire felt pride in her. She captured the kind of strength a woman needed to rule in her husband's absence.

Shushing through the underbrush beyond them, huntsmen appeared, ready to take their horses. Dru rolled his eyes at Gregoire and threw down Catherine's reins to one of the men. Shaking his head, he guided his own horse to the edge of the forest where more huntsmen gathered with sniffing hounds.

Gregoire rode over to Catherine, and considering her stiff posture, he remembered the lore he'd overheard about her. Supposedly, she could hold her own with a bow and attended small hunts when her father entertained guests. Yet, something about her seemed off. He attempted to lighten the mood. "Joining in the hunt?"

With one hand, she lifted her reins from the huntsman and returned them to their proper place, then turned to face him. "I had no idea men were so fragile."

"Dru? He is far from fragile. You saw him in the mêlée." Gregoire eased around her. "He hates to lose. Probably best if you try not to antagonize him."

He had come as close to warning her about Dru as possible. Once married, there would be nothing he could do. His stomach churned, and he wished there were some way he could protect her. But none of this was his affair; best not make it that way. He led Fiérsabo away.

Drumbeats approached and musicians crested the hill. Behind the performer, brightly garbed hunters on horseback pranced along the road. Gregoire headed down to the wood's edge and dismounted. Huntsmen tended to dogs and folded netting, much too busy to pay much attention to the crowd pouring into the field.

The Master of the Hunt came charging through the woods, his horse pulling at the bit. He motioned to a few men grappling with the snuffling dogs. Giving a brief nod, he pointed in two directions, and the huntsmen immediately disappeared into the woods. He rushed over to Dru and Gregoire.

"Mount!" he yelled. He lifted his arm in the air and made a circular motion. A horn blasted a high note and punctured the air.

Lord de Gray and his honored guests stopped. Suddenly, the hunters among them left the road, raced past the tents, and ignored Catherine.

Master of the Hunt shouted through cupped hands. "They have sighted the Giant Stag! The Lymer is on its trail!"

Pounding toward the forest ahead, de Gray yelled. "A fortuitous sign! Let the hunt begin!"

Chapter Ten

Catherine stood with Perrine under the tent, watching men, late to the hunt, lope into the woods. She silently played with a loose string hanging from her sleeve.

"Dru is not like your father." Perrine sighed and touched Catherine on the back.

"I am beginning to realize just how little he is like anyone I know." Catherine shrugged Perrine's hand off her back. She did not want to be calmed.

She resented the exclusion from the actual hunt. Her father had never required her to stay behind, in fact, most hunts he asked her to participate. He proudly laughed when she cleverly stalked animals that most men were too cumbersome to track. Being petite had its advantages. However, Sabina had come to her room earlier in the morning and announced that Catherine had hostess duties instead. Upon leaving the room, Sabina added that Catherine must leave her bow and quiver behind, taking away even the most remote possibility of hunting.

Catherine wanted to prove her hunting skills. How else could she show Dru her accomplishments? After all, she didn't have a trunk full of embroidered bedclothes or tapestries. It had been a foolish desire. She now saw her mistake. He cared not one whisker for her prowess as a hunter. She began to wonder if he had any real interest in her at all.

Sabina's horse ambled over. She dismounted and came over to Catherine. "Luckily the men were called to hunt straightaway. What came over you? It was rude to bolt away in front of our guests."

"I...." Catherine didn't finish. What was the use? No one would believe she panicked over a little congestion and noise. Ever since her reoccurring dreams, crowds and confined spaces made her feel trapped as if someone tightened a press. Everyone preferred to believe she was ill mannered and thoughtless.

"These are your guests. They are our neighbors. Unlike Rayne, you will live in Pître the rest of your life. People never forget an offense. You will do well to remember that."

Catherine pinched her wrist. She kept her eyes even with Sabina. Her nature made her want to grab her horse and gallop to the end of the earth just to escape all the expectations. Tears threatened, and the back of her throat burned, but she would never let her stepmother know how she really felt.

"One day you will host your own hunt with your husband. You must treat your guests with dignity. We have gone over this. Now offer the women the special tansy cake made especially for them. There is plenty of spiced wine and a good hostess will make sure each guest's glass is never empty."

Catherine scanned the tables set with fine white linen brought from the Eastern trade routes. At the very end of the table, she spotted red rose petals. Her favorite soft pink candies were sprinkled with hard sugar then wrapped inside the petals. At least Dagena watched over her. Would probably be the only bright spot in her day.

Women huddled together in groups of four or five; their voices wafted over a gentle breeze while they watched the dark gap in the forest where the hunting party entered. A couple of women wore sticky perfume in their hair, and it seeped through the diaphanous fabric of their wimples, dripping onto their necks. They swatted flies that gathered to lick away the sweetness, spoiling the entire effect. While Catherine knew this was part of a new trend, she also found it silly and thumbed the cincture around her waist, clamping her teeth around her lips to keep from giggling.

A young woman accompanied Lady Amée into the tent. Immediately, Catherine recognized her. Dru had given her the silver cup at Rayne's wedding. She wore a robin's egg blue woolen bliaut; the rich color signified that she had been elevated in status to a handmaiden. Her hands folded into her skirt, and she made every effort to seem small and invisible. She was never farther than two paces from the lady. Every so often, Lady Amée pointed to her cup or raised her finger to beckon the young woman. When she approached the older woman, she drew her body inward as if she feared Lady Amée might strike her.

The women in the tent didn't hold Catherine's attention for long. Several large dogs dashed back and forth from the meadow to the forest, howling and barking, the de Gray colors strapped to their backs.

"A stag brings luck, does it not?" Catherine couldn't stop watching the men though they were gray shadows in the shaded forest.

"More than luck. A prosperous year to follow. Good crops, fat babies, and enough livestock to sell at market." Perrine stood perfectly still.

It unnerved Catherine how little energy Perrine used when she wasn't mixing elixirs or gathering plants. As if she were saving all her strength for something bigger. Maybe she simply called as little attention to herself as possible, but Catherine wasn't convinced.

Catherine let her gaze wander over the tent's silky fabric from one angled post to another. In the middle, a musician played a simple flute ditty, the tune perky enough to dance if the women wanted; yet no one began. Instead, they continued to gossip and sip wine.

Standing around was not to Catherine's liking. She much preferred to be in the woods and agitation built like smoke in a charcoal kiln.

To her right was a shuffling sound, followed by a whine. It grew in intensity. Perrine swayed into the sunlight as if she'd forgotten her aversion to scrutiny. Sweat streamed over her brow, and she placed her hand on her chest as if in pain. Catherine closed the space between them, but Perrine brushed her away. The healer's breathing labored. She released another high-pitched whine. All the women in the tent stared at her. Just as quickly as it started, it stopped. Perrine came to her senses and grabbed her forehead, looking around in confusion. Red blossomed on her pale face, and she covered her cheeks with her palms. Catherine reached out for her again, but Perrine ran from the tent, leaving her behind.

Catherine bunched her shirt and stepped out. Horns sounded from deep in the woods and halted her stride. In such a short time, the hunt was over. Impossible. Catherine strained to see into the woods. Red, yellow, purple, and green tunics ran between the trees like rabbits fleeing a burrow. From a break in the trees, men coursed into the meadow, their overwrought hounds bounding all around. A few women from the tent dashed to the meadow with their cups lifted in the air. They shouted over the barking dogs.

Contagious laughter floated over to Catherine. Her eyes shifted over the grounds, but she didn't see Perrine anywhere. De Gray colors raced past her as anticipation rose. A festive atmosphere filled the meadow, and she wished Isabelle were with her. Her little sister would have adored all the excitement, but Sabina squelched the idea from the beginning, saying her sister was too young and would only be in the way.

A lone huntsman blew a long horn as he marched to the center of the meadow. Once he was surrounded by the crowd, he played three short clear notes. Dru pranced out on his horse, holding a massive stag head mounted on a blood-streaked pole. The Stag's antlers jutted out well past Dru's shoulders. It was a magnificent sight. He was the only hunter mounted on his courser; the other men led their horses in his honor.

Inside the tent, musicians started a celebratory song, and women clapped along, reentering with smiles and empty cups. Men whistled and shouted, finding partners among the women, swinging them into the air. To add to the sense of good fortune, a light breeze rained orange flower petals across the meadow. It was truly a magical sight.

Sabina came up behind Catherine, placing her hand on her shoulder. "The Stag's power belongs to Dru, now. He will also have the luck."

"I hope his mood is much improved."

Sabina lifted a brow. "I've seen men determined to master the hunt as if their lives depended on it. Dru is keener on winning than any man I've ever seen."

"If only it was a simple matter of winning or losing. He said I was reckless and needed to be tamed." Catherine hated to repeat his words to her, especially if it proved Sabina right, but from whom else could she seek advice?

"Hmm. He has already forgotten." Sabina pressed her lips together in a small smile and lifted her cup in Catherine's direction. "His attention is diverted elsewhere. With all his prizes and victories, his mood will be high. You will soon learn his temperament and how to please him."

Catherine had not expected this response. After all, Sabina had earlier said that everyone had long memories.

"Best to keep men a little off balance, or they lose interest." Sabina tweaked her brow again. Mauve wine stained her upper lip, and her breath smelled thick with it. She cupped her breasts, pushing them toward her chin. "Once the bee tastes the honey, he will stay close, but never give out your honey all at one time––otherwise he will search for more elsewhere. Maintaining their interest is always challenging, though. Surely your friend the healer has discussed these things with you. She gives women enough potions and powders."

Catherine was disgusted. Sabina talked about sex with her ridiculous bee analogy, but the thought of her tantalizing Catherine's father was a sickening thought, and she scrunched her nose in disgust.

"It will all come in good time." Laughing, Sabina pushed Catherine into the cluster of women, right beside Lady Amée Devreux who watched her son with such intensity, she was completely unaware of Catherine.

According to Rayne, her mother made no secret of her favoritism for Dru. Catherine had to agree when she saw that Lady Amée smiled and waved a scarf in Dru's direction. She proudly wended her way through the crowd. The timid servant girl stayed behind and concentrated on the tips of her toes. Catherine wasn't sure why the girl held her attention, but Lady Amée had kept her close since Rayne's wedding.

Dru spotted his mother, then Catherine, and nodded at them, making his way through all the people congratulating him. He jumped from his horse, landing with his legs spread wide. With a grunt, he rammed the wood pole into the soft ground, bringing the Stag's dead eyes even with his. The crowd drew in a gasp. He pinched one of the smaller tines between his finger and thumb. His eyes widened, and he roared with laughter.

"For you." Dru lifted a glistening white sac from his saddle and dropped it into his mother's waiting hands. The Stag's round, white testicles bulged against the slick membrane. He leaned down, kissing her cheek. "Enough luck for this year and the next."

Lady Amée made a show of bowing before her son, lifting the testicles for everyone to see. She took a step back and searched until she caught the eye of her new handmaiden. The girl slid through the crowd, and Lady Amée dropped the slippery sac into a leather bag. The girl made a quick bow in Dru's direction, but he took no notice.

Catherine held her breath. Dru's mother kept this girl close, but something else was at play here. His gaze had brushed right past the handmaiden. He had seen Catherine. She knew he had. He had briefly nodded to her, but he pointedly ignored her. Other women noticed, some gestured toward her, shaking their heads, tilting their heads to the back of the tent.

He pushed through the crowd, stomping to the tent. "Wine. I need wine."

His eyes appraised her as he drank—for an instant Catherine felt like an errant child after a scolding. A feeling she wanted to chuck away. He appeared to revel in his anger. Perhaps Perrine could help. Maybe it was just a matter of correcting his humor. Possibly, he had too much black bile or a buildup of phlegm in his colon. The people he seemed to have a friendly relationship with were his sister, Rayne, his mother, and Gregoire.

Catherine became aware of Lord de Gray standing beside her. Engrossed in her thoughts, she had not heard him draw near. She turned to address him and was shocked to find Gregoire on the other side of him. He put a hand at his daughter's back and guided her to a corner of the tent, continuing a conversation with Gregoire.

"It has become considerably more dangerous to travel Castle Road. Boars have marked their territory up and down Bracken Woods. We've allowed it to go on too long. It's time we thinned them. If we don't, they will take over Gabriel's Stream, and no one will be safe."

Gregoire obviously considered it, his expression distant as if he were already devising a plan. Lord de Gray thrust a goblet in Gregoire's hand.

Perrine slipped silently to Catherine's side. Gregoire turned to them and handed Catherine the goblet. Perrine coughed into her fist, giving an almost imperceptible shake of her head in Catherine's direction. Without hesitating, Catherine gave her the wine. Perrine swirled the liquid, and Gregoire chuckled.

"In case you didn't notice, Lord de Gray gave the wine to me first. Do you think I had the time or the inkling to put something in the drink?"

Perrine focused on him over the lip of the cup and sipped.

Gregoire lifted his eyes to the heavens, then spoke directly to Catherine. "I will return with another."

When he turned his back to them, Catherine heard him speaking under his breath, "As if I need potion for love."

He slipped through the crowd past Lord de Gray to a table peppered with wine goblets. De Gray leapt onto a portable dais, hoisting his goblet. Perrine fanned her face, her skin a bright pink. She spoke to Catherine from the side of her mouth, "I still don't trust him."

"You have said that before." Catherine crowded Perrine. "What happened to you earlier? You looked so strange. Don't tell me it was nothing."

"Nothing" Perrine's expression remained bland. "No need to worry about me. Wasn't a premonition or anything of importance. A shared experience, perhaps."

"What aren't you telling me?"

"When I understand it, I'll let you know." Perrine touched the notch at her throat. "I promise. For now, you must remember what we spoke of earlier."

"You told me to stay away from Gregoire, but maybe the one I should worry about is Dru."

"Hmm." Perrine's attention had moved on, yet she remained at Catherine's side.

Gregoire returned with two goblets, and he let Catherine choose. He looked so relaxed; Catherine could see why Dru felt comfortable with him. He clinked his goblet against hers.

"To Dru." He grinned like a mischievous little boy.

Catherine saw the reason so many women chose him. He had the most seductive smile. He gave Perrine a salute and melted into the crowd.

Lord de Gray motioned to the musicians, and the music stopped. One hundred goblets rose in unison. "In all my years of hunting, I have never seen a more magnificent animal. Dru Devreux slowed the beast with one quick thrust of his spear. He finished the slaying with a single slash of his blade. A masterful kill."

Goblets clinked, and everyone drank to Dru. Lord de Gray held up his hand for silence a second time. "With great appreciation we toast you for the luck this kill will bring. We can anticipate a fine harvest, warm winter days, and above all, healthy baby boys to carry on the names and traditions in Pître."

"Hear, hear!" echoed through the tent.

Catherine drank, but her heart wasn't in it. She watched Dru interact with the adoring crowd. He enjoyed all the attention, flashing an exaggerated grin as his gaze swerved over the uplifted faces. He gave a flourished bow before lifting his glass. He seemed to spot someone. He grinned broadly, then his smile disappeared while his drink hovered in midair. Everyone turned.

Lord Devreux clutched his chest, his face paler than chalk. His drink splashed on the ground, and his lips were ringed white with pain.

Dru threw down his cup and dashed to his father. Lord Devreux collapsed, falling backward. He hit the ground with a thud. Lady Amée shrieked and ran through the crowd. Devreux rolled on his side, pressing his chest with his fist.

Catherine felt a breeze. Perrine had pushed past her and now kneeled beside Lord Devreux.

"When did the pain start?" Perrine placed her tiny hand on his forehead. Catherine had seen her do this many times. The skin's temperature told Perrine whether the illness could be cured with a simple willow tea or required a combination of herbs.

"Just... started." Lord Devreux could hardly speak; his teeth ground together.

"Is the pain in the front or back?"

"Center." Lord Devreux croaked.

"How about your left arm? Pain there?"

"Yes. Mon Dieu... make it... make it go away."

Lady Amée knelt on the other side of her husband. He tilted his head back, the veins in his neck distended. Suddenly, he stiffened and began to shake. His eyes rolled back until only the whites showed, and he kicked in all directions, his arms flailing wildly. Perrine tried to hold his head, but foam oozed between his teeth, dribbling down the sides of his cheeks. Dru grabbed his legs to hold him still.

Perrine aimed her words at Dru. "I need my bag. It's on my horse."

Dru's clasp on his father tightened.

Perrine leaned over Devreux. "Release him. Let him thrash... holding him will only hurt him."

"Get my bag!" Perrine motioned to Catherine.

Before Catherine made it to Perrine's horse, Gregoire passed her carrying the satchel. She spun around and followed him back to the tent. Lord Devreux had stopped convulsing by the time they returned. The crowd had parted, giving Perrine room to work.

Devreux writhed on the ground. Gregoire handed the bag to Perrine and stood beside Dru, wrapping an arm around his shoulder. Dru stiffened, then leaned into Gregoire. Quickly, Perrine removed a mortar and pestle, a bundle of foxglove, and a dark brown vial. She stripped off one leaf, folded it into fourths, then tore off one corner. She placed it in the mortar and shook a drop of clear liquid from the vial. Mint scented the air when she mashed the leaf, creating vivid green oil.

As Lord Devreux rocked back and forth, she dipped her finger into the oil and forced his mouth open. She smeared the oil along his gums and tongue, then closed his mouth. Within a few breaths, his pain visibly eased, and his restlessness subsided. Perrine pulled a wooden object from her bag. It resembled two cups stuck back-to-back. She put the larger cup on Lord Devreux's chest before placing her ear to the smaller one.

"Everyone must be still and quiet. Not a word," she said.

A few onlookers placed fingers over their lips as if they might forget the order. Perrine listened. Her face remained impassive. After a moment, she sat up, motioned to Catherine, then rummaged in her bag. She brought out a willow branch and some hemp seeds. Catherine recognized it easily from childhood, when her mother was treated with willow tea to assuage the pains during her lie-in. Perrine's mother worked the cure. And now Perrine stripped a section of bark and swished it in a goblet of wine. She crushed the hemp seeds and dropped the crumbs into the red liquid. Lord Devreux tipped forward so he could drink it. He took three sips, then laid back.

Perrine rocked on her heels and eyed Lord de Gray. "He needs to rest for at least three days, possibly longer before he can travel."

"Our castle is close. We will go there," Lord de Gray commanded.

Perrine nodded and gave Lady Amée the goblet. "Have him drink the remaining solution to the last drop."

Lady Amée mumbled an expression of thanks as she took the potion from Perrine. Her hands shook almost sloshing the wine onto the ground.

"He has had a serious injury to his heart. Do not thank me yet, my Lady."

Lord Devreux waved his wife off. "Feels like a horse sitting on my chest."

"Keep drinking. The pain will ease." Lady Amée put the cup up to his lips.

When Perrine rose, Gregoire held out a hand. She took it with a slight shiver, stepping over to Lord de Gray and Catherine. "My Lord, he must have nothing but rest for the next few days. It can make the difference between life and death."

"Of course. Whatever he needs." De Gray curled his fingers into his beard and tugged the whiskers along his jaw. "We can transport him using one of the carts."

"Once he finishes the wine, his pain will be lessened. Only then can he be moved." Perrine thumbed the wooden listening cup.

Lord de Gray nodded to Perrine and left to prepare the

entourage. Gregoire pointed to the object resting in Perrine's palm. "I have never seen a healer use one. What is it?"

"I call it a listening bell. You can cup your hands and do the same thing. It magnifies sound."

"What do you hear?" asked Catherine. She saw Perrine as a true healer, but she worried others may see her as something else.

"The rhythm of life." Perrine demonstrated how to use the listening bell on the back of her hand. "Close your eyes. Sounds like someone beating a drum inside your chest. God made all creatures with a similar sound. Unless I hear a disruption, all is fine."

Perrine walked away, leaving Gregoire with Catherine. From the easy way Perrine spoke to him, her distrust of him had disappeared for some reason. Though surprising, Catherine would ask her about it later.

Gregoire held the larger bell against his palm and listened. "Hmm, my hands make a swishing noise as if under running water. Interesting object."

Catherine held out her hand. He released the device and turned. All his recent humor had drained away, and he'd become deadly serious. Perrine readied her bag, while de Gray and Lady Amée mounted. Dru came up beside them just as Catherine handed Perrine the listening bell. She turned to see Gregoire tap his chest, a sign to his friend that he was ready to do anything necessary for him. Her head whipped back toward Dru. His eyes clouded, and he gave a stiff nod. These strong men shared a strong friendship, and it made Catherine glad to think that Dru wasn't alone.

"Can you retrieve my other medicinal bag from the cottage, Catherine?" asked Perrine.

Lord de Gray ran his foot along the lip of his stirrup. "I can send someone else. Catherine should leave with the rest of the guests."

Perrine's brows drew together. "Will you allow someone to escort her? She knows what the bag looks like."

Lord de Gray huffed and sat in his saddle, his eyes on Perrine as if to say his mind was made. Gregoire trotted over. "I will go. Can you describe the bag to me?"

"It is a sack with a large pine embroidered on the outside. My mother would know, but she and Papa are beyond Bracken Woods preparing new beehives for the coming year. Catherine knows where the medicines are kept."

"I'll escort her my Lord," Gregoire said.

Lord de Gray grunted. Obviously, he didn't like the idea of sending his daughter with a single man, no matter how much he trusted him. He regarded Gregoire with two fingers resting on his temple, then he sighed before speaking. "I will send my most trusted men with you. Keep my daughter safe."

Gregoire tapped his chest for the second time since Lord Devreux collapse. "With my life, sir."

Catherine scampered onto Moncadeau. "If we hurry, we can arrive back at the castle before the vesper bells."

Gregoire drew up beside her. She urged Moncadeau into a gallop. She glanced back at her father trotting next to Lady Amée. Dru sat in his saddle, watching Catherine and Gregoire leave. The rest of the hunters and guests, including Sabina, were forming a line back to the castle.

Before long, she urged Moncadeau faster and only Gregoire's horse kept up. If she'd slowed for the other men, they'd still be traveling on Castle Road. Gregoire rode beside her in silence, until they approached a familiar bend in the road. They slowed, and Catherine craned her neck, anticipating the thatched cottage. She looked over at Gregoire. Mon Dieu, he stared back with those watery green eyes. They would cause the death of her.

"Perrine has an unusual amount of skill for such a young healer," he said. "You know more than you say."

"It's an easy explanation. She grew up under her mother's skirts, attending to the sick in Pître. Her mother comes from a long line of healers. And her papa knows more about herbs than anyone." Catherine looked off into the distance. "Her father has intimate knowledge about which herbs can cure, and which ones can kill. Perrine has the advantage of learning from both parents."

"Dru says she has magic powers, too. Is that true?"

"You saw her. Do you think she practiced magic?" Catherine didn't want to reveal too much about Perrine.

"I watched her today when Dru's father collapsed. She was beside you one moment and beside him the next." He shifted in his saddle. "No one can move that fast. Others may have seen her. You should know so you can caution her."

A smile pulled at Catherine's mouth. "She is more healer than anything. You may have thought she was faster than normal, but she would be surprised to hear you say it. The cottage lies just ahead."

Catherine jutted her chin toward a single room thatched house. A newly built stone chimney rose at one end. Gregoire dismounted and helped Catherine to the ground. His now familiar musky scent filled her head, and if playing games, she would have pretended dizziness. Descending from the horse, she noticed his scarred wrists. In time she was determined to find out what had happened to him, but it could wait until they returned to Castle Road.

"Wait here," said Catherine.

"What?" Gregoire ground his heel into the soft earth.

"She would never reveal her hiding places to anyone else. If I hadn't come..."

"Ah." Gregoire crossed his arms over his chest. "Don't tarry."

Catherine entered, standing for a moment to gain her bearings in the dark room. A wooden table and a small bench were outlined in the gloom beneath a low window. Two rope beds topped with hay-stuffed mattresses lined the back wall. A blue wool curtain with stitched yellow starbursts stretched along the sidewall, adding a unique touch to the room. Bundled dry herbs hung from the rafters, and the cottage smelled like mint and lavender. A nearly invisible crack ran along the ground beneath the table. Had Catherine not known it was there, she would have missed it. She ran her hand along the seam, slowing to lift a latch the same color as the earthen floor, exactly as she had seen Perrine do many times before. Hidden inside a narrow chamber was the embroidered bag. She lifted it, heard a few items clatter, and hurried back to Gregoire.

Catherine handed the bag to him and smiled. "Thank you for understanding. Perrine would have never revealed where she hid it. We all have our secrets."

The corner of his lip quirked up. "She is lucky to have such a loyal friend. I hope she is as faithful to you."

"More so," Catherine replied mounting Moncadeau.

Quickly, Gregoire secured the bag to his saddle. Catherine reasoned her father's men would wait for them on Castle Road. Regardless, Gregoire scanned the horizon, his back rigid, his hand on the pommel of his sword. Cantering into a fallow field, Castle Road lay beyond, but de Gray's men weren't visible. Catherine slowed and Gregoire followed her lead.

"We made good time. There is plenty of light. Not to worry, though, I know the way, even in the dark. Papa taught me to use the stars."

Gregoire's head swiveled in her direction. "By the stars, did you say?"

"My father went with Geoffrey of Rancon on the Second Crusade. Papa was a very young man, and he hadn't ever left Pître before then." Catherine fingered her reins as she told the story. "Eleanor of Aquitaine held temporary court in Antioch. Father couldn't believe that she spoke to many men in their native languages. King Louis teased that she read better than anyone at court, but she could be stubborn. Father said she gave her opinion too freely, and soon men listened to her as much as the king."

"I've heard the same. And your father wanted an education for you. Is that it?"

Catherine held up a finger in the air and freehanded her name. "He hired Frère Cyril, a wise priest to instruct me in Latin, mathematics, and calligraphy. I must admit, while reading is my favorite, calligraphy is my personal enemy." She stroked the air with an invisible pen. "Frotlina says I am too impulsive."

She laughed out loud, and Gregoire chuckled, seeming to enjoy her little confession. "You are full of surprises. Your father allows you to think for yourself. Is this not a dangerous thing to do?"

"He regrets it from time to time."

Nearing Castle Road she pointed at a massive tree husk, its burnt, blackened top scraping the afternoon sky with gnarled, twisted fingers.

"You're looking for my father's men. See that tree?"

"The burned one?"

"Yes."

"Lightning took all the life from it, leaving behind that shell. Some say they hear strange voices coming from it... day and night. Father's men are probably too afraid to wait for us near Burned Tree Meadow."

Gregoire reined in his horse. "Do you believe it?"

"Me?" Catherine studied the tree. "No. Someone probably made up the tale to keep others away. With good reason, too, boars roam from here to Bracken Woods. With dusk coming, we'll need to be cautious."

Gregoire sniffed the air.

"I hate boars. I hope to see the hairless head of the one that killed John spiked on the castle wall one day soon."

"Ah yes.... Unfortunate. I've noticed you and your father with Faith. You seem to have a special fondness for him."

"Faith came to Castle de Gray when my parents were newly married. He can train a courser to race and turn a stallion into a warhorse. He is immensely gifted and can fashion a lumpy piece of metal into a beautiful pendant. Once, he made a fine chair for my mother. Is in my room now. Also, Faith is kind. His son was the brightest spot of his life. It's hard to see Faith grieve and not be affected."

They had slowed to a stop. Gregoire stretched over his horse and

119

placed his hand over hers. "Sometimes horrible things happen to good people like Faith. There is no reason for it."

Catherine gaped at Gregoire. No one had ever touched her with such tenderness. She took in every angle of his face. His actions should have made her uncomfortable, instead she yearned to pull him closer. Yes, this was the trouble Perrine warned her about. Catherine resisted the urge by pretending to examine her horse's mane, just above their hands. But then her gaze fell on his arm, and she traced the thick scar encircling his wrist with her other hand.

"What happened to you? Who did this?" Her voice came out softer than she realized.

Unexpectedly, Gregoire grabbed his reins and goaded his horse forward, leaving her behind. She had misread the moment, but then he slowed and allowed her to catch up. His hands curled and uncurled into tight fists, but he considered her as she approached. He held up his wrist, exposing the wicked cuts. "My first lesson in bad things happening to good people."

Chapter Eleven

Gregoire's head pounded. Tension pulled at his shoulders. Why did this woman have command of him? It didn't make sense. He felt compelled to tell her the truth, but still he had a wall to break down in his own mind.

"You never let down your guard," Catherine said.

"I learned long ago; you can't be too careful." He rubbed the scars on his wrist. Fire ran the length of the marks. "You ask me about my scars, and I will tell you. Although, I think it is more fascination than empathy."

Low afternoon light picked up the gold specks in Catherine's eyes. She pinched her lower lip, then spoke, "Cristobel said she knew why you had scars..."

"I would never tell her anything." Ridiculous. Cristobel whipped nonsense with air and called it a discussion. He felt the strain in his neck and shook his head.

Catherine angled her head, taking in his remark. Nothing about her pointed to deceit or manipulation. It intrigued him more than he expected. She was lovely, but he thought of Dru, his fellow knight and true friend. How could he allow his feelings to rule him?

He swallowed hard but continued. "When I was young, I was a lot like you. I rode across my father's land, carefree as a bird traveling on the wind. I had no fear and spoke to anyone, including the charcoal burners in the woods. My father cautioned me over and over, but I disregarded his warnings and roamed without fear. For my safety, he assigned a knight—Bertrand the Bull—to protect me. The Bull did more than that. He taught me how to hold a sword and throw a spear." He winked. "And other important things like how to empty an entire cup of ale, how to belch louder than a bellowing cow, and how to leap onto a trotting horse from atop a wall.

Catherine laughed. "He sounds like a great man."

"*Yes*. He was brave and worth more than ten bold knights." Gregoire plucked a string from the bottom of his tunic. Using his fingertips, he rolled it into a ball. "The time came for my brother to leave for King Louis's court. As you know a tremendous honor for him and my father. Two years later, I would leave for Henry de Champagne's court, but that is another story."

Fiérsabo's ears twitched. De Gray's men were gathered just ahead on Castle Road. Gregoire noticed the men fanned out into the crowded wheat field. With Catherine approaching they should be regrouping. These weren't lazy or undisciplined men. Their actions made him anxious, and he kept his voice modulated so Catherine wouldn't notice a change in his demeanor.

"Before my brother left, I wanted to give him a special gift. I knew of a skilled woodcrafter who made excellent crossbows, but he lived beyond our border, a three-day ride. My father had his doubts about the trip; there had been several abductions. But the Bull knew how much it meant and agreed to accompany me."

Gregoire paused. Only two of de Gray's men stood on the road, on guard as Gregoire and Catherine drew near. An overturned cart lay precariously at the edge of an irrigation ditch. His gut told him to keep her distracted. He glanced at Catherine to be certain he still held her attention. Her eyes were on him.

"The nights were clear filled with stars and an infant moon. We traveled for two days, sleeping in the open. But on the third evening, as darkness closed in, several men charged out of the woods, surrounding us. At first, I thought they were the friendly charcoal burners, but the Bull knew better. He jumped from his horse, knocking three men down with just his body, swinging his sword in a broad killing arc. I saw him slay three men before I was jerked from my horse and blindfolded."

Catherine drew a sharp breath. A de Gray man galloped toward them, the lowlight creating an orange halo at his back. Even from a short distance, Gregoire could tell the man's face was grim. For the first time since they entered the road, Catherine turned away from Gregoire.

"Ho. An accident ahead. Another boar attack!" De Gray's man called out, holding up his hand. "Appears to be the miller and his wife."

Before Gregoire could respond, Catherine cried out, "Alice!"

Goading her horse with her heels, she galloped down the road. Gregoire charged after her until Fiérsabo pulled ahead. He leapt from the horse, solidly hitting the ground. Catherine reined in and vaulted from her horse. Gregoire was ready for her. He blocked her with his body, pinned her arms to her sides, and shielded her face.

"Let me go!" she howled.

"Please. Allow me to check, first." Gregoire held her so tightly he worried he was bruising her arms. "I promise, I will take you over to them, but let me examine them first."

Catherine stopped squirming and sagged against him as she dropped her head into the center of his chest. She murmured. "She is my friend. Please, let her be safe."

Gregoire loosened his grasp, setting her on the ground. He grabbed her horse's reins and handed them to her. "Stay here. I will return as quickly as I can."

Before stepping away, he checked her once more. Catherine's chin quivered, and it took every fiber in his body not to take her in his arms, stroke her hair and tell her it would be all right. An overwhelming sense of protectiveness filled him, yet she could care for herself.

He took a few steps into a ditch toward the field. Blood spooled out over crushed wheat. Between the rows, de Gray's men had bound a body in a tattered blanket, but another body lay closer. Gregoire plodded over to a young woman. Her plump breasts, wet around the nipple, caught his eye first. A red rash marked her face. Obviously, a boar had not killed her; her head was turned at an impossible angle. Her neck had snapped when tossed from the cart. At least, she was not ripped apart by a beast. One of de Gray's men draped her with a woolen cloth.

Gregoire headed back to the ditch, and as he passed the over-turned cart he noticed a very slight movement, reminding him of a salamander's tail swishing the dirt. He knelt to get a better look. Several baskets were overturned, stacked in a bizarre heap, thrown clear of the cart. He lifted a basket and a tiny leg appeared.

"Does the miller's wife have a baby?" he yelled to Catherine.

"*Yes.* A little boy," she shouted back, dropping the reins and running toward him.

Dirt covered a small lifeless form. Gregoire dug like a dog uncovering a bone. He rotated the infant, cradling its head. Once the baby faced up, he ran a finger through his mouth and around his bare gums, removing moist debris. He watched for respirations, then covered the child's chest with his hand. He felt no movement. He rubbed the center of the baby's back briskly with the heel of his hand.

At his first lusty cry, Catherine grasped the infant, cradling him cautiously against her chest.

"Catherine..."

"Don't say anything just yet." Catherine made cooing noises over the baby, his cries eventually turning to whimpers. When she glanced up, tears brimmed and spilled onto her cheeks. Gregoire eased his hands over Catherine's shoulders, but then stepped back. He'd not touch her in front of de Gray's men though she needed soothing.

De Gray's men huffed around them, bringing up the bodies.

Gregoire gently nudged Catherine away from the cart so the men could right it. He patted the child's head. It was the best he could do. Gregoire moved his hand to a space just beyond the small of her back. His fingers itched to guide her.

"What happened?" Her voice broke.

"The baby's mother was killed quickly, not by a boar. She broke her neck."

Catherine angled herself closer to Gregoire, her voice tight with pain. "I spoke to her only days ago. She came to the castle with her husband to deliver fresh root vegetables and visit her mother. Who could believe it?"

A man approached them from behind. "Boar tracks are everywhere. We heard screams from a distance, but by the time we arrived the damage was done. The miller obviously tried to draw the animals away from his wife by using a dagger. Not much of a weapon. Poor man. He probably never knew his wife was dead. The sound of our horses must have chased the devil's creatures away."

"A shame we were not close enough to help. This must be stopped. I will talk to Lord de Gray upon arrival. We will form a hunting party. As it is, no one can travel safely along this road."

Gregoire scooped up a thick-handled basket from the road and, carefully taking the child from Catherine, tucked it inside. Then, he helped her onto Moncadeau, handing her the basket once she settled into the saddle. She deftly looped the handles over the saddle pommel. The infant continued to mew.

"Who will care for the child?" he asked.

"Our cook, Dagena, is Alice's mother. She will know what to do." She stroked the baby, shushing him. "His mother grew up in our castle. We care for our own. If anything ever happens to Dagena, I will take him."

Gregoire handed her the reins and mounted his horse. Her words stayed with him. She cared greatly for the mother and would take the child, no question. Petite, she appeared weak. It was a mistake to think thus. She was determined and strong-willed. Lord help him. He was hopelessly falling in love with her.

* * *

Catherine rocked along on her horse, watching the sleeping baby. What a day this had been. She shuddered when she thought about the foolish race with Dru. Her feelings had been hurt when he reprimanded her like a small child, making her feel less loved than a clumsy servant. But it paled in comparison with the rest of the day. Lord Devreux might be dead for all she knew. Tragically, Alice and the miller lie dead as husband and wife in a fallow field.

And yet, Gregoire had extended kindness and protection when needed. All the warnings about him from Perrine and Dru dissipated when he unexpectedly used his own body as a shield. Genuine compassion isn't something someone learned. It was part of Gregoire's nature.

While tending the baby, sorrow burrowed into the marrow of her bones and despondency set in. Along with the shock of another friend dying, she fought with her unwanted feelings for Gregoire. Dru valued this man and his friendship. Watching the de Gray colors rise and fall ahead of her, it only made her more aware of Gregoire's position behind her. A thoroughly misplaced fondness wrecked every idea she'd shared with Rayne about chivalry and love. Her feelings should be for Dru and no one else.

If only she could remain on Castle Road, riding forever with Gregoire by her side. She really needed to pull her emotions together. Sabina would call this an imaginary concern. Real live issues stared her in the face. She lifted the sleeping child's hand and ran her finger over several tiny red pustules; insects must have bitten the child while he lay on the ground. This child had no mother. Catherine suspected he would never know the unconditional love or true devotion of a mother. The idea broke her.

Thankfully, Gregoire had taken full control and sent a man

ahead. When they finally arrived at the castle, darkness had fallen, and gummy torches flickered against the wall along the Outer Bailey. The Inner Bailey was lit with both torches and brass oil lamps suspended from rings. Heat licked the stones, making the inner courtyard hot and stuffy.

Dagena waited alongside Sabina and Perrine near the outer kitchen, an open tent set up for all the extra guests. Dagena trudged into the courtyard with her arms extended, whimpering with each step. Catherine gave her the baby. He wailed when Perrine pulled aside his wrappings and examined him.

"He seems sensitive to touch." Perrine used two fingers and pressed along the child's head, backbone, arms, and legs.

"He was thrown from the cart. It is what saved him," said Catherine.

"Unusual for a fall to break a child's bone, but not unheard of. His eyes are red. Has he been crying?" Perrine placed her hand over the infant's forehead.

"Some whimpering at first. Sleeping until you unwrapped him," said Catherine.

"Keep him warm. I will check him first thing tomorrow." Perrine turned to Dagena.

She wound the cloth tightly around the infant, tucking in the corners with a shaking hand. With Sabina's help, Dagena started for the castle kitchen, but just past the garden, her shoulders began to shudder, and she buried her face in the child's wrappings.

"What a horrid day." Catherine handed Perrine the woolen embroidered bag. Items shifted in the exchange, and a muffled clink caught her hearing.

"*Yes.*" Perrine answered in a tired voice, pulling back her hood. Her irises were the color of bloodstones. "You found everything?"

"*Tu Dieu*, your eyes. You must be under tremendous strain. You tell everyone else to rest, maybe you should listen to your own advice. And, yes, I found your bag just where you always leave it."

Perrine waved with her free hand. "Good. As for me, I am

nowhere near exhausted. It's something else, but we can talk of it later."

Too much had happened for Catherine to argue. She could barely put one foot in front of the other.

Perrine gathered her long hair in one hand, coiling it into a loose bun. "I gave Lord Devreux and his wife something to help them sleep. Dru is passed out in the Main Hall. He was caught between celebrating and worrying about his father. Probably for the best."

"How long do you think his father will need rest?"

"A few days I would think. Not more than five." Perrine squeezed a tiny bag between two fingers. "My concern now is about you. Gregoire was with you when you found Alice and her husband?"

"Yes." Catherine bowed her head. "He kept me from seeing them. He–"

"Some things will never be the same after today." Perrine pushed her fingers together forming a steeple, her eyes focused squarely on Catherine. "I was wrong about Gregoire."

This was no small acknowledgement. Her friend had never admitted to Catherine, or to anyone else as far as she knew, that she was wrong about anything. But Perrine had been here at the castle when they found the bodies. What exactly did she mean, she was wrong about Gregoire?

"Catherine." Lord de Gray called across the courtyard. "Come here my dear."

Perrine handed Catherine the tiny pouch. "Pour half the contents of this bag into boiling water, let it steep, and drink it right away. It will help you sleep tonight. We will have time to talk tomorrow."

Pulling her hood back over her hair, Perrine retreated to the castle. While she made her way to Lord de Gray, Catherine ran her finger over the coarse bag, wondering what was happening to her friend. She wished this day had never begun.

"No need to wake everyone. We can start in the morning." Lord de Gray stroked his beard, talking to Gregoire. "But you are right, we must rid Pître of these vicious beasts. I appreciate your volunteering to stay until the job is done. We will need every available man."

Gregoire maintained his rein-hold on Fiérsabo. His squire had not taken the horse to the stable, whereas Faith had personally taken Moncadeau. Catherine assumed her horse was already fed, brushed, and put away. She lifted one shoulder, where today's stress had decided to settle.

"Catherine, Gregoire told me where you found the bodies. Can you tell me exactly which field?"

"The wheat field that runs between Castle Road and Bracken Woods. The larger one with the irrigation canal."

"Par le sang de Dieu!" Lord de Gray flipped the end of his beard. "They are spreading out, claiming more territory. We will start just after Matin bells. Pître must be assured this will not happen again."

Faith joined de Gray with an unfurled map. The two men walked away, tracing lines and plotting strategy. When Catherine faced Gregoire, she was surprised by his visage. He seemed to have lost his spirit.

"Has been a hard day. Once all the boars are all dead, I will leave." He spoke without enthusiasm, and his eyes lacked their usual brilliance.

Pain clouded her brain. She could have sworn her head was going to break right off her shoulders. After everything else that had happened, those were the last words she wanted to hear tonight. She had tried to ignore her attachment to him, and she was tired of fighting something that felt right instead of forced and false.

"I thought you were staying with Dru through the hunting season."

"True. Originally, I planned to stay." Gregoire tugged on the reins, leading his horse to the stable. "Do you know much about a knight's vows?"

He did not wait for an answer. "They are sacred, and I will not betray them. I have come close to making a mistake already."

Catherine wanted to believe he referred to her. Surely, he could tell. She berated herself for her selfishness. After all that happened today, surely, he referred to something else. Perhaps, his father had sent for him. He speaks of vows and betrayal. He must be referring to his brother. It was all in her mind. She glanced over the stable roof into the sky in time to see a shooting star.

"Behold! A star! Make a wish!" She closed her eyes, wishing for the impossible.

"If only wishes did come true." Moonlight reflected off the side of Gregoire's face; fine gold stubble ran along his jaw. She wanted to reach up and touch it, to feel the roughness beneath her fingertips and give him some small comfort.

He sidestepped Catherine and picked up his pace. She scooted in behind him after he placed Fiérsabo in the stable. He took his time with the horse pulling on each blanket, carefully—almost reverently. She ran her hand over a rough board in the stall.

"You take better care of your horse than most men their wives."

Gregoire removed the reins, guiding his horse to a grain-filled trough. "Every knight knows his horse is sometimes the only thing standing between him and death on the battlefield. If I am good to him, he is good to me."

Catherine spotted a brush hanging inside the stall. She went to lift it off a wooden peg, intending to brush Fiérsabo. As she entered the stall, the horse cross-stepped, his rump knocking her directly into Gregoire just as he placed the reins over a high railing. When his arms came down, he naturally folded them around her, steadying her.

They stared at each other, and the air around them stopped moving. Gregoire's eyes reflected the conflict in his soul, but all she felt was the heat from his arms. The world tipped on its side, and Catherine felt she might slide off. Instead of steadying herself, she rose on her tiptoes just as he came down to meet her. She felt his body harden against her. Her fingers skimmed his waist, his muscles contracting beneath her touch.

The pressure of his lips overwhelmed her. Simultaneously apprehensive yet eager, she couldn't make sense of her feelings. Dizzy with emotions and burning with desire the most she managed was a hope that the kiss would never end.

"Ahem."

Gregoire's head jerked up. A cool breeze caressed her moist lips, but his arms stayed warmly around her. Catherine would have spun around, but her knees wobbled in protest. From the corner of her eye, Faith leaned against his cane just beyond the stall.

Chapter Twelve

Faith walked Catherine to the castle. Neither spoke. Words spun in her head, but any kind of conversation was impossible. Gregoire had awkwardly moved aside so that she could make her way to Faith. The silence between them echoed off the courtyard walls emphasizing the scrape and tap of Faith's cane. This only added to her discomfort when Faith offered her his hand and guided her from the stables to the castle. Upon reaching the entrance, Faith leaned all his weight on his good leg and cleared his throat.

"I have known you since you were born. I want nothing but the best for you." He grasped the massive iron handle. "We will never speak of this after today. It will be our secret. And if Gregoire is a man of honor, which I think he is, no one ever need know of it."

He pushed the door open, and Catherine reluctantly slipped inside. If he thought his words were the end of it, he was wrong. After the door closed, she stood in the hallway with every emotion from betrayal to euphoria swirling inside her heart. Her steps lightened as she climbed the stairs. Slipping into bed, sleep evaded her, but she didn't care. No matter the cost, she had experienced love–the passion troubadours sang about, poets wrote about, and saints died for. Wars had been fought over love, and until tonight, she couldn't fathom why.

Gregoire's eyes, his lips on hers–it all came back to her over and over even as she angled her head to gaze at a misty morning through the arrow slit. A knock sounded on the door, and Perrine returned from the kitchen with freshly baked bread alongside a slurry of mashed berries and honey.

"The kitchen is a hushed place this morning." Perrine smoothed a linen cloth over a simple table two paces from the bed, then placed the berries, clotted cream, and bread atop it. "The other cooks are doing what they can, but Dagena is a walking shadow. She has no tears left to cry, but clings to the baby, only allowing him out of her sight to go to breast."

"Poor woman. She is strong though and will recover. Is Frotlina with her?" Catherine ran her hand over Bijou's black furry back, not turning to look at Perrine.

"Yes. She is helping, but the child is sickly. He is strangely warm to the touch, but mayhap he is not suckling from the wet nurse. A shock can do that to a child."

"I hope he will recover. Dagena came to the castle soon after her husband was killed several summers ago. Since Frotlina lived here, it made sense she would want to be near her sister, someone to help her with Alice. Not that she was any trouble. She was such a shy little thing, unlike me, who seemed to stay in trouble. Dagena cares for everyone; now it is time to care for her and the baby."

"She refuses to take anything to ease her grief, saying her daughter would want her to attend to her child with a heavy heart. Something about the depths of despair. Everyone is different, but I did leave her something anyway. Also, your father and Faith were in the gardens outside the kitchen door this morning." Perrine stood next to the table, running her finger over the fine cloth, apparently waiting for Catherine. "They were talking about choosing the oldest hounds for the hunt. Faith's bad leg bulges to twice its normal size this morning. He is much weakened by John's death, but he wouldn't miss being part of the boar hunt for anything."

Perrine was working her way around to another topic. She rarely talked this much, but Catherine let her continue uninterrupted as she adjusted her position to see the activities in another part of the court-yard. Huntsmen brought out muzzled hounds. Once the dogs were on the boars' trail, the huntsmen would remove the leather straps and the dogs would go crazy. Much to her surprise, she understood the feeling. Last night it was as if a binding had been ripped from her heart, allowing it to beat freely. Since then, all she wanted to think about was Gregoire.

"Many strange things happened yesterday. You said we would talk about it today." Catherine left the window.

Perrine dropped onto the bed and licked the cream spread across the bread. Her pink eyes glazed over. "I'm not sure I can explain everything. But I'll try. You talked me into going to the Stag hunt. Yet, I felt that I should go with you, as if something or someone willed it. The sensation clung to me. I couldn't get out from under it."

"Strange things have followed you all your life. But during the hunt, you were so odd... everyone noticed," said Catherine.

"Do you remember hearing a loud clap of thunder before the men reappeared?" Perrine asked.

"There was no thunder."

"You heard no thunder?" Perrine's response was incredulous.

"No. Only horns and hounds."

Perrine swallowed, placing the bread back on the table. She cleared her throat, a sure sign she had something to tell. "I knew the exact moment Dru killed the Stag. A force struck me in the chest, halting my breath. My heart stopped beating. I sensed a shift in power much the same as when a crown is placed on a man's head. Then as quickly as it came, it left. The strangest part wasn't the changes in power but the changes in me. I felt reborn. I would have sworn my body had been struck with a burning arrow. For several moments my heart remained stopped. When it began again, a new power surged within me."

Catherine sidled closer to Perrine. "Instead of Dru receiving the great Stag's power, you did. Is that what you are saying?"

"I am not speaking of the power of the hunt. This is different. The only way I can explain it is... like a gift. The Stag gave me his power, perhaps the power to see beyond today or this moment."

Catherine's hands went to her face. "A sorcerer? Everyone said the Stag was no mere animal. You can change into a stag now?"

"No, no." Perrine took Catherine's hands. "I assure you, I will not be turning into a hart or bounding out of the castle. No. But, I see things in my head I never saw before, like you and Gregoire finding Alice and her husband. The only thing is... I saw it before we left the hunting park–before it happened."

"A premonition." Catherine pulled her hands away. Fear clouded her head. This was a dangerous discussion. She went to the door and checked under the crack to make sure no one heard them. "You should be careful who you tell."

"I may never have another. But there is more." Perrine touched Catherine's forearm.

"I sense energy coming from other people. This is not unbalanced humors or anything of the sort. It's as if I can read your emotions." Perrine took a breath, then folded her hands together. "For instance, I know you kissed Gregoire."

Catherine covered her mouth with her hands. Someone had seen them last night. She'd been a fool to think only Faith saw them. "Who told you?"

"No one told me." Perrine sat on the bed and patted a spot next to her. "This is all so new. I'm learning through observation like before, but my senses are heightened. Let me see if I can explain a little better. When I crawled into bed last night, you practically glowed. Something inside you was altered. You might say that I know you better than anyone and could easily determine the cause, but when I touched your shoulder something incredible happened. Sparks, like exploding stars, went off in my head and Gregoire stood before you. I knew he had kissed you. I have no other way to describe it. Through the ages it is said that when a stag dies, it loses its power. Some legends claim the hunter receives the power, other stories say the stag chooses another animal or human. Whatever the truth, I simply know that there are changes in me."

Catherine put her arms around Perrine, sitting beside her. "This is dark magic. No one can do those things but a..." She pushed the words before they could stick to the back of her throat. "...sorceress."

Perrine leaned her head on Catherine's shoulder. "I am far from being a sorceress. I have no desire for dark magic. Yet, think of what I can do as a healer."

Catherine remembered the day at the cave, how Perrine had lit the torches with a snap of her fingers. She had said the spark was the combination of two elements that marry and create another element, but this went beyond lighting candles and reading lines on someone's palm. Knowing someone's thoughts and practicing sorcery meant a death sentence. The church forbade executions that spilled blood, so sorcerers and witches were burned in France. It was the worst death imaginable.

"Perrine, if you tell anyone else about this, they will think you are practicing dark magic. Promise you will talk to no one until we figure this out."

"I hardly speak to anyone, only you and my parents. Who else would I tell?"

Catherine removed her arm and slipped back to the window. The men were mounted and heading to the Lower Bailey. "What are we to do? You and your new powers, and me with an unrealistic love."

Below her, Gregoire's squire divided and distributed spears among the other men. Gregoire sat on Fiérsabo and maneuvered through the riders to the front of the line beside Dru. Both men wore lower armor on their legs for extra protection. Just seeing Gregoire made her heart squeeze harder.

Lord de Gray led a larger group of men a little way ahead, his standard fluttering in the breeze. Catherine clutched through her thin chemise and clasped her wrist, resisting the urge to pinch and claw at her arms There was a real possibility that someone would come back maimed or draped over a horse, never to see the world again. The thought stuck to her. A hand snaked around her waist, and Perrine tipped her head on Catherine's shoulder.

"This will be hard, but I think you should try to forget Gregoire. He will leave and return to Henry the Liberal's court in Champagne or join his father; either way you will remain in Pître. You would never disgrace your father or sully the family name by running off with him no matter how much you love him. Soon you will marry Dru, and your union will combine the two wealthiest families in Pître. This is what your father has planned for you."

Watching Gregoire leave the castle, Catherine knew Perrine was right, but it made no difference. She had tried not to love him. No one would understand how much she had tried. Tears dripped off her cheeks as she shuffled away from the window. If she could not have him, she would have to find a way to stop thinking about him. She had to close her heart to him, impossible as it sounded.

The afternoon came quickly. Catherine helped Frotlina make new linens for the baby before she left to brush Moncadeau. On her way to the stables, crossing the Upper Bailey, she stopped at the pigeonnier, built to match the stone towers at the front of the castle. Over fifty trained messenger pigeons belonged to her father. Some birds carried messages as far away as the Normandy Coast or Paris. Pigeons were much faster than a human messenger, but not as secure. They could be lost, captured, or killed easier than a man. She considered the days she sent blue-footed pigeons to Devreux Castle delivering messages to Rayne and red-footed pigeons to Perrine. Would her secret messages continue once she married Dru?

Bijou sniffed the pigeons, causing them to scatter into a side pen where Catherine could feed them. She watched the plump birds strut around and reconsidered her conversation with Perrine. What would it take to snuff out her affection for Gregoire? Dru showed no real fondness for her. He showed more consideration for a servant girl than for her. His only devotion seemed to be for Gregoire. More than his indifference was the idea of living under his mother's expectations. Would she be trapped in a loveless marriage? Lord de Gray had signed a betrothal agreement with Lord Devreux; it was nearly as binding as the marriage contract. He would never break it, not even for her. He was a man of honor, his word his bond.

This was her fate, spun out, cut, and measured by the men around her. If she thought for one moment she could change it, she would. Horses skittered into the courtyard, interrupting her thoughts. Catherine whisked up Bijou, dropping her into the small bag that hung from her neck.

De Gray rode in first, covered in blood all the way up to his furry eyebrows. Catherine dashed through the garden eyeing all the knights and huntsmen as they entered the courtyard. A cart rumbled past, piled high with boars' carcasses. Dru's squire guided a horse draped with the body of a man to the stable. Her heart dropped to her toes.

By the time she reached her father, her throat had tightened with anxiety and her voice squeaked out. "Papa! Papa!"

He dismounted, handing his horse off to a stable boy. He glanced at Catherine, then grimaced at the mess on his leather armor. "Boar's blood, not mine. Stinks worse than a bucket of piss. I was lucky though. We lost one man and a hound when one of those sorry bastards charged."

Dru sauntered over, jutting his chin toward the wounded man. "Could have been worse. Your father fell from his horse and was nearly trampled, but the boars were in a hurry to escape."

"Tomorrow, we hunt the rest of the revolting creatures and then feast on their bones." Lord de Gray removed his dagger from its sheath. "Faith has the pots boiling and will send the hides to the tanner. What is it, Catherine? You are shaking all over."

"Look at you. Not for nothing do I tremble." She felt Dru's eyes on her and turned to face him. He held a bloodied spear, and his face held concern, causing her to blurt out, "A man was injured. You returned without Gregoire."

"He will be along soon," said Dru. "Never fear, Gregoire has the luck. I would fight with no one else."

Lord de Gray laughed and patted his middle. He wended through the crowd and stepped toward the castle entrance. "One thing about hunting, gives me an appetite."

Moving aside for the men, Catherine nearly stumbled with relief. Then she felt guilty for the dead man. Someone expected him to return, she knew not his name, but would make it her business to find out. Once Lord de Gray disappeared into the castle, Dru stepped to the door, holding it for her. "The world has altered much since the bell rang two mornings ago. And as such, we must discuss our future."

Catherine stopped at the threshold. This was unexpected. More had changed than he suspected. Fear coursed through her. Did he know of the kiss? He showed no anger.

"Since my father's illness, I have reconsidered our wedding date. An entire year is too long to wait. I will confer with my father, but we should marry at Michaelmas. There would be no need for the wedding party to leave. Gregoire and the other knights could stay until then."

His mood had improved. Apparently, he had discussed this with someone—her father? Catherine smiled, but her insides turned to liquid. She twisted her fingers in the ties of her cincture until they hurt, too shocked to speak. Mordieu, what did she do now?

He opened the door wider, waiting for her go through. A look passed over his face. There was more. "Your father will consider your feelings. It's best you encourage haste."

So, he had not discussed it with her father. She was in no hurry. Dru had said more to her in the last few moments than ever before. There was some hope she could ask him to consider the original betrothal. He motioned for her to enter. His cheek quirked with impatience.

"Forgive me, but I left something at the pigeonnier. Please, go ahead. I will return before supper."

She raced down the steps before he had time to counter. Remembering Bijou slept silently curled into a ball, she stuffed her hand into the padded pouch and fingered the animal's wiry fur. For years she had happily anticipated Dru's homecoming, and their families uniting as one. There was a time when she would have rejoiced at hearing him say he wanted to marry her sooner, but that was because she had envisioned him differently. He seemed to have hidden his true feelings behind a hard shell. He didn't pretend to care much for her beyond the marriage contract.

Behind the pigeonnier was a small shelter used for training the birds, nothing more than a roof top for them to land on. She slipped underneath and dropped to her knees on the soft ground. She pulled Bijou from her pocket and pressed the tiny dog to her cheek. She squeezed her eyes shut, clamping her teeth together to stop tears from gathering.

Her head buzzed. Michaelmas marked the change in season. Maybe she would be ready by then. Yet, when she thought of him touching her, she couldn't imagine it. If she'd not seen him give the servant girl the token and cup, she might think him incapable of feeling. She rocked back on feet until her head touched the stone wall behind her. The birds scratched and cooed on the other side.

Running away wasn't a viable option. The chances of a lone female surviving in the surrounding countryside were risky. She needed the protection of either her father or a husband. Perhaps she could hide until the Devreux left the castle. If only she had a horse with wings to carry her to a distant land or an angel to whisk her away and take her to heaven. Bijou's warm, wet tongue licked her chin and brought her back to the difficulty at hand. It did no good to wish for things that could never be.

Lower light and lengthening shadows meant night approached. A white pigeon flew above her head, circling before landing at the door to the pigeonnier. A miniscule note was coiled around its foot, and

Catherine knew right away it was meant for Perrine because of the red ribbon. She scooped up the bird and removed the delicate parchment. Slanted figures filled the small note.

Horses pounded cobblestone, and the sound of hooves echoed against the Bailey walls. The other riders were back. Catherine tucked the parchment, along with her dog, into her pouch. She heard Gregoire's voice, but she did not wish to see him. She was afraid she might do something ridiculous, like ask him to take her away.

Scurrying through a garden of newly trimmed trees heavy with ripening pears, she made her way to the castle and crept up the stairs to the Upper Hall. Trestle tables for the men were set up on the dais while a smaller one for the ladies sat closer to the hearth. A large, blackened pot filled with charred mutton, stewed cabbage, and creeping thyme took up a spot in the center of each table. Dark thick slabs of bread were stacked on wooden trays.

Seated in a carved wooden chair, de Gray's head nodded on his chest. Dru spooned mutton onto a bread trencher for his father, Lord Devreux. Faith sat at the end, massaging his bad leg and paying little attention to the rest of the men at the table who vied for trenchers, waiting their turn for chunks of cabbage or mutton.

At the women's table, Sabina spied Catherine and patted a spot next to her on the bench. Catherine dropped Bijou at her feet and looked over at Lord de Gray's hound, daring him to pester the little dog. Isabelle snuggled close.

"You smell like a puppy. Have you been sleeping with the dogs?" teased Catherine, holding her nose.

Isabelle stuck out her tongue. "Ty-Ty, why do you say that? The sun made me sweat."

Sabina blotted her mouth with the edge of her sleeve. "Girls, don't forget we have guests. Did you find what you left at the pigeonnier?"

"Yes. A message came for Perrine. Where is she?" Catherine felt inside her bag for the tiny roll of velum. Only then did she note

Perrine's absence. Lady Amée casually ran her hand down her throat, her gaze falling first on Sabina, then back to Catherine.

Surely, she hadn't requested that Perrine eat in the kitchen with the servants; after all Faith sat not but a few feet away. Catherine tipped toward her stepmother.

"Where is Perrine? Not in the kitchen pray tell."

Sabina whispered back. "She is tending to the candlemaker's sick child. The poor little soul has an unusual rash and complains of a sore throat. Finish your meal, and you can wait for her in your room."

Catherine felt her face flush. Perhaps she did jump to conclusions too easily. "I fear my appetite has left me. All the excitement. I probably should go to my room. The food, while it smells delicious, might not settle well."

"'It would be nice if you could stay. Lady Amée has requested coarse cloth and will show how she prepares a pattern for a new tapestry," said Sabina.

"You will be designing your own tapestries soon." Lady Amée pulled a corner of moistened bread with narrow fingers. It seemed that Lady Amée smirked at her. It was common knowledge that Catherine hated needle work. Rayne had tried to encourage her in the art of tapestry, but Catherine had no eye for it and sitting for hours only made her anxious.

"Please excuse me. I really must go." Catherine briefly bowed to Sabina and Lady Amée, then headed to the left side of the Upper Hall. A double door opened to the family chambers: a master chamber for her father and Sabina and a smaller room she shared with Isabelle. Orange flowers painted into a grid hid several squints between the rooms and the Upper Hall. If she'd desired, she could have spied on Dru and his parents, but she felt drained and the whole idea seemed childish. She'd leave that to Sabina or the servants.

Rayne's absence weighed heavy on her. Catherine wondered if she missed Rayne's companionship or if her friend's leaving only reminded her of what lay ahead. She sat opposite the arrow slit. A full moon rose and reminded her of a giant pearl. Her mother had once said that she only wanted to remember the best days, like a strand of choicest pearls. Catherine reflected on her mother's words; for even when she lay dying, she chose to remember the good over the bad. But what of people who have no choice, and each day is only a repeat of the intolerable days before? She shook her head to clear her thoughts. Wasn't she clothed, fed, warm? How dare she compare her life to those less fortunate. The pressure in the room changed.

"Good evening, my friend," Perrine moved away from the door and washed her hands in a wooden basin. She meticulously scrubbed each finger, one by one, one side at a time, then dried her hands on a linen cloth.

"How is the candlemaker's child?" Catherine quickly remembered that life could change faster than the beat of a butterfly's wings.

"Her throat is filled with fine white pustules. Thankfully, she has none on her body, only a rash upon her chest. I gave her a willow tea and massaged her skin with lavender oil." Perrine came to the window and peered out into the courtyard. "I heard boars rutted the field around Bracken Woods, nearly ruining the entire crop of wheat. Pray, they were easy preys with their full bellies."

Catherine leaned into the window and tried not to show how discouraged she'd grown. Perrine pushed back her hood and unwound her colorless hair. "I walked with Lord Devreux today, rebuilding his strength. He assured me boars once removed, rarely return, preferring new territory. The way is clear, and we can go to the cave tomorrow."

"My greatest desire is to be anywhere but here." Catherine removed her pouch and fished around for Perrine's message. "It's from your mother. I recognized the writing."

"Ah." Perrine unfurled the parchment strip, tracking the words from one end to the other. Once read, she twirled the message round her finger.

"News?"

"I asked her advice about Lord Devreux." Perrine beamed, looking out the window. "I did everything she would have done... and

143

more. He will heal. Do you smell that? The cooks are roasting a huge boar on the side court. Will be enough for everyone in the Bailey. Would you like some?"

"No. I lost my appetite earlier."

"Do you think I didn't notice? Dismay does not suit you. Just as Dagena will survive, so will you. You must have nutrition. When was the last time you had anything to eat?"

"I broke my fast this morning." Catherine forced a tight smile. Why make Perrine worry, she had enough on her mind? "Maybe my appetite will return if I share a meal with you."

Perrine nodded and pulled on her hood, then hurried away. Catherine glanced back through the window into the courtyard. Polished metal lamps gave an eerie glow to the stones below, and shadows resembled creatures with eerie pointed talons. Perrine's robe flashed in the light on her way to the side court. A tiny shadow twirled behind her across the cobblestones.

Catherine shook her head at the cat brave enough to take its chances in the courtyard among the knights, their dogs, and horses. However, at second glance, she realized with horror, it wasn't a cat, but Bijou. She must have followed Perrine down the steps.

Catherine flew out of her room. At the top of the stairs, she crashed into Dru, nearly causing him to tumble to the bottom floor. He reached for her arm. "Why such haste?"

"Bijou is in the courtyard. I must get to her before the hounds. They will make a meal of her in no time."

Dru maintained a grip on her arm. "When this business with the boars is over, we will ask your father about Michaelmas. My father is in favor of it. *We should be done with this business soon.*"

Dread crept over her. Why did he have to refer to their marriage as business? She felt certain he could see it on her face. His hold on her only increased her unease. She tried to slip her arm away, her composure ebbing. "We can talk of this later. I really must go."

"We have been betrothed from birth. It is our duty to the community." He kept her attention by maintaining pressure on her arm. He crowded her, his voice dropping to a whisper. "It doesn't have to be more. A male child–a necessary heir."

His eyes had darkened. His words held contempt, but for whom she wasn't certain. Catherine stumbled to the next step when he released her arm. "I really–

Laughter swirled up the stairwell. And the outer door to the castle closed with a bang. High-pitched barking echoed off the walls.

"I never knew something so small had such a long tongue." Gregoire's mellow voice carried above all the other noise.

Perrine rounded the steps, Gregoire beside her. Bijou wriggled in his arms, nipping his chin and ears. Perrine carried a tray full of meat and bread with an amused expression. Catherine had rarely seen her so animated. Perrine paused on the next step, and she laughed at Gregoire as if they shared a good joke. Unexpectedly, her head whipped around, and she stared up at the top landing.

Gregoire followed her gaze, and when he saw Catherine, he held up Bijou. She wanted to race down the stairs and crush him and the dog in an embrace. For some reason, it was as if the moon and all its power were playing with her. Gregoire's small gesture beckoned her to him and promised safety. His eyes locked on her. Her heart felt pierced, truly stung with regret. This had become her reality, stuck between desire and despair.

Gathering Bijou in her arms she stuttered, "Thank you, sir."

Perrine, one step below, continued to stare at the top of the stairs.

Catherine spun to go up. With her foot on the next step, she caught Dru glaring not at her, but at Gregoire. His face was set in a stone-cold grimace, not the jealous glare a man gives another for over-stepping, but the look a man gives a lover after catching him in an act of betrayal.

Chapter Thirteen

Once the boars were cleansed from Pître, Gregoire would leave. After he handed Catherine her dog, he hurried to the stables. He wasn't surprised when Dru followed him.

"What was that?" Dru stood only a hand's breadth away.

Gregoire had suspected Dru felt more for him than friendship, but until this moment, he'd not been certain. Relationships between knights were forbidden by the church. Vows taken before the king included the same understanding. Dru risked gossip by following Gregoire into the night. Gregoire ran a hand over his face.

"I can explain. It's nothing." Gregoire didn't have an explanation or a remedy for this situation. He had fallen for his best friend's betrothed, and his best friend had fallen for him.

"Dru cleared his throat and took a step. "What happened when you took her to the healer's hut? Did you do something to put her virtue at risk?"

"Nothing. And de Gray's men will tell you we only had time to gather Perrine's bag of remedies." Gregoire was close to lying. Yet, Dru seemed to be trying to lay blame at his feet for another reason.

This was a dangerous game. A man, even a noble's son could find himself isolated, without allies. They had been like brothers.

Dru had taken the conversation in a different direction. Gregoire never expected to be so attracted to Catherine. Whatever the reason for the change in Dru's approach, Gregoire would not make trouble for her. He had no claim on her. Their kiss had been a mistake, a moment of weakness. Faith had assured him he would never tell a soul. The seneschal had more honor than he.

Dru touched the dagger at his waist. "I saw the way you looked at her in the stairwell just now."

And not only Gregoire, but Catherine and Perrine had seen the look on Dru's face. With so many reputations at stake, Gregoire pretended to not understand Dru. "You are a lucky man, Devreux. You must become accustomed to other men thinking your wife is handsome and charming. But no man would dare act on it." Gregoire hooked his thumbs in the folds of his belt close enough to his dagger to let Dru know he wouldn't back down. "She will be the star in your crown if you let her."

Dru narrowed his eyes. "My father says those who flatter most are the least trustworthy. Do I need worry?"

"I have fought and hunted with you since our earliest days. I have no wish to betray you." Gregoire's shoulders tensed. He felt like a traitor saying those words.

If Dru felt something for him, he was also at fault. He allowed their relationship to be incredibly close. Other men had commented on it. There were times when he had suspected more, there had been talk among the squires, but he had paid little attention. Dru, though impulsive, was a knight, loyal to his vows. It did explain one thing. He'd noticed that Dru held no special attraction for Catherine. Perhaps, when he sensed Dru's reluctance to pursue her, he thought it gave him permission to cross the line and kiss her. He could reason a crooked path to his heart, but it didn't change things. Gregoire wanted more than a fortunate life; he wanted what he couldn't reach.

He had given his word to Lord de Gray to stay until the boars were under control. With luck, the hunt would be finished tomorrow. He would return to Champagne without fail.

"Foolish notion. She belongs to me." Dru ran a hand through his hair, and the muscles along his jaw relaxed. He recovered his composure. "Enough of this talk. Water under the bridge."

Dru patted Gregoire's shoulder, but he looked out over the courtyard. "Too much pressure with Father's sudden illness. Our wedding has been moved forward. Once done, Catherine will stay in Pître. You and I can return to court."

Gregoire was surprised at the revelation. Dru had never pushed for the marriage, leaving that to his father. He seemed complacent about the decision as if some greater plans were unfolding. Gregoire hated discord between himself and Dru, but his suspicions had been piqued, and he wondered if he'd misread Dru all along.

"You scouted the lower fallow fields, the ones closer to Devreux territory. What did you find?" Dru was back on familiar ground.

"There are boar tracks all the way to Hawk's Bridge. Luckily, they have not crossed into Devreux territory. For some reason, they stay in one group. Could be a family. If we are clever, we can kill them in one day."

Dru held up a hand and clapped Gregoire on his shoulder a second time, but immediately drew his hand away. Their relationship had changed. Now that Gregoire suspected Dru's feelings for him, nothing between them would be the same. But surely their love of sport would keep them connected.

Gregoire returned to the topic, content to stay on familiar ground.

"Upon return to Castle de Gray, we saw a giant boar. Haunches on the fellow would feed a family for an entire winter. He disappeared into Bracken Woods just beyond the fields we hunted this very day. Tomorrow, I will return with two men and search for the beast. The remaining men will ride with Lord de Gray to the lower fields."

"Tomorrow then." Dru pivoted on his heel and walked toward the castle.

Gregoire noticed a sort of swagger to his walk. Dru was a proud man and just established that the woman Gregoire had an eye for belonged to him. Misery like grief didn't creep into people's lives, it flung open the door and took over.

At daybreak, Gregoire saddled Fiérsabo and rode with a few good men to Bracken Woods. Boars had rutted the field, tearing into the soil, and feasting on small rodents. Wheat stalks laid in messy clumps. Peasants would come later and scavenge what they could. Another reason the boars needed removal; the wheat fields had to be saved before harvest in the fall.

Gregoire searched the field's perimeter for any fresh tracks with three of his best men. The day before, they dug a fresh pit lined with spikes. Unfortunately, the pigs were smart and not a single animal fell into the hole. Assured the field was clear, he lifted a sack from his saddle. He shared leftover roast from the night before, cutting off a chunk for each man. The cook included bread and a pot of stewed fruit.

Apparently, Lord de Gray had opened an extra barrel of wine and his men had drunk their share. A downed tree near the edge of Castle Road provided the perfect place to rest. His men spoke little and gnawed on their food while Gregoire stared into the sky, waiting on Lord de Gray to appear on the rise. He had hoped to find the boar first and end this madness. Although Dru wanted him to stay for the upcoming wedding, Gregoire desired to visit his father and meet Dru back at court. No matter how hard he tried, his mind kept returning to Catherine's appreciative smile just before he noticed the expression on Dru's face.

He felt as if he'd sinned twice and no matter how many times he confessed, he'd never be forgiven. The mess belonged to him. He'd encouraged it all. He had made a vow before God, promising to protect his fellow knights. He had also vowed to tell the truth above his own life.

Gregoire called himself a man of honor. He had never promised any woman to wed, and he never crossed a fellow knight; he could be counted on to defend his brethren to the death. But in only a few days, everything had changed. Here he sat, wishing he could take back the previous day. He desired his old friendship with Dru; however, with all honesty, he still wanted a relationship with Catherine. These thoughts weren't doing anyone any good.

Sunlight brought along sticky heat. Beyond the rise, the tip of a flag appeared, followed by the sound of jingling bells attached to the leather bridles. Soon Lord de Gray and Dru came into sight. They led several men with grim, determined faces. Today, they would rid Bracken Woods of the murderous boars. Gregoire and his men rose to meet them.

De Gray sat on his saddle and waited for Gregoire to mount. "I need a full night's sleep. All I dream about are these damnable boars damaging my crops and killing every man, woman, and child in Pître." His overgrown brows emphasized each word as he spoke.

Gregoire acknowledged Dru with a quirk of his chin.

"You should ride in the rear, stay ready. I'll ride with de Gray. He will be my father-in-law soon enough. I need to establish my place." Dru said then tilted his head to the rear of the line.

He meant it as an insult to Gregoire and his men. So, this was how Dru wanted it? An uncomfortable truth. So be it. Best to be far away from Pître by tomorrow.

Clicking his tongue, Gregoire goaded Fiérsabo with his heels and led his three men. They joined the remainder of his men already riding at the back of the line. As they neared a second wheat field Gregoire stretched and ran his hand over his scabbard. It was empty. Quickly, he searched his person, including the sack wrapped round his saddle horn. He must have dropped his dagger in the wheat field when he fed his men.

"Ho!" Gregoire yelled. His men stopped. "I lost my Le Sage dagger where we broke bread. I'll return for it. Continue with Lord de Gray. I'll catch up later."

One of his men tossed him a spear. "A treacherous beast it is. Certain you don't want us to come with you?"

"Lord de Gray will need you more. The tracks go in the direction of Gabriel's Stream. Stay with him" Gregoire pointed his horse toward the wheat field and set off at a gallop.

Catherine threw back her hood and shook out her hair. Despite the heat, the sun felt glorious on her scalp. She was free of the castle, of prying eyes, and of the Devreux. She had crossed under the portcullis with ease dressed in a robe made to mimic Perrine. No one seemed to notice the bow and quiver strapped across her back.

Earlier, she and Perrine were set to leave the castle when the chandler sent for Perrine.

"I will see to the child. I feel certain it's not much." Perrine collected her healer's bag. "But I should check on Dagena's baby before we leave."

"Since the harvested wheat field is cleansed of boars, we are safe to enter Bracken Woods. I will go ahead." Catherine finished braiding her hair and flipped it over her shoulder.

"Will be safer if you wait until I finish," said Perrine.

"If Sabina or Lady Amée find me first, they will have me sit at the new tapestry–a fate worse than death. Pray tell. They talk of nothing but the wedding now. Don't fear, I will not enter Bracken Woods without you."

Perrine pinched her lower lid and pulled it down, exposing the glistening red part of her eye. "Take care. You will be beyond my sight."

Catherine hated when she did that. It sent a shudder over her. "I will be careful. Promise."

Once Perrine left the sleeping chamber, Catherine gathered her bow from under her bed along with a quiver and five arrows. She opened a trunk and pulled out a robe like the one Perrine wore, then she scooped up Bijou, tucking the dog into her padded pouch. A rush-reed basket sat by the threshold, and she snatched it up before she closed the door. She tugged her hood forward, covering most of her face as a precautionary measure.

Wearily, she traversed the Upper Bailey. Sleep had evaded her and left her more depleted than usual. The last few days ran again and again in her mind, leaving her with a plethora of new emotions. All these years, she'd thought Dru inattentive, but it had been more than that. Regardless, he still declared her his property, a courier for his sons and a means to expand his wealth and power. Perrine had seen his face, too, but neither potions nor magic could help Catherine when it came to promises and duty.

If only she had never kissed Gregoire Le Sage, she would never know the difference. Perrine had warned her. Sabina had warned her about frivolous emotions. Even her father had warned her to be realistic. No matter how much she wanted to believe Gregoire had actual feelings for her, the truth was, it didn't matter. Marriage to Dru was inevitable. However she approached her father, he would do the prudent, honorable thing and join both families as soon as possible. Her future was set.

Catherine set off for the wheat field with her thoughts tangled. She lifted Bijou, nuzzling against her fur as she ambled down Castle Road. She passed a field plump with ripe greens; purple blossoms shot out of the ground in search of the sun. She spotted a silver fox jumping from furrow to furrow. Her eyes widened. Not two paces behind sprinted a lean, red fox. A silver fox meant luck. Were two foxes double the luck? She would hold tight to the omen.

When she reached the destroyed wheat field, Catherine slipped Bijou into her pouch. She leaped over the irrigation canal separating the road from the field. Long ruts and bent wheat stalks screamed boars. Thank God, the disgusting beasts had been routed. Lifting the hem of her robe, she avoided the muck and stayed along the drier margins. Wild berries grew there, and she could pick as many as she wanted while she waited for Perrine.

She chose a low, mounded bramble loaded with ripe berries. With her hood pushed back, she heard the wildlife scuttling about the woods: squirrels scrambled from tree to tree, birds called to one another from high above, and a vigilant owl hooted in the distance. The brambles were thickest over the ripest berries. Catherine separated the stems and smiled at the bounty. Time passed quickly, and she popped as many berries into her mouth as she plucked for her basket.

When she shifted the basket to her other hip, she realized the woods had become peculiarly quiet The birds had ceased their chatter. With her senses alert, she tipped her head to listen. Had she been a cat, her tail would have twitched. Sound shifted from high in the trees to a heavy rustling through the underbrush. Suddenly, all was still.

The wind picked up, carrying the rotting stench of a killer boar.

Catherine dropped to the ground. Fear shot up her spine. She hugged Bijou to her chest while peering through a maze of wheat stalks. A black boar zigzagged through spiky ferns, snuffling and grunting, scarring the earth with its ugly snout and disgusting cloven hooves. Only the devil could create such a creature.

Catherine curled around Bijou. She had two options: stay where she was, praying the beast never spotted her—or look for a way to escape. She knew better than to bolt. That was certain death. That wicked beast ran faster than a horse. One clip with its tusks, that's all it took. Again, she watched the boar through the wheat stalks with its grinning mouth and bony tusks.

The wind billowed and gusted around her, pulling at her hair, and pushing it across her face. She fought to see and grabbed a fistful of wafting strands. To her horror, the boar stuck its snout straight into the air and smacked its hideous thin lips. The animal let out a high-pitched squeal. Catherine resisted the urge to run. The demonic boar tore the ground in a frantic search for her. She had no choice—she had to escape.

From the corner of her eye, she watched the boar pass. She pressed Bijou further into the pouch, and then eased her bow into position. Despite her trembling hands, she nocked one of her arrows. Her expertise depended on enough time to carefully aim with a steady hand. Would she have the strength to send the shaft through the thick hide of a crazed boar? They were harder to kill than a leaping hart. An arrow had to enter at just the right spot, between the shoulder and spine.

Catherine rose, level with the wheat buds. On her toes and ready to move, she watched the beast working itself into a murderous rage. White foam dripped from the swine's mouth. She focused on the triangular space between the shoulder and spine. Taking in a slow breath, she reminded herself to stay calm, act decisively.

The boar's eerie squeal carried across the field. Catherine rose to her full height. Traditionally, hunters rush the animal, circle it, and trap it before striking a blow or shooting an arrow. But the boar must be closer for the arrow to pierce its thick hide, making it all the more dangerous.

Catherine planted her feet a shoulder's width apart, stabilizing her legs for the shoot. Inadvertently, she knocked over the berries, and they trickled beneath her feet. The boar's terrifying squeal changed to a high-pitched whistle and meant only one thing—it had spotted her. With a shuddering jerk, it bounded toward her.

She pulled back the bow with more strength than she ever remembered having. The beast came straight for her, clacking its lower tusks. It was nearly in range. Catherine's heart beat in her ears, while her arms trembled from the strain.

The swine spun. Her heart sank. It charged chaotically through the towering stalks. She tried to keep the arrow trained on the animal, unable to escape.

The animal darted to her right. Catherine shifted her foot and slipped on the spilled berries. Overcorrecting, she stepped into a hole and dropped to all fours. Panicked, she glimpsed the boar less than three body lengths away. Catherine scrabbled with her weapons. Her hand had clipped a rock when she braced for the fall, yet she clinched her bow. Her robe snagged a bramble, pinning her in place. She'd not realized she'd die today.

Without warning, a horse and rider bolted past her. Too confused to react, she sat with her arrow nocked and her arm strained to the point of numbness. Shaking her head to clear it, she came to her senses. Escape. She bolted toward Castle Road, her bow grazing the pouch bouncing against her side. Bijou had formed a ball and hid safe inside.

Just as she reached the irrigation canal, she whirled around. Gregoire Le Sage sat straight, focused on his prey. He circled the boar, keeping his horse out of range of the deadly tusks. Catherine stood her ground. She was too far from the castle to summon help. Gregoire fought the boar alone; he might need her.

The forest grew silent once more. Gregoire beckoned the boar toward the forest, then darted out of the shadows with his spear angled at the beast. Filled with rage, it blindly followed. Gregoire rounded on the animal, forming a tighter and tighter circle. Catherine twisted the skin on her arm until she felt nothing but pain. Gregoire had to be precise, his aim perfect. His spear had to slice between the shoulder blades for a rapid kill, piercing both heart and lungs. She wanted to scream and warn him to be careful.

On his last pass, Gregoire stood high in his stirrups. He whipped around and came up behind the beast. With the blade angled vertically to the ground, he struck the devilish beast with the spear, but the boar veered off. Blood spurted around the tip of the blade.

Enraged, it clacked its bony tusks, then jerked under the horse, clipping Fiérsabo's fetlock. The snap caused Catherine to cringe. Although injured the courser continued to gallop ahead of the boar, gaining more ground, and reaching the forest first. Blood oozed down the horse's leg. Catherine had to do something. She ran into the field.

"Gregoire!" she yelled.

Gregoire met her gaze and leaped off his horse, disbelief etched on his face. He knelt at the forest's verge, then stretched his hands out to form a human cross. The image startled her, and she stopped in her tracks. Somehow, she needed to distract the boar. She let out a scream and flapped her arms, but the boar knew its prize and had eyes only for Gregoire.

Catherine clasped her bow to her chest and ran with all her might. In shooting range and with the boar fixed on Gregoire, she ground her feet into position.

Gregoire stood up. "Go back!"

Incensed, the boar continued to hammer toward him. She made her arm one with the arrow, pointing it at the boar's neck and chest, pulling the cord until her arms throbbed.

"No!" yelled Gregoire.

Chapter Fourteen

Gregoire could do nothing but watch in horror. He yanked out his daggers. His legs were in motion before he fully rose. His heart flipped in his chest. If she hit the boar anywhere but between the shoulder blades, it would turn and tear her to pieces. With arms pumping, the distance between them narrowed, but she had yet to hear him. He doubled his efforts when she released the arrow.

It sliced through the air. A sick feeling rose in him. With a marksman's proficiency, the arrow hit its target and knocked the boar backwards into the freshly dug pit. Catherine began running as soon as she released the arrow, seemingly unaware the disgusting creature had dropped from sight. Gregoire bolted for her.

"Catherine! Stop!" he shouted.

With horror he watched as she disappeared right into the killing pit.

Skidding even with the open hole, he immediately thrust his hand into darkness. His fingers latched onto her bow. He stared down into the blackness until his eyes adjusted. Catherine clung to a root, dangling in the open space, her shoulder hooked to the bow.

"Hold!" Gregoire yelled. Nothing in his past could have prepared him for what just happened. He had ordered a pit dug then filled it with sharpened sticks to trap the giant pig. Now he wished he'd set up a snare or cage. He felt added weight and a slight thrum on the bow. Looking down, he saw Catherine had let go of the root, clinging desperately to the bow. Cleverly, she faced the dirt wall and braced her feet. When she shifted to gain purchase, pellets of earth fell to the bottom of the pit. Although the stakes held the boar in place, if Catherine fell onto the needle-sharp points, she would certainly die.

He dropped flat to the ground and extended his arms over the edge until he touched the top of her head, but this left him precariously unbalanced. He dug the tips of his boots into the earth. "Hold onto the bow. I'll hoist you up."

"I'm ready." Her voice trailed off, swallowed in the darkness.

Gripping the bow, he lifted the wood hand over hand. Finally, he felt the hollow beneath her arm. With one last effort, he pulled upwards. The momentum sent Catherine reeling into him. They tumbled over the ground.

Her heart thundered against his ribs. He rubbed the knobs along her backbone in no hurry to rise. She was safe. He held her closer when she shivered. Her head nestled into the crook of his arm. He stroked her hair, tracing it over her shoulder and down her back until she quit shivering. She rubbed her cheek against him. He would love to stay with her, his heart racing next to hers forever.

"Why are you alone and dressed as Perrine?" He made sure his voice contained no accusation.

"I was waiting for her." The way she said it made him feel like she regretted it.

"Neither your father nor Dru warned you about the boars in this area?" He found this not only incredulous, but reckless.

"I have not seen either one." Catherine had managed to brace herself with one arm. "Perrine was coming with me, at first, but the candlemaker sent for her. I decided to come alone. Apparently, a foolish decision."

"I've heard you escape the confines of your father's castle from time to time. A dangerous scheme in the best of times, but I'll not chastise you." Gregoire sat up, bending his knee to support her.

"The very reason I wear a robe to resemble hers. It's easy to fool others; they fear Perrine." Catherine faced Gregoire; her expression was a mix of sadness, and if he were right, longing. "She cannot help that she was born with no color. When people see the robe, they turn their back or hasten away. I become invisible. Protection is in the deception."

Gregoire lifted his hand to remove a strand of wheat from her robe. She caught his wrist, wrapping her fingers around the most vulnerable place on his body.

"Thank you." She blushed.

"I am the one who should be thankful." He gave a quick laugh. "Never dreamed a maiden would save me. Your arrow was true. And once hit, the boar fell into the pit. No hunter could ask for a better result. I shouted a warning. Did you not hear it?"

"No. I concentrated so hard on the arrow's path I blocked out everything else. I overheard Papa talking about digging pits. Foolishly, I forgot about them. This isn't the only field with one." She drew in a breath, her robe clinging to her small breasts. "I only knew you needed help."

He wanted to lie with her again, to feel her body against him once more. He felt a nudge at his back. Fiérsabo blew a hot blast of hair across his head. Catherine gaped at something over his shoulder.

"His fetlock." She reached out, touching the horse's leg just above a jagged, bloody cut.

Gregoire examined the injury. "Not too deep. But one can never be too careful about an injury from a rank tusk. It could fester. I will care for it upon return."

Catherine looked around the field. "I do not understand. Why are *you* alone?"

"I came to search for the dagger my brother gave me. From Castle

159

Road, I saw you before I saw the boar. Had I not come back, I hate to think of what might have happened to you."

Catherine tipped her head, taking in a slow breath. "You risked too much. On your knees with a wild boar around. It might have gone around the pit. You wouldn't have had a chance."

"It was my intent to confuse the beast. To draw it away from you." She was bewildering. All the questions—interrogating him instead of just being thankful. "Do you not think... you are worth the risk?"

"My father complains I court danger." Catherine closed her eyes. "Perhaps I do."

Gregoire gently lifted her chin, and her eyes focused on only him.

"You feel it, too. Do you not? The feeling between us. I try to ignore it, but it's too strong," she said.

He cupped her entire face. "What do you suggest?"

Her gaze never wavered. "The priests say prayer is the answer, but I have heard Papa say prayer is little good without action. You must know...I am hopelessly charmed by you."

He could hardly believe what she just said. He placed his other hand at the back of her head. He yearned to kiss her, to feel the softness of her lips beneath his. More shocking to him was the realization that he had a greater need to tell her he would find a way for them to be together. If only there *was* a way, but he could not give her false hope. He let his hands fall away.

Horse's hooves pounded over the field. In less time than it took to clear his throat, the rider galloped to them, cloaked by the sun. Instinctively, Gregoire felt for his missing dagger.

"What is this?" Dru made no effort to hide the disdain in his voice.

Gregoire rose before he dismounted. "It is good thing I returned. That devil's spawn of a boar lies in the pit below."

Dru's eyes drifted from Gregoire to Catherine and back. "What is she doing here?"

"She intended to meet–

"I can answer for myself." Catherine stood brushing dirt from the woolen robe.

"And why are you dressed as the healer?" Dru made no pretense about his displeasure and lifted his crop from his saddle.

"I came here to meet Perrine." Catherine gathered her bow, lifting her chin in Dru's direction. "The boar meant to attack me. I fell into the pit. Gregoire halted my fall. The boar, however, was not so lucky."

Dru peered into the hole, then jutted his head toward Gregoire. "You lost a spike."

He made no mention of the arrow stuck between the boar's shoulders. Gregoire took a step, hovering over the dark pit. In the gloom, the boar slumped between two spikes as if prepared for the spit.

Dru faced Catherine. "Gregoire saved you from a terrible end. You should not be out alone."

"True..." Catherine slid her fingers along the bow cord. "I have tested my luck for too long."

Her response tugged at Gregoire. "She had her bow—

Dru cut off Gregoire, punctuating each word with flick of his crop. "Luck or no. This is not the first time your actions could have gotten someone killed." He stopped talking and paced about three steps, then pivoted to face them. "You risked not only your safety this time, but Gregoire's."

Gregoire started to retort; Catherine spoke first. "I had no reason to think the fields were not safe." She glared at Dru.

"It's useless talking to you." He flicked his crop in the air. It snapped too closely to her face.

Gregoire shot between them. He stood eye to eye with Dru. His insides were boiling, but he remembered how Dru looked the night before. He placed his hands on his friend's shoulders. "My horse is wounded. His injury needs to be treated and bound as hastily as possible."

Dru lowered the crop to his side, but his gaze never left

Gregoire. The color in his face dissipated, but he looked more hurt than angry. "I will follow you back to Castle de Gray. Someone will need to accompany Catherine and see *she* falls into no more misadventure."

At her name, Gregoire stepped aside. Catherine frantically patted her robe. She bounced on her toes and ripped the padded pouch over her head, then turned it inside out. "Bijou?"

When the pouch proved empty, she ran her hand over her clothes as if her dog might be clinging to her. Her hands trembled when she shoved the empty pouch arm's length. "Bijou... my dog. She must have tumbled out when I fell into the pit."

Before anyone could speak, Catherine scrambled over to the yawning black opening. As soon as she reached the lip, she dropped and dangled her legs over the side.

"What do you think you are doing?" Dru asked.

"She was in the pouch when I shot my bow. I felt her curl into ball." Catherine scrunched her bag to her body. "We have to find her."

"When did you shoot your bow?" Dru angled his head as if he couldn't believe her.

"When she felt my life was in more danger than her own." Gregoire spoke to Dru with regret. He had felt Dru's discontent had to do with Lord Devreux, but he wasn't convinced anymore. This was a situation he had never thought to be in. Yet, he owed Catherine his life. For that alone, he had to search the pit. "I will do it."

"This is madness. It's nothing more than a dog. You expect too much." He faced Gregoire. "And you give her too much. Enough of this nonsense."

Gregoire pulled a twisted hemp rope from a satchel draped over his horse. He looped one end around the saddle horn. "The boar has been silent and is either dead or close to it. I think I can search for your dog without harm."

Catherine yelled into the pit. "Bijou!"

A faint yelp rose to the top of the pit, and she gasped. "Hurry, please hurry."

Gregoire knotted the rope around his waist, but just as he descended, Dru grabbed his tunic. "If the boar is alive, I will not come for you."

Gregoire shrugged Dru's hand away. "I will give two tugs on the rope. Fiérsabo will know what to do."

He descended and could just make out Catherine's worried features as the murky pit swallowed him. When his feet met the bottom of the hole, he had to cover his nose. The boar smelled of old blood and death. It made not a twinge. He heard a yelp. He extended his hand into the dark corner where the noise came from. Bijou slid into his hand, shaking so much he could barely hold her. He slipped her into his tunic and noticed her fur covered in blood. He yanked the rope, twice.

Briefly nothing happened. Gregoire jerked the rope a second time, then heard a guttural snort behind him. He flattened himself against the wall as best he could. If the boar started thrashing, he was a dead man. The rope became taut. He pushed against the wall with his feet and practically flew up the rope.

Light cut into the pit as he emerged. He squinted into the midday sun. Catherine clutched her hands together as if in prayer, and Dru stood beside her with his hand on the rope. He had tied it to his own horse.

"Fiérsabo is injured. My horse was the better choice," said Dru.

Gregoire handed Bijou to Catherine. She brought the dog to her chest, examining her from snout to tail. "Poor thing, she is covered in blood."

"Yes." Gregoire caught the rope when Dru tossed it to him and replaced it in the leather satchel. "The dog feels whole to me. Most likely the boar's blood."

"She is all I have left of my mother. Bless you." Catherine stroked Bijou, and her eyes glazed over. For a while it seemed she left them for some far place, then her forehead crinkled. "I've had dreams about falling into holes and dying there. It's a thing to fear. But Perrine... she... where is she? I expected her by now. Do you think some mischief has befallen her?"

Dru mounted his horse. "No harm can come to her. Clearly, everyone, but *you*, knows there is dark magic around her."

Catherine didn't respond with anger as Gregoire expected. Instead, she swallowed hard and held her little dog close. He needed to return to Castle de Gray and dress Fiérsabo's wound. Also, he had to distance himself from Dru and Catherine. Confounded by his attraction to her, he could not get enough of her, the way her eyes lit up when she was happy, how she pinched her arms when she thought no one saw, how she tossed her braid over her shoulder as if her hair were an irritation instead of part of her beauty. But she did not belong to him, or anyone else for that matter. Her father brought her up to think freely and gave her the skills to do just that. Did he truly expect his daughter to blindly accept a marriage without a say?

Gregoire led his courser to the road. He shifted his eyes to the ground, picking his way over the uneven furrows in the field. There next to the stump laid his dagger. Sunlight danced along the edge of the blade. If he had not come back for it, someone would have had a treasure as surely as night turns to day.

He stepped onto the road, glad for the blade, but glum when his thoughts returned to the situation between Dru, Catherine, and himself. She was more than a treasure, but apparently not to Dru. It wasn't as if Gregoire had not heard of knights who fought exclusively for one another, who slept away from others, but that was before King Louis made his vows before God and the church. Rules for knight-hood were strict, and the king's laws were more than mere rules to abide by–duels, hell, battles were started over them.

Two men riding palfreys came over the hill and trotted swiftly toward them. Both wore de Gray colors and came to a halt when they set eyes on Catherine. The taller of the two spoke first, "Lady Sabina sent us to find you."

"And you have found me." Catherine's voice was subdued. She opened the pouch, and Bijou's nose poked through.

"You are to return to Castle de Gray at once. Lady Sabina demands it." The shorter man puffed out his chest and dismounted. "You are to take my horse and make haste. Perrine is attending your sister. A fever has entered the castle."

"A fever?" Catherine asked. "My Isabelle is ill?"

In answer, the shorter man held out the reins. "Every child..."

Gregoire wished with all his heart that Fiérsabo weren't injured. Dru pulled up beside the palfrey, while the shorter man held the small horse still for Catherine to mount.

"Make haste!" Catherine clasped the reins and checked on Bijou.

Dru nodded to her, and they galloped down the road, becoming dust on the horizon.

The two men stayed behind. The shorter man walked a few paces behind Gregoire.

"No need to hang back, you may walk with me. What is this about a fever?"

The taller one was quicker. "The chandler's daughter died this morn. Five other children woke up before first bells with fever and swollen eyes. So far, only children are sick. They say the miller's babe drinks nothing and has no more tears to cry. And now the young Miss Isabelle is sick as well."

"I heard was more than children. A young woman large with child is sick as well. Some say may be a pox." The smaller man held his hands together as if in prayer. "The babe is covered from head to toe with tiny red pustules."

A chill ran up Gregoire's spine. The pox. *Lord save us all.*

Chapter Fifteen

Catherine jumped from the old palfrey's back into the stone courtyard. Holding back tears, she pounded up the stairs with Dru on her heels. Entering the Upper Hall, she careened into Perrine carrying a basin. Water sloshed all over her. It broke her. Tears coursed down her cheeks.

"That's not helpful. Clear you face. I have plenty for you to do." A sweaty sheen covered Perrine's forehead; her hair hung about her face as if she'd never combed it. She continued with the basin in the direction of Catherine's chamber.

"Isabelle?" Catherine had twisted the skin on her wrists raw.

"She has a fever, but thank God, no rash." Perrine stopped at the door. "Pray, her skin is so hot she babbles about night creatures and other scary things. She needs you by her side."

Catherine felt Dru's breath on her hair. If he meant to be supportive, it made little difference. He could not reassure her that all would be well.

"Rash? What does it mean?" asked Catherine.

Perrine propped the basin on her hip. "Dagena's daughter

complained of a sore throat on the day she and her husband left the castle. No telling how many people she visited while here. Her baby had a slight rash but seemed content until last night. I'm not sure if he'll live. The other children have varying degrees of illness from a runny nose to those like Isabelle who are so hot they can only sleep."

Catherine braced herself against the door. Dru squeezed her shoulder, then prodded her forward. Isabelle looked like a mite in a too big bed. Only her wan face, drained of color, appeared above the covers. Sabina sat on the bed and mopped her daughter's face with a moist cloth. When she saw Catherine, she shook her head, then dropped her head on the same pillow as Isabelle.

Catherine slipped to the other side of the bed. Sabina lifted her head as if it were too heavy to hold upright. "I let her sleep with us last night. She woke this morning throwing off the covers. When I lifted her, her skin burned me. I have prayed and given her recovery to God."

Perrine threaded her way between Dru who stood behind Catherine to the child. "I crushed willow bark and elderflower in the water to bring down the fever and draw out the bad humors." Perrine handed the basin to Catherine "Bathe her until the fever is gone. Remove her gown if needed. Once she awakens, keep her calm."

Catherine looked into the cloudy water. "May your wish reach God's ears."

Perrine's eyes narrowed at Dru. "Hear my words. Lord Devreux and Lady Amée are leaving. They were packing when I left them. He can't afford to catch this fever. He still needs rest—at least a fortnight."

Catherine had never heard Perrine speak in such a severe manner.

Dru drew back, either baffled that Perrine would speak to him thus or taking her words to heart. "Boar, illness, and now fever have come to this land, yet you seem to have ready answers. You practice strange medicine. What says your mother?"

"My *mother*? I have no time for this. The candlemaker's daughter died this morning. Dagena's grandchild might be next. More children have fevers with each clang of the bells. I must make a paste to soothe the rash. If you have nothing to do, go to the chapel and pray." Perrine left, her words echoing in the room as she rounded the stairwell.

Catherine shifted the basin against her hip. "Is good news of your father. Be glad. Will you accompany your parents?"

"I must, but in a fortnight, I will return to speak with your father." Dru stepped so close Catherine observed the coppery shadow forming along his jaw. His fingers encircled her wrist where the sleeve of her robe had slipped back, exposing her raw skin. He noticed it and studied it briefly, then shook his head. "Your sister's illness makes our marriage imperative. I will bring the marriage contract with me. No more delays."

He gave a quick bow and exited the room. Catherine didn't want to think about Dru, marriage, or her independence. She only had eyes for her younger sister. The one person who held her heart without expectations. She took the cloth from Sabina and dipped it into the basin. Sabina laid her cheek next to her daughter's thin chest and listened. Catherine wrung the cloth until just moist, and bathed Isabelle's heated little body.

"She is my mourning dove. I would give up all my jewels, every luxury for her life" Sabina's voice sounded thick with sorrow.

"Perrine is the best healer in Pître." Catherine smelled the strong herbal scented water. "She has added her own knowledge to what her parents taught her. We will do exactly as she says, and Isabelle will be healthy in no time."

"I remain hopeful. Perrine says the bad humors must be either sweated or bled out. The rash is a sign that all is going normally, but if the fever stays high..." Sabina swallowed. "Perrine has never seen this illness. She said the rash starts on the stomach and chest, then travels to the legs and arms. She said it is not a pox. But the chandler's daughter died. Her father said she was not so ill at first, but later her eyes turned red, and she stopped breathing."

Catherine exhaled and considered her tiny sister. "You have been with Isabelle all morning; I will stay with her while you rest. Where is Frotlina?"

"Helping Dagena with the baby. He has completely stopped taking the breast even though the wet nurse produces enough for all the babes in the castle. But Perrine says little about him. I think she wishes us not to worry, but according to Frotlina he may soon meet his mother in heaven."

"Perrine can do nothing for him?" Catherine found this difficult to believe. "What about her special skills?"

Sabina's eyes narrowed. "What kind of skills?"

Catherine swallowed slowly. She had to be careful and give away nothing that might be interpreted as dark magic. "She observes and learns quickly, studies plants, special herbs. She makes new potions and tries them on animals. Beyond good and bad humors, she believes the heart's rhythms tell you much if you listen. No one else has as much knowledge for one so young."

With a small groan, Sabina rose from the bed. "I will go to the chapel and pray. For once, I wish Perrine had magic. Anything to help our little Isabelle."

Catherine continued to dab her sister with cool water and blow across her forehead. Sabina shuffled from the room. Catherine had never seen her stepmother so worried or so weary.

"Can you hear me little dove?" Catherine whispered in Isabelle's ear. "You must be well. You are the sweetest in the castle. Everyone loves you. I will not let you leave me. I love you."

Isabelle moaned and turned on her side. Her head and neck were cooler than before. The herbed water was working. Folding Isabelle's chemise to her chest, Catherine bathed her sister's entire body. Oddly, afterwards she was worn to the bone. She never realized caring for another was so exhausting.

Her head throbbed. The water was so inviting–cool and fresh, tiny white petals floated on the surface. It mesmerized Catherine. Her throat felt parched and sore. She sponged the water over her face, but there was nothing cool about it. The water felt as if it had been boiled.

The light in the room stung her eyes. Her head split down the middle with pain. If only she could rest. Catherine lay next to Isabelle. Where their bodies touched, a flame kindled between them. She closed her eyes; the stinging eased. But the temptation to rest overwhelmed her, and she drifted to sleep.

* * *

Dragons flew overhead spewing fire over her. Boars chased her until her legs buckled. Demons laughed and pulled her into the pit of hell. There was no escape; her bones refused to move. She screamed, but her throat had been cut open. Blood filled her mouth. She tried to spit it out, but then her head fell into her hands.

Perrine's voice floated above her. Catherine lifted her hand to bat it away. The room blurred from dark to light over and over. Then she heard Lord de Gray barking orders, quickly followed by the patter of footsteps. Someone cried. The light in the room glowed too bright. She pressed her arm over her eyes to block it.

"She moves." Lord de Gray stood near her bed. "Mon Dieu. Mon Dieu. Catherine, can you hear me?"

Her throat felt as if someone made her drink hot coals. She tapped her mouth, unable to speak. She wanted to see her father, but her eyelids were too heavy to lift.

"She has been in a deep sleep much longer than Isabelle. It will take her longer to lift from the fog." Perrine spoke to someone. "The rash has let the bad humors escape. She will heal now."

The bed undulated near Catherine, and then she heard Sabina's voice, droopy and airy. "We must go to the chapel and give thanks. Also, you should let Dru's poor friend, Gregoire, know she lives. He has left the Main Hall or forecourt only to attend to his wounded horse."

"I wonder if he has slept these past days." De Gray's voice faded. The door closed with a soft whoosh of air.

Perrine lifted Catherine's head. "Bonjour, mon amie. Can you drink a little wine? It will make you feel better."

Her head lolled to the side. What had happened? She felt the cool edge of the cup against her lips and sipped the wine, but each swallow was liquid fire. Perrine said something else, but she barely heard it. Sounded like—he used his horse as an excuse to stay.

* * *

Lord de Gray stepped from the Keep with a light step, his arm around Sabina. A broad grin spread across his face as he approached Gregoire. "Her fever has lifted. God is good. Perrine says she will recover. Let us go to the chapel and give thanks."

Gregoire exhaled, unaware he had been holding his breath. "I promised to bring these herbs to the healer when I returned. I shall meet you for Vespers."

Lord de Gray winked at Gregoire. "Perrine asked for those earlier. Make haste young man. The healer needs you."

Gregoire opened the door to the Keep and started up the stairs. He hid his concern for Catherine behind caring for his horse. Throughout the ordeal, he had done Perrine's bidding. Anything to help the situation. The misunderstanding created good cover though. The last few days had been the worst he ever remembered. When the boar pursued Catherine, he knew the beast could be killed, but this illness was a deadly fog he could not slay. The waiting had been excruciating and had helped him make up his mind. The world without her in it was unthinkable. He prayed to God that he was willing to change everything to be with her.

As he bounded into the room Perrine recoiled from the bed. She pulled back her hood and her white hair glistened in the light. "She is better. I brewed a drink to speed the healing. You may speak to her, but she must rest a few more days more."

Gregoire tentatively approached Catherine. She opened her eyes. And a beautiful smile graced her lips. He knelt by her bed and kissed her palm.

"I dreamed of you." She cupped his chin. Her voice sounded raspy and weak.

"I never left. Perrine snuck me in a few times. Your father thinks Fiérsabo's injury kept me from leaving or... he may have gotten the mistaken idea that I'm interested in Perrine." He rose, yet his finger-tips lingered on her wrist. "When you are well, we will talk. I know you shared a glass of wine and a piece of fruit with Dru. But contracts can be broken even by kings and queens."

Catherine brought Gregoire's hand to her lips. Her eyes fluttered closed, but she clutched his hand. Her fingers were dry and warm. She was alive. He could ask for nothing more.

Perrine had mixed a concoction with fresh garlic bulbs, and the scent wafted around the bed. She steadily watched Gregoire, then pointed to the door.

"She must rest. You may return tomorrow." She whispered, pushing him past the threshold. "Please do not give her hope where there is none. She is more fragile than you think."

"You are not the only one to work miracles, Perrine." Gregoire strode away, his mind clear, his goal certain. Fiérsabo was healed, and he could leave at any moment. He had used his horse as an excuse long enough.

Crossing the forecourt, Gregoire heard the clomp and jangle of horses. Four knights, one of them Dru, rode into the Upper Bailey. They circled the courtyard, dismounting next to Gregoire.

Dru held up his hand. "Ho. How is the maiden?"

Gregoire grimaced. "If you speak of Catherine, she is recovering."

"Ah. It is good to know." Dru clapped his horse, then gave a trou-blesome grin. "Lord de Gray hasn't betrothed the younger sister, but I don't relish waiting."

"I am meeting Lord de Gray in the chapel to give thanks. You should come and give thanks as well." Gregoire smiled and hoped he appeared convincing.

The knights took Dru's mount and left the two men in the courtyard.

"We've been partners, friends, God's breath... brothers. I don't want anything between us. Surely, we can work this out," said Gregoire.

"You understand nothing about brotherhood. Life is not about what you want or what I want. It's about duty, not desires." Dru studied Gregoire for a reaction. "If it were about attraction life would be much different. My father demands I continue our line if I want any power handed down to me."

"But you don't care for Catherine. You only want her father's wealth." Gregoire dared to speak the truth. "You can have the land. Let her go. Let her marry someone who will give her a good life."

"Who? You?" Dru crowded Gregoire, looked fixedly eye-to-eye. "Tell me you didn't know. That all these years you thought we were only close friends. Pray, God would have to strike you blind or ignorant not to notice my preference to you. Perhaps I mistook your attention for caring. And now, it comes down to a woman. Are you jealous of Catherine being with me?"

"Dru, you weren't wrong. I have stayed beside you when you fell ill, have celebrated our victories together, have taken our vows for knighthood together. We are bound with something stronger than mere attraction." Gregoire held out his hand as if to touch Dru instead pulling his hand back to his side.

"It's dangerous to speak of this so openly. Someone could overhear." Dru growled. He spat on the ground. "It isn't me other men are suspicious of. They accuse you of a gentle heart. Some have suggested you have a fondness for *me*. Pray tell it isn't an unnatural yearning. Because I'll not lose the king's favor over it or my father's influence."

Gregoire hadn't expected Dru to threaten him. They were

friends, after all. Or was this Dru's personal fear—the dread of discovery. He had completely misread the situation for years. How could he be so dull-witted? That was one thing, but the other thing this conversation brought to light was Dru's true feeling and motives for marrying Catherine. He cared nothing for her. The thought of him laying hands on her, mistreating her made Gregoire willing to do anything to keep her safe.

"You have nothing to fear from me. You will always have the king's favor and your father's regard. However, I think we can work something out concerning your duty and inheritance. I only want what's best for Catherine." Gregoire didn't move and stood his ground. "There is no need for misunderstandings between you and me."

"So, you choose Catherine." Dru made a move toward the chapel, then stopped and spoke over his shoulder. "You don't recognize love when you see it. You'll be left with nothing in the end."

Gregoire's guts turned on themselves. He had to be careful until he could convince his father and Lord de Gray of an alternative. If Dru had wind of his plans, he would marry Catherine in the very bed where she lay. Luckily, he'd already sent a messenger to his father in Champagne.

Five nights had passed since Gregoire visited her. Or had her imagination tricked her? Wispy clouds dusted a dark ocean of flickering stars. She held her hand up to the window and remembered Gregoire's kiss on her palm. It had felt like an eternity that she had dreamed Gregoire came to her. He begged her to stay...to live. One time, he promised God that he would protect her with his life. His sincerity was the reason she clung so hard to life.

Catherine rubbed her slender arms together. No longer raw, she vowed to stop chafing them. Her illness had changed her. Death twisted around the bed, eager to have her. There had been a battle for her soul, and she had won only because she yearned to be with Gregoire. Before she even opened her eyes, Catherine decided she was ready to do whatever necessary, run away if she must. The idea gave her much needed strength. Somehow, he had become the blood that ran through her veins and gave her life. Beating Death made the impossible seem possible.

Now that she was able to sit up, Dru visited, alongside her beloved father.

"We bring happy news," her father said, settling on the bed near her. "We will no longer wait until next year for the nuptials."

She'd been languishing in bed cloaked in a fantasy. Reality had a bite. Her father sat beside her in the flesh. Dru stood next to her bed with his hand on her father's shoulder.

"We thought telling you would speed your recovery. Everyone is in agreement." Dru leaned forward, his smile the same he wore when he won the sword and gauntlets.

Her father patted her cheek. "Good news indeed."

Catherine couldn't go against his wishes. It would not only destroy him, but she would find herself without a defender. Her choice would carve a wedge so deeply between them she would never be able to repair it. Her cough returned. Gasping for breath, she doubled over, motioning for everyone to leave the room.

"Ah, is too much for her." Dru moved aside.

Her father leaped up and they left together, reminding her of a father and son. Fever had left her lungs weakened. Dizzy, she forced herself to the edge of the bed. Compline bells clanged in the distance. Even though the bells meant the last prayer service and the beginning of curfew, they also meant the forecourt would soon be empty.

Once the arrow slit in her room darkened, she crept past Isabelle, sleeping as only a child can sleep, deeply and soundlessly. Luckily, Frotlina still rested with Dagena and the baby everyone thought would die. Perrine said he had become so thin, they nearly gave up all hope, but Dagena took him to Gabriel's Stream and dipped him in the water three times. When she brought him back to the castle he latched onto the wet nurse's breast and suckled until he fell asleep. He was one of the lucky ones. Earlier, Perrine had set out for the cottage to replenish her remedies and would return on the morrow, so Catherine had only her sister to sneak past.

The door to the forecourt opened with barely a sound. Fresh air curled up her legs beneath her chemise and linen robe, reminding her of the days she'd missed walking the meadows. In the kitchen garden, a wooden bench occupied a space between two pear trees. Moonlight scattered across the little seat. With a contented sigh, Catherine sat and took in the dark shimmering shapes around her. Her room had become confining and smelled of illness. Only in the garden did she feel truly alive.

A shadow crossed the pebbled path in front of her. Apprehensively, Catherine slipped to the edge of the bench. No one should have been out. Whoever it was should have been in bed.

"I prayed you might come to the garden...alone. I didn't dare visit you." Gregoire eased to the seat.

Her heart picked up its beat. Was she imagining him? She'd hoped as much, yet hope was a potent thing. It billowed through her filling her with strength.

"Perrine says I will overtax myself if I am allowed to wander. She is probably right."

"And you are much better?"

"I am neither in bed, nor in my room." She smiled resting her hands in her lap.

"Well enough to travel?" His thumb skimmed over her fingers.

His words should have shocked her, but she actually expected them. Her memories were so confused, but of one thing she was certain. She would go with him anywhere, despite her father or Dru. "Mayhap."

When he swallowed, the moonlight caught the knot in his throat as it traveled up, then down. She wanted to kiss it. The idea excited her yet frightened her with its boldness. Her illness had given her courage. Death and solitude encouraged her to assess her life. If there was any way to be with this man, then she'd find the resolve to see it through.

"So be it. I have wanted to tell you something for a very long time." Gregoire knelt beside her.

Chapter Sixteen

Catherine's face felt hot like the fever, but this was different. Gregoire continued to run his thumb over her hand. She wasn't sure what to think, but Gregoire comforted her with his steady grip. It felt the most natural thing in the world.

"Until I came here and met you, I thought the troubadours' songs were puffery. Invented by lonely ladies at court." His eyes gleamed when he spoke. He stopped speaking and scraped his teeth along his lower lip. "I never truly understood what love meant."

Catherine focused all her attention on him. Silver light pooled at the opening of his tunic where sand-colored hair curled along the edges. His voice slid over her like silk over satin.

"I once heard that love is when you care for someone more than you care for yourself. I thought this meant duty and responsibility. Now, I realize it is bigger than duty. Love is stronger than a human. It won't be denied."

Gregoire looked tenderly at her.

"I admit to hearing tales and yearning to see if they were true. I became infatuated with an ideal I'd created in my head. In some ways you were more than I imagined. You have enchanted my mind, body, and soul."

Blood coursed through her head and made her giddy as if she had drunk too much. A part of her wanted to dance, another part wanted to cry. Her entire body was so confused all she could do was sit and listen.

"I have tried to ignore what I feel, but it has proved impossible. When knighted, Dru and I took a vow. To betray a fellow knight is a serious offence; other knights will no longer trust me if I follow through with what I have planned." He paused to catch his breath.

Catherine realized nothing could stop the torrent of words. He was a wall with the foundation stones removed, nothing and everything made sense.

"When Perrine told me you might die, I thought my life over. In the moment of her telling, I understood that if you belonged to another, it would be the same as death. I struggled to walk to the stables and the weight on me so severe I fought to catch my breath."

Catherine murmured. "I thought I was one of many. Dru told me you broke hearts wherever you traveled. As if you had no care."

"True. I was guilty of carnal pleasures, but not as many as supposed. It seemed a trifle, a game to play." He touched the tip of her chin. "I thought of you so differently after we found the babe. You immediately let it be known you would take responsibility for him if no one else did. You have strength bound in compassion, and you let no one tamp it down."

His fingers glided along her jaw, leaving a warm trail. "When you shot the boar, everything changed—few men would have chanced death, but you came back. Duty set us on different paths. And until recently, I would have fallen on my sword before I broke my oath or turned my back on duty."

"I, too, have tried to control my attraction, but it's a useless struggle. I saw your face when you found Alice's babe; you showed great concern. Formidable power comes from men with merciful hearts." Catherine searched his face for any evidence of guile. "You talk as if you plan to turn your back on duty, even break your vows. Bold words. What are we to do?"

"Do you have the courage to go against your father's wishes? To leave everything you have ever known behind?" asked Gregoire.

"If it means we will be together the rest of our lives, I will gladly leave everything behind. I do not wish to displease Papa, but if it means eloping with you, then I will go."

"I want you to think about this. You must be certain."

Catherine opened her mouth. Gregoire placed a finger over her lips and resumed speaking. "I have a plan. But for now, we must be careful and tell no one. If Dru discovers we are meeting, he will force you to marry, and I will lose you forever."

Relief flooded her. She had never cared much for tradition, but she did care for her father, and as much as she loathed to admit it, she had affection for Sabina as well. They might never forgive her, might never allow her to see Isabelle ever again. But if she did nothing, she'd have to endure a life of suffering and discontent. "I know my heart. There will never be anyone else. If you ask, I will leave with you this night."

"There is a plan in motion. I have sent a message to my father. Once he approves of my plan, he will send a formal request for betrothal. Of course, your father may reject it. But with my father's consent, you will be under my protection." He stopped talking and tucked a strand of hair behind her ear. "You do know I love you with all my heart."

If she owned wings, she would have flown into the sky. Her heart was beating there already. She reached for his hand and held it to her cheek. "I love you, too."

Gregoire twisted his finger into a curl, leaned forward, and kissed her hair. "May I have a lock to carry with me?"

Catherine motioned for his dagger and opened her palm. She took the blade and cut a blond curl. Then she twisted the strands into a small circle. Using the blade, she sliced through a blue silk cord around her neck, then tied the ends of her hair together. Gregoire tucked the circlet of hair into the pouch of prize sapphires and returned it to his tunic.

No one had ever asked her for a strand of hair before. She gladly gave it to Gregoire. Placing a hand over his heart she said, "The priests talk of duty, but never of love. The troubadours sing of love, and it seems a mythical notion. When it is real, there is no retreat, no refusing it."

He rose, holding out his hand. When her fingers touched his, she felt as if her warm humors were pleasantly out of balance. His cheek bristled against the side of her face. He whispered, "I love you farther than the wind can travel the earth. And I promise we will be together. I will make my plan work if it's the last thing I do."

Moist heat ringed her earlobe. Yet, his words sounded like a forewarning. A chill raced up her spine.

* * *

Two days passed before Perrine pronounced Catherine's humors fully in balance. Finally, she was healthy and free to do what she wished. Light danced with dust along the window, and Isabelle slept with her arm around Bijou.

Catherine touched her sister lightly on the nose. "Would you like to keep Bijou for me for a few days?"

Isabelle rubbed her nose and squinted up at Catherine, pulling her arm around the little dog. "Can she be mine?"

"For a few days. Can you keep her away from Papa's hounds?"

Isabelle mumbled, "Yes." Then she turned on her side, lifted her arm, and wrapped it around Catherine. She gave her a peck on the cheek. She smelled like old cheese, and Catherine nearly laughed. When did her sister start smelling of old cheese instead of sweet things like honey and bread?

She tucked her sister and the dog under a thin wool blanket. Even if the outside were hot, the interior of the castle never seemed warm enough. She bent and kissed Isabelle's forehead. What a precious gift this child was to her, precious enough to leave Bijou in her care.

Shaking off the last remnants of her illness, Catherine felt nearly dizzy with expectation. Her first trip was to the stables. Faith brushed Moncadeau; the horse's saddle lay close by.

"I heard you were well and content." Faith limped away from the horse, grasping his cane from the stall's corner. "Good to see color in your cheeks. You have been much missed. I assumed you would want your horse today?"

"*Yes*. Perrine has been so busy with all those ailing, she finds herself without many of her remedies. I am to help her search for herbs beyond the castle walls."

Catherine nuzzled Moncadeau's nose, enjoying the velvety muzzle. Fatigue plagued her, but she'd not let it win.

"Perrine needs a palfrey to ride. Do not expect our return on the morrow. I shall return on the third day."

She knew good and well that she and Perrine would go to the cave before traveling to the cottage, but she never spoke of it to anyone. Remedies and concoctions occupied every shelf, and Perrine had expressed a need for several. The entire time Catherine was speaking to Faith, her gaze drifted away from the stables to the castle grounds. The Upper Bailey appeared busy, as usual with squeaking carts, barking dogs, and shouted good wishes. She saw no sign of Gregoire, but his horse was still stabled in a front stall near Dru's.

Catherine ambled to Fiérsabo's stall. The horse blew a whinny, tossing his head, as if greeting an old friend. She noted his leg lacked even a scar. "His fetlock... how?"

"Perrine heals not only humans. She looked after the horse along with its owner. She gave Le Sage a salve to use. He comes every day and works with the horse no matter how crowded the stables are with all the extra messengers. Fiérsabo has been well for days." Faith leaned against his cane.

Catherine took in a breath and met Faith's gaze. "Things change from day to day since Dru Devreux came home. A time may come when I need a trusted friend."

Faith hobbled closer to her. "I will do your bidding until my last breath. You are as my own child."

He paused and stared beyond the stable door as if gathering his thoughts. "You were always kind to my John... I have kept so many things to myself over my life. Secrets burden a person as much as an injury. Things are not always as they appear."

The skin between Catherine's brows pulled into a frown. Where was Faith going with this?

"My John was not going to the villages the day he left, this I know. He would have been leery of the boars and smart enough not to enter a field where they rooted. And what became of his horse? It has yet to be found. There are whispers that he was soon to be seneschal for another Lord. I saw him just before he left, and he was preoccupied often of late. He suggested we toss knucklebones when he returned and bet me that he would win."

"I have never doubted you. Your John was a good man. If he were to become seneschal to another, he would have told you. Now...worry not" Catherine lowered her voice. "You may hear ill of me over time. Pay no attention. Just as you have said, things are not always as they appear. From this day forward, be prepared to have Moncadeau ready at a moment's notice."

Faith made a motion as if locking his lips. "The less I know the better. I would never think unkindly of you, Catherine. Even as a child, you had a good heart. I will have your horses ready when you return."

Catherine wended her way back toward the castle and noticed Sabina coming toward her. Her stepmother rested a shallow basket of roses against her hip as she made her way from the gardens beyond the forecourt. She smiled and waved when she spotted Catherine.

"Were you up before the Matin bells? I came to your room as the bells were clanging. Isabelle slept, but your side of the bed felt cold.

Did you sleep at all?" Sabina gingerly stepped over the uneven stones, her countenance peaceful.

"Father gave me permission to accompany Perrine in her search for herbs and remedies. I went to the kitchen before first light. Dagena was there with the babe, and I held him while she prepared foodstuffs for us to carry." Catherine kept an eye on Sabina. Her stepmother's calmness was unnatural, and the way she bit her lip was an indicator she had something else on her mind.

"Dru is speaking to your father. Do you know why?" Sabina cocked a brow.

Catherine's stomach clenched. She had heard nothing from Gregoire over the last two days and was unsure what to do. Dru had become obsessed with the wedding. Hopefully, her father would speak to her before he came to a final decision.

As she and Sabina ascended the stairs to the Upper Hall, she heard male voices. Blood thrummed so loudly through her ears she thought she might tumble backwards on the stairs. Sabina turned to her.

"You've gone pale as chalk." Sabina reached out and touched Catherine's arm. "You skin is like ice. Pray you aren't sick again?"

"It's nothing like that." Catherine stopped under the arch leading to the Upper Hall. She balanced on the last step, pushing Sabina's hand away. Attempting to appear unruffled, she smoothed the hair around her face. The urge to pinch her arms was strong enough to cause her to look down at her skin and pretend to examine a few scaly patches, all that remained from the pustules that ruptured on her body to remove the bad humors. "Perrine warned me of cold humors attacking the warm humors until the spots are completely gone. Sometimes it chills me to the bone. No need to worry. All is well."

Sabina narrowed her eyes. It was obvious she suspected Catherine of lying. Before she commented further, a slap sounded, and they hurried round the corner. Standing in front of the massive fireplace, Lord de Gray shook Dru's hand.

"Then it's settled." Lord de Gray cocked his head toward the stairs. "Ah, the women have arrived. I have much to discuss with them."

Sabina placed the basket of roses on a trestle table and sauntered over to her husband, slipping her arm in his. Catherine stayed rooted on the last stair. Dru sidestepped the dais near the fireplace, ending up next to Catherine. He clasped her fingers, and she felt the hard callouses left from many hours of sword training.

"Your father and I have come to an agreement. He will explain it to you," said Dru.

She bit her lip, afraid if she opened her mouth, she might shout about the injustice of it all. They hadn't included her in any aspect of their discussion. Truly Bijou meant more to her than she did to her father.

Dru released her. "All will be as it should be."

Catherine wanted to ask exactly what that meant, but he gave her no time for a retort and descended the stairs. She stared at the floor, wondering when the green rushes became brown. Her insides churned, and she knew it had nothing to do with humors. Her strength came from inside. All her wishes and dreams ended if she were not willing take a chance. Her father had his pride, but so did she.

Lord de Gray tapped the fireplace mantel as Catherine made her way to him. He smiled at her and played out a jaunty tune such was his frame of mind. "Good news my dears. Dru came personally to speak to me of your coming marriage. The Lord sees all and the Devreux are anxious to have nuptials before Christmas or Michaelmas."

Catherine had mistakenly thought her illness might slow the process, not hasten it. How was she going to tell her father that his plans are for naught?

"What say you to a wedding toward summer's end, at the Feast of Saint Peter's?" Lord de Gray opened his arms, obviously anticipating a joyous response. Sabina drew in a quick breath and clapped her hands. Catherine twisted the fabric of her bliaut but remained where she stood.

"Papa, I liked the idea of exchanging vows during Michaelmas. It's not a great difference. Can we wait?" Catherine took a tentative step to her father.

Sabina's excitement was palpable. She would finally have the house all to herself if all went as her father planned. "There is no reason to delay. We have a feast and Mass for Saint Peter's each year. This year will be a bit grander. Dru is here, and with his father's illness, not to mention your own, more reason to hasten the wedding."

Apparently, this was not the first time the marriage had been discussed among Lord de Gray, Sabina, and Dru. The signs were all there. The way Dru spoke to her before she became ill. The looks Sabina gave her after the fever lessened when it was certain she would survive. When Dru told her his father wanted the marriage to take place before the seasons changed. In the past, she paid little attention to messengers or others coming to the castle, but Faith knew. He had tried to warn her in the stables. She should have spoken to her father on her sick bed. It would have been harder to turn her down.

"Saint Peter's Feast is less than three weeks away. I have no say in this matter?" she asked.

Lord de Gray hit the mantel with his fist. "Time to begin life with your betrothed. He is acting on your behalf. The families should be as one, especially if anything should happen to his father."

"You say he is acting on my behalf, yet I have no say. What if I have no desire to marry Dru?" Catherine squared her shoulders and kept an eye on her father.

"What... did you just say?" Sabina's voice cracked in the middle of the question.

"I knew you were spending too much time on your own. The world is not made of troubadours' tales and wandering about on your horse or with your healer friend. Time belongs to God. We belong to

God. There is duty and there is pleasure. Duty comes first." Lord de Gray furrowed his bushy brows.

"But I have no love for Dru Devreux, and he has none for me. The marriage would be doomed." It had to be said. Now it was out. But what she left unspoken, what she wanted to scream to the roof, was that she cared for Gregoire Le Sage and wanted to marry *him*. He had promised to protect her and love her. No one else would do.

Sabina plopped onto a small stool near the fireplace, scrubbing her hands over her face. It was the most unladylike thing Catherine had ever seen her do. Sabina sighed. "Only once have I known anyone refuse to marry. And there was a reason. You must be in love with someone else. Who?"

Catherine felt her eyes widen. Lord de Gray smacked the mantel a second time and stepped away, shaking his head. "*Love.* Love has nothing to do with it. You may love someone else, but Dru is your betrothed. This was decided long ago. You have no choice. We are an honorable family and are bound by our word. The wedding will take place at the Feast of Saint Peter's."

"Papa, you can change this. It's not too late." Catherine knew her whining would not convince her father, but her temper grew. She felt it rising like an ill humor. Her father cared for her, but he would not go back on his word or his honor. Unless, unless she could think of another way, another argument to convince him.

"You are speaking of a fleeting, youthful desire that will be gone when the knight—I assume you are in love with a knight—leaves your sight. You have a duty, and we will speak no more of this."

Sabina stood and rested her hand on Catherine's shoulder. "Love grows over time. My father desired a good match for me. I had never met your father, but we have grown to love each other over the years. It will take time, but you will grow to love Dru. More things bind two people than duty. You will become a family and your children will bind you to him as well."

The thought of bearing Dru's children was more than Catherine could take. She grimaced at her father tugging on his beard. The walls in the room drew in on her. She had one last idea.

"Papa... you loved *my* mother. I remember. I remember how you adored her, the way you stroked her hair. When she was sick, you sat next to her in the bed and read to her. When the sun shone strong, you had the servants place her bed in the forecourt because she wanted fresh air."

Tears slid down Catherine's cheeks. Sabina gaped at her. Lord de Gray rested his forehead on the mantel.

"Mother once told me that if I were lucky, I would marry someone like you one day. That she had loved you from the first moment she spoke to you. She said you promised to always care for her. You loved her more than anything, and it killed you when she died. I watched you carry her body to the chapel, then refuse to leave her for two days. The priests amassed outside the chapel and wrung their hands, fearing you had lost your mind. When they finally convinced you to let her go... you mounted your stallion and charged beyond the Baileys. I thought you were leaving forever. You loved her more than your life, more than *me*."

Catherine swiped at the tears on her face and took in a stuttering breath. She knew what she said next would make an enemy of Sabina, and she had no desire to do so, but she had to convince her father somehow. "I want to marry someone I love, like you did. Not someone I will grow to love."

When Lord de Gray turned from the mantel, his face went dark with fury. "You have not lain with him?"

Sabina groaned and crossed herself. "No... Mon Dieu. Saints save us."

"I have not been disgraced. But I wish I had." Catherine's voice shook. She allowed tears to flow freely, not with anger, but with disappointment.

"You have said enough. *There will be no changes.* I have given my full blessing. Dru leaves tomorrow to confirm the date. He travels with papers that will bind our families for generations to come. His father has three days to consider and return them. I will not hear another word on the subject. You *will marry* within the month!"

Her vision blurred to a watery blindness. She collided with the dais and fell to the floor. Catherine swiped her hand over her eyes. Through her lashes, she noticed her father supporting Sabina by the arm as they made their way to their chamber. She had tried to use his own love to change his mind, but it only made him angrier. She was heartbroken.

Rising, she darted to the edge of the rush mat. Dru stood still as stone between the Upper Hall and the stairs to the Keep.

He reached out and touched her shoulder with just two fingers, enough to stop her momentum. "Few men can resist a woman with tears. I admire your father for staying with his convictions."

"So you heard." Catherine's throat felt raw and strained. "I was unaware you were here."

"I never left. Heard it all from the Keep. Your actions have betrayed you. Did you and Gregoire honestly think your pitiful love for each other would change anything?" Dru shook his finger as if he were speaking to a petulant child.

"You assume too much. Perchance it's not Gregoire, but someone else. You still want to marry me?" She knew the answer. She staunched her tears and pleaded. "Please allow me to be released from the betrothal."

Dru tossed back his head and laughed. "Love and duty have nothing to do with this. You are a stupid young woman who knows nothing of power or love. You think you know Gregoire Le Sage. Half the women at court are in love with him. Do you honestly think he would give up everything for you? I know he told you he had a plan... he tells all the women the same thing. Then he leaves. Have you seen him? No. Because he plans to leave you here with some ridiculous pining for him."

"That's not true."

"Does it matter? You are a fool." Dru caught her collarbone

between his fingers and twisted. "Our fathers want this, have always wanted this. You mean nothing to anyone except a name on a page."

Dru squeezed harder. Pain spread across Catherine's collarbone. "I will never love you... You disgust me, but I'll never let you have him."

He bent so his face was level with hers. "We will marry. I will be Lord over all Pître one day. This is only the beginning. As for you— once married, you will be locked behind castle walls so thick you will never see the sun. You will never wander or be seen by anyone ever again. And as for your little friend, her magic cannot reach or save you. You will be all alone. Your father has allowed you too much freedom. Someone must protect you from yourself."

"I will never let you hurt me again." Catherine yanked her shoulder away. "I will throw myself from the parapets before I ever let you touch me."

"Go ahead." Dru smirked. "You father has two daughters."

Catherine drew back. She wrapped her arms around herself, countering the chill running up her spine. She whispered, "She is just a child."

"No matter." Dru bowed with a snicker. "One sister or two. Makes no difference to me."

He stalked away. After he turned the corner, Catherine scanned the room. A shadow passed behind the floral squint painted on the wall to Lord de Gray's chamber. If either of her parents had seen and heard Dru, why hadn't they come out? She felt as if she might collapse under the weight of what she would remember all her life as her day of reckoning. Because Dru was right, she meant nothing more than a name scrawled on a matrimonial page. No one could or would help her. Her world tipped on its side, and she feared she would slide into oblivion. She bolted from the room desperate to find Perrine. They had to leave the castle before anyone thought to stop them.

Chapter Seventeen

Gregoire strolled up the hill from the Lower Bailey. He held a securely wrapped message sent by carrier pigeon between his fingers. The outer stone wall loomed before him, and he found a handhold to pull himself to the top. Sitting on the cool ledge, he unrolled the tiny parchment. Immediately, he recognized his father's precise handwriting across the ribbon-thin parchment. Anxiety collided with excitement as he read the missive.

To my loyal and much beloved son, Gregoire.

I must admit shock upon receipt of your most recent letter. For a father to know his son's true heart is a rare thing. After a day of contemplation, I well understand every point and find myself in full agreement. Upon writing this missive, I dispatched a trusted messenger with the anticipated contract.

God's Blessings.

William Le Sage

The overall tone of the letter surprised him. Although his initial apprehension eased, Gregoire couldn't yet relax. It had been with considerable risk that he broached the subject of an engagement to Catherine with his father. Gregoire had presented his case with eloquence and intelligence just as his father would have done. He had requested a document set aside for his future engagement—an ornate velum document outlining William the Wise's lineage and lands. The information recorded on the page was more valuable than gold. Per Gregoire's request, his father gifted him the document and added important alliances along with other forms of wealth. Also, included in the missive—an elaborate engagement contract. The offer would be more than any man could refuse, even Lord de Gray.

Gregoire wrapped the message around his finger, thought better of it, and secured it within his tunic. The scent of bread filled the air, and he scanned the horizon where a bold, bright sun gave him confidence. With his plan now in motion, he could finally share his ideas with Catherine. The last two days had been nearly impossible. Every time he saw her crossing the forecourt or entering the stable, he had longed to feel her heated breath sweep across his shoulder when he embraced her. At night, he hungered for the press of her body against his. It had taken all his strength to stay away from her. At dawn, he left the castle on the pretense that he searched for the last of the killing boars.

He planned to meet his father's messenger before he reached Pître. With that thought in mind, he had little time to inform Catherine about the documents and their importance. He dropped from the wall, landing like a cat. Morning-prayers bells, lauds, rang, and each metallic clang solidified his desire to see his mission to the end. Across the Lower Bailey, a small boy, his biscuit-shaped knees pressing against his tights, swung a stick at a lumbering cow. The child stuck out his tongue at the blacksmith who moved into the shadows and laughed before he shoved cold bacon into his mouth. The cool gray shade made Gregoire think about lengthening days he hopefully would spend with Catherine by his side. Ducking into the large stables in the Upper Baily, he immediately relaxed. Fiérsabo snorted in his direction.

A crop snapped right before his eyes. Startled, Gregoire dropped into a fighting stance, his hands balled into hard fists. Just beyond Fiérsabo's stall, Dru stepped from behind a post, and he flicked the crop against his thigh. A high-pitched whoosh filled the air. Gregoire dove at him, knocking the crop from his hand. Dru had anticipated the move and stepped aside, causing Gregoire to sail past. He had overshot the mark, and Dru was on him before he regained his balance. Gregoire's left cheek slammed into the ground. He pushed back, ramming his head into Dru's nose. The element of surprise had given Dru the advantage, and he kicked Gregoire in the side, forcing him on his back. Gregoire grabbed Dru's foot before it crashed into his chest. Dru grinned despite his bloody nose. Using his weight, he pinned Gregoire to the stable floor.

"I have watched women surrender to your charms in every town, vale, and stable. You and your soft words and courtly manners." Dru leaned in, his nose dripping snot-lace blood on Gregoire's face. "They all desire the title of Lady Le Sage. But you will not have Catherine de Gray. For once I have something you want. She belongs to me."

Gregoire threw off Dru's foot and rose before him, using every bit of strength to control his anger. "You do not own her."

"Wrong. She is my property. We are betrothed. The marriage is a formality." Dru wiped his nose, then scooped his crop off the ground and went back to slapping his thigh. "Dowries have been set, land, and inheritance are all in order. You must realize it's too late. Catherine is making ready for the wedding in a fortnight."

Gregoire's body buckled in response despite his best effort to control his emotions. Dru appeared to be waiting for it. His eyes gleamed with malice, then something else filled them. Gregoire had seen that tender expression before and reached out for Dru. The look vanished, and Dru jerked back as if burned.

"You think you are so clever."

"Not so," said Gregoire. His hand dropped.

Perplexed he wondered exactly when his opinion of Dru changed. He had thought him a true knight. Had been proud to joust and train beside him, but his friend had changed once they entered Pître. His father's influence was apparent in every decision he made. Any friendship or sense of brotherhood they shared had vanished. Cautious, yet bereft over the widening distance between them he was now certain Du had become a power-hungry mongrel, but his actions were driven by something stronger than his father's expectations.

"Troubadours will sing of my conquest for decades to come." He paused, then tapped the crop to his lips, seemingly searching for words.

"We can remain like brothers. You can rule Pître. I have no desire for the land. You have no need for Catherine. Let her go."

"You think it's about the land?" Dru closed his eyes, then sneered. "Winning is all you know. Did you think you achieved fame alone? No, I helped you. It is what *you* wanted. I've stayed by your side when I've had other offers, but still you refused to see. I deserve happiness, too. Your decisions have nothing to do with me any longer."

Dru edged to the door and sputtered over his shoulder as he left.

"Luck has left you, Le Sage. I own the luck, now. Final contracts arrive in my father's hands within two days. His advisors will then make copies. Next I return, this land and Catherine will belong to me. You will never have her."

Terce bells rang through the Bailey signaling midmorning. Gregoire had to speak to Catherine and leave at once; otherwise, he wouldn't be responsible for what he might do to Dru.

Heavy clouds drifted over the castle grounds. Gregoire brushed off his tunic and stepped into his horse's stall. Behind him, he heard a shuffle. His body tensed, weary but ready to fight. Faith walked toward him with his odd three-point gait, leading with his cane. Gregoire relaxed.

"Pardon. I felt it best not to interfere." Faith hesitated, leaning his weight against his carved stick.

"Wise man." Gregoire spoke under his breath.

"Will you be needing your horse?"

"Yes. But first I might ask if you have seen Perrine the Healer." Gregoire let compassion reenter his voice. Faith had recently lost his only son. Anyone with a heart would pity the man.

"She left with Catherine. Today the first time they could replenish the healer's herbs." Faith grimaced and shifted his weight from one hip to the other. "Did you not see them as they left the stable, earlier?"

"I was in the Lower Bailey." Gregoire threw a wool blanket over Fiérsabo's back. "Alone? Just the two of them?"

"The only reason Lord de Gray allows Catherine to go unescorted is because everyone fears Perrine more than the sword. The healer's mother started the myth. She said the child had powers beyond her own. I have never seen her use those so-called powers but that means nothing. If Catherine is with her, she will be fine."

"Do you have any idea where they might have gone?"

Faith moved to Fiérsabo's side and helped fasten the saddle. "Catherine and Perrine usually begin their search for plants along

Castle Road or the woods beyond. If you hurry, you should find them."

Gregoire picked up his bag and draped it over the saddle horn. "And if I do not find them?"

Faith produced a pouch from the folds of his tunic and gave it to Gregoire. "I passed by the kitchen on my way here. You've eaten little in the past couple of days. You'll need your strength. Not much passes my notice." Faith sighed. "Search the woods, not the fields for Catherine. They have no plans to return and will be resting at the healers' cottage tonight."

Gregoire mounted. "Thank you for your aid. You have been very kind."

"Catherine de Gray is dear to me. I only want the best for her."

Gregoire observed how Faith favored his crumpled leg. He remembered the beautiful medallion Faith crafted for his son. Pain grayed the man's rheumy eyes. This was a person to be trusted, and Gregoire understood Catherine's devotion to him. Prodding Fiérsabo, Gregoire trotted from the Upper to the Lower Bailey. A storm was moving in. Wind whipped through the lower gates funneling dust behind it. Dru's words were trapped in his head. If Catherine had given up hope and was indeed preparing to wed, he truly must find her.

Gregoire sidestepped a thicket of thorny undergrowth, disappointed he had not found either Catherine or Perrine in the forest. He had given up the road and fields earlier after questioning a few peasants gathering legumes in brown baskets, but no one had seen the young women. Heavy clouds reflected his mood. He couldn't shake a dark foreboding.

Faith had told Gregoire to keep to the woods, but the sun had all but disappeared and what little light was left fought through tightly woven branches. His anxiety crept alongside him though the forest, time gaining an upper hand. He thought he heard a horse snort. He slipped off Fiérsabo and crept toward a small pool. A shallow stream gurgled past, mayhap a branch off Gabriel's stream. Beside it, Moncadeau flicked her tail. A pale palfrey noisily slurped water. Gregoire took a breath. Moncadeau pulled against a twist of ivy at the sight of him. He would need to calm her, but there was no sign of Catherine or Perrine.

Leaving Fiérsabo tethered to a tree, he allowed Moncadeau to sniff his palm. The horse went back to leisurely nipping ivy leaves. Gregoire searched the pond and noticed a footprint heading in the direction of a thick wall made completely of moss and ferns. He pressed his hand to the wall, and it separated, revealing a dark yawning cave. He jumped back, then cautiously stepped inside. A torch fluttered at the end of a corridor. Blue light cast purple shadows along a grainy surface. He'd never seen a cave of this sort and touched the walls. Moisture seeped into his riding glove, and he removed it, wondering at the slightly salty smell.

Deeper into the cavern, a translucent oval occupied most of the ceiling. Gregoire suspected on a clear day the opening provided enough light to rival the open sky and fields. The walls sparkled as if sugarcoated. A grand mirror stopped him in his tracks. How it came to be in the cavern intrigued him. In the smooth metal, he spotted Catherine, and his thoughts flew to her.

Seated on a bench in the middle of the ledge, her head bowed, she studied a green token. Dust motes caught in the light floated past her. If she were not a mythical creature, she should be. Gregoire had no desire to frighten her, so he trod lightly over the stone floor to the ledge.

His shadow fell over her. She gaped up at him, her hands immediately covering her mouth, the token still in her hand. A mangy black swan, with a petticoat of feathers flounced over a nest. It belched out a long, discordant note, sounding more like a bleating lamb than an imperious swan.

"What are *you* doing here?" Catherine rose, shoving the token through a slit hidden in the fold of her bliaut and into a pocket beneath. She spoke in a soft whisper. "I... I..."

"Are you alone?" His voice echoed off the walls, startling him. He murmured, "Where is Perrine?"

"How...how did you find me? The cave?" Her eyes had taken on the blue hue of the entrance lanterns, giving them a haunting beauty saved for saints and angels.

"Was not difficult." He stepped within a foot of her.

"No one knows of it. Only Perrine, Rayne, and me."

Gregoire grinned, trying to reassure her. "No one is with me. I came alone. Your horse stood near the stream. An odd wall of ferns caught my attention. I ran my hand through the tangle and discovered this natural hall."

"No one followed you?" asked Catherine.

"No one," said Gregoire. His gaze went to the ceiling. "How did you find this?" He opened his arms, motioning to the space surrounding them. He had no words to describe it.

"We discovered it when we were children, but it has been *our* secret. It is a refuge, a safe place to meet away from the prying eyes at the castle. It has special powers and changes at will. The cave is never the same." She swiped at her cheek, smearing a streak of dirt.

Gregoire reached out and thumbed away the remaining smudge. He wanted to hold her close, but she hadn't made any sign that she desired the same.

"I left home in search of solitude. Dreams haunt me, and the fever made them worse. I am terrified to sleep, but if by chance I rest, even briefly, I awake with my covers twisted in a furious tangle around me. Papa and I had words. He refuses to discuss my betrothal, and I displease him at every turn. He has contempt for me with no more care than a trampled leaf in winter and has sided with the Devreux. He reveres duty over me."

With her last words, she threw herself into Gregoire, nearly knocking him off his feet. He slid his arms around her, drawing her warm and inviting body to him. She shuddered, and a sniffle escaped.

He carried her, and she gently rested her head on his shoulder. A tear dropped onto his neck. Its heat nearly undid him. He sat on the bench, holding her securely while she cried. There had been times in his life when the emotional release was more important than a soothing hand. After a while, her breathing returned to a regular rhythm. He smoothed a loose strand of hair behind her ear.

"Your father is a man of his word, and I honor him for that." Gregoire swallowed hard. "He is unaware that my father and I will offer a new contract. He doesn't expect it, but he won't turn it down. It would tempt even the King."

"The future is upon me, pins me like a hawk. I don't know what to think anymore. You haven't spoken to me in days. I thought I might never see you again." Her voice was small, childlike.

"Only this morning I received news from my father. I have a plan. You have no idea how much I ached to be with you, but I feared if we saw each other, we would be in each other's arms as we are now. It is too hard to be near you without touching you." He perched her on his knees while continuing to stroke the side of her face with a single finger. She felt so light; he feared he could easily hurt her. "Dru waited for me in the stable earlier. He delighted in telling me of your coming nuptials. You are right. He only wants the marriage to increase the Devreux power. The laws are on his side. He won't push for a duel or risk death."

Tears filled Catherine's eyes again. "Even though I had not heard from you, I trusted what you said to be true. I tried to persuade Papa to postpone the wedding until Michaelmas, but he has his mind made up. Nothing anyone says will change it."

"My father has a great deal of influence with Henry the Liberal, as well the kings, Louis and Henry. Why do you think so many women want to be with me? It isn't simply because I am outrageously handsome." He grinned, then became serious again. "There is an expectation of power associated with my father. One day all he owns will be mine. Small-minded men think this an easy task, but to inherit his land and maintain his substantial influence will be a challenge."

Catherine lifted her chin, tipping her head to listen. Gregoire took her hands into his. "I didn't tell you I sent a message to my father for fear he might not agree. For years, being the second son, he told me to marry an intelligent woman. That she would bring me true happiness. But then my brother died, and my father pressured me to marry his widow. In reality, it would be the simplest thing to do. Overtime, he stopped pushing me, but I felt his original wishes were still there. Honestly, I never foresaw my feelings for you. This calls for diplomacy or Lord Devreux could call foul and demand justice. Father trusted me enough to send a charter designating what belongs to me. He will promise your father that Pître will always belong to you. A marriage of equals, like Eleanor of Aquitaine and King Henry. Father had the papers drawn up, and a messenger is on his way now. Your father, for all his honor and duty, will have a difficult time dismissing the offer."

"But Dru will deliver binding papers to Lord Devreux in three days. Papa said as much."

"Dru told me. But if all goes well, I will have the contracts in your father's possession before then. I will leave tomorrow and deliver the missive to your father myself."

"Can you trust the messenger?"

Catherine absentmindedly traced the scars along his wrists.

"We can trust him. He is the son of Bertrand the Bull and my squire. Earlier, at my request, I had him return to my father's. Waiting until tomorrow will be the hardest part."

Gregoire cleared his throat. He had never wanted to tell anyone about how he came to have the scars. He was not particularly ashamed of how they came to be, yet neither was he proud. But she needed to know. "You circle my scars and seek the tale behind them."

"Only if you wish to tell."

"I will continue where we left off before with the charcoal burners. As I said earlier, they had fooled me completely. In the past, they had always been kind, but a new man led them. When they abducted me, he came forward, thumbs tucked in a leather vest, boasting how he would make them all rich. He swayed the men with big words and a loud voice. He demanded a ransom from my father. The charcoal burners did not see the man for what he was. A gambler who would run away with it all.

"Their leader bound my wrists with heavy metal cuffs, ringed on the inside with sharp teeth. He warned me they would tighten the bonds each day until my father paid the ransom. If he didn't pay, eventually my hands would fall off. I told them my father would refuse, and as certain as my words, my father denied he had a son. The leader sent Bull's body back with the next demand, but my father still denied I existed. They tightened the bonds every evening, and the metal cut into my flesh. I never cried out or let them know the damage, but my fingers were starting to go numb and change color. I gave them a lofty figure for the next demand, telling them I was worth it, and my father would pay. They scoffed at me, saying he had already denied I even lived. Eventually, the leader relented, mainly because they had no choice; I had been with them for so long, I had the stench of a man dying.

"My father paid the ransom with a warning attached. If they accepted the ransom, he would hunt them down, kill them, and spike their heads up before the castle gates." Gregoire pretended to jab a spike in the ground.

"The ransom was delivered late in the afternoon, and I knew they would soon kill me. I wedged myself into the base of a tree, twisting the metal away from my wrists as best I could. Then I waited for them to jump me. My abductors did not realize my father had sent me a message when he accepted the ransom and said he would have their heads on a spike. He was at their backs." Gregoire placed Catherine on the bench beside him, leapt to his feet, and re-enacted the scene.

"When the leader came to kill me, the light flickered low, mostly firelight. I grabbed his feet and flipped him onto his back. He yelled out and all became mayhem. I choked my captor with the very bindings round my wrists. But I was weaker than I knew and after I felt his last breath wither from his body, I flopped over him. It soon became quiet; the fighting had stopped. I rested until a foot nudged me. My father stood over me. My bonds were removed, my hands useless at this point." Gregoire opened his palms facing Catherine. She kissed his palms. Her sweet scent rising to him. She smelled so good; her kindness reassured him, and he continued.

"My father had warned me, and I was a fool who did not listen. He was well known for his wisdom, but the charcoal burners underestimated him. I learned later he led the attack. A man fueled by fear for his family is a dangerous man. He is driven beyond rage. My father cut off the heads of all the charcoal burners and had them hoisted on long spikes, all except one. The man who planned the abduction had his hands and feet cut from his body so he could admire them before his head was hacked off. Then Father lined the road to the castle with spiked heads as a warning."

Catherine touched his scars. A chill ran over him, and for the first time in his life, he understood his father's fear. He would kill anyone who tried to harm Catherine.

"But you are whole now. God watches over you, so the priest would say, and you have been rewarded with a good and healthy life. I am confused, though. Why did your father deny you, then agree to pay a high ransom? To leave your life to chance seems too great a risk."

"Not a risk...Caesar did the same with the Sicilian pirates when they captured him. My father and I had discussed the story many times. If I had persuaded them to demand a higher ransom too early, my father would not have had time to track them down. When they raised the ransom, he knew to attack."

Catherine's lips met his scars. She covered them with tiny, light kisses. He desired her more than ever before. He slid his hands to her waist, flipping her legs around him so she straddled him on the stone bench. Her face was only slightly lower than his, and he kissed the tip of her nose. She wrapped her hands around his neck and drew him to her. He felt the heat of her body through his clothes and thought he would go insane if he could not have her. But that would have to wait. He wanted to take his time. Pleasure her as well.

He pressed his lips to hers. Her tongue slipped between his teeth, and moist heat spilled into his mouth. He rose clasping her buttocks with his hands as she wrapped her legs tighter around him. He nuzzled the skin at the base of her ear.

"I love you, Catherine." He kissed and nipped the length of her neck, loosening two strings knotted at the notch of her throat, slipping her bliaut off a shoulder. He flicked his tongue over her entire collarbone, tasting the salty tang of her skin. The need rose in him; he thought he might die.

She caught her breath, then slid down the length of his body, setting him on fire. Languidly, she stood before him and shrugged the last of the fabric from the other shoulder. She reached up, pulling him to her. He glanced down, marveling at the rise and fall of her breast.

"I love you, too." She took a step back and placed a finger under the material near her shoulder.

She was magnificent.

"Look what I found..." Perrine's voice rang through the cave. She carried a spiral-shaped wooden staff and halted with one foot hovering in the air. "God in heaven. How did he come to be here?"

She stalked across the ledge, thrusting a basket of fresh plants and herbs onto the soft stone floor. Her hood fell away, and her hair furiously streamed out around her. She flicked the staff above her head.

Gregoire reached for Catherine and placed her behind him. But Perrine stopped several feet from them. "You betrayed our friendship by bringing *him* here. We swore a sacred oath to tell no one."

The entire cave seemed to tremble. Gregoire realized Perrine was angry over something more than his being with Catherine. He started to speak, but Catherine stepped from behind him, retying the strings at her neck.

"The cave revealed itself to him. I was just as surprised as you."

Catherine stepped between Gregoire and Perrine. "You said you felt differently about Gregoire. Do you think the cave senses this, too?"

Perrine lowered the staff, but her eyes pierced him. Her glare diminished. She sighed and leaned against the twisted stick. "The cave has never been a secret. It has always been open to anyone. You like to believe the cave is special. You have since your mother died. But the real reason no one dares come here is because they think they will be cursed if they enter."

Catherine stepped back into Gregoire. "But the cave is enchanted. Think about the way it has grown with us."

"I will not deny this to be true, but just because you desire the cave to be magical does not make it so. Magic is an inference, a tool used by healers to create wonder and hope. You, like so many others desperately want to believe in something extraordinary. If a healer can grant the illusion of hope, then what is the harm? It hastens healing in many cases."

"Why are you saying this?" Catherine touched Gregoire's hand as if needing reassurance.

"I study to heal the sick and injured, but there is more to my expertise than just making elixirs. Do you honestly think my mother has magical powers or my father? Their superior ability to heal others is the result of knowledge handed down from one generation to another. It is you and others who make more of it than it is, you who constantly warn me to hide my skills as if they are due to some kind of wizardry, Under my parents roof I have been allowed to try new things without the interference of priests or jealous men. I will never be able to use everything I've learned." Perrine's voice cracked. "I am not angry at you...only at the inability to do anything for you."

Catherine swayed under the weight of Perrine's words. Every living child in the castle owed their life to Perrine or her mother. Only now did Catherine realize the risk her friend had taken coming to the castle and caring for those stricken by the fever.

"Catherine, you allowed him not only into our sanctuary, but also into your heart. You may love him, but he cannot protect you."

Perrine spoke wearily and dropped to the very bench Gregoire and Catherine recently occupied.

Gregoire stiffened, ready to defend himself. Catherine put out a hand, warning him not to move. Then she knelt beside her friend. "You have always been the stronger one. It pains me to see you this way. You changed your mind about Gregoire, you told me this. Yet, you are clearly distressed. Why are you so distraught?"

Gregoire had heard enough and planted himself beside Catherine. "You may have caught us in an embrace, but I am not leading her on a fool's trail. Please believe I would never hurt her and will always protect her."

Perrine studied him. Sadness tinged her expression. "I believe you truly think you can save her. I'm aware you sent a messenger bird to your father, but unless you have a plan that contains the magical ability to disappear—nothing else will help."

Catherine leapt to her feet, shaking her head. "I never told her... about a plan."

"I sent a message the same day to my mother and noticed a missing dove. Doesn't take a sage to ask around and find out who sent it. If I know, so does Dru." Perrine pinched the bridge of her nose and closed her eyes. "He is made miserable by his circumstances. If he can't be happy and contented, no one can."

Catherine pulled back from Perrine's words. But Gregoire stood closer to her, his understanding of the situation becoming even more clear. Not that he thought the situation easy, but Perrine's fears were real. He knew Dru better than anyone or thought he did. Now he wasn't sure of anything. "I will never give him the chance to hurt her. Betrothals are broken from time to time. It's not unheard of. Catherine and I will wed soon. Never doubt I will protect her with my life if need be."

Perrine twisted the pilling along the edge of her robe. "It may come to that. Dru will never give her up, especially to you."

Her words rang true to Gregoire. Dru would not only see

Catherine as the key to power, but the obstacle to everything he truly wanted.

"You seem so certain." Catherine clasped Gregoire's hand. "What if I left with Gregoire today?"

Perrine stood before them. "You think your love is stronger than any force in this world. You still do not understand. Lord Devreux has plotted for years. He has conspired with someone in your father's castle, I know not whom, but too many messengers travel Castle Road. Dru has been promised Catherine and Pître all his life. He is determined to have it. There is no question that if he marries you, he will make your life a living hell. If he cannot have you, he will marry Isabelle and make her life worse. If he is denied both daughters, he will start a war, and Pître will never be the same. Misery will rule the land.

Chapter Eighteen

C atherine stepped away from Gregoire, and cool air replaced his warmth. "You are too certain in your tone. Why do you say these things?"

Perrine lifted her eyes to the shelves crowded with bottles and clay pots. "God forgive me. As a healer, I am bound to curing the afflicted which means keeping secrets. But today I will break my oath; too many lives will be ruined if I do not speak. Have you noticed that Dru's mother, Lady Amée, travels with a young woman, a handmaiden?"

"Yes," Catherine answered. Dread wound up her like a viper. She had noticed a young woman at the hunt, the same one from the wedding. Before then she would have sworn, she had never laid eyes on her.

"Before the boar hunt, Lady Amée sent a messenger, but mother wasn't home. I intercepted the request for help. Her handmaiden was ill. At first, I thought her sick like many others with the spring illness. I started to collect salves and scented water, but the messenger stopped me and said was more an injury than an illness. When I arrived, Lady Amée took me to a storage room attached to her bedchamber. Before we entered, she pulled me to the side. She made me promise to tell no one about the handmaiden." Perrine lifted a clear ampule. A clear, syrupy liquid dripped like honey into a polished stone mortar. "My mother always dreaded when Lady Amée's messenger came for her. She left in a silent huff and rarely returned the same day. She walked the forest to clear her mind, yet she never said a word to me. I knew. A novice healer would have worked it out. Mother carried her delivery tools and more than enough medicine to cut pain, yet I was unprepared for what I saw."

Catherine took care in walking over to the shelves. Gregoire placed two fingers at the small of her back and followed. Those two points of pressure along her backbone were a comfort. Perrine continued talking, bottles rattling beneath her touch.

"Lady Amée's poor handmaiden lay on a pallet. I could tell from the doorway; she was terribly hurt. But I was unprepared for the depravity of her injuries. Someone had ravaged her. Her clothes were torn around her shoulders and hips. Bite marks ran down the length of her body, deep and vicious. Blood smeared the insides of her legs, and her arm had been twisted behind her, the bone broken in more than one place." Perrine took a breath. "I wondered how someone could be so cruel. More so, curious why no one stopped the brutal attack. Surely the poor girl must have cried out. Then, I saw why she was so silent... a thin blue line circled her throat. Her voice box was injured. Someone had choked her, nearly killing her. I wondered if she had been left for dead."

Bile surged in Catherine's throat. She swallowed it before speaking, but the burn stayed with her. "Did Lady Amée know who did this?"

Perrine cradled a bundle of bright leaves from a box. The disparity between the florid greens and Perrine's bleak tale made Catherine feel disjointed and even more unsettled. Perrine gave a quick nod.

"After I had done everything possible for the young woman, Lady Amée escorted me down the steps to the kitchen. Her concern was not for her handmaiden. She only questioned if she would carry a child." Perrine rolled the fresh leaves between her fingers.

Water dripped, echoing throughout the cave, interfering with Catherine's thoughts tumbling in her mind like blocks scattered by an angry hand. Even though she knew Lord Devreux to be harsh, she couldn't deny Perrine's rendition of that night, and the realization frightened her.

"Rayne ... She never said anything—acted innocent."

"I think she probably was. Lady Amée is clever and knows her husband better than anyone. When Rayne said she escaped the guard at her door, I doubt it was the first time a guard stood there. Her father and mother knew her value, but only if she remained pure." Perrine flattened the rolled leaves into her palm.

"Lady Amée would not want anyone to know her husband was habitually unfaithful. Until I saw the damage done to that poor girl, I never understood some of my mother's conversations with my father. She talked about Lord Devreux, and the women he jostled for pleasure. They came to her for salves, many hoping for a pregnancy, but he liked it so rough he ruined them for childbearing. Dru was raised to think he had to answer only to a father who delights in cruelty. But something else has happened to Dru. Something snapped in him when his father became ill. Perchance a taste of power. Now he waits for the day he has more. Did you ever suspect him of such brutality?" Perrine raised a brow at Gregoire.

His eyes glazed as if he were remembering something. "His temper is well known, but I never heard of him defiling a single woman. He had no interest in anyone besides Catherine and even then, he only spoke of her in terms of the contract between families. However, since we arrived at Pître, he has become more unpredictable." Gregoire ran his hand over his face. "He nearly beat a boy to death while hunting. I'd never seen him lose control like that before."

"The kind of pain his father inflicted on this poor girl was not about seduction. It was about power with a ruthlessness that knows no bounds. I fear the day his father dies will be a day blood runs slick between heaven and hell. Something beyond power fights within him."

Catherine had heard of men without a conscience; they rarely changed. Someone had been watching through the peephole in her parents' bedchamber. For him to witness Dru threatening her was bad enough, but if he knew about Dru's brutality and still wished her to marry him, then words were insufficient to describe the ragged hole left in her soul.

She shivered and Gregoire hugged her to him, but his closeness could not reduce the injury swelling in her heart. Her father had turned his back on her. If Gregoire's plan didn't work, she would run away, even if it meant death. She'd not become Lady Amée and hide her husband's savagery from others.

"More the reason for me to meet with Lord de Gray," Gregoire said "Catherine will stay at my side until I leave. She shall remain at the cottage; your family can hide her if need be." He turned to Catherine and grasped her by the shoulders. "You are not to go back to your father unless I am with you."

Catherine braced herself. She knew Gregoire was right. Returning to her father put her in more peril than she originally imagined. But why delay? Surely, he understood her father would not change his mind. There was no longer a reason to stay.

"We should leave now. Nothing else matters." Catherine reached up and held Gregoire's face in both hands.

"Pître will be yours one day. Your father has been good to his people. I find it hard to believe that once he is presented with an alternative, he will not hasten to do what is right. With the marriage contract in hand, I will seek your father's blessing."

Perrine mashed the leaves into the golden solution, releasing a thick, yellow vapor. "You cannot protect her."

Gregoire pivoted toward her. "I will protect her with my last breath."

This was the third time Perrine had said Gregoire could not

protect her. It sent a cold streak, death's finger, up Catherine's backbone. "Have you had a premonition? A vision? Whatever it is. You must tell us."

"I have a solution to this..." Perrine poured the billowing vapor into a thin-lipped clay vial, sealing it with hot wax. "I will return to Castle de Gray and slip this in Dru's food. The poison works quickly. He will never hurt anyone ever again."

"No!" Catherine lunged for the vial. "It would kill your soul to take a life. And if caught, have you considered what will happen to you? You won't be held beneath water until dead for practicing plain magic. You will be killed for practicing black sorcery and burned at the stake."

Side-stepping Catherine, Perrine successfully evaded her.

Gregoire angled himself between Catherine and Perrine, clearly assuming he would take command of the situation. But Catherine knew better. She had seen Perrine escape from under rockslides and over castle walls like a worm on hot rocks. Gregoire seemed to have missed the reference to a vision.

"*You* cannot save her." Perrine walked away from them, heading to the exit. "I *have* seen the future. This is the only way to be truly safe. He must die."

In one stride, Gregoire was across the floor, his tunic billowing with air. He tried to grab the vial, but Perrine spun as easily as a column of dust and in one motion, she snatched up the staff. She disappeared through the arch with Gregoire on her heels. Catherine ran after them and in the widening gap, she saw Perrine's hair streaming blue under the muted light cast by heavy rain clouds.

Their horses whinnied as lightning streaked across the sky—quicksilver over black silk. Perrine bolted past the animals, charging through the trees. She knew the woods better than Gregoire, and soon he fell behind. When Catherine caught up with him, he matched her pace.

"It's impossible to follow her," he puffed in between breaths.

"She is headed in the opposite direction of Castle de Gray." Catherine's voice sounded reedy with strain.

"Going where?" Gregoire asked.

Catherine stopped and thought about his question. She had an idea. She turned in the opposite direction and yelled at Gregoire over her shoulder. "The only chance we have of catching her is to mount and ride parallel to the woods. Eventually, she will have to exit."

He caught up with her in a couple of footfalls. It didn't take long to reunite with their horses. Catherine untied Moncadeau and mounted, Gregoire sat astride Fiérsabo. He clicked his tongue, and they bolted to the fields, followed by the slower palfrey.

They traveled twice as fast on the road as in the field, but soon rainclouds pulled all the gaps in the sky closed. Fat raindrops pelted their shoulders. She thought of the tears she'd shed since Dru arrived in Pître. Two of her childhood friends had died, she had nearly died herself. The most astounding revelation was the bond her father shared with the Devreux even after he spied on her and knew of Dru's disrespect for her. She never expected him to continue with the vow once he'd witnessed it. But he had. She'd never expected him to abandon her. The movement behind the spy hole struck her as hard as any sword or weapon. Her heart would never heal.

Only Gregoire gave her hope. She trusted him more than her father, even more than Perrine. A philosophical revolution was occurring. Troubadours and pilgrims talked about nothing else. Gregoire exemplified the new definition of love—her needs eclipsed his own. He would risk everything to protect her. The idea overwhelmed her.

Darkness cloaked time, and it was difficult to know how long they tore down the road. Lightning increased, crackling all around them. Gregoire urged Fiérsabo off the road into a muddy field. A sustained flash spun out across the sky, and it seemed as if a decrepit tree walked across the land—they were at Burned Tree Meadow. Catherine watched Perrine trudging through the mud, clutching at her soggy robe. She headed directly for the Burned Tree.

"Stop, Perrine! Please! Come back!" Catherine screamed. A

thunderclap crashed directly over her head, overpowering her voice. Perrine's poor little palfrey skidded to a stop. Off to their left, Gregoire goaded his horse but gained little traction in the mire. Lightening sliced the darkness again, this time so close to Catherine, she felt her scalp prickle. The palfrey bolted.

The scene played out in fractured moments as if pieces of time had gone missing. The storm grew in intensity; wind swirled around them picking up Perrine's white hair and pulling it in all directions. Catherine had never seen such a force of nature and to say she was frightened didn't begin to describe the terror that consumed her. Perrine looked across the field at Catherine, her expression calm, her face ghostly white. As if someone called her name, Perrine lifted her face and stared into the heavens. She raised her wooden staff in one hand and the sparkling vial in the other.

Before Catherine could blink, the world glowed blindingly white. Perrine shouted a jumble of strange words. An earsplitting crack opened the sky into two halves. Silver lightning spiked the ground, and heat sucked all the breathable air from the meadow.

Perrine thrust the staff to meet the light, and wood shattered like brown glass. Light blazed and crackled over Perrine's body. Her clothes caught fire. A narrow orange flame surged up her arm and ruptured the poison vial, sparks jumped from the vial into the air, casting an eerie glow.

Moncadeau reared, catapulting Catherine into the field. Dazed, but unhurt she called out, "Perrine? Mon Dieu! Perrine?"

Fiérsabo charged over to Perrine's slumped figure. Gregoire vaulted to the ground. Catherine picked up her skirts without thought. Mud sucked at her shoes, and she slogged across the field.

By the time she reached Perrine, Gregoire had lowered his head to her chest and listened for the sounds of life just as Perrine had taught him. He rocked back on his heels.

"She breathes, but barely." He kept a hand on her shoulder. A worried expression passed over his face.

Smoke curled off Perrine's white hair; her ears and nose were smudged with soot. Catherine pulled her into her lap. She hugged her close smoothing away the singed strands from her face. "You have always said: You can only heal what wants to be healed. Please, listen. The world is a wonder. You are part of it. Without you, the skies will never be blue or the sun as bright. You must stay, for we cannot fully live without you."

Gregoire stood. "I will find the horses. But what do we do? Who can heal her?"

"Only her parents can heal her."

Catherine caressed Perrine's brow and concentrated on her shallow breathing. It was then she noticed the ground around them. Splintered wood mixed with shattered glass enclosed them in a circle. Flames shot from the Burned Tree.

Catherine's fear had not been unwarranted. Perrine lay listlessly in her arms. Whatever made her do it? Catherine could think of no plausible explanation. The stench of charred flesh filled her nose. She coughed, and a voice inside told her to be brave. Now was not the time to weaken, now was the time to show strength.

Gregoire returned with only two horses. "The palfrey is gone. We will find it another day. If I lead Moncadeau, could you hold Perrine against you? She weighs but a trifle."

Catherine mounted before Gregoire finished speaking. "We must hurry. And pray her parents are at the cottage."

He gently pressed Perrine into her arms, then led the way through the field. A few villagers from the hamlets surrounding the fields had gathered along the road. Catherine felt their puzzled gazes on her back. Their mumbling rose into gasps, and she glanced backwards. Two men pointed at the field. Following the direction of their hand, she watched the final remnants of Burned Tree flickering to nothingness on the ground. Oddly, in its place eight golden flames trailed the circle that had surrounded them.

Catherine faced forward and continued. She let her mind go blank while Moncadeau led the way. In no time, Perrine grew heavy, but Catherine kept her close. Finally, the cottage came into sight, and welcoming smoke coiled from the chimney.

Gregoire galloped toward the little house, yelling for the healers. Perrine's mother came out, wiping her hands on a leather apron. Her hand over her brow, she searched the horizon. Her husband sauntered around the corner and pointed toward Gregoire. In a flash, they ran to him.

Perrine's mother raced past Gregoire never giving him a second look. She reached Catherine and grabbed Moncadeau's lead, then grasped her daughter's dangling arm. Her fingers rested on Perrine's wrist. Perrine's father darted back to the cottage. He reemerged with a blanket and met his wife as she made her way. By then Gregoire had dismounted and waited beside Fiérsabo. Neither of Perrine's parents spoke, instead they drew Perrine down from Catherine's arms.

"What happened?" Perrine's mother asked.

Catherine tried to squeak out an explanation, but never got the words out before Perrine's father slipped his daughter into Gregoire's arms. "Bring her to Gabriel's Stream." The old healer directed them to follow him. He whispered something to his wife and continued to the stream. She dashed back to the cottage.

Perrine moved her head to the side, and a moan escaped her lips. She was gaining consciousness. Her father spread the blanket on the ground. Gregoire gently placed Perrine where her father directed. The old healer wrapped her in the light fabric like a cocoon. Her mother appeared and tucked an amber block of what looked like soap under her arm. She also brought a sloshing, muddy liquid in a bowl.

"We will need to clean those burns." Perrine's father carried her into the stream, letting the frigid water flow over her.

Catherine felt a gentle hand at her waist and knew without looking that Perrine's mother was beside her. "It's unlike her to practice folly. How did this happen?"

"We followed her to Burned Tree Meadow. It was a terrible storm full of thunder and lightning. Perrine threw her hands into the air just as lightning shot from the sky." Catherine couldn't keep the image of Perrine burning out of her mind if she'd wanted. "It was as if she challenged God..."

"Not God, the Stag." Perrine's mother sighed. "We will care for her. You can do nothing. Would be best for you to go."

"We can help."

"You have done enough, and we thank you. From here, we will care for her." She dropped her hand from Catherine's waist. "I never thought to care for my own daughter, but I will do what I must. Now you must leave."

Gregoire stepped softly away from Perrine and her father, tenderly clasping Catherine's hand. His look suggested silence. They grabbed their horses' reins.

"We should stay," whispered Catherine.

"I have seen burns like this before. They will need to bathe her and remove the charred bits from her body before it molders. Leave them be."

Part of Catherine's strength came from her friendship with Perrine. They faced the world together, supported one another, and encouraged each other in the bleakest times. Their relationship had conquered loneliness, but now a larger threat faced them. A mystical incident Catherine couldn't fathom had changed Perrine. This type of thinking did no good. Her own problems stared back at her. "Where shall we go?"

Gregoire walked around the horses and drew her to him. "There is no place to go, unless you wish to return to the cave."

The cave no longer felt like a sanctuary. Perrine had seen to that. A memory blossomed in her mind. She knew a place. Somewhere no one would search for them. "Stone Mountain."

Gregoire stood between Fiérsabo and Catherine. "Stone Mountain is a myth, something from a minstrel's tale."

"No, It's real." She stood toe to toe with him, looking up into his face. In a soft voice, she said, "I know how to get there, although I have never seen it myself. Only a half-day ride. Couples seeking

Stone Mountain pass through Pître regularly. Did you not wonder about this before?"

Gregoire looked dubious; he arched one brow and stroked her hair. Then he grinned, reminding her of an errant boy about to do something naughty. "Lead the way, my angel. I will follow you to hell and back and believe it is heaven if you tell me so."

They mounted their horses, and Catherine tipped her head toward the East. "In this direction."

Before she nudged Moncadeau into a gallop, she glanced back at the stream. Water tumbled around the healers. Perrine's father held her in his arms while her mother stripped her blackened clothing from her body. Catherine offered a silent prayer.

Chapter Nineteen

Though the sky had cleared, Gregoire worried when Catherine remained quiet throughout most of their journey. He would not describe her as sullen, but the change in Perrine had affected her deeply. Only once had they stopped to rest the horses, eat a loaf of barley bread, and share a few kisses. He had his doubts about the legend of Stone Mountain, but Catherine would not be swayed. The day waned, and the sun dipped into the afternoon.

"Stone Mountain." Catherine pointed to a purple haze and a small mountain before them.

A narrow path snaked through the meadow, dotted here and there by ancient rock cairns. Stones were stacked in all manners, some taller than Gregoire with thick block bases, others with round pebbles shaped into pyramids. A few cairns looked as if they might fall over any moment, but somehow, they boldly stood as if God himself had placed them there.

"Why the stone monuments?" asked Gregoire

"They are left by pilgrims coming to the mountain to profess their love." Catherine tipped her head toward the mountain. "We'll be there soon. You know the tale of Stone Mountain? Marie de France's fable called it the Mountain of Two Lovers."

"More than once from a passing troubadour, but I know it not by heart."

Their horses plodded along, and Gregoire examined a cairn as they passed. Smooth green river slabs formed the base. Matching rectangular stones, one atop another, until they created twin pillars. Nearly identical, someone had carried the rocks a great distance. He couldn't help but wonder the reason and story behind the unique cairn.

"Marie de France gave the tale to King Louis as a gift." Catherine's eyes grew bright as she spoke, and whether she meant to or not she had prodded Moncadeau. They were not quite trotting, but they had picked up speed. "Stone Mountain is where the two lovers are buried."

"Was never real." Gregoire eyed Catherine for her response.

"A troubadour once told me all stories are born from truth. I heard some pilgrims refuse to marry until they have stood before the two lovers." She gazed ahead. "The tale starts with a father's love."

"And that is why the story makes no sense," he said.

"You do not believe it possible for a father to love his daughter so much?"

"For a father to order men to fight for her affection, I can believe. But to have them carry her to the top of the mountain seems madness," he said.

"Ah, you missed the whole point of the story," she said.

"You mean the secret lovers."

"No." Catherine drew up in her saddle. "The king knew his daughter would leave if someone appealed to her, and she fell in love. He devised a way to keep her near him. If a suitor carried her to the mountain top, then he would not only marry the princess, but inherit the kingdom as well."

"An impossible task. No one could carry his daughter all the way to the top without stopping. His darling was a dumpling?" Gregoire grinned at Catherine.

"Ack. It's a love story. You are mocking me."

"My apologies. Continue, please." Gregoire realized she did not put up with teasing well and suppressed a chuckle.

"I imagine the princess was beautiful, like me." Catherine returned his grin and continued with the tale. "The princess fell in love with a count's son, not someone her father would have chosen for her. He asked her to run away, but she refused. Truly, if her father had trusted the love she had for him, he would have known she would stay. This tale has a familiar ring."

Gregoire faced her because her voice had faded. This story had significance to her beyond a troubadour's tale. If not for the distance between the two horses, he would have given her a reassuring touch.

She swallowed hard and began again. "The princess begged her love to climb the mountain and win her hand. She knew of a special potion that would make him strong. The young man agreed, relying on her to find the potion. Her father joyously set the day, thinking the young man would fail like all the others before him."

"The princess hid the potion in her lightest dress, and when they were halfway up the mountain, she offered it to her beloved. He refused it and pressed on, feeling strong in his love. He grew weaker as they ascended, and she begged him to take the potion. Again, he refused. He wanted to prove he was worthy of her father's request. As they crested the top, he collapsed, dropping the princess. She knelt and attempted to pour the potion down his throat. He died in her arms. She was so distraught, she smashed the vial, spewing the potion across the mountaintop. Then she embraced him one last time and died."

Gregoire shifted in his saddle. "No dagger or poison. She simply died. Do you believe that?"

"She died of grief." Catherine gave him an incredulous look. "You do not believe you can die of a broken heart?"

At one time he might have answered that the entire concept was absurd. However, the world had changed. Now, love was more than an idea. It was included in the rules of chivalry, discussed in Royal Courts, and brought into contracts. At first, he had no real understanding and thought the concept silly. Duty trumped love, period. But then he met Catherine.

They were caught between the new ways and the old—bound by duty. Yet, desire was God given. The Courts of Love proclaimed it. When Catherine lay motionless, too ill to respond to his voice, something happened inside him. It was as if someone had turned a key, and nothing mattered but her. Without her the world would lack light and substance. It would be meaningless. He could no longer scoff at the tale of a broken heart; such grief existed.

"The story ends badly for the young couple. What then is the point of love? Why would Marie de France invent such a fable?"

"Ah. Then, you agree; it is conceivable to die from a broken heart." Catherine surveyed the mountain as she spoke. "A tragedy for the young lovers if the king let it remain so. However, he wanted the world to learn from his folly. By holding his daughter too close and denying her love, he lost her forever. Thank the Saints, the tale does not end there. He placed his daughter and the love of her life side-by-side in the same marble coffin and buried them at the top of the mountain as a testament to love everywhere."

"Ah. I only heard of the two lovers' deaths." Gregoire gave Catherine a weak smile. He was no different than the count's son. He wanted Catherine to be included in his life and would do whatever it took to make it so.

They started up a dirt switchback. Stone cairns stretched as far as the eye could see along the horizon. Gregoire had always heard about faith, trusting in the unseen, but he had never contemplated what it meant beyond God or priests. He was overcome by the beauty of the stones, especially what they represented. Thousands of couples had trekked to this mountain to pledge their love.

Catherine pulled up on a trail wide enough for three or four horses, and Gregoire rode adjacent to her. In the afternoon light, an old woman approached, descending the mountain trail. She looked as if she had borrowed someone else's skin; it didn't fit and was loose in all the wrong places, but she had lived in it anyway. She stepped aside for them to pass and bowed her head.

"Ho. Have you come from the mountain top?" asked Gregoire.

The woman opened her mouth to speak, revealing but three gnarled teeth through her skinny lips. "Yes, but not for the first time. I came here with my husband long ago."

"He is not with you?" asked Catherine.

"No. He was a good man, but he died of the sweating sickness last spring." The old woman reached between the folds of a woolen tunic and pulled out a water bladder. Then she tilted it back for a slow drink. She wiped her wrinkled mouth with the back of her weathered hand.

"When we were young, many couples had just started making the pilgrimage. We heard of it and decided to leave our cairn. The only time in our whole lives we ever left our hamlet. Together we brought stones from our home and made a small cairn and left it at the top. He thought and worried about those rocks all his life. He wanted them to rest on our graves. I came here to gather them." She patted a drooping leather sack, draped across her body.

She flipped a worn flap back to show the precious stones, then stepped next to Catherine's horse. "It was his last wish, my good husband. I will not lie; it has been a struggle without him." Her voice was crusty and full of air as if she had scrubbed her voice box with sand.

Gregoire grew concerned over her condition. "The sun is nearly set. How will you get down the mountain?"

"Do not worry about me. I broke the cairn so I can have peace." The old woman rifled around the bag and pulled out a small round pebble. "Take this. Place it on top of your cairn. It will bring you luck all your days. It brought us seven babes and full bellies."

She reached up and placed it in Catherine's palm. As she walked past, Gregoire reached into his pouch and pulled out a small lump of silver, opening his hand to the woman.

"Please, take this as a token of our appreciation."

"I have no need of silver or gold where I am headed. Only my husband's arms will satisfy me." She grinned again, stroking the sack. "Be kind to each other."

The woman doddered down the trail. Catherine's mouth drew up at the corners. "We need to hurry so we can build our cairn before nightfall."

Gregoire raised his chin in the direction of the upper peak. "Lead the way."

Catherine nudged her horse. When they reached the summit, the light across the sky had changed to a swirling pink sea, streaked with orange and yellow. Gregoire helped Catherine dismount, and he kissed her before her feet touched the ground. He interlaced his fingers through hers and walked into a meadow peppered with flowers of every size and color. Bright grass bowed and swayed in a light breeze.

"It's beautiful." Catherine drew in a breath.

He pressed Catherine's hand to his chest. The air smelled of honey. Bees nestled within open petals, then quickly fluttered away. In the center of the meadow, a three-sided cairn, taller than the pillars supporting his father's castle glowed in the receding light. Silver-flecked white-marble rose into fog-banked clouds. Etched into the stone was an epitaph. Catherine knelt and traced the words with her fingertips.

Two Lovers Embrace
Never to be Parted
Resting As One

"The tale is real. They are buried beneath the cairn. They have given us their blessing." Catherine rose, searching Gregoire's face. "We are actually standing before the Lovers, not a stack of stones."

"Then we should quickly build a cairn and do the same." He pulled her to him and kissed her hard. She rested her head on his chest, her hips pushed against him, but he drew her back. "If we stand in the Lovers' shadow, let's begin our adventure with their blessing. Hurry, check the ground for stones."

Catherine spun away and laughed. Her voice reminded him of water trickling through a creek bed, wild and carefree. They searched along the mountainside carrying rocks of all shapes and sizes, piling them close to the trailhead. Gregoire hefted several large ones to form a strong base. The cairn rose, taking a circular shape. The sun had settled below the horizon, but an odd light emanated from the marble stones and fanned out across the mountaintop. In silvery light, Catherine and Gregoire completed a knee-high cairn. She pulled the round pebble from her pouch and started to place it on top. Gregoire blocked her hand.

"We should pledge our love before placing the last stone." He touched the small of her back, clutching a jeweled pouch. "I have a gift for you."

He pulled the drawstrings and poured a necklace into the cup of his hand. Teardrop shaped loops formed a chain: at the end dangled a perfectly round pink pearl the size of a robin's egg. Catherine ran her finger across the sphere.

"All the women in my family have worn this necklace. My mother gave it to me before she died, and I have been carrying it for a long time, saving it for my bride."

Gregoire fought to breathe normally. He had never loved like this, never would again. No one had to explain it to him. It was something he knew as surely as the stages of the moon.

He slipped the chain around her neck and dropped the pearl to the notch of her throat.

Catherine covered the pearl with her hand. "As long as I wear this, I will be reminded of your love, lest I ever forget."

He knelt before her, taking her hand. "I pledge my love to you–all I am and all I ever will be. You shall want for nothing. All I have belongs to you. I will protect you and our children with my body and soul. This I vow until my last breath."

Tears pooled in Catherine's eyes as Gregoire rose and tipped her head back. Half of her face glistened in the light cast by the glowing Lovers' cairn. He leaned in and kissed her. She wound her arms around his neck.

"I have nothing for you. No gift of any kind," she whispered.

Gregoire held her tighter than before. "You are my gift. Nothing else matters."

Catherine still had the round pebble in her hand. She held it up. "Let me say my vows."

They moved slightly apart, but before she started, she bent and kissed the scars on his wrists, sending a surge of blood through him.

"I pledge to always be true to you. To love no other but you with all my heart. Just as all you have belongs to me, all I have belongs to you. I vow these words before God, the moon, and the stars."

Gregoire enveloped her hand in his and together they placed the old couple's pebble on the cairn's crest. He kissed the back of her hands and the inside of her wrists. She angled her body into his, then slipped her arm around his waist. He felt the roundness of her breasts and the sharp bones at her hips.

He groaned. A puff of air caressed her hair. Clutching her to him, he said, "This will be the hardest night of my life."

"We have said our vows. There is no reason to wait."

"True. But until we have said them before witnesses and in the church, they mean nothing to anyone else." He ran his hand down her back. She gave a soft whimper. He sensed her urgency, but he would not expose her to shame.

"I just took a vow to protect you–body and soul. If I were killed, and our child grew inside you... what kind of man would I be to leave you so?"

Shaking her head, she brought her face to him. She kissed him, then loosened the strings of her bliaut, letting it fall to her waist. "Did you not receive a message from your father? Did he not agree to protect me if you should bring me to him without my father's consent? I will never belong to anyone else."

Every argument he had dissipated like mist on a sunny day. Her smile broke him, and he kissed her bare shoulder. Heat shot upwards from his legs to his gut. He traced the deG along the base of her shoulder and felt her shudder. She fell into him, her hands scrambling over his skin.

They tore at each other's clothes, kicking off shoes in between kisses. Her skin shimmered in the diminished light, and he ran a single finger down her side to ensure she was real. She kissed the entire length of his collarbone as he slipped his hands beneath her breast. Being with a woman had never felt like this before. Lust thrummed through him. Desire claimed him, and he could no longer hold back.

He ran his thumbs over her nipples, covering her breasts with small hasty kisses. She fell back, arching her back. He was so lost. She was so beautiful. Nothing in life could ever compare to this moment.

The stars looked brighter and lovelier than Catherine ever remembered. Gregoire's arm covered her, and she carefully rolled to her side. She stared at the monument still glowing and competing with a shower of shooting stars. She experienced lightness in her soul that could only have come from the Two Lovers. The sensation bloomed within her, bringing inner peace. Her love for Gregoire overshadowed any previous doubts and reassured her that their future was together. Now, they just needed to convince her father. Beyond his approval, she dreaded what Dru might do.

Chapter Twenty

Catherine woke to Gregoire stroking her hair. It spilled casually over his chest and abdomen. His laugh rumbled against his breastbone, and she felt it along her cheek. He shifted away from her as if to rise. The next morning dawned, and the meadow flowers looked as if they'd been brushed with droplets of sunshine.

"Where were you going?" She gave a lazy grin, smoothing her hair back on his chest.

"The day is on us, and we have much to do. Remember? If we were not so hurried, we would stay until our hearts desired or we ran out of food." He lifted her, giving her a quick peck. "I want that missive in my hand by tomorrow."

Catherine stretched. She frowned at Gregoire. "The mountain's beauty caused me to forget, but I must return to help care for Perrine. If only we could stay here forever."

Gregoire draped Catherine's bliaut over her shoulder and gave it a pat. Then he slipped his gambeson trousers over his legs, tying them at his waist. "Forever is a long time. We only have enough bread to break our fast."

Tugging on her sleeves, she giggled, then reached out for his leg, running her hand over his trousers. She reached the tie and pulled, giving Gregoire a mischievous raise of her brow.

Gregoire grinned and stilled her hand. "And I for you, but we must be on our way. The sooner I have the missive in your father's hands, the better."

They prepared the horses, mounted, and started down the mountain. When they passed their cairn, Gregoire reined in, aiming his chin at the stack of stones. "We will return someday soon and celebrate. I feel the luck—like before a tournament. This will turn out well. Have faith."

The small round stone at the top of the cairn glistened in the morning light. Catherine was not as confident as Gregoire, but she put a smile on her face so he would not worry about her. Papa was not easily convinced once he made up his mind, but she felt he might have met his match with Gregoire. He rode before her, leading the way off the summit. He sat so straight and confident. She adored him. He, Gregoire Le Sage, belonged to her.

Catherine saw a twist of smoke when they rounded the stream. She expected as much but dreaded seeing a weakened Perrine. Catherine had only known of one other person struck by lightning, but they had died instantly. Perrine survived the ordeal, but how could she possibly be anywhere close to normal? From Catherine's perch on her horse, she spotted the older healers standing on either side of the cottage door. They appeared to be arguing with someone inside. Perrine's mother used short jerky gestures. Bent and exhausted, her words drifted on the wind to Catherine.

"I will not have it! You must do as we say!" She placed her fisted hands on her hips.

Catherine reined in and looked at Gregoire. He shrugged and they eased closer.

"Ho. How is Perrine?" Catherine asked.

Perrine's mother glared at Catherine. Yanking a bucket from a wooden peg, she swept her hair off her forehead. "See for yourself. She listens to no one! I'll be at the stream."

"You will not recognize her. She is much changed." Perrine's father grabbed Moncadeau's reins as Catherine leaped to the ground.

"Go. Go at once." Gregoire urged Catherine on before dismounting. "You have talked of nothing else since we left the mountain this morning. I will discuss your stay with the healers. Then I must be on my way."

She blew him a kiss and ran to the door, stopping at the entrance. The old healer had just warned her, and she needed to prepare herself. She had once seen a woman whose clothes had caught fire while cooking; her face and hands looked like melted candle wax. She pulled the skin on her forearm, resisting the need to pinch the tender skin. If Perrine were unrecognizable, she would have to act naturally. She plastered a smile to her face and pushed past the door.

Perrine stood near the window and partially hid her face with one hand. Light played over her, creating an illusion of health. Catherine knew better. She couldn't move farther inside, something about the way Perrine stood. As if the weight of her body was too much for her to bear.

"Perchance you would like to come in?" Perrine moved closer to Catherine and let her hand fall away from her face.

The shock of seeing Perrine caused Catherine to stumble. "Do my eyes deceive me?"

"Is it better or worse than you expected?"

"I know not what I expected. Maybe you in bed with the covers pulled to your chin. Instead, I find you standing in a white chemise, as if newly born." Catherine craned her neck to better see. "Are you blind?"

Perrine blinked. "I can see better than before. Yet, my eye color has changed."

Confused, Catherine tried not to crowd Perrine, but she couldn't help staring. Perrine's eyes glowed lavender blue, and her skin glowed soft like a ripe peach. "But I saw lightning strike you down. You barely breathed. Your parents bathed you in the spring, and your skin fell off dead and shriveled. How can you be standing here talking as if, as if..." Overwhelmed, Catherine choked. "You are newly born."

Perrine removed a linen kerchief covering her head. She ran her fingers though what was left of her colorless hair. It had been cut short around the ears, like a man. Salty sprigs stood up like a bristling hedgehog. "My hair burned to the scalp in some places. The smell hung about me all night. This morning, my mother cut it. You should see your face."

"I thought you close to death. In your place stands a woman so strange to me I know not what to think," said Catherine.

"My father once spoke of a man made deaf by lightning. There is also this." Perrine turned her palms upward. A black streak ran up the center of each arm. She traced one line all the way to her heart. "I looked far worse earlier. The skin was raised and puckered. My life force thundered in my ears, and I fell into a dark place. A great power held me there even when I tried to leave. Yet, my soul was at peace in the darkness, and I never feared death.

"My parents put me in the stream to revive me. The water shocked me, pulled my humors back into balance. Confused, I initially had no memory of what happened. Apparently, when lightning shattered the poison in the bottle, the solution misted me. It should have killed me. When my parents removed my clothes, I smelled worse than a Saint-Jean bonfire. My skin sloughed off and, in its place, new pink healthy skin remained. Most of my hair floated down stream in great clumps. Father says only time can tell if the color remains the same."

Catherine felt like a mute. Not a sound left her lips. There was no need to hide her shock. Perrine's transformation was so unexpected; Catherine couldn't think how to react.

"Do not worry. It's for the best." Perrine bowed her head. "I have lived all my life with people fearing me because of the color of my eyes and the paleness of my skin. Perhaps, they will no longer fear me. Yet, I have no illusions; my existence will never be easy. I was born different and will always remain so." Perrine scrubbed her hand over what remained of her hair, then replaced the linen cloth, tying it at the nape of her neck. "By the time the moon rose high in the sky last night, I had assessed my injuries and knew what to do. My mother and I ground oak leaves with the mud near the stream. We applied it, and most of my pain disappeared. The mud dried and pulled out all the poison, leaving behind unblemished, nearly perfect skin. Was wrong to contemplate killing Dru. I will never use my gift to harm others again."

With Perrine's confession still in her ears, Catherine thought of her own transformation since her illness. She now understood the bond between lovers. Her beliefs had changed, and she had chosen Gregoire over duty. She also had defied her father. Would he ever forgive her? Did she have the right to make her own choices? This was the real question, and a novel concept even for a noble woman. Watching Perrine, she was reminded that change was fraught with conflict.

Overnight, Perrine became a different woman, physically and mentally changed forever by a bolt of lightning. More than her appearance, she had a new perspective. She seemed fearless as if the worst had brought out her strength. When death comes, one must decide whether to leave or stay. With all her changes, she had lost her youth and resembled something ethereal. No longer a common healer Catherine feared for her more now than ever before. Always confident in her own abilities, Perrine's strength would be her undoing.

The days of going to the cave for refuge were gone—shattered and broken like wintery ice. Of the three, Perrine might find sanctuary there, but it would never be the same for Rayne or Catherine. By law, their refuge rested in the men they married. It made Catherine shiver. What if Gregoire was on a fool's errand?

She hugged Perrine. Her bristly hair, no longer wispy, chafed

Catherine's cheek through the smooth cloth. There was no better reminder that life as they knew it was gone forever. They could only move forward into their own destinies.

"Gregoire is waiting outside. Come see him before he leaves." Catherine took Perrine's arm. "He wants me to stay with you until he returns. I will explain all of it to you later."

Despite her strong spirit, Perrine leaned into Catherine. Her gait remained steady. "Last night my dreams came to me more vividly than before. The visions were clear, but not the messages. I sensed a warning concerning you and Gregoire; however, each time I concentrate, it slips away."

Catherine wanted to run away from Perrine's dreams. Why couldn't she and Gregoire be happy? Exiting the cottage, Catherine overheard Perrine's parents talking in hushed tones to Gregoire. He lifted his head when he saw her, and the healers swiveled to face her.

His eyes widened when Perrine appeared from beneath a spray of healing herbs placed above the door. Immediately, he composed himself and said, "I did not expect to see you on your feet. You are much changed. Your parents tell me you are well and good."

She gave a shy grin. "I will not lie. A little crisp, but healthy."

Catherine laughed as did the healers. Gregoire stood amongst them confused. This was a new side of Perrine, and Catherine liked it.

Gregoire took Catherine's hands. "You will be safe with them until my return. I shall deliver the missive to you father within two days."

Perrine's mother cleared her throat, then spoke. "You must never return to Devreux Castle. I foolishly believed the danger was only with the father. Dru carries anger deep inside. He is careful around de Gray, but I overheard him yelling your name while whipping a servant on Castle Road. Luckily, he didn't see me. Assuredly, I would have met the same fate. Heed my words."

Perrine's mother wrapped an arm around her daughter, and her parents led her back inside.

Catherine felt pressure on her fingers and looked up to see Gregoire staring at her. "I must leave now. If your father signs anything before I return, it will be harder to take you from Pître without starting a war. Accepting my father's offer would mean he would be aligned not only with my father but Count Henry the Liberal. It would give him more power than he has now and make him a formidable foe. He will give more than a second glance at such an alliance."

"I worry there will be some misfortune, and we will never be together again." Catherine gripped Gregoire and felt his muscles clench with strain. He held her close, his woodsy scent enveloping her for too short a time.

"I will return." His face betrayed him, his eyes dark with worry. He kissed her and quickly mounted his horse. He spoke with conviction. "I will come back for you. Do not ever give up. We will be together."

Catherine twisted the skin along her forearm, wishing the pain would take away the pain in her heart, as she watched him disappear past the noisy stream. Tears stung and threatened to spill down her cheeks, but he had asked her to stay strong, and she was determined not to fail him.

Alone, she stared at the open meadow that led to Stone Mountain. If only they could go back. But it did no good to wish for the impossible. Anxious with worry, she murmured, "He has to come back. He has to."

But no matter how much she desired Gregoire, she knew her father. This was not going to be easy. The days of reckoning were on them. With every dram of courage, she sucked in her apprehension and tramped to the cottage. Each step was a promise. No matter what happened, she was a woman with choices. Duty may have bound her, but love had set her free.

* * *

The ground remained damp from the earlier rains, and Catherine's clothes soaked up moisture, making her skirt heavier with each step. Perrine had asked for a walk, gaining more strength as the afternoon wore on. They kept the cottage well within sight. Faith would eventually tell her father where she had gone. She half expected his entourage to charge up, but the only thing moving or making noise was the passing stream. Though Gregoire had left only hours before, she already missed him.

Plots of lavender cut across the meadow and shaggy herbs grew in their shade. Perrine explained how some plants followed sun cycles while others followed the moon. Lavender, a moon plant, had stronger properties at night. Sap ran up the stalks and had to be harvested when the moon rose to its highest peak.

"Your mind is not on plants." Perrine pulled a stalk from a yellowing plant and chewed the end while watching Catherine. "You vacillate from one emotion to another. Even with Gregoire's reassurance, you are uneasy about the future."

"You warned me about Dru before Rayne left. I fear you've known about his unpredictable nature long before you said anything to me. What are your visions worth if you can't help me?" Catherine felt for the folds in her bliaut to stop the urge to rub her forearms raw. "Usually, you rely on your premonitions as much as your remedies. Since Gregoire's leaving, you've said nothing to ease my mind."

Perrine bit off the tip of another plant, sucking the sweet droplets from the end. Then, she said, "My visions and dreams were once clear and easy to interpret, but now they have been replaced with hazy images. It's as if the storm broke that part of me that communed easily with the elements. But it's only been one night. Perchance they will return. We can only wait."

Catherine grimaced. "If nature works against me, how will we know?"

"When I try to force a vision, it only worsens. I cannot give something I do not have. Warning you to stay away from Dru comes from scrutiny not visions." Perrine tapped her cheek, studying Catherine. "Let us talk of you. I am not the only one to change."

Heat filled Catherine's cheeks. "Is it noticeable?"

"When your friend's eyes glaze over at the mention of a certain man's name, you do not have to be a healer to know something deep inside has changed."

"It is strange—the joining. The connection, the bond between two people is stronger than I ever thought possible. Everyone talks about desire—a spark, a flame, quicksilver love—but no one mentions devotion, affection, trust, or adoration. That you truly become one person instead of two."

"My mother says it's like being tethered, one to the other."

Catherine smiled at the thought. It was true. She felt Gregoire even when he was not with her. "But a tether only stretches so far. Concern for him consumes me, and yet, I know he has no need for my disquiet."

Perrine reached for Catherine's wrist, lightly touching the inside of her arm. Catherine shivered at her touch and snatched her wrist back, cradling it to her. "What are you doing? I haven't hurt myself."

"No one said you did. Your skin is flushed but could be the sun. Your humors appear to be in balance. Do you feel different?"

"Perrine, you have been talking about plants, the seasons, the stars, and the moon all morning. Why do you ask about my health? What do you really want to know?" Catherine pressed her foot into the moist ground and felt it give. She left an impression, not that it mattered. The motion caused her to lean forward, and her new necklace dangled against the smooth silk of her bliaut.

"The necklace. How did you come by it?" Perrine grazed the notch at Catherine's throat when she scooped the heavy pearl into her hand.

"It belonged to Gregoire's mother. He gave it to me."

"I dreamed of it." Perrine, clearly in awe, studied the pearl between her two fingers. "Last night my head ached so badly, I hardly slept. Nothing I dreamed made sense. Images blurred as if someone dropped a rock into a pool. One remained, and until this moment, meant nothing. A moon hung from a woman's neck. At first it shone like an ordinary full moon, then it changed to pale pink and became so heavy it nearly burst."

"What does it mean? Your dream?" Catherine clasped the pearl as soon as Perrine let it fall.

"More proof we are still connected. I am not the only one who slept in fits and starts last night."

Catherine felt the familiar warmth creep up her throat and into her cheeks. She stared into Perrine's eyes, attempting to read her friend's emotions. "We should go back to the cottage. Storm clouds are moving in, and you should not chance another encounter with lightning."

Perrine shoved back the hood of her robe, almost as a challenge. "As long as you wear that necklace, you are protected. Don't ask me how I know. It has some special quality. And as for me... not too much frightens me anymore." She tugged on the linen covering her newly shorn head before replacing the hood. "Gregoire told you nothing about the pearl other than it belonged to his mother. He never claimed it has special powers?"

"I had little time to ask. Remember I was hardly sleeping." She laughed.

Despite the conversation, it felt so good to let her worry go. Their relationship had always been that way. Since childhood, they shared the ability to comfort one another.

Perrine grinned, picking up a basket of lavender. "Keeps stinging bugs away. We'll scatter it when we return to the cottage."

Catherine picked up a bundle of herbs left on the ground and shook them out. She noticed a hoof print pushed into the mud. It came from a courser or a warhorse, too deep for a palfrey. But neither she nor Gregoire had been this way. It was north of the cottage. Catherine spun, looking in all directions. She saw nothing, but in her heart, she knew someone watched them.

* * *

It was impossible to sleep past dawn at the cottage. A big-chested rooster crowed on the window ledge each morning. Once done, he drifted down to a brood of cackling hens and strutted past them. Catherine had mentioned the hoof print to the old healers, but they said many people shortened their route though that meadow.

Even after their assurances, Catherine felt uneasy. After a light breakfast of mixed-grains, honey, and almond milk, she went out to feed Moncadeau. With a light step, she stood on a swell of ground and avoided the mud. Her spirits lifted when battling clouds separated, and the day gleamed gold and green.

Moncadeau twitched her ears and sidestepped Catherine to reach fresh grain in a wooden bucket. Although Perrine's parents gave little heed to the print in the meadow, it paid to be cautious. Catherine scanned the fields for riders, but the morning seemed quiet. Sleeping in a bed with Perrine reminded her of childhood, especially the tossing and turning. However, Perrine's restlessness seemed more turbulent. She had called out numerous times. At the deepest part of the night, Catherine discovered her standing at the open window, staring into the sky, starlight bouncing off her prickly hair. She raked her hand over her head, clearly not happy with the fresh cut. It was heart-wrenching to see Perrine so restless. She had always been the calm one.

Resting her head against her horse, Gregoire drifted into her mind. He represented her future happiness. He had become her life. It was as if all the elements had joined together and formed this one perfect human. When he laughed, she was certain the heavens opened. He had lit a fire in her, and she wondered if it would keep her alive or destroy her.

Bits of grain stuck to Moncadeau's chin, and Catherine led her to Gabriel's Stream. She watched a leaf swirl and dip as it wound its way downstream. It occurred to her, not for the first time, that if she followed the current, she would come to Hawk's Bridge and pass over into Devreux territory. The location of their castle, so close to Castle de Gray, had until this point, been a comfort to her.

She looked upstream. Today, Gregoire would make his way back to Pître. If he failed to change her father's mind, she would not be safe staying with the healers. She couldn't put them at risk any more than she already had. The best place to stay would be the small habitats built near the beehives for honey harvesting. No one except the bees themselves, would think to look for her there. Deep in her thoughts, Moncadeau jerked and startled her.

Catherine reached out to soothe the horse. But before her hand touched its sleek coat, someone yanked her off her feet, throwing her over the arch of a saddle. She gasped when the broad horse bolted into the stream, splashing her with bracing water. Struggling to right herself, she lifted her head, and her captor slipped a leather noose around her neck. One quick yank, and the leather tightened. She dug her fingers under the loop. It helped temporarily. Batting at her captor, she saw that he hid under a woman's filthy wimple. Another yank blocked any air coming into her lungs. She battled to scream, yet no sound could pass her lips. The landscape around them swirled into liquid, and darkness consumed her.

Chapter Twenty-One

G regoire arrived at Castle de Gray just as the noon bells clanged, reminding all to gather for prayer. Once his father's messengers slapped the precious missive into his hand, he made double-quick time. As much as he yearned to see Catherine, he had never planned to have her with him when he presented his plan to Lord de Gray.

There was no problem getting past the gatehouse. De Gray's men passed him with a jovial nod. Aimless riders with nothing do now that the boar hunts had dwindled to only one a day ignored the call to prayer and clogged the Inner Bailey. Faith spotted him over the back of a lively young colt and waved him over.

"God's blessings. Good to see you. The castle is in an uproar. Catherine has not returned. Lord de Gray is beyond worry and in a mean mood. I hope you bring good news." The old man leaned most of his body weight into his cane; his face was set with a deep frown.

"Is she not with the healers? I left her with them. She is safe there. You told her father she was with Perrine?" Gregoire dismounted and noted more men racing to the stables. "Why the uproar?"

"I'm not certain. I told him she went with the healer. He took the news almost as a relief, though he would never admit it." Faith chewed his bottom lip. Something bothered him and Gregoire wanted to know more.

"I have a missive for de Gray, but it may be best to keep my horse at the ready," said Gregoire. "He is expecting me?"

"Not at all," said Faith. "Other things have occupied his mind since you left. It was not until this morning he grew concerned at Catherine's extended absence."

Le Sage's youngest squire exited the stables. His eyes brightened when he saw Gregoire. "Good trip? All is well with your father?"

"All is well. Gather our belongings and be ready to fly at a moment's notice." Gregoire clapped the boy on the shoulder. "You wanted adventure. Today may be the day."

Gregoire rubbed his gloves together. "You are keeping up with my groom and the other men's costs? I brought payment."

Faith tapped the side of his head to suggest he kept it all in his brain.

Gregoire noted the response and gave him his gloves. "If you would, please give these to my squire."

The old man unsettled him. He had acted on his side, now he seemed spooked by something. Gregoire swallowed hard, thinking of what he was about to do. He'd practiced the conversation a hundred times riding through Pître. In all his days, he never had such a difficult time summoning courage. So much depended on whether he could convince de Gray to break a lifelong bond with the Devreux and form an alliance with the Le Sages. Could be, nothing he had ever done meant so much.

A commotion spun his head to the castle steps. Lord de Gray pounded down the first few with Lady Sabina hurrying behind him. He carried his sword, she, his scabbard.

Lord de Gray shouted. "Faith, my horse!"

"At once." Faith nodded at Gregoire.

Gregoire pushed himself into the forecourt. Lord de Gray

fidgeted with his sword. Raising his arms, Lady Sabina tied his scabbard and took a step back. When she turned, they saw Gregoire and looked at him much like two cats studying a mouse that accidently left a cozy niche in the castle wall. Gregoire cleared his throat. All the practicing he'd done for the past two days left him. He was unmoored. He had to convey confidence, or he was lost from the start.

"Lord and Lady de Gray." He bowed deeply and said a silent prayer.

De Gray leveled his gaze at Gregoire. "My daughter, Catherine, should have returned yesterday. She has never been gone this long. I sent someone to the healers, but no one was there. Please tell me you have nothing to do with this," he growled.

Best not to answer directly and give de Gray reason to rebuff him from the start. "I have traveled in great haste to present this missive from my father. A proposal if you will. Instead of the usual messenger, I wanted to present this to you myself. It's of great importance to the future of our families."

This took the de Grays by surprise. Lady Sabina seemed to elongate. She drew her head close to Gregoire. Her eyes followed one man to the other as they spoke.

Gregoire gave him the rolled velum. A gold ribbon circled the thick missive. Lord de Gray wound the ribbon around his finger as the message unfurled. Gregoire had not seen the actual contracts. His father had included a separate message for him, explaining the contracts in detail. The pages made a shushing sound as they unfurled.

For what seemed like an eternity, de Gray squinted at the pages. He glanced up at Gregoire, then immediately dropped his head and traced several sentences with the tip of his index finger. He tugged on his beard more than once and stared at Gregoire every now and again. Finally, he came to the end of the missive and rolled it back up.

"This is unexpected." Lord de Gray gave Lady Sabina a cursory look. "Have Frère Cyril and Faith meet me here at once."

Lady Sabina swept past the men, giving Gregoire a smirk of sorts as she gathered her silken skirts. De Gray narrowed the distance between him and Gregoire.

"A generous offer." Lord de Gray's face remained impassive. "You are certainly aware that Catherine is betrothed to Dru Devreux. The betrothal ceremony was performed many years ago. I am afraid what is done cannot be undone. I sign the final documents tomorrow."

"The very reason for my haste. I know you are a man of your word. Your daughter has said as much, and she honors you. My father is a man of great wisdom, as you well know. When I explained the situation, he recommended this course."

"And what is the situation you speak of?" Lord de Gray tapped the rolled pages.

Gregoire felt his throat dry up as if he had swallowed a desert. "I am in love with Catherine, and she loves me. This is the new way, much discussed in the courts of Marie de Champagne."

"What? Love again." Lord de Gray thrust his hands to the heavens, maintaining a grip on his sword and the missive. "What of duty? What of a man's word, his honor? You act as if discussions by lonely ladies and young knights make the law. I am bound by the law, not by my whims."

"I, too, believe in honor, my Lord. But honor should never be taken for granted. Are there not men who would use your honor for their gain? Lord Devreux for instance?"

"Of what are you accusing him?"

Before Gregoire could answer, Lady Sabina led Frère Cyril and Faith to the castle steps. They appeared bewildered, possibly by the request to come so quickly, for both sucked in rapid breaths as they approached Lord de Gray.

"Faith, can you examine the documents for merit? Frère Cyril, you know the law better than any man in these regions. Make sure these documents are legal and binding." He gestured to the door, and the two men disappeared into the castle, hastily unwrapping the expensive vellum. Faith squinted through a coin of thick glass and examined the top pages, while the priest perused the others. Lord de Gray motioned at Lady Sabina. "Stay with them. I will walk the grounds with Gregoire."

Lord de Gray rested his hand on Gregoire's shoulder. "Mayhap, you do have something to do with Catherine's disappearance." De Gray gave Gregoire a knowing look and gestured to the ramparts, continuing to walk through the forecourt. "Shall we?"

Gregoire considered de Gray's demeanor as they entered the noisy Inner Bailey. Though he casually clasped his hands behind his back, he kept his sword. Gregoire did not have the luxury of wishing things different. He let an uncomfortable silence remain between them.

"I am not a man to throw my daughter to the wolves. She is the sun and the moon to me, but her disobedience has never gone unnoticed, though she has never outright defied me. It is one thing for her to leave with the healer's child for a day or so, not unexpected. She was angry when she left. I suspect she was being influenced. Why else would she think she had an alternative?"

Lord de Gray cleared his throat and studied Gregoire. "You come here as a man of integrity. Offering more than a promise to wed."

"True. I offer her protection above and beyond my lands. As you have witnessed in the documents, she will keep anything she inherits. They belong to her. But I personally will protect her with all that is mine. You are not the only one surprised by this turn of events. She is an amazing woman."

"You have suggested there is some dishonesty in what Lord Devreux offers."

"Not in what is offered, but in what is being taken." Gregoire followed Lord de Gray up the stairs to the ramparts between the Inner and Outer Baileys. The time had come for the truth. If he truly loved his daughter, he would make the right decision.

"Lord Devreux has planned to marry his son to your daughter for the land alone. They hunger for power, nothing else. They have no intention of ever treating her as anything cherished, far from it. Dru Devreux will never cherish or love your daughter. Because he is incapable of honoring her, he will never protect her. He has always had a temper, no great surprise there. But he has shown a different side since he returned to Pître. His father is a heartless creature and I worry Dru will never honor whichever daughter of yours he marries. He is an unhappy man in Pître. To assuage his anger, I saw him beat an innocent boy with a whip. Could have just as easily been Catherine."

"These are strong accusations." Lord de Gray pulled at his beard with such fierceness Gregoire feared he might pull it out. "Do you stand behind them?"

"Not only do I stand behind them..." Gregoire straightened his back, positioning his shoulders into a rigid line. "I pledge my life to you and your daughter. I will defend her to my last heartbeat, even if it means exile from this territory."

A glint entered Lord de Gray's eyes. "I overheard Dru arguing with my daughter. At first, I thought they were having a lover's quarrel. But I heard my daughter and the strength in her voice. I thought Dru was calming her, at first. He stood over her, and I could not make out his words, but her reaction made me realize she would never accept him. She is a good judge of character, has had to be, growing up without her mother to guide her. But she is headstrong, I will tell you that. You will have your hands full. Are you sure you are ready for the challenge?"

Relieved, a grin shot across Gregoire's face. "I look forward to it."

Lord de Gray sighed. "This will not be easy. Likely, Devreux will cry foul and there will be war. He will not sit idly on his hands and let my daughter go to another. I have lived long enough to know men seeking power never turn up their bellies like sweet-tempered dogs. Instead, they bare their teeth, ready for a fight. Ah, the priest and Faith are seeking us in the forecourt."

Gregoire knew de Gray spoke the truth. However, what he really wanted was to race down the ramparts and ride away to meet Catherine. De Gray started down the rampart steps. With his joy impossible to contain, Gregoire clapped his hands together and aimed them to heaven. If all went well, they would be celebrating by nightfall. Catherine would be safe and never have to worry about Dru Devreux or his devious father again.

Faith stood precariously on uneven stones in the forecourt. Gregoire knew a satisfied expression when he saw one. Faith gave him a nearly imperceptible nod before addressing de Gray. "My Lord, it is a generous offer. Gregoire will inherit all the lands owned by William the Wise. Everything he inherits will pass to the firstborn male. The alliance formed would be extremely powerful. William the Wise is also true to his name. As an example, he writes of another betrothal broken where the daughter of royal blood ran off with another man. The case was tried before King Henry and he found in favor of the young lady's father, for he was blameless in the breach of contract. Also, the daughter was married in the eyes of God. Included in the missive is all the documentation to remake the case–if need be. It has been done before; it can be done, again."

Lord de Gray glanced at the priest. "What say you?"

"Parts of the missive appear to have been drawn up previously with recent additions made to include Pître and outlying territories accumulated by William the Wise. I agree. It is an extremely gracious offer, including the dissolution of the betrothal. Everything appears to be in order. All it needs are the appropriate signatures and witnesses."

Lord de Gray kept his head bowed in deep thought. Gregoire adjusted his footing, waiting for a signal. He tamped down his excitement. Regardless of his love for Catherine, he had to consider her father's integrity. Not only her father, but he and his father would be changing the lives of every resident in Pître. If he didn't believe all would be for the better, he wouldn't risk the problems this would surely bring.

Horses' hooves clattered across stones in the Inner Bailey. Shouts and cries charged the air with urgency. Gregoire turned to see what created such a commotion. Surrounded by de Gray's men, Perrine rode Moncadeau. The sight of her sitting atop Catherine's horse buckled Gregoire's heart.

De Gray's man leaped from his horse and pointed back at Perrine. "We intercepted her coming down Castle Road. She claims your daughter was with her earlier today but is now missing. When we stopped for her, two village children approached us. They claimed to have seen someone wearing upper body armor charging down Gabriel's Stream. His face was covered with a woman's veil. Someone was draped over his saddle."

Perrine dismounted so quickly, neither Gregoire nor Lord de Gray moved to help her. Lady Sabina tore into the forecourt just as Perrine tossed back the hood of her robe. Everyone, including Gregoire, gasped at her shorn hair. But even Gregoire was unprepared for her icy blue irises. They reminded him of a keen-eyed nesting hawk. She fixed him with a stare, and he felt the full weight of responsibility. It had been his idea to return Catherine to the healers. He had vowed to keep her safe, and he had failed.

"Missing?" Lord de Gray's voice rose above all others.

"Since this morning," said Perrine.

"And you did not think to raise an alarm?"

"She went to feed her horse——

"So you say!"

"I searched in vain for her." Perrine reached into her sleeve. "I found these."

She held up a marble figure of some sort. The token, Gregoire remembered from the cave, and he had no idea what significance it carried other than it belonged to Catherine. Perrine pulled out a necklace. Dangling from the gold chain was a perfectly round pearl the size of his thumb. He recognized it right away. Fear and dismay pulsed through his guts. Catherine would never have removed her necklace willingly, not after they exchanged vows.

"What is it?" Lady Sabina crowded in.

"A gift to Catherine." Gregoire held out his hand. "It once belonged to my mother."

Perrine handed the necklace to Gregoire. "Surprisingly, the necklace was whole. Whoever has her has a horse with an injured leg. Churned up the meadow, but one leg left an odd imprint. The hooves are large, belongs to a courser."

Lord de Gray shouted orders. "My horse! Mount up! Make haste, make haste!"

Faith hobbled next to him, throwing hand signals to the men around them. The Upper Bailey crackled with sudden movement. Orders split the air.

Gregoire plowed past men toward the stable, throwing a question at Perrine. "Did you follow the tracks?"

"To Castle Road. There I met Lord de Gray's men." She caught Gregoire's arm.

"You've experienced nothing? No forewarning?" His voice sounded desperate.

"Only the pearl." Perrine's eyes darted from one man to another as they hurtled through the forecourt, but her expression contemplated something else. "From where did this pearl come?"

"It belonged to my mother and to my father's mother before her. It's said to protect the wearer." Gregoire grimaced and held the pearl in the sunlight. He had no time for this and wished Perrine would have her say.

"I too gave her a token for protection. But she wears neither now." She held up a small green bird. Then she gestured to the pearl. "May I see it, again?"

He handed the necklace to Perrine, yet his anxiety built while they stood in the narrow entrance joining the forecourt and the Upper Bailey. She examined the thick gold clasp at the top and twisted.

"Perrine, I must go. Whatever magic you think this necklace holds..."

The gold snapped. Gregoire and Perrine leaned in.

A tiny piece of shell shaved into the shape of a miniature sword was attached to the top of the pearl. Liquid swirled inside. Perrine's eyes went wide.

"Stand back."

Gregoire eased back. A scowl crossed his face. "What is it?"

"Poison." Perrine quickly replaced the top, giving it a quick turn. "I fear the fumes from it may be enough to kill someone. A talisman indeed. The original wearer probably knew it held poison, but over the years the secret was lost. The small sword is tipped with the poison. A skin prick is all it takes to kill someone."

Gregoire had a new respect and a greater fear for the necklace. His own neck felt as if it might break; he reached up and massaged the ropey muscles at the base of his head. His mother had worn it all her life, a decoration, nothing more. Or so he thought, and he gave it to Catherine, never realizing it could kill her.

Perrine studied the clasp. "Nothing leaked. Will be safe but be careful with the contents if you or anyone else ever uses it."

Gregoire gingerly hooked the chain with a finger, keeping the necklace at arm's length.

"The clasp is strong. Press it inward until you hear a click, or it won't open," explained Perrine.

Gregoire placed the necklace inside the same jeweled pouch he hid it in before he gave it to Catherine. He secured the small bag to his belt.

"Heavens and stars above us! Catherine dreamed bones for so long until this instant, I thought it connected to her past fears of her mother's death." Perrine balled a fist and held it to her breast. "Bones mean danger or death. All this time, she has carried this fear. And now...."

"Bon sang! We must go to Gabriel's Stream. The trail begins there." Gregoire hadn't removed his upper chest plate, while those around him, including Lord de Gray, tussled with their armor and bindings. He raced to Fiérsabo, shouting at Perrine over his shoulder. "Use Moncadeau! She is faster than the others. I will follow you."

Once mounted and trotting though the Upper Baily, Lady Sabina chased behind them. Gregoire looked back in time to see her shout out a blessing, then drop solidly to the ground; her skirts billowed around her, as her hands folded in prayer. The remaining men and Lord de Gray hurried to catch up.

Gregoire ground his teeth as he passed under the portcullis. He shared such a strong bond with Catherine, he wondered why he had not sensed her terror. A veiled rider pointed to abduction. With everything in him he prayed that whoever took her would not harm her.

Chapter Twenty-Two

Catherine's head jostled violently. Slowly the ground came into focus. Her ribs simmered with pain. What had happened? Where was she? She tried to lift her head, but someone forced it back down. She smelled sweat, too acid for a human, and she remembered that she was draped over a horse.

"Ah ha, the ice maiden awakes," said a gruff voice.

She knew immediately it belonged to Dru. She shut her eyes, wishing him away. Mon Dieu! He was cruel.

"Did you honestly think staying with the healers would protect you? For once, my father will be glad I took the initiative. No, that was a lie. He is never pleased." He tracked a line over her back. "If he only knew..."

Chills crept over her skin where his finger had slid over her. There was no chance of escape while she hung upside down. Her size put her at a distinct disadvantage. She could not anger him by fighting or breaking away. She would have to use her wits.

Catherine attempted to speak, but her lips flapped together and refused to form words. She tried to grab the saddle and pull herself up, but her hands were tied together with the laces from her bliaut, of all things. The front of her dress bloused open, her breast unbound.

"Please, can we stop for just a moment?" Finally, her lips worked. "All the jostling. I feel unwell."

He mashed the side of her face into the horse. Its damp coat stuck to her cheek. Her mind sharpened. She had to stay calm and think. This took more effort than she expected. Everything from her head to her toes cramped. Closing her eyes, she concentrated on her breathing until she was calm. With her mind less jumbled, she formed a plan. First, she needed to determine where they were.

She noted that the horse could not break into a full gallop due to the mossy stones beneath them. Slippery rocks meant a water source. Gabriel's Stream was still close. Soon they slowed. The horse deftly avoided black roots reaching across the forest floor. Suddenly, they came to a halt.

Dru flung her to the ground. She anticipated the fall and angled her body so that she landed on her feet. Dru had other ideas. His sudden grab startled her before she touched the ground. He threw her like a bag of oats over his shoulder. His metal chest plate dug into the soft tissue beneath her already bruised ribcage. Deep in shade, he dropped her on an ancient root bed. She turned to her side and threw up.

"Disgusting woman." Dru stood akimbo over her. Sunlight filtered through a fan of green leaves behind his head. He had pushed the wimple behind his ears and looked like the fearsome gargoyles lodged at the corners of the chapel roof.

Catherine swallowed hard and pretended to suppress a gag, buying time. He towered over her, so she gingerly rolled to a sitting position. "My father will be searching for me."

He removed the crop from his horse and tapped his leg. "He will never find you. No one will ever find you. You have been outfoxed. A hard thing to admit, but you brought it on yourself."

"Dru, think about your father. He has wanted our families to be united for years. This is a mistake." She used measured tones, trying anything to slow him down, though she knew it was foolish to believe logic would stop him.

He slid the tip of the crop along her neckline, tossing back her hair. "You are so naïve. At first, it was rather endearing. You think love is an overwhelming emotion between a man and a woman. Just the opposite was right under your nose—your beloved John gained power through methods you never suspected. A handsome man, he found out other men's secrets. Men have needs beyond what a woman can give them. And you, disgusting creature, could never begin to please me."

He nudged her with his foot as if she were a dirty field cat. "Duty is duty. We both know love has nothing to do with marriage. You were born a pawn. I thought you clever enough to figure that out before we became grand partners. You are right though; my father *has* been planning this for years. It would all fall in place the moment your father signed the marriage contracts."

Catherine's stomach lurched. She clung to the fabric around her waist to fight the urge. "What do you mean?"

"Come now. Did you really believe John died from a boar attack?" He spat out the words. "Tell me you never noticed a change in him. Favors were exchanged. Eventually, he knew too much."

Catherine searched the ground for something she could use as a weapon. Of course, she had noticed a change in John. Childhood was a time for growing and learning. They always knew they would go down different paths; he would follow his father, and she would marry Dru...but he was suggesting something more.

When she thought about it: Before his death, John had barely spoken to her, had avoided her. Several days in a row, he left before the Matin bells, supposedly to check newly planted fields. He came back later each time, and each time he went straight to see her father, who had trusted John to handle all the correspondence between families. Faith's crippled hands and knees made traveling unthinkable, and John took over more and more responsibilities.

"What are you saying about John?" She slid one finger under her wrist bindings. It was a tight fit, but the ties from her dress gave way easier than she expected.

Dru shook his head. "What is it about you that makes men fall in love with you? Makes them betray their very nature. John grew up knowing he would be seneschal for your father when Faith died. A neighboring lord offered him a higher position. My father saw an opportunity and offered John land, a chance to walk free of the de Grays. My father's proposal included an exchange of information. De Gray never knew the offer made. Like all foolish old men, he believed in loyalty. John, ever the fool, jumped at my father's offer."

"John would *never* do that. You are suggesting sacrilege and deception. I'm not so naïve." She dropped her hands to the middle of her skirt, rolling them along the material, and loosening the bindings about her wrists.

"Oh, but he did. Well, he did for a while." Dru ran the crop lazily down Catherine's throat, tracing her collarbones. He tapped the little well in between them three times. "Three times is lucky. But I think your luck has run out, my dear."

A vicious gleam in his eye caught her. Had he always been this way? Catherine held his gaze and slid a second finger beneath her bindings.

"For the past two years, John has carried messages to your father and your father losing his eyesight and being the trusting fellow he is, never truly appraised the documents John had him sign. Little by little he signed away his property." Dru guided the crop's tip between Catherine's breasts.

She wiggled the binding over her thumb, loosening one hand enough to start unwinding the braid. She had to keep him engaged. "But you still have to marry me for the land to transfer to the Devreux."

Dru cocked a brow and grinned so broadly his back teeth showed. "That is the tricky part. John began to have remorse, an emotion he could not afford. And refused to bring any other missives to your father. Stupid man, he claimed he would testify, if need be, that Lord de Gray never realized what he was signing. In the end, John proved to be useless. God's breath, what can you expect from a traitor?"

Dru sucked on the tip of the crop, wetting it. "My father had planned for years, and he would never let an ant spoil the pudding. He bound John and threw him in a sack. Once the moon rose, he had his men take the traitor to a newly rutted field. Oh, I forgot to mention, my father smashed John's knees. He could neither walk nor run. Of course, just as planned, the boars made a meal of him and were blamed for his death."

Hot tears gathered in the corners of her eyes. John had been so gentle and kind. A trustworthy servant. She was no fool. Dru's father never offered John land. The despicable man had threatened to expose John's true nature. The priests would never condone his behavior any more than they would approve of Perrine if she were charged with sorcery. Crimes against the Natural Law were dealt with swiftly. The accused were castrated, dismembered, then burned at a stake. There could be no other explanation for John's betrayal. Intuitively, she had always known John was simply too kind for this world.

Lord Devreux was pure evil. After the things Perrine told her, Catherine knew why Lady Amée had feared for her daughter and had kept her away from her father. All along, it had been more than saving her for a good marriage. Lady Amée, while she seemed harsh, may have done her very best for Rayne.

The idea that she would have to spend the rest of her life with Dru and his family made her feel as if someone had dropped her into an icy pond. She froze under his gaze. She would never go with Dru. Never.

"I carry the final marriage contract––it transfers Castle de Gray to me upon marriage." Dru stuck the wet crop against Catherine's skin, pushing her bliaut fully open. She felt the cold air race over her skin.

"With the new contract, I have decided to wed your sister instead. She is not too young after all. Within a few years she will have her first blood and by then... I will train her to be submissive. If you keep an animal in the dark with limited food and water, they will eventually bend to your will."

The revelation about John and his death shocked Catherine. The thought of Isabelle in his monstrous hands made her queasy. She gritted her teeth, determined to change his mind. She clenched her hands together now free under her loose bindings. Dru would never have her sister, not if she had anything to do with it.

Catherine thrust her fingers directly into Dru's eyes and snapped to her feet. He fell backwards, but his training had made him resilient. Blinded, he leapt up, extending one arm in front of him, searching the air. He covered one eye while squinting with the other to see.

She bolted to the stream, tugging her bliaut to keep it from tangling in her feet. Dru's long strides put him on her faster than a hungry falcon. He grabbed her by the braid and yanked her back-wards. She tumbled into the water. He rammed his knees on either side of her hips, trapping her. He drew back his hand to slap her. Catherine rammed her leg upward, connecting with the mound between his legs. He screamed and cupped his hands over his groin. Twisting away, she rose to her feet and staggered out of the stream. Her dress was saturated, but despite its weight, she gathered it to her and ran for the horse.

Dru whistled. The horse obediently returned to him. As it pounded past her, she tried to catch the reins, but they slipped through her grasp. She took off toward the woods; a thicket was just ahead. If she made it there, the dense understory would hide her. She had barely finished the thought when she heard the horse thundering behind. The next thing she knew, the animal head-butted her from behind and sent her flying. She landed with a sickening thud, all the air in her lungs whooshed out. Dru leapt off his horse and once again, Catherine was at his mercy.

* * *

When she came to, her hands and feet were numb from their bindings. Dru's plan to marry Isabelle banged around in her head. Power hungry, he would be able to do whatever he wanted once he was Lord of the land. Her sister would never survive a life caged in Devreux Castle.

The horse threaded its way through recently coppiced trees, stumbling over spindly branches growing directly from trunks cut to the ground. A spiky new branch thrashed her across the face. The horse startled several times, clearly struck along its legs by sharp branches. With no sense of direction, she listened for a stream or wildlife to identify in which direction they were headed, but she heard neither. Lost. She might as well have worn a blindfold. She'd run out of time and had to act now.

Marrying Gregoire was a dream, but it was a chance she had been willing to take. Unbeknownst to her, Dru had wanted Gregoire, too. An impossible situation. Dru knew this better than anyone, and it had filled him with hate. His misery now belonged to everyone. She had not realized that by following her heart she would put her sister in danger.

Her chest felt as if it had cracked into two pieces. Gregoire had vowed to protect her. And she had no doubt he would. Somehow, she had to convince Dru that she would be the best choice. Riches, land, power meant nothing to her. He could have everything. If that meant she could never see Gregoire again, so be it. No matter how much she loved him, she could never let Dru destroy Isabelle.

"Please, listen to me." Catherine choked out the words. "I will never create trouble for you again. I can bend to your will with pleasure. Please, listen. As your wife, we can live however you like. Whatever you want. There is no need to change the contract. The land makes no difference. All can be as it was before."

The horse crept on. Dru remained silent.

His crop raked across her back. Her muscles tightened, and she fought back a scream. Her bliaut fell about her in shreds. Any pride she had was completely gone.

He growled above her. "You think you know misery, but you would never understand true anguish. To love someone you know the world will never let you have is a torment worse than death. But why should I be the only one to endure loneliness? If I suffer, we will all suffer."

"You *must* understand." Desperation crept into her voice, and she tried to sound normal, but what did it matter? She *was* desperate. "You have broken me—body and soul. Please, I will do whatever you say. We will marry, and I will live at Devreux Castle for the rest of my days. Just tell me what you want me to do."

They had started up an incline. Coppiced trees were no longer underfoot. She heard a horse neigh, and at first it sounded just behind them. She listened but did not hear it a second time.

"Too late." He reined in his horse and dismounted, leaving her on the horse. "If I thought whipping you, starving you, or putting you behind bars would break you, I might try. But you are unbreakable, and I do not have the will or the desire or the time to do it. My father and I will present a new marriage contract. Isabelle will live with me. She will bend like a green branch to our will. Make no mistake, this is your doing."

He slapped her bottom and dropped her to the ground. She stifled a sob. "I will do whatever you say. Please take me. She is innocent."

"True. She is innocent." Dru smirked. "An admission of your own sin?"

Catherine bit the inside of her lip until she tasted blood. "I never meant—

"Do not think you can play games with me. You are no virgin. You betrayed me with someone who means more to me than you could ever perceive." He held his head as if the words weighed more than his neck could bear. "Many times, all it took was a touch. His arm around me. Sleeping under the stars, in a shelter with him an arm's length away. Bathing in streams. His reassurance that we'll fight together forever. That was until we returned to Pître. It has driven me crazy. My own father would throw me to the priests if he knew of my true feelings for Gregoire. And in their court, I would be castrated, tortured, and burned. But you. You can love him openly with no repercussions."

He moved in close and pulled a dagger. "Misery yearns for a partner. You want to be with me, mean something to me."

Dru held the dagger high, and the sun glinted off the blade. His hands clasped her ankles. The blade plummeted. She squeezed her eyes shut. He cut her bindings. Eyes wide open, she knew not to flinch when he held the dagger to her face.

With a jerk, he grabbed her bound wrists, drawing her hands to his cold chest armor. His breath smelled like sour wine and stale bread. Concentrate on the smells, she thought. She stared into his eyes, as he sliced cleanly through the leather ties. She resisted the desire to grit her teeth and show defiance. With her head bowed, she pretended defeat.

"You have no idea where we are, do you?" He kissed the top of her head. "We can become man and wife right here. You can scream and kick all you desire."

He was softening. No, she was doomed. He'd never care for her or her sister. What he most desired would never happen. He wouldn't be happy until he destroyed her and most likely, Gregoire.

"There is a cave just beyond." He gestured with his chin.

Catherine stiffened, then reached out for his arms. His muscles hardened at her touch, and she pushed her body against him. She felt his leg come between hers, entangled with what was left of her skirt. Mordieu!

"Not here." He sniffed, then said, "Follow me."

He started up an overgrown path. She staggered behind him. Passing over a rock-strewn path, something sharp cut into her shoe and blood slickened the sole. No more than a few steps ahead, the mouth of a small cave yawned open as if the underworld welcomed them.

Dru placed his hands on her shoulders, spinning her so that her back faced the cave. She felt a slight breeze ruffle her hair. She would never look back to this day. If she did, she would never survive, but she would know her sister was spared.

Dru pinched her chin and tipped her head back. Overhead ancient drawings covered the ceiling. She focused on a group of dark men racing ochre horses. Her mind detached from her body. Nothing mattered anymore. He whispered, but she had drifted so far away, his words meant nothing. She arched and tilted back farther, becoming one with the primitive riders. One of the men pointed to her, and she wished for him to take her into the stone with him. Dru shouted something. The words sounded familiar, but far away. He pushed her.

She flew backwards, reaching out at the last moment for Dru. His grin widened; his teeth shone white in the dimming light. Full realization hit her—she was falling.

It didn't take long, and she landed on an accumulation of stones and debris. When she shifted, the mass undulated beneath her. The stench of rotting meat overpowered her, and she gagged. Splaying her hands in front, she knelt and felt around her. What she found horrified her—a shoulder blade, a hip, and a chest plate with ribs still attached. A small animal scurried over her outstretched hand and emitted a distressed squeak. Terrified, she snapped and let out a scream. Dru shouted down at her.

"Did you think I would be fooled? Only an idiot would believe you." His voice chilled the very air between them. "I saw how you looked at Gregoire. You are no better than a hound's bitch. He probably took you right on the stable floor. Did you like it squirming around in the mud, where you belong? No one wants you. You are revolting!"

Dru spat at her. A sickening glob of sputum hit her right in the face. She swiped away the nauseating mass with the back of her hand. A realization twisted through her. If he left, she was trapped. The stony edge loomed beyond her reach.

"You can't do this. They will know you left me." Her voice bounced from wall to wall.

"Just as I suspected, you are plotting to escape even now. I will leave you with one last thought." He bent over the ledge, his eyes narrowed. Hate pierced her as surely as an arrow. "Your father will search for you. But he won't get this far. However... if he does, I will be waiting with my men. It will be most regrettable when he meets with an unavoidable accident. Then no one will be left to protect your stepmother or your sister. They will belong to me."

He moved back from the opening. Catherine watched his shadow recede. "Dru? Please, you cannot do this."

Her chest heaved, her breath the only noise filling the space around her. He had to come back. He had to.

"Dru?"

Fear threatened to consume her. Despite the darkness and the scrabbling sounds beneath her, she clenched her teeth and resisted the urge to scream again. There had to be a way out. Catherine felt around past broken and shattered bones. Mad thoughts of the dead, their dancing bones rising and joining her, filled her head. Quickly, before she lost her courage and believed her own twisted mind, she ripped her dress, wrapping her hands so she wouldn't cut them. She felt around her, pushing her terror away, until finally, she touched something large and cold–a rounded boulder. With a huff, she pulled herself onto it. The light shone brighter in this part of the cave, and she could finally make out what lay under the rock ledge.

Tiny claws tugged at her skirts, attempting to climb on her. She slapped them off, only to have three filthy beasts attack her. Her nightmares had become real. Beneath the rock were thousands and thousands of bones. This was no ordinary cave. It was an ancient burial pit.

Chapter Twenty-Three

P errine pointed out the distorted hoof print to Gregoire. He
had seen that imprint before, rare in coursers, but common
in smaller horses. The hoof on the forefoot was compressed
in the middle instead of a nice half-moon shape. The irregular shape
was caused by an irritation along the horny part of the hoof, possibly
a blistering thorn. Either the rider had access to only one horse, or the
animal had little value to the rider. The last thought made him more
fearful for Catherine than the first.

They followed the trail where it left Castle Road, lost it near
Hawk's Bridge, then relocated it on the Devreux side of Gabriel's
Stream. Lord de Gray and his men caught up with them there.

Gregoire continued to identify fresh tracks along the stream until
he came to a hollow in a thicket of trees. He held up his hand and
leapt to the ground. He had difficulty interpreting the prints; they
overlapped, as if the horse pranced in one place for some time,
distorting the shapes in the mud. "They stopped here."

Lord de Gray and Perrine dismounted. Perrine asked. "Any
traces of a woman?"

Gregoire knelt to examine the indentations. A piece of leather thong had been trampled into one of the indentions. "Impossible to say. A scuffle of some kind occurred here."

Perrine bent and studied the chaotic trail "It's amazing this horse still carries a double rider. And I agree, a fight occurred here. The impressions circle each other. Look, human footprints—I'm thinking a man. They are deeper than the others, as if carrying something. Perchance, Catherine?"

"My thoughts, too." Gregoire scanned the area for more clues.

"There is no blood, no signs of injury." Lord de Gray wiped sweat off his forehead with the crook of his arm. "We can pray she is without harm."

Gregoire spied something strung across the underbrush near the forest's perimeter. He hustled over, recognizing the braided cord immediately. "Belongs to Catherine. We are most assuredly on the right trail."

Perrine moved away from the stream. "Then, it's definitely the same horse, a single rider with Catherine." She motioned to the north. "They are headed toward the rise."

"Where could they possibly be going?" Lord de Gray trudged to his horse. "Nothing ahead but coppiced trees and uninhabited mountains."

As Gregoire prepared to mount, Perrine stepped over to him. She placed her hand on his shoulder, stopping him. Her sleeve fell away from her wrist. Pink skin mottled her arm. He had forgotten it had been only days since her transformation.

She whispered. "There is a rumor about an ancient burial site just beyond the forest. Catherine dreamed of bones. I told her it meant nothing, gave her another explanation. But what if they are bound for the old cave? What if whoever has her, intends not to hold her for ransom, but to kill her? Perhaps bury her where we will never find her?"

"You know more, or you wouldn't make such suppositions. What is it?" Gregoire tired of the game. Why couldn't she express her concerns straight out?

"I no longer have clear visions. In the past, I might have had some notion of what happened to her. Today, I had no forewarning." Her expression was marred with worry." I am useless. Though no one will speak his name, we both have an idea who this mysterious rider is. We are all at his mercy."

Gregoire put his foot into a wooden stirrup. "As long as there is breath in my body, I will search for her. I will never give up and neither should you. We have tracks ahead. It may be all we have, but it is more than nothing. I suggest we take heed and follow them as long as we have light."

Once Perrine mounted, Gregoire bolted ahead. He wanted to shake the feeling of helplessness she pushed on him. Catherine was as attached to her as a sister, but he did not share those feelings. Perrine's damage went beyond her physical appearance and her muddled visions. She wrestled with something more, and for some reason, she had chosen Gregoire to confide in. He had no patience for it. What use was she without her visions? He needed to find Catherine before his worst fears were realized. If he could leave Perrine behind, he would.

Catherine was in unspeakable danger. She would not willingly have taken off the pearl necklace, that much he was certain. But the braided cord he held in his hand worried him more than anything else, even though he didn't reveal his concern to Perrine or de Gray. He knew exactly what happened to a woman's bliaut without the cord to tie it together. But he saw no evidence she had been ravaged. All he had was hope. It would have to be enough.

* * *

Overhead, a spinning Merlin hawk dodged screeching sparrows. Gregoire shielded his eyes and watched the birds. The sparrows swooped the predator, pecking at the back of its head. They would defend their nest to their last breath. The tiny birds voices filled the thinning forest. Tension ran high. Gregoire dreaded entering a field of newly hewn or coppiced trees. The woodcutters left behind gnarled stumps where stiff green branches stuck out like splayed fingers. For horses, the fresh branches were more dangerous than a whip and impossible to trot through. The coppiced trees funneled into a small open field at the base of a craggy mountain.

A glint of metal flashed ahead. Gregoire leaned forward in his saddle for a better look. He signaled Lord de Gray, who halted his men at the forest's edge. A lone rider trotted in the open field. De Gray's men quickly lined up within the forest. Gregoire, Perrine, and Lord de Gray maneuvered to a small clearing beside the forest.

Perrine whispered. "Dru. His horse. Watch how it favors the right leg."

Gregoire noticed it at the same moment Perrine spoke. Fury flew over him like a fever. He prepared to charge him when Lord de Gray growled, "Hold your anger. Let him come to us. I suspected he had something to do with Catherine's disappearance, but I did not think him fool enough to do it himself. Let him think there are only the three of us. If he bolts, we may never find Catherine."

Lord de Gray was right. Gregoire resisted the temptation to race out and run his sword through Dru. Earlier, wending their way through the trees, Gregoire thought back to the time he and Dru were boys just beginning their training together. Dru lashed out at other trainees with his fists. His bouts of anger were famous, and the other boys challenged his at every opportunity. Ignoring Dru's temper, Gregoire had enjoyed his company. They practiced for hours when everyone else retired. Until their arrival in Pître, Gregoire had thought Dru's father a proud man who expected too much, but now Gregoire saw clearly that it was rejection Dru truly feared.

Though Gregoire offered friendship, Dru's confession revealed his desperation. He had risked his father discovering his deepest secret. Gregoire knew Dru well enough to realize that he feared banishment as much as death. He meant to kill Catherine and Gregoire. His family would not be the only one to suffer.

The horses were jittery. Gregoire's courage was at its peak. Why did Lord de Gray delay?

"Before we enter the fray, I have an admission." De Gray cleared his throat. "I made a terrible mistake trusting Devreux and his son. It might very well cost me my daughter's life. You claim to love her and have gone to great lengths to show it. When Catherine laid ill, I thought your concern was for Dru and his attachment to my daughter, but clearly it was more than that. It did not go unnoticed by me or my wife that you stayed long after your horse was healed. You have earned my respect and my trust. It will be an honor to fight beside you."

Gregoire bowed to Lord de Gray. "My sword will protect Catherine until I can no longer hold it."

He experienced the familiar rush of anxiety, fear, and excitement he normally had before a joust. Only this time, sadness filled his heart. Instead of fighting with Dru, he now fought against him. He couldn't bear the thought, but he wouldn't let it distract him. He closed his mind and concentrated on a path through the dangerous coppice. Dru slowly made his way to the tree line. His horse came to a standstill, and he made a show of pulling his sword from its scabbard.

"What brings you uninvited to Devreux land? A death wish, perhaps? This I can easily grant." Dru's voice carried to the forest.

"He has glass balls," said Lord de Gray with a sneer as he grasped his sword. "Time to shatter his damned arrogance."

Gregoire had an uneasy feeling. Dru had fought enough to plan a clever assault. Lord de Gray's horse sidestepped a large fern entering the coppice. Both had drawn their long swords and were at the ready. Perrine hung back when de Gray's men trotted into the clearing and stood at the ready.

"Something is amiss," said Gregoire, scanning the forest on either side.

"I agree," said Lord de Gray. "I fear we may have walked into a trap. Whatever happens, ride straight for Dru. You have trained with him and know his weaknesses. If anyone can beat him, it will be you."

Just as de Gray finished his last sentence twenty or more armed men darted from either side of the woods and charged into the clearing. A full quarter of the men carried maces, and all brandished swords save one; he clutched a loaded crossbow. Gregoire forced Fiérsabo into the frenzy of chopped stumps. He heard but did not see Lord de Gray clashing with Devreux's men. Metal rang against metal, horses snorted, and men shouted God's name. A bolt whizzed past his head. He ducked just in time.

Dru bounded into the coppice field. Fiérsabo pulled at the bit but picked his way forward. Gregoire glimpsed Perrine gliding along the forest's border, thankfully unhampered by the Devreux men. She seemed to be working her way to the mountains.

Once Gregoire was near the edge of the field, Dru shouted at him, "If I die, you die. No mercy. There is no turning back."

Training with Dru had put Gregoire at a disadvantage. Dru knew he would not risk hurting Fiérsabo. For that very reason, Dru had chosen the coppice area for a fight. Gregoire would be unable to gain any speed weaving through the stumps for an attack.

Another whiz sounded just above Gregoire's ear. He guided his horse through the coppice, starting and stopping, going wide as well as narrow, hoping to fool the next bolt. He ducked and shouted. "Where is Catherine?"

"No mercy, I said. We all die today." Dru gave a harsh laugh. "You never understood. This misery will be thrice shared."

"Tell me where she is." Gregoire directed Fiérsabo around several newly chopped trunks. Talking to Dru was futile, but it helped fuel Gregoire's anger to its peak.

"You will meet her in heaven." Dru guided his horse closer to the coppiced trees. "You will arrive first, but she will follow in time, never fear."

Gregoire looked past Dru's shoulder; Perrine had stealthily goaded Moncadeau into the mountain's pass. She dismounted and checked the ground for tracks. He prayed she was on a trail to Catherine. He might never know.

Dru charged. Gregoire prepared as best he could, but without speed his downward sword stroke would lack the momentum he needed for a clean cut. Fiérsabo jumped the last stump. Another bolt whizzed past them but went wide and made a loud thunk when it speared Dru's horse in the haunches. The animal bucked, and Dru clung to it as it spun and hurtled in the opposite direction.

Gregoire gave chase as the horses galloped across the clearing. They were at the base of the mountain when Dru's horse stumbled. He leapt clear before the courser crashed to the rocky loam. Dru fought to stand, holding his sword in the front, his legs planted and ready.

Gregoire anticipated Dru's next move—undercut Fiérsabo's legs and bring him down. His horse had been good to him. He would never give Dru the chance. Gregoire pulled to the right and jumped from his horse. He gripped his sword in one hand and his dagger in the other. He felt the cool tremor that ran through him before a mêlée or a joust.

A movement just at the fringe of his vision registered in his brain, but he focused on Dru too intently to look away. The muscles in his legs were ready to spring, yearning for release like a snake before it strikes. Then he heard Perrine scream.

Chapter Twenty-Four

Catherine's throat ached from screaming, but it was useless. No one could hear her. The noise had scared the rats enough to scuttle them into dark corners and coiling tunnels alongside the disgusting nest woven through the bones. The rat's lair had broken her fall and saved her. The stench of decaying animals and years of urine burned her nostrils.

She searched for a way to climb out. The nesting tunnels ran clear to the top of the pit. She attempted to climb one, but it was in vain. Each time she grabbed a section, it fell apart, leaving a foul substance smeared on her hand. Beady eyes blinked red in the low light, and it became clear that she could never rest or sleep. She would have to fight to the end. If she didn't, the revolting creatures would smother her to death long before she bled to death. Every time she lifted a leg, reached for the wall, more ancient bones shattered beneath her feet. She pulled her bliaut high enough to protect her upper body from the knife-like edges.

With her hands on her hips, she grabbed a thighbone to ward of rats hanging outside the upper nesting tunnels. It gave her an idea. She tore long strips from her skirt, then gathered as many long bones as she could find. Wrapping the fabric around three thighbones, she created the bottom rung of a ladder. She prayed for enough bones to reach the top lip of the pit.

Rats poured out of every conceivable narrow space and lined the tunnels. Catherine hastily wrapped more fabric around the bones. With each twist of material, she batted away several bold rats leaping at her skirts. She continued in this manner building rung upon rung. Finally, she leaned the ladder against the cave's wall and tested it, knocking several skulking rats off a rung with her hand.

Stretched between one bony rung and the next, she heard her name.

"Catherine!"

She shook her head. Could not be true. Sounded like Perrine. No matter if real or a demon, she cupped her hands around her mouth. "Here!"

In the muted light, she made out Perrine's face hanging at the cave's ledge. Her head was uncovered, and her short silvery hair caught light from the entrance.

"Where are you? Grand Dieu. Are you injured?" Perrine shouted.

Tears nearly choked Catherine. She stomped at a hissing rat before placing her foot on the next rung. "Hurry. You must hurry. We need a rope."

"Yes. Luckily, I rode Moncadeau. I have the one from your saddle. God in heaven! This place is crawling." Perrine threw down the twisted hemp; it unfurled and ended just above Catherine's head. "Make haste. Can you reach it?"

Catherine wrapped the rope the best she could around her wrist. "Now! Now! Pull me up. I'll tie it around me."

Perrine grunted and tugged, bracing her legs against a solid rock, but Catherine's grasp slipped away. The nesting rats became crazed. A brush of fur skimmed Catherine's cheeks, her arms, her waist. Frantic teeth tore into her ankle.

"Moncadeau?" called out Catherine. "Get her double quick."

Perrine left.

"Make haste before these stinking animals make a meal of me!" Catherine shouted, swinging her leg against the cave wall, crushing two of the pests sucking blood on her leg.

She squeezed her eyes shut and prayed she would not die in this stinking pit. More rats scrabbled out of the giant nest. More determined than ever, she pulled on the rope and began to ascend the rickety bone ladder. Each step brought another wave of animals leaping from the nesting tunnels, some landing in the void below, others clawing at Catherine. She stared eye to eye with a feral rat clinging to a bony crossbar.

"Die, you filthy beast." Catherine crushed the rat with a thick femur. It fell into the seething nest below, and immediately disappeared under a mass of furry bodies. Above, a horse snorted. Catherine clung to the center rung. Perrine's face appeared over the ledge again.

"The cave is too low for her."

Catherine could not afford another failed attempt. "Tie the rope to the saddle."

Perrine scuffled above. Catherine teetered on the cobbled ladder, fighting off more advancing rats, swinging her fists and stamping her feet. She gripped the rope with all her strength. The line went taut, then jerked upward.

Rats dropped from above, landing on Catherine's back, arms, head... everywhere. Hand over hand, she made progress, but then she lost her footing and slipped a rung. She had to reach the top rung. This was her last chance.

Dizzy with fear, she yelled, "Pull me up. Otherwise, this is the death of me!"

Her palms burned, but she refused to let go. Even when a fat rat plopped on the back of her hand and began to chew on a knuckle, she bared her teeth and bit it back. The creature drew back, but Catherine had had enough and flung it into the cave wall. Last step.

Light burst out around her. She grabbed a cleft in the floor and pulled herself over the ledge and immediately collapsed. Tears of gratitude threatened to spill over her cheeks, but she sniffed and bared her fists. Perrine bashed every rat that dove off Catherine with a mottled sword.

Her legs too shaky to stand, Catherine rolled on her side. Perrine dropped beside her, embraced her, and whispered, "My sweet friend. You are safe now."

Rats pushed and jostled their way to the cave's entrance. With Perrine by her side, Catherine fought off a river of angry rats as they plowed out of the cave. Moncadeau stomped on the despicable animals, squishing bodies, and splattering blood over shifting rocks.

Catherine heard men shouting and a horse's whine when she took her first breath of freedom. She leapt on Moncadeau and thrust out a hand to Perrine.

"Another time you have saved me."

The corners of Perrine's mouth gently lifted as she pulled her hood up securely covering her soft new hair. She grasped Catherine's hand and swung her leg over the pitching horse.

Catherine goaded Moncadeau and dashed to the clearing. It wasn't as far away as Catherine imagined though trees and under-story blocked her sight until she rode into the clearing.

Riding in earlier, draped over Dru's horse, she hadn't known the copse field so large. Hemmed in by the forest and the mountain, the men had no choice but fight. There was nowhere to run. Her father swiped men with his sword from atop his horse. Dead men lay motionless, while bloody men writhed on the ground or sat at odd angles on stumps. Muffled horses' hooves mauled the ground. Metal clanged and showered men with sparks. Adjusting her vision through the dusty haze, Gregoire appeared. She gasped at the sight of a deranged Dru lashing his sword.

"Hold tight." Catherine prodded Moncadeau.

Perrine nearly fell off the horse. Clutching the saddle, she screamed.

In response to her voice, Gregoire lifted his head long enough for

Dru to slash his belt into two pieces. The strike hit his scabbard just beneath his breastplate. Jumping into a crouch as his belt, dagger, and pouch hit the ground, Gregoire's sapphires along with the pearl necklace tumbled on the rock-strewn ground between the two men.

Catherine rode in a circle around them, but they ignored her. Using her knees, she prodded Moncadeau into a tighter circle. Perrine pointed at the ground. "The pearl necklace. Mayhap, I can reach it."

"How can you think of pearls at a time like this?"

Perrine whispered. "The pearl contains a deadly poison. Certain death."

Over her shoulder, Catherine gave Perrine a hard glance. She needed to hear nothing more and jumped from the horse. She spied Gregoire's dagger and scooped it up with the necklace. Standing there, she watched in horror as the men hammered at one another, then circled and lunged. Blood streaked their clothing, smearing their armor.

They were so engaged, neither saw Catherine—or so she thought. Perrine somehow was by her side.

With confidence, Perrine said, "Careful. Simply press the top until it clicks. Inside is a small dagger with enough poison to kill a warhorse. Neither smell it, nor prick yourself."

Catherine never took her eyes from the two men. Warming the oversized pearl in her palm, her instincts took over, and she hid the deadly poison in the folds of her filthy, shredded skirt.

Gregoire gave her a side-glance and clasped his sword in front. "Stay away. Go back, Catherine."

During that fleeting moment of distraction Dru rushed Gregoire. He sliced Gregoire's fighting arm at the junction of his breastplate. Blood gushed from the cut, drenching his sleeve. Gregoire grimaced but maintained his grip on his sword.

He swung the blade hard, aiming for Dru's breastplate. It bounced off, metal ringing in the silence. Gregoire's arm dangled at his side, blood dripped from his fingertips, his sword slipping from his grip.

Catherine struggled to concentrate. Gregoire's sleeve was saturated with blood, yet he lured Dru away from her by stepping away. Catherine calmly moved between them. Moncadeau snorted and reared, coming down with a thud.

Dru grabbed Catherine, spinning her to face Gregoire. His dagger nicked the notch between her collar bones. His attack happened so quickly she hardly realized it.

"She will die before I let her go." Spittle flew from Dru's lips and splattered against her cheek. "Come, Gregoire. See if you can save her before I slice into this pretty neck of hers. You have always underestimated me. Thought you could have what is clearly mine when I offered you better. Both of you will die today."

Blood trickled down her chest. Gregoire's face turned dark; his body shook with rage. She wanted to move her head, wanted to warn him to stay back, but it was impossible. With two fingers she pressed the sides of the pearl's cap. She felt it separate. Everything but the tiny shell dagger fell from her grasp.

"You and Lord de Gray walked right into my trap." Dru pressed his dagger harder against Catherine's neck. "She is a nuisance, not worth all this worry. What do you value in her?"

Gregoire took a step. Dru backed up, landing in a shallow crumbling trench. He tilted off balance. Catherine jabbed the bit of pearl, slick with poison, into his groin. As she moved away, she dropped the piece of necklace and cupped her hand against the cut on her neck. Gregoire charged Dru, using his body like a battering ram and knocking Dru's sword out of his hand.

Blood spurted from Dru's nose. Bent over in pain, he searched for his sword. Suddenly he swiped at his eyes, swinging his fists wildly as if fighting off a swarm of bees. He staggered in a circle. He opened his mouth as if to scream; instead his tongue, swollen to twice its normal size, rolled out of his mouth. Dru collapsed facedown into the shallow trench, reminding Catherine of tales where giants topple over into a cloud of dust.

Gregoire crawled over Dru. He rasped, "It didn't have to be this way."

"No other way." Dru slurred his final words. A torrent of blood gushed from his mouth, filling the powdery trench.

Swaying, Gregoire picked up Dru's sword stained with his own blood, then prodded the man he once called his friend. Dru did not respond. Gregoire's knees buckled, and he held out his arm. Catherine ducked beneath it, and they dropped to the ground. Against her ribs, she felt Gregoire's heartbeat, reassuring her he was truly alive. Only then did she dare to dream this entire ordeal over.

Perrine sidled up beside them and knelt beside Gregoire. "The injury is deep. I will sew and bind it before you mount your horse. Pray you keep the luck and do not lose your arm."

"I have the luck." Gregoire's voice croaked with exhaustion. He gave Catherine's shoulder a gentle squeeze. "When I vowed to protect you with my life, I did not expect to be tested so soon."

Engrossed in Gregoire, she barely felt Perrine's fingers on her neck.

"Thank the saints, he scratched only the skin," said Perrine.

A look of genuine relief passed between them. Catherine flicked her chin at a ring of dead grass. The tiny shell dagger sparkled in the sunlight. Perrine sighed, then rose and retrieved her bag filled with healing remedies. She began her solemn round of inspecting the fallen men.

Catherine brightened when she heard her father's horse approaching, but her joy was tempered when she realized her father rode with only three other men from Castle de Gray. How many men would leave this field maimed or draped over a horse today?

Her father dismounted so rapidly, he reminded her of a hawk falling to earth. He ran a hand over Catherine and then over Gregoire, kissing the tops of their heads. He drove his sword into the ground and knelt facing the east.

"The Second Crusades taught me many things. Among them—with privilege comes responsibility. Pride can turn a man into a beast if he so chooses. He bowed his head and made the sign of the cross. "Par le sang de Dieu, we praise God for the lives before us..."

Lord de Gray's words faded as Catherine leaned closer to Gregoire. His blood smelled of metal. It overwhelmed all her other senses. Exhausted, grimy, and flat on his back, he was still the most impressive man she had ever known. He wound his uninjured arm around her waist and placed his head in her lap. Her gaze took him in, and she smoothed his hair off his forehead. An understanding sprang to life in the moment. He belonged to her, and she belonged to him.

Chapter Twenty-Five

Catherine stood in the forecourt of Castle de Gray, ruffling Bijou's soft fur. The entire courtyard was bathed in peach and gold. Lord de Gray crossed the swept stones in the rose garden. He spied Sabina and flashed a smile.

"I do not think those carts can hold another thing. Only Queen Eleanor travels with more, and everyone knows her taste for luxury." He sauntered to the first four-wheeled cart in a line of three. "You have inspected these at least one hundred times. Will you ever be satisfied?"

Sabina slipped a finger under a taut rope knotted to the cart. "It is a long way to Champagne and more than a visit. Upon our return we shall leave behind a daughter and all her belongings."

"True. But more than twenty loyal men travel with us." Lord de Gray rested his hand on the last cart containing hay-filled mattresses, posts, and tents. "We have prepared for foul weather and marauders, my dear. Stop fretting and make sure our youngest traveler is prepared to leave."

Sabina wended her way around the carts one last time, making eye contact with Catherine. She grinned, then tucked her hands inside her sleeves and sauntered to the kitchen.

"She will not be satisfied until the smallest detail is seen to," said Lord de Gray, tugging at his beard.

Her father seemed worn, like the thinning leather on an old saddle. Clouds streaked behind his head much like the day Dru and Gregoire arrived in Pître. She would never forget that morning. Her father had been so agile on his courser; anyone could have seen he was a formidable lord. Dru had not sought to challenge Lord de Gray then, or at least, he did not appear that way to her.

In the end, his angry words on the way to the cave would forever haunt her. Perchance evil is not in the person, but in the men who create the laws we live by. Gregoire said Dru changed once they entered Pître, more so under the influence of Dru's father. There had been those who knew more than they admitted, yet out of fear never spoke a word.

John had been too trusting of others. When Lord Devreux discovered that every missive, every parchment, every bit of velum passed through John before reaching Lord de Gray, he came up with his plan. Devreux discovered John's secret life and threatened him to do his bidding.

In the end, John found his honor too high a price. When he realized the extent of the betrayal, he returned to Castle de Gray and burned all the documents de Gray had signed. Later, when he was caught destroying Lord Devreux's copies, he was murdered. Without John as his witness, Devreux would have difficulty proving the agreements were legal. All his scheming brought him nothing.

Lord Devreux, unaware of Catherine's abduction, took none of the blame. Power hungry, he was blind to his son's needs. Dru had hidden behind a mask to protect himself, yet, discontented, his resentment grew and possessed him. All he had left was a fractured spirit, full of misery.

Upon returning to the castle after Dru's death, Lord de Gray, Catherine, and Gregoire stayed within the castle grounds to heal.

Without delay, Lord de Gray had to contend with Lord Devreux who created a stir among the neighboring nobles, demanding justice for his son's death. It took less than a week for neighboring families to hear about Catherine's abduction. Lord de Gray had issued a decree condemning Dru Devreux and his actions, thereby absolving Gregoire of any wrongdoing.

Once the other nobles learned the truth, no one dared stand with Lord Devreux. It was said he became enraged and killed all his hunting hounds after the last noble refused to join him. The next morning Lady Amée found him crumpled at the base of the stairs, his speech rambling, his body curled in like a wilted leaf.

A full month after Dru's death, Catherine's future father-in-law arrived. He appeared much older and surprisingly more stylish than expected. When he dismounted and stood next to his son, Catherine saw an older version of Gregoire before her. They shared the same dewy green eyes and sharp cheeks. Not to be left out, Frère Cyril prepared a Thanksgiving Mass welcoming William the Wise to Pître.

As part of the Homily, the priest spoke about greed and made veiled references to Lord Devreux, a bold, yet dangerous move to reprove him in public. A rustle of fabric swept through the chapel when several nobles shifted and glared directly at the priest. He opened his arms to all, reminding them it was the sin of Judas. Catherine worried for Frère Cyril. With William the Wise in attendance, it seemed the frère took advantage of a crowded chapel. Later that day, Gregoire and his father shared a simple meal with Lord de Gray. Catherine wasn't allowed to attend, but for once she stayed still. The next day the men settled into the Upper Hall and agreed on dowry, inheritance, and marriage charters. Although she had no place at the table, she had made her desires known. It was her fervent hope that during Queen Eleanor's reign more women would be included in decisions made between families.

Catherine and Gregoire married a week later. Time passed in a whirlwind of activity. Sabina had become a hummingbird flitting from flower to flower. Castle de Gray was transformed with late summer peonies strung together in rich orange, pink, and green swags. Ivy garland decorated the doors and gates to the castle. Linens normally packed in trunks and stored in a small room behind Lord de Gray's bedchamber were spread across trestles in the main hall. Catherine had wanted to help, but Sabina insisted she continue to rest.

The day Catherine and Gregoire exchanged vows, Sabina surprised her with a bliaut of yellow silk stitched with gold thread. She had prepared it herself over the years. Just before the ceremony, Sabina cinched in the fabric at the waist with needle and thread until Catherine thought she heard her ribs crack. She plucked nervously at the trumpet sleeves sweeping the floor. Sabina liked to show her embroidery skill and lined the sleeves with lavender silk studded with pearls.

Catherine stared across the chapel until she met Gregoire's gaze. He meant everything to her, and she could not believe her good fortune. If not for him, her life would be so different now. Had he not been exposed to Marie de Champagne's Courts of Love would he have taken the chance to be with her? His father represented the few who even listened to their son's wishes. At this moment, her mind allowed her to think of nothing else but the life she would share with him. She felt the skin at the corners of her eyes crinkle and knew her smile reflected her feelings.

Someone shook Catherine by the shoulder, and she snapped into the present, still standing adjacent to the traveling carts with Bijou in her arms. Her wedding had been a month ago. Bijou licked her chin. Lord de Gray stood next to her. He asked, "Where is your mind, ma petite chou? I have asked several times if there is anything else you wish packed?"

"No, Papa."

"Faith is readying your horse for the last time. Mayhap, you should go to the stable." Lord de Gray tugged on her braid. "He will miss you. I worry about him once you are gone."

"He will not be without adventure too long. Isabelle may be

quiet, but she has her ways."

Lord de Gray embraced Catherine with a chuckle. She headed for the stables.

She twisted the pearl given to her by Gregoire while walking across the Upper Bailey. Perrine had searched the ground until she found the pearl and small dagger. She wrapped them and then carefully neutralized all the contents before replacing the cap and chain. She had presented it to Catherine the morning she exchanged vows. The vile poison had been replaced with scented rose water.

Following the ceremony Perrine left, but when she returned two weeks later, she had a surprise, an apprentice—Lady Amée's young handmaiden. She kept a hand to her throat, covering a thin scar. Most of the time, she stood quietly by Perrine with her head bowed. When asked, Perrine admitted she had not the proper permission to harbor or train the young woman. This put Lord de Gray in a precarious position. He could not allow another man's servant to live on his property no matter how much he detested Lord Devreux or wished her to stay with the healer.

He spoke to Perrine. A missive would be sent to Lord Devreux suggesting the handmaiden live with the Perrine and learn the art of healing, later to return and care for those at Devreux Castle. If Lord Devreux agreed, then the young woman could live with the healers without fear of reprisals. Otherwise, she would always live in fear of being captured and hanged or worse.

The following day, Lord de Gray sent a messenger on the slowest horse, on the longest route to Devreux Castle. At least the young woman had some time, and if need be, she could hide, but de Gray assured her a healer was highly prized. He had done what he could do, and felt the odds were in her favor.

Before coming down to inspect the carts for the last time, Catherine had run into Perrine and her new apprentice. The young woman smiled and bowed deeply, then placed her hands to her throat. She touched her fingers to her mouth and made a sign. For the first time Catherine realized the girl could not speak. She truly believed the girl would be safe with Perrine as she made her way to the stable.

Faith was returning from the pigeonnier when Catherine's foot came to rest on the dense hay floor. Gathering her skirt in hand, she made sure she didn't step on anything displeasing. When she looked up, she realized Faith carried a slatted cage holding two traveling pigeons.

"Thought you might like to have them with you. They are trained to return here." He set down the cage. "It's not too far for them to fly."

"Thank you. In all the packing and shuffle I forgot about the birds." Catherine set down Bijou. The dog immediately raced to the pigeons and stuck her muzzle into the cage, causing the birds to flutter about.

"There is something else I have for you." Faith hobbled to the other end of the stable and returned dragging a small wooden trunk. He placed it at her feet, and then rose, rubbing the knee on his crippled leg. A tight smile appeared when he looked at her.

Catherine ran her hand over the polished wooden box, too small for clothes, but the perfect size to store jewels and embellishments. The wood had been rubbed to a rich caramel gloss. A forest and meadow were painted on the top. In the foreground a young woman with a long wheat-colored braid held out an amulet suspended on a strip of leather. A young man held out his hand to the woman, his eyes bright green like Gregoire's.

"This is beautiful." Her throat constricted with emotion.

"When John was a child, I dreamed he would one day care for his own manor." Faith opened the box and fingered the soft cloth lining the small chest. "I had painted the background waiting to see whom he brought home as a wife, but life is like a river and never runs straight. I hoped by painting your images together, it would secure your luck."

"And so it has." Catherine knelt and ran her hand over the precious figures. "The day you met my father during the Crusade was a fortunate one. You are a good man, Faith."

He blushed at his name. "The world is a dangerous place, but you have found someone who cares for you more than his own life. It is a rare thing to find love like that."

"I am looking for a traveling companion to accompany me to Champagne." Gregoire entered the stable, and it was as if the shutters were opened, and the sun came in. "Would you like to accompany me, Madame. I've heard you love adventure, Catherine Le Sage of Champagne."

Catherine could not stop the grin on her face, and she gave an exaggerated bow. "If my husband is in agreement, then let it be so."

Gregoire stroked her cheek and said, "Lady Sabina needs you. Perrine is with her in the herb gardens. Something to do with you and a pouch of herbs?"

"Ah. Perrine insists the fresh herbs must be picked in the early morning. She made me a sack with some healing herbs. Always meticulous, she has directions on how to care for you ..." Catherine tipped her head at Gregoire, then she dipped to Faith. "I will miss you. Thank you for the lovely gift. It will stay by my side the entire trip, and I will find a special place for it in my new home. Come Bijou. Let us take our leave."

Once she left the stables, Gregoire turned to Faith. "Ah, the stable has been good cover. She has not discovered me stopping to visit you these last months."

"She is occupied with dreams for *her* home." Faith removed a pouch from his belt and shook out a golden ring into his palm. "'Was a pleasure to make, sir. She is well worth the price of sapphires and rubies."

"My thought as well." Gregoire took the ring and closed it inside his fist. "It will be my pleasure to visit with you when we return."

"It has been my joy to help. Take good care of her, she is dear to us all." Faith turned, and a tear dripped into the wrinkles of his cheek.

Gregoire tucked the ring into a small pouch attached to his belt and left the stable just as his squire entered. He addressed the young man, "Bring the horses to the forecourt. We will leave when the Prime Bells sound."

He crossed the Upper Bailey and entered the herb gardens. A large-leaf vine climbed a trellis on his left. He picked an over-sized leaf and a stringy tendril, then tucked them into his belt next to the pouch. Lady Sabina and Perrine were in deep conversation with Catherine. Bundles of herbs and little sachets of seeds were piled into a reedy basket. He sat on a bench and watched with fascination.

For all his years of training as a knight, nothing had prepared him for Catherine de Gray. She consumed his thoughts every waking moment, and he nearly laughed at the idea. He had been approached by some of the most alluring women in France, but this little waif of a woman had captured him, heart and soul. He had nearly lost his life twice since he arrived in Pître, but he would do it thrice over to be with her.

When she entered the chapel on the day they were to exchange vows in front of witnesses, his heart had pounded so loudly against his chest, he wondered the reason no one commented. Catherine wore her hair entwined with lavender and pearls to match the inside of her sleeves. Her eyes flickered from watery gray to the intense blue of a tempestuous sea, and it made him nearly giddy with delight. No doubt their lives would be an adventure.

Gregoire closed his eyes and felt the day's warmth around him. A shadow passed, but he knew before he opened his lids there would not be a cloud, and he was not disappointed. Hovering over him, Catherine tilted her head to the side and studied him, tapping her finger against her temple. He patted the space beside him. When she sat beside him, her thigh brushed against his. It was no accident.

"Resting before we leave, kind Sir."

Catherine ran her fingers up the inside of his arm, and he wanted to take her right there in the garden. He could not wait until they reached Champagne and his bedchamber. Not that being at Castle de Gray had dampened their desire, but his own bedchamber was in a hall all to itself and away from others.

"I have a surprise for you." Gregoire took the herb basket from her lap and set it on the pebbled ground. "Hold out your right hand, my dear."

"What have you done?" Catherine asked.

Cupping her hand in his, he dropped the leaf into her palm. He had tied the long tendril to the top creating a pouch. A tiny violet rested between the tendril and the leaf, much like a flower stuck in a cap. Catherine stared at the gift and then tossed it into her hand as if checking the weight.

"How did you make such a treasure? I will place it by our bed. Such a delicate flower shouldn't take long to dry, and then I will hang it over our bed. Does it have a meaning this leaf shape?"

Gregoire drew her to him. "It's meant to be opened."

"Open it? But it is too pretty." She tugged at the tendril, and the leaf slowly unfolded. Catherine gasped at the extraordinary ring.

She picked it up. Sunlight reflected off the rectangular shaped sapphire encased in miniscule copper leaves. Each leaf held a tiny diamond dewdrop. Tears glistened in her eyes, and he wiped one away with his thumb.

"It's the most beautiful ring I have ever seen."

Gregoire took the ring and slid it onto the middle finger of her right hand. "I have been committed to you since Stone Mountain where we said our vows to each other and before God. I love you, Catherine Le Sage of Pître."

He touched her chin with his fingertips and kissed her lips. They tasted slightly of basil and mint. Yesterday she tasted of salt and honey. He loved the way nothing was ever the same with her. He backed away.

Catherine said, "Seems luck has not deserted me. Each day is better and better with you."

"Do you like the ring?"

"Silly question. I will never remove it from this day forward."

"Faith and I designed it. He mentioned you had loved the forest since you were a child. He showed me the box he was painting. He told me of an artisan who specializes in rings. When I met with the man and showed him the stone, he suggested nestling it in a bed of lover's metal."

"You are thoughtful and kind, Gregoire Le Sage." She placed her head on his shoulder. "I will love you until the day I die."

Gregoire wrapped his arm around her. "We have tested that vow more than my liking. I suggest we live a long, happy life. Love is already a given."

The Prime Bells rang out, and the forecourt became a hive of activity. Gregoire stood and pulled Catherine up to him. He kissed her lashes and whispered. "I felt the bulge at your belly this morning. How do you feel?"

Catherine's eyes widened. "Perrine insisted I take mint and basil the last few mornings to soothe my stomach. Can it be...so soon?"

"I know nothing of these things, but I am very observant when it comes to your body."

Catherine's face turned crimson. Gregoire gave a deep laugh and placed his hand at the small of her back as they wended their way through the servants adding fresh eggs and pots of butter to the carts. Isabelle jumped out from behind one of the servants carrying Bijou in her arms.

"I found her wandering in the garden. May I hold her in the cart?" She tucked the tiny dog beneath her chin while she addressed her sister. "She will be safe with me. Please, oh please..."

Catherine nodded, then lifted the dog's pouch over her head. "Mayhap, it is time for someone else to care for her as well. Two can watch over her better than one."

Isabelle dipped her head so Catherine could adjust the pouch on her shoulder. "Thank you. I will never let her out of my sight–especially around Papa's hounds."

The sisters embraced with the small dog between them. Isabelle skipped away, clearly anxious to share the news. She ran right to Frotlina, who rolled her eyes and led the child to the middle cart.

Gregoire walked beside Catherine to their horses. Perrine stood beside Moncadeau with a satchel she meant to hang from Catherine's saddle. Gregoire noticed two women servants standing to say farewell to the de Grays. When Perrine passed, they scuttled backwards. Although an accomplished healer, Perrine still frightened them.

Perrine took Gregoire to the side, raising a finger to Catherine and causing her to stop. "I will speak to him alone if you please."

Catherine pretended to inspect Moncadeau for the journey, but Gregoire knew she would pelt him with questions the moment they were alone.

Perrine pinned her gaze on him, and he felt like a bug trapped under glass. "You made your promise and are taking her away. She is strong, but vulnerable. Please take care of her."

Her brows wrinkled into a frown, and she murmured. "My dreams have returned. Last night I had a premonition. A body floated underwater–I know not who. Ice drifted along with the body, sending a shiver through me. Above Castle de Gray, you soared with hawk's wings, but pulled a cloak tightly around you, concealing your identity."

"I have just married the woman of my dreams, and you wish to dash those feelings under your shoe with a death." Gregoire had had his fill of Perrine and her dreams.

"Not so. I do not discern an immediate threat, but I have no control over my dreams. It is my duty to tell of a premonition." She tapped her bag and squeezed Gregoire's arm. "Fare thee well and safe travels."

She spun so quickly, Gregoire had no time for a retort before she spoke to Catherine, her voice soothing, yet commanding. His attention shifted to Catherine.

"I have all the herbs and remedies you shall need." Perrine opened the bag and let her fingers dance across tops of several sachets, each filled with colorful herbs and spices. The mixes had heady scents. She closed the bag and directed her chin at Gregoire. "Sir, she may have need of the mint in the morning. Should relieve any distress she may have. This shall pass by Michaelmas."

She grinned as if she knew something he did not, and a tingle ran up his spine. Catherine hugged Perrine and adjusted the nubby hood around the healer's face. "I worry for you. You will be alone."

"I have an apprentice. I have begun her education not only with plants and herbs, but she is learning to read and write." Perrine lowered her voice. "We found another cavern the other day, and it will make a perfect hiding place if need be. Never worry. My fate is set, and I am content. I shall expect a pigeon after a fortnight."

Catherine squeezed Perrine once more, then mounted Moncadeau. She and Gregoire rode past the retinue. She had told Lord de Gray earlier she wanted to see Pître from the summit one last time and would meet him there. She nodded to Gregoire, and they trotted through the Upper Bailey before dashing into the Lower Bailey. Well-wishers waved from both sides of Castle Road.

She was quiet until they crested the upper ridge beyond Castle de Gray. She turned in the saddle facing Gregoire and gave him a sad smile. "I grew up in these meadows and forests and shall have many adventures to regale over the years. It is a region to be proud of."

Gregoire dismounted, then helped Catherine down. "In Champagne, we will have many warm mornings to linger in bed and many cold nights to burrow under the covers. I have been told upon good authority we will return to Pître."

Catherine kissed his fingers and tipped her head to the side. She wanted to say this right. "Once you said you would follow me to hell and think it was heaven. A bold statement, but I've come to learn that love cannot be torn apart by man or nature. Though we may grow old, we will always be young at heart. Gregoire Le Sage, you are my joy, my forever, my everything."

Castle Road Series

Will continue in 2024

Acknowledgments

Unending gratitude to **RaeAnn Ebarb** who deserves her own page. She is more therapist than friend and lets me read unfinished chapters out loud. Her kindness knows no bounds.

Special thanks to **Isabelle Pace** who checked my French names and references despite my Anglo-Saxon stubbornness. Incredible appreciation of **Stacey Hand** who made line edits in-between her job and infinite hours of volunteering. Always thankful to **Cherie Mathis** and her eagle eyes, especially when she detects the tiniest flaws on the last edit.

Laura Crawford, Bryan Sullivan, and **Megan Conway** were my first readers. Lord, their eyes must have been bleeding, but they powered through and encouraged me as good friends will do. Artist, friend, and beta-reader **Sharon Waddell** wanted more sex scenes and has a closed-door moment tucked away somewhere. **Darla Rackozy, Wallace Rackozy,** and **Dottie Reeser** also gullibly read one of the first drafts–God does make special people.

My Posse friends–**Vona Weiss, Diane Buseick, Melanie McCook, Elena Duke, Lory Evensky, Sherri Skrivanos, Sally Hardin,** and **Lee Collier**–bring comfort and laughter along with great wine to every meetup. Kindness runs strong through their veins.

Some days are tricky. After spending a day at the keyboard, my moods swing from disagreeable to euphoric. Despite the kaleidoscope of characters my husband **David** watches K-dramas with me, tells me he loves me every day, and kisses me the last thing before the lights go out. For more than forty years he's defined the word love for me.

Imagination needs oil, and playlists are a must. Mine include Medieval Estampie by various artists, **John-Henry Crawford**, **Shinwha**, and massive amounts of **BTS (OT7-2025.)**

About the Author

Originally from Texas but raised in Louisiana and Mississippi, Phylis found her creative calling in Shreveport after pursuing her education at Northwestern State University. Her writing journey began in earnest once her youngest child started high school, allowing her the time to follow her passion for storytelling.

In 2015, Phylis made her literary debut with the release of her first book, *Skinny Dipping in Cane River*. Rooted in her Southern upbringing and inspired by the mystical tales passed down by her grandfather, this work set the stage for her writing career.

One of Phylis's most noteworthy accomplishments is her captivating historical adventure novel, *The Wind Has a Voice*. Drawing inspiration from the ancient discoveries of Jeannine Davis Kimball in the 1990s, who uncovered a woman encased in permafrost in the mountains of Mongolia, Phylis weaves a mesmerizing fictional account of this courageous nomad's life. In her hands, the story unfolds into an epic narrative of a woman who rises to become a revered warrior.

Originally conceived as an episodic tale for Vella and titled *Windrush*, this extraordinary work quickly gained acclaim and soared to the top of historical adventure charts on Amazon, where it remained for weeks. Phylis's gift for storytelling shines through in her ability to transport readers to distant times and places, immersing them in the rich tapestry of history.

Connect with Phylis on Facebook, Instagram, or Twitter to keep up with her latest literary adventures and to engage with a writer who values her readers' voices and stories as much as she does her own.

www.ingramcontent.com/pod-product-compliance
Lightning Source LLC
Chambersburg PA
CBHW032154190626
46814CB00005BA/1988